MINDSTAR RISING

MINDSTAR RISING

PETER F. HAMILTON

TOR®

A Tom Doherty Associates Book
New York

MINDSTAR RISING

A Tor Book
Published by Tom Doherty Associates, Inc.
175 Fifth Avenue
New York, NY 10010

Tor Books on the World Wide Web:
http://www.tor.com

Tor® is a registered trademark of Tom Doherty Associates, Inc.

Design by Basha Durand

Library of Congress Cataloging-in-Publication Data

Hamilton, Peter F.
Mindstar rising / Peter F. Hamilton. —1st Tor ed.
        p.   cm.
"A Tom Doherty Associates book."
ISBN 0–312–85955–4
I. Title.
PR6058.A5536M56   1996
823'.914—dc20   95–53847

First Tor edition: August 1996

Printed in the United States of America

0 9 8 7 6 5 4 3 2 1

To my mother and father, Hazel and John, of course

MINDSTAR
RISING

Meteorites fell through the night sky like a gentle sleet of ice-fire, their sharp scintillations slashing ebony overload streaks across the image Greg Mandel's photon amp was feeding into his optic nerves.

He was hanging below a Westland ghost wing, five hundred meters above the Purser's Hills, due west of Kettering. Spiraling down. Wind strummed the membrane, producing near-subliminal bass harmonics.

Ground zero was a small crofter's cottage: walls of badly laid raw stone swamped with some olive green creeper, big scarlet flowers. It had a thatched roof, reeds rotting and congealing, caked in tidemark ripples of blue-green fungal growths. A two-meter-square solar-cell strip had been pinned on top.

Greg landed a hundred meters downslope from the cottage, propeller spinning furiously to kill his forward speed. He stopped inside three meters. The Westland was one of the best military microlights ever built—lightweight, highly maneuverable, silent, with a low radar-visibility profile. Greg had flown them on fifteen missions in Turkey, and their reliability had been 100 percent. All British Army covert tactical squads had been equipped with them. He'd hate to use anything else. They'd gone out of production when the People's Socialism Party came to power, twelve years previously. A victim of the demilitarization realignment program, the Credit Crash, the Warming, nationalization, industrial collapse. This one was fifteen years old, and still functioned like a dream.

A time display flashed in the bottom right corner of the photon amp image, spectral yellow digits: 21:17:08. Greg twisted the Westland's retraction catch, and the translucent wing folded with a graceful rustle. He anchored it with a skewer harpoon. There'd be no danger of it blowing away now. The hills suffered frequent twister-gusts, and this was March, England's rainy season: squalls abounded. Gabriel hadn't cautioned him about the wing in her briefing, but Greg always followed routine, ingrained by sergeant majors and way too much experience.

He studied the terrain, the amp image gray and blue, smoky. There were no surprises; the Earth-resource satellite pictures Royan had pirated for him were three months old, but nothing had changed. The area was isolated, grazing land, marginally viable. Nobody spent money on barns and roads up here. It was perfect for someone who wanted to drop out of sight, a nonentity wasteland.

Greg heard a bell tinkling from the direction of the cottage, high-pitched and faint. He keyed the amp to infrared and upped the magnification. A big rosy blob resolved into a goat with a broad collar dangling a bell below its neck.

He began to walk toward the cottage. The meteorites had gone, sweeping away to the east. Not proper shooting stars after all, then. Some space station's waste dump, or an old rocket stage, dragged down from its previously stable discard-orbit by Earth's hot expanded atmosphere.

"At twenty-one nineteen GMT the dog will start its run toward you," Gabriel had said when she briefed him. "You will see it first when it comes around the end of the wall on the left of the cottage."

Greg looked at the wall; the ablative decay that ruled the rest of the croft had encroached here as well, reducing it to a low moss-covered ridge ringing a small muddy yard.

A yellow blink: 21:19:00.

The dog was a Rottweiler, heavily modified for police riot-assault duty, which was expensive. A crofter with a herd of twenty-five llamas couldn't afford one, and certainly had no right owning one. Its front teeth had been replaced by monolattice silicon fangs, eight centimeters long; the jaw had been reprofiled to a blunt hammerhead to accommodate them; both eyes were implants, retinas beefed up for night sight. One aspect Gabriel hadn't mentioned was the *speed* of the bloody thing.

Greg brought his Walther eight-shot up, the sighting laser glaring like a rigid lightning bolt in the photon amp's image. He got off two fast shots, maser pulses that drilled the Rottweiler's brain. The steely pumping legs collapsed, sending it tumbling, momentum skidding it across the nettle-clumped grass. In death it snarled at him, jaws open, eyes wide, crying blood.

He walked past, uncaring. The Walther's condensers whined away on the threshold of audibility, recharging.

"At twenty-one twenty and thirteen seconds GMT, the cottage door will open. Edwards will look both ways before coming out. He will be carrying a pump-action shotgun—only three cartridges, though."

Greg flattened himself against the cottage wall, feeling the leathery creeper leaves compress against his back. The scarlet flowers had a scent similar to honeysuckle, strong sugar.

21:20:13.

The weather-bleached wooden door creaked.

Greg's espersense perceived Edwards hovering indecisively on the step, his mind a weak ruby glow, thought currents flowing slowly, concern and suspicion rising.

"He'll turn right, away from you."

Edwards's boot squelched in the mud of the yard, two steps. The shotgun was held out in front, his finger pressed lightly on the trigger.

Greg came away from the wall, flicking the Walther to longburn, lining it up. Edwards was a bulky figure dressed in filthy denim trousers and a laddered chunky-knit sweater, neck craning forward, peering through the moonlit gloom. He'd aimed the shotgun at the ramshackle stone shed at the bottom of the yard.

The goat bleated, tugging at its leash.

Edwards was somehow aware of the presence behind him. His back stiffened, mind betraying a hot burst of alarm and fear to Greg's espersense. He tightened his grip on the shotgun, ready to spin round and blast away wildly.

"Drop it," Greg said softly.

Edwards sighed, his shoulders relaxing. He bent to put the shotgun down, resting its barrel on a stone, saving it from the mud. A man who knew weapons.

"Okay, you can turn now."

His face was thin, bearded, hazel eyes yellowed. He looked at Greg, taking in the matte black combat leathers, slim metallic-silver band bisecting his face, unwavering Walther. Edwards knew he was going to die, but the terrified acceptance was flecked with puzzlement. "Why?" he asked.

"Absolution."

He didn't get it; they never did. His death was a duty, ordered by guilt.

Greg had learned all about duty from the Army, relying on his squad mates, their equal dependence on him. It was a bond closer than family, overriding everything—laws, conventions, morals. Civvies like Edwards never understood. When all other human values had gone, shattered by violence, there was still duty. The implicit trust of life. And Greg had failed Royan. Miserably.

Greg fired. Edwards's mouth gaped as the maser beam struck his temple, his eyes rolling up as he fell forward. He splashed into the thin layer of mud. Dead before he hit.

Greg holstered the Walther, breath hissing out between clenched teeth. He walked back down the hill to the Westland without giving the body another glance. Behind him, the goat's bell began to clang.

He refused to think about the kill while the Westland cruised over the countryside, his mind an extension of the guido, iced silicon, confirming landmarks, telling his body when to shift balance. It would've been too easy to brood in the ghost wing's isolated segment of the universe, guilt and depression inevitable.

Rutland Water was in front of him, a Y-shaped reservoir six and a half kilometers long nestling in the snug dark valleys of the county's turbulent rolling landscape. A pale oyster flame of jejune moonlight shone across the surface. Greg came in over the broad grass-slope dam at the western end. He kept low, skimming the water. Straight ahead was the floating village: thirty-odd log rafts, each supporting a plain wooden cabin, like something out of a Western frontier settlement. They were lashed together by a spiderweb of cables, forming a loose circle around the old limnological tower, a thick concrete shaft built before the reservoir was filled.

He angled toward the biggest cabin, compensating for the light gusts with automatic skill. At five meters out he flared the wing sharply. Surging air plucked at his combat leathers; his feet touched the coarse overlapping planks that made up the roof, legs running, carrying him up toward the apex as the propeller blurred. He stopped with a meter to spare. The tart, scrumpylike odor of drying waterfruit permeated the air, reassuring in its familiarity.

The Westland's membrane folded.

"Greg?"

He watched Nicole's bald head rise above the gable end. "Here." He shrugged out of the harness.

She came up the ladder on to the roof, a black ex-Navy marine-adept dressed in a functional mauve diving bikini. He couldn't remember her ever wearing anything else. Even in the moonlight her water-resilient skin glistened from head to toe; she looked tubby, but not overweight, her shape dictated by an all-over insulating layer of subcutaneous fat, protecting her from the cold of deep water.

"How did it go?"

"All sorted, no messing," he replied curtly.

Nicole nodded.

Two more marine-adepts swarmed briskly up the ladder and took charge of the Westland. Greg appreciated that, no fuss, no chatter. Most of the floating village's marine-adepts were ex-Navy; they understood.

They'd colonized the reservoir around the time Greg moved into his chalet on the shore, seeding and harvesting their gene-tailored water-fruit. Their only concession to the convulsions of the PSP years was to store Greg's military gear for him and, very occasionally, provide sanctuary for an activist on the run from the People's Constables.

"I'll be back tomorrow," Greg told Nicole as he climbed into his ancient rowing boat. When the neurohormone hangover had gone, when the memory of Edwards had faded, when he felt human again.

She untied the pannier and tossed it into the boat after him. "Sure, Greg. Take care."

Back on land he headed for the pub to forget the kill. The Army had taught him how to handle that as well. How to suspend human feelings in combat, to refuse the blame for all the deaths, the pain, suffering, horror. Greg had never woken screaming like others in the regiment had.

He knew what he needed: the release that came from drink and women, gluttoning out, sluicing away the memory of Edwards in a wash of basement-level normality.

He had a good feeling as he walked into the Wheatsheaf at Edith Weston. Esper intuition or old-fashioned instinct, it didn't matter which, the result was the same. Static-charged anticipation. He opened the taproom door grinning.

The Wheatsheaf's landlord, Angus, had come up trumps; his new barmaid was a tall, strapping lass, twenty years old with a heart-shaped face, wearing her thick red hair combed back from her forehead. She was dressed in a long navy blue skirt and purple cap-sleeve T-shirt. A deep scoop neck showed off the heavily freckled slope of her large breasts to perfection.

Eleanor Broady. Greg stored the name as she pulled him a pint of Ruddles County, topping it with a shot of Angus's homemade whiskey. It lasted longer that way; he couldn't afford to knock back pints all night.

Greg sat back and admired her in the guttering light of the oil lamps. The Wheatsheaf was a run-of-the-mill rural pub, which reverted true to the 1900s ideal with the demise of the big brewery conglomerates. Flash trash fittings melting away surprisingly fast once mains electricity ended and beer had to be hand-drawn from kegs again. Either relaxing or monumentally dull, according to individual sensibilities. Greg liked it. There were no demands on him in the Wheatsheaf.

He was wedged in between a group of local farm workers and some of the lads from the timber mill, billeted in the village's old RAF base. The resident pair of warden dodgers were doing their nightly round, hawking a clutch of dripping rainbow trout they'd lifted from the reservoir.

Eleanor was a prize draw for male attention. Slightly timid from first-night nerves but coping with the banter well enough.

Greg weighed up her personality, figuring how to make his play. Confidence gave him a warm buzz. He was seventeen years older, but with the edge his espersense gave him that shouldn't be a problem. What amused her, topics to steer clear of, he could see them a mile off. She'd believe they were soul twins before the night was out.

Her father came in at eleven-thirty. The conversation chopped off dead. He was in dungarees, a big stained crucifix stitched crudely on the front. People stared; kibbutzniks didn't come into pubs, not ever.

Eleanor paled behind the bar but stood her ground. Her father walked over to her, ignoring everybody, flickering yellow light catching the planes of his gaunt, angular face.

"You'll come home with me," he said quietly, determined. "We'll make no fuss."

Eleanor shook her head, mute.

"Now."

Angus came up beside her. "The lady doesn't want to go." His voice was weary but calm. No pub argument was beyond Angus; he knew them all, how to deal with each. Disposal expert.

"You belong with us," said her father. "You share our bread. We taught you better."

"Listen—," Angus began, sweet reason.

"No. She comes with me. Or perhaps you will recompense us for her schooling? Grade four in animal husbandry, she is. Did she not tell you? Can you afford that?"

"I worked for it," Eleanor said. "Every day I worked for it. Never ending."

Greg sensed how near to tears she was. Part of him was fascinated with the scene: it was surreal, or maybe Shakespearian, Victorian. Logic and lust urged him up.

Angus saw him closing on the bar and winced.

Greg gave him a wan reassuring smile—no violence, promise.

His imagination pictured his gland, a slippery black lens of muscle nestled at the center of his brain, flexing rhythmically, squirting out milky liquid. Actually, it was nothing like that, but the psychosis was mild enough, harmless. Some Mindstar Brigade veterans had much weirder hallucinations.

The neurohormones started to percolate through his synapses, altering and enhancing their natural functions. His perception of the taproom began to alter, the physical abandoning him, leaving only people. They were their thoughts, tightly woven streamers of ideas, memories, emotions, interacting, fusing, and budding. Coldly beautiful.

"Go home," he told Eleanor's father.

The man was a furnace of anger and righteousness. Indignation blooming at the nonbeliever's impudence. "This is not your concern," he told Greg.

"Nor is she yours, not anymore," Greg replied. "No longer your little girl. She makes her own choices now."

"God's girl!"

It would've been so easy to thump the arrogant bastard. A deluge of mayhem strobed through Greg's mind, the whole unarmed combat manual on some crazy mnemonic recall, immensely tempting. He concentrated hard on the intransigent mind before him. Domination really wasn't his suit, too difficult and painful.

"Go *home*." He pushed the order, clenching his jaw at the effort.

The man's thoughts shrank from his meddling insistence, cohesion broken. Faith-suppressed reactions, the animal urge to lash out, fists pounding, feet kicking, boiled dangerously close to the surface.

Greg thrust them back into the subconscious, knowing his nails would be biting into his palms at the exertion.

The father flung a last imploring glance to a daughter who was genuinely loved in a remote, filtered manner. Rejection triggered the final humiliation, and he fled, his soul keening, eternal hatred sworn. Greg sensed his own face reflected in the agitated thoughts, distorted to demonic preconceptions. Then he was gone.

The taproom slowly rematerialized. The gland's neurohormones were punishing his brain. He steadied himself on the bar.

There were knowing grins, which he fended off with a sheepish smile. Forced. A low grumble of conversation returned, cut with snickers. An entire generation's legend born, this night would live forever.

16 Peter F. Hamilton

Eleanor was trembling in reaction, Angus's arm around her shoulder, strictly paternal. She insisted she was all right, wanted to carry on, please.

Greg was shown her wide sunny smile for the first time, an endearing combination of gratitude and shyness. He didn't have to buy another drink all night.

"Kibbutzes always seemed a bit of a contradiction in terms to me," Greg said. "Christian Marxists. A religious philosophy of dignified individuality, twinned with state oppression. Not your obvious partnership." He and Eleanor were walking down the dirt track to his chalet in Berrybut Spinney, a couple of kilometers along the shore from Edith Weston. The old time-share estate's nightly bonfire glimmered through the black trees ahead, shooting firefly sparks high into the cloudless night. A midnight zephyr was rucking the surface of Rutland Water, wavelets lapping on the mud shallows. He could hear the smothered-waterfall sound from the discharge pipes as the reservoir was filled by the pumping stations on the Welland and Nene, siphoning off the March floodwater. The water level had been low this Christmas, parched farmland placing a massive demand for irrigation. Thousands of square meters of grass and weeds around the shore that'd grown up behind the water's summer retreat were slowly drowning under its return. As the rotting vegetation fermented it gave off a gas that smelled of rancid eggs and cow shit. It lasted for six weeks each year.

"Not much of either in a kibbutz," Eleanor said. "Just work. God, it was squalid, medieval. We were treated like people-machines; everything had to be done by hand. Their idea of advanced machinery was the plow that the shire horses pulled. God's will. Like hell!"

Greg nodded sympathetically; he'd seen the inside of a kibbutz. She was chattering now, a little nervous. The restrictive doctrine that'd dominated her childhood had stunted the usual pattern of social behavior, leaving her slightly unsure, and slightly turned on by newfound freedom.

Greg felt himself getting high on expectation. He was growing impatient to reach the chalet and bed with that fantastic-looking body. Edwards's face was already indistinct, monochrome, falling away. Even the neurohormone hangover had evaporated.

The tall ash and oak trees of Berrybut Spinney had died years ago, unable to survive the Warming. They'd been turned into gigantic gazebos for the cobaea vines Greg and the other estate residents had planted around their broad buttress roots, dangling huge cascades of purple and white trumpet-flowers from stark skeletal boughs.

He'd spent long hours renovating the estate for the first three years after he moved in, putting in new plants—angel trumpets, figs, ficus, palms, lilies, silk oaks, cedars, even a small orange grove at the rear: a hurried harlequin quilt thrown over the brown fungal rot of decay. The first two years after the temperature peaked were the worst. Grass survived, of course, and some evergreen trees, but the sudden year-round heat wiped out entire ecological systems right across the country. Arable land suffered the least; farms, and the new kibbutzes, adapted readily enough, switching to new varieties of crops and livestock. But that still left vast tracts of native country-side and forests and city parks and village greens looking like bat-tlefields scoured by some apocalyptic chemical weapon.

Repairs were uncoordinated, a patchwork of gross contrasts. It made traveling interesting, though.

Greg and Eleanor emerged from the spinney into a rectangular clearing that sloped down to the water. The dying bonfire illuminated a semicircle of twenty small chalets and a big stone building at the crest.

"You live here?" Eleanor asked in a very neutral tone.

"Yes," he agreed cautiously. The chalets had been built by an ambitious time-share company in conjunction with a golf course running along the back of the spinney and a grandiose clubhouse-hotel perched between the two. But the whole enterprise was suddenly bumped out of business thanks to the PSP's one-home law. The chalets were commandeered, the golf course returned to arable land, and the hotel transformed into thirty accommodation modules.

Greg always thought the country had been bloody lucky the PSP never got round to a one-room law. The situation had become pretty drastic as the oceans started to rise. The polar melt plateaued eventually, but not before it displaced two million people in England alone.

"I never asked," she said. "What is it you do?"

He chuckled. "Greg Mandel's Investigative Services, at your service."

"Investigative services? You mean, like a private detective? Angus told me you had a gland."

"That's right. Of course, it was nothing formal in the PSP decade. I didn't go legit until after the Second Restoration."

"Why not?"

"Public ordinance number five seven five nine, oblique stroke nine two. By order of the president: no person implanted with a psi-enhancement gland may utilize their psi ability for financial gain. Not that many people could afford a private eye anyway. Not with Leopold Armstrong's nineteenth-century ideology screwing up the economy. Bastard. I was also disbarred from working in any state enterprise, and social security was a joke: the PSP apparatchiks had taken it over, head to toe, by the time I was demobbed. Tell you, they didn't like servicemen, and Mindstar veterans were an absolute no-go zone. The Party was running scared of us. As well they might."

"How did you manage?"

"I had my Army pension for a couple of years after demob." He shrugged. "The PSP canceled that soon enough. Fifth Austerity Act, if I recall rightly. I got by. Rutland's always had an agriculture-based economy. There's plenty of casual work to pick up on the farms, and the citrus groves were a boon; that and a few cash-only cases each year. It was enough."

Her face was solemn. "I never even saw any money until I was thirteen."

He put his arm round her shoulder, giving a little reassuring shake. "All over now."

She smiled with haunted eyes, wanting to believe. His arm remained.

"Here we are," he said, "number six," and blipped the lock.

The chalet's design paid fleeting homage to the ideal of some ancient Alpine hunting lodge, an overhanging roof all along the front creating a tiny veranda-cum-porch. But its structure lacked genuine Alpine ruggedness: prefab sections that looked like stout red-bark logs from the outside were now rotting badly, the windows had warped under the relentless assault of the new climate's heat and humidity, there was no air-conditioning, and the slates molted at an alarming rate in high winds. The sole source of electricity was a solar-cell strip that Greg had pasted to the roof. However, the main frame was sound; four-by-four hardwood timber, properly seasoned. He could never understand why that should be—perhaps the building inspectors had chosen that day to put in an appearance.

The biolum strip came on, revealing a lounge area with a sturdy oak-top bar separating it from a minute kitchen alcove at the rear. Its built-in furniture was compact, all light pine. Wearing thin, Greg acknowledged, following Eleanor's questing gaze. Entropy digging its claws in.

The corners of her lips tugged up. "Nice. At Egleton, there'd be five of us sharing a room this size. You live here alone?"

"Yeah. The British Legion found it for me. Good people, volunteers. At least they cared, did what they could. And it's all paid for, even if it is falling down around me."

"They were bad times, weren't they, Greg? I never really saw much of it. But there were the rumors, even in a kibbutz."

"We rode it out, though. This country always does, somehow. That's our strength, in the genes; no matter how far down we fall, we're never out."

"And you don't mind?"

"Mind what?"

"Me. I was in a kibbutz; that made me a card carrier."

His arms went round her, hands resting lightly on her buttocks. Faces centimeters apart. Her nose was petite and pointed. "Only by default. Nobody chooses their parents, and I'd say you unchose yours pretty convincingly tonight." His nose touched hers, rubbing gently.

She grinned, shy again.

The bedroom was on his right, behind a sliding door. A tiny pine-paneled room that was nearly filled by a huge double bed: there was a half-meter gap between the mattress and the walls.

Eleanor flicked him a quick appraising look, and her grin became slyer, lips twitching. Greg leaned forward and kissed her.

He cheated with her, just as he'd done with all the others. His espersense was alert for exactly the right moment. When it came, a minute into the kiss, his hands found the hem of her T-shirt and pulled it off over her head, muffling her giggles. She undid the skirt catch herself, allowing him to slide it down her legs; the silky panties followed.

Her figure was just as spectacular as his imagination had painted it for him. Eleanor's years at the kibbutz had toughened her, more so than most of the girls he'd had. He found that erotic; her flat, slightly muscular belly, wide hips, broad, powerful shoulders, all loaded with athletic promise.

Greg's own clothes came off in a fast heated tussle, and they moved onto the bed.

It lasted for an age, building slowly. With his eyes he watched the blue and black shadows flow across her smooth damp skin as she stretched and twisted below his hands. With his mind he sensed cold shooting stars igniting along the glistening trail left by the tip of his tongue, then fire along her nerves into her brain, adding to the glow of arousal. He saw what excited her, the words she wanted to hear, then exploited the discoveries, whispering secret fantasies into her ear, guiding her into the permutations she'd never dared ask from a partner before.

After the initial astonishment of making love to someone who not only shared her desires but actually relished them, Eleanor shook loose any lingering restraint. Greg laughed in delight as she let her enthusiasm run riot, and told her how she could repay him.

When he asked, she rose up in the way he loved, poised above him, light from the slumbering bonfire licking at her flesh, deepening her mystique. His hands finally found her breasts. She grinned, seeing his weakness, and played on it, drawing out the poignancy before she twined her legs around him and pulled herself down. Her mind became almost dazzlingly bright as she used him to bring herself to orgasm, all coherency overwhelmed by animal instinct.

Greg let go of Edwards and duty and guilt, and concentrated solely on inflaming Eleanor still further.

2

Julia Evans sat at the dresser in her bedroom while the maid brushed daytime knots out of her long chestnut hair. It had to be done every night; she hadn't allowed her hair to be cut for years, and now it hung almost down to her waist. Her best feature, everyone said, striking.

She studied her face in the mirror, plump cheeked and bland, wearing a slightly sorrowful expression. It wasn't an ugly face, by any means. But at seventeen some allure really ought to be evolving.

Access Vanity#Twelve, she told her bioware processor implant silently. At least she had had a sense of humor when she began this memory sequence.

A mirage of her own face, six months younger, unfurled behind her eyes. She compared it to the one in the mirror. There was some change. A burning-off of puppy fat, her cheeks were rounder then. Fractionally.

There had been a time, a couple of months back, when she'd considered *plastique*, but eventually shied away. Having herself altered to match some channel-starlet ideal would be the ultimate admission of defeat. As long as there was still some development there was hope. Perhaps she was being impatient. But how wonderful it would be to make the boys ogle lustily.

Commit Vanity#Twenty-five. The mirror image, with all its melancholia.

"Thank you, Adela," she said.

The maid nodded primly, and made one final stroke with the brush before departing. Julia watched her go in the mirror, some deep instinct objecting to ordering people around like cattle. But it was an instinct that was nearly dead, the Swiss boarding school had seen to that. Besides, Adela wasn't one of the grudging ones. At twenty-two years of age she was close enough in years for Julia to feel comfortable with her, and she was certainly loyal enough—to the extent of sharing Wilholm Manor's considerable quantity of below-stairs gossip.

Julia shrugged out of her robe and flopped down on the big circular bed, stretching luxuriously on the apricot silk sheets. The room was huge, so much empty space, and all her own. So very different from the little stone burrow she'd lived in for the first ten years of her life at the First Salvation Church warren. Space was undoubtedly the best part of being rich.

The bedroom was a celebration of opulent decadence, with its satin rose ceiling, thick pile carpet, walk-through wardrobes, a marbled bathroom. It was a feminine room: a boudoir, foreign and exotic.

She'd spent a fortnight with an increasingly harried interior designer selecting exactly the style she wanted. A distant memory of an old memox video cartridge, a costume romance of handsome dukes and willowy heroines in a more genteel age.

Her grandfather had come in when the bedroom was finished, his eyes rolling with bemused tolerance. "Well, as long as *you're* happy with it, Juliet."

He hadn't paid many visits after that. Not that she minded him. But it was delicious to be left alone; privacy still seemed a bit of a novelty. Her security hardline bodyguards accompanied her everywhere outside the mansion, not nudging her shoulder—they were too professional for that—but always close, always watching. And once inside Wilholm's 'ware-saturated perimeter nothing went unseen.

Some part of Julia's nature rebelled against being a cosseted princess, treated like some immensely precious and delicate work of art. Yes, she was valuable, but not fragile. However, there were subtle ways to defy the surveillance, to indulge herself without suffering the silent censure of the hardliners' ever-vigilant eyes, keeping some little core of personality secret to herself.

Open Channel to Manor Security Core. The 'ware came on-line, a colorless menu of surveillance circuits and defense gear streaming into her mind, all of it listed as restricted. She fed her executive code in, and every restriction was lifted.

Access Surveillance Camera: West Wing, First-Floor Corridor. Route Image Into Bedroom Three.

She rolled over and rested her chin in her hands, legs waving idly. A picture formed on the theater-sized wall-mounted flatscreen opposite the bed. It showed the corridor outside, a slightly fuzzy resolution. Adrian was walking down the thick strip of navy blue carpeting, dressed in a long burgundy toweling robe. Barefoot, she noted, and no pajama trousers either.

Peeping Tom, her mind chided. Her cheeks were suddenly very warm against her palms, but Pandora's box was open now.

Adrian stopped outside one of the bedroom doors and looked

furtively both ways along the corridor before opening the door without knocking.

For one glorious instant Julia allowed herself to believe it was her bedroom he'd entered, even twisting around to look. But of course her door was closed.

Access Surveillance Camera: West Wing, Guest Suite Seven.

Katerina's room, bathed in a musky green light. Now, here was something very interesting. By day it was Adrian who took charge of their little group; Julia and Katerina listened to him, laughed at his jokes, followed him when he wanted to go swimming or horse riding or playing tennis. But here in private the roles were reversed; Adrian did as Kats told him.

Julia studied her girlfriend as best as the irritatingly grainy image allowed. Kats had lost some of her youthful daytime frivolity, becoming imperious, a confidence verging on arrogance.

Open Memory File, Code: AmourKats.

So she could retain all the impressions she saw on the big screen and then retrieve them at any time for future consideration. AmourKats was going to be an objective study in seduction.

Kats was kneeling on her bed as Adrian came in, dressed in a provocative taupe-colored silk camisole top and a short waist slip, blond hair bubbling down around her shoulders. A real-life sex kitten. She told Adrian to take his robe off.

It was more like an order, Julia thought. Her heart leaped at the prospect of seeing Adrian naked at last, jealous and excited. Seeing him in his swimming trunks all afternoon had been a real treat.

Adrian was nineteen years old, ruggedly handsome, and possessed of a truly heavenly physique, each muscle perfectly proportioned, nothing like the ugly excess of a bodybuilder, just naturally lean. **Mesomorph**, her implant dictionary subsection told her.

The toweling robe formed a dark puddle around Adrian's feet.

Julia slowly turned onto her side, looking away from the flatscreen, shame finally overpowering greed.

Exit Surveillance Camera.

Adrian had been so nice to her, treating her no differently than he did Kats during the day as the three of them roamed Wilholm's vast grounds. She'd really hoped the attraction was mutual this time. She never seemed to be able to attract, much less hold, a boy as desirable as Adrian.

The memory of Primate Marcus, leader of the First Salvation Church, floated out of that little dark core of anguish to haunt her once more. He'd favored her mother for several months when Julia was eight. The patronage had enabled her to walk like a queen through the desert commune's airy underground tunnels, the happiest time of her young life. Daughter of the Primate's chosen one.

Primate Marcus was an obese fifty-year-old, wrapped in a huge toga to hide his slovenly frame. With her eyes closed she saw the big round head with its full gray beard leaning down toward her. Fat fingers adorned with gold rings tickled her ribs, and she shrieked her joy. The air had been thick and sweet from his marijuana. "One day soon, I'll fill you with Jesuslove," his slurred voice rumbled.

She had laughed then. Shuddered now.

But then, she thought miserably, that was always the way when it came to men—boys. She just never seemed to have any luck. So far they had fallen into two categories: the first she hadn't even believed existed until afterward. More handsome than Adrian, wittier than a channel comedian, with the culture and manners of a royal. But most of them had no real money—executive assistants, flavor-of-the-month artists, impoverished aristocracy, men who could make deals to retire on if they just had backing. They haunted the fringes of society, sharks who homed in on her name, her money like fresh meat, which in a way she was. She had been too young, too stupidly blind with the whirlwind of holiday romance. And in bed his immaculate body had made her scream out in glory. Only afterward did she find out she was simply part of his grand scheme.

She had fled from one extreme to the other. Back to her exclusive Swiss school, and into Joel's arms, a boarder at the boys' school down the road. He was the same age as her, the sensitive type, mild-mannered, caring, just perfect for a true first love. She knew he would never exploit her. And in bed he was an utter disaster; she would lie in his twitchy embrace and remember how sensational sex could be. Thankfully it had fizzled out soon enough—her leaving her school, him returning to France, neither making much effort to keep in touch.

The soul-bruising knocks and disappointments had set up a barrier, a psychological flinch. And the boys seemed aware of her mistrust, finding it difficult to breach. Anyone who could was too smooth; those that couldn't would be like Joel. What she wanted more than anything was one good-looking boy who didn't know who she was to look at her and think: yeah!

Then Kats had come to stay at Wilholm, injecting some much-needed laughter into the long procession of warm, wet, boring days, and she'd brought Adrian with her. Adrian, who fit the bill as though he had been born for her: mature, athletic, no doubt very experienced in bed, fun, intelligent, not at all arrogant. And when he had smiled and said hello there had been no barrier, no hesitancy at all. It would've been utterly sensational, if Kats hadn't enchanted him first.

Julia shivered slightly at the involuntary recollection of Primate Marcus and the cult. She'd been ten when the upheaval came. The big Texan, known later as Uncle Horace, had arrived to take her away. Over the sea to a near-mythical Europe and a grandfather she'd never even known she had. Lady Fauntleroy, the other commune kids had teased before she went, bowing, curtseying. She'd giggled with them, playing along, secretly terrified of leaving the gently curving sandstone passages with their broad light wells and the eternal magnificent desert above. Her mother had stayed with the cult; her father had accompanied her.

The bioware processors helped Julia suppress the name, the whole concept of *father*, pushing him below conscious examination, a fast, clean exorcism. He brought too much pain. Childhood ignorance was a blissful existence, she reflected.

Europe and Philip Evans, her grandfather, and the astonishing revelation of Event Horizon. A company to rival a *kombinate* in size, heroically battling the British PSP, which surely made Grandpa a saint. Socialism was the ultimate Antichrist.

Her grandfather had sent her to the school in Switzerland, where starchy tutors had crammed her with company law, management procedures, finance; twittery grande dames teaching her all the social graces, etiquette and deportment, refining her. She'd dropped her American accent, adopting a crystal-cut English Sloane inflection to lend a touch of class. A proper Lady. Then on her sixteenth birthday she'd left the school and spent a month in Event Horizon's ultra-exclusive Austrian clinic.

She was given five bioware implants, nodes of ferredoxin protein meshed with her synaptic clefts—three memory-cell clusters, two data processors—a whole subsidiary brain to cope with the vast dataflows generated by Event Horizon. The parallel mentality didn't make her a genius, but it did make her analytical, objective. A conflation of logic and human inspiration, she was capable of looking at a problem from every conceivable angle until she produced a solution. An irrational computer.

"It's the only way, Juliet," Philip had told her. "I'm losing track of the company; it's slipping away from me. All I ever get to see in cubes are the summaries of summaries, a shallow overview. That's not enough. Inertia and waste are building up. Inevitably, I suppose.

Department heads just don't have the drive. It's a job to them, not a life. Maybe these nodes will enable you to control it properly."

Julia let desire war with her conscience. How did you captivate a boy like Adrian?

Access Surveillance Camera: West Wing, Guest Suite Seven.

A laughing Kats was straddling Adrian, playing with him, her hands caressing, tongue working slowly down his chest. He was spread-eagled across the mattress, clutching the brass bedposts with a strength that came close to bending them, face warped in agony and ecstasy, pleading with her.

Commit AmourKats.

Julia had never done anything like this, not leading, not making all the moves. She wasn't sure she would have the nerve. Kats seemed so totally uninhibited. Shameless. Was that the key? Could boys home in on abandon? Kats sat back on Adrian's abdomen, then crossed her arms and gripped the hem of the camisole. She peeled it languidly over her head, shaking her hair out. Julia felt a sharp spasm of envy at seeing her friend's well-developed body. That was one reason why Kats had Adrian, she acknowledged bitterly: they looked like godlings together. At least she had longer legs than Kats. Skinny, though; nothing like as shapely, two beanpoles really.

Exit Surveillance Camera.

Her mental yell was contaminated with anger and disgust. Peeking on the lovers had seemed like a piece of harmless fun. Certainly using the security cameras to spy on the manor's servants had been pretty enlightening. But this wasn't the gentle romantic lovemaking she'd been expecting. Nothing near.

Pandora's box. And only a fool ever opens it.

Anger vanished to be replaced with sadness. Alone again, more than ever now that she knew the truth.

Boys were just about the only subject she never discussed with her grandfather. It never seemed fair somehow. He'd taken over every other parental duty, a solid pillar of comfort, support, and love. She couldn't burden him with more. Not now. *Certainly* not now.

Part of the reason for her being at Wilholm was so she could be his secretary. Philip Evans needed a secretary like he needed another overdraft, but the idea was to give her executive experience and acquaint her with Event Horizon minutiae, preparing her to take it over. A terrifying, yet at the same time exhilarating prospect.

Then this morning at breakfast he'd taken her into his confidence, looking even more haggard than usual. "Someone is running a spoiler operation against Event Horizon," he'd said. "Contaminating thirty-seven percent of our memox crystals in the furnaces."

"Has Walshaw found out who was behind it?" she'd asked, assuming she was being told after the security chief had closed down the operation. It was the way their discussions of the company usually went. Her grandfather would explain a recent problem, and they'd go over the solution, detail by detail, until she understood why it'd been handled that particular way. Remote hands-on training, he'd joked.

"Walshaw doesn't know about this," Philip Evans had answered grimly. "Nobody knows apart from me. I noticed our cash reserves had fallen pretty drastically in the last quarterly financial summaries. Forty-eight million Eurofrancs down, Juliet; that's fifty-seven million New Sterling for Christ's sake. Our entire reserve is only nine hundred million Eurofrancs. So I started checking. The money is being used to cover a deficit from the microgee crystal furnaces up at Zanthus. Standard accounting procedure; the loss was passed on to the finance division to make good for our loan-repayment schedule. They're just doing their job. The responsibility lies with the microgee division, and they've done bugger all about it."

She'd frowned, bewildered. "But surely someone in the microgee division should've spotted it? Thirty-seven percent! What about the security monitors?"

"Nothing. They didn't trip. According to the data squirt from Zanthus, that thirty-seven percent is coming out of the furnace as just so much rubbish, riddled with impurities. They've written it off as a normal operational loss. And that is pure bollocks. The furnaces weren't performing that badly at start-up, and we're way down the learning curve now. A worst-case scenario should see a five percent loss. I checked with the Boeing Marietta consortium that builds the furnaces; no one else is suffering that kind of reject rate. Most of 'em have losses below two percent."

The full realization struck her then. "We can't trust security?"

"God knows, Juliet. I'm praying that some smartarse hot rod has found a method of cracking the monitor's access codes, however unlikely that is. The alternative is bad."

"What are you going to do?"

"Sit and think. They've been gnawing away at us for eight bloody months; a few more days won't kill us. But we're taking a quarter of a million Eurofranc loss per day. It's got to stop, and stop dead. I have to know the people I put on it are reliable."

They couldn't afford major losses, Julia knew. Philip Evans's post–Second Restoration expansion plans were stretching the company's resources to breaking point. Microgee products were the most profitable of all Event Horizon's gear, but the space station modules tied up vast sums of capital; even with the Sanger space-planes, reaching orbit was still phenomenally expensive. They needed the income from the memox crystals to keep up the payments to the company's financial backing consortium.

The fact that he'd admitted the problem to her and her alone had brought a wonderful sensation of contentment. They'd always been close, but this made the bond unbreakable. She was the only person he could really trust in the whole world. And that was just a little bit scary.

She'd promised faithfully to run an analysis of the security monitor programs through her nodes for him, to see if the codes could be cracked, or maybe subverted. But she'd delayed it while she went horse riding with Adrian and Kats, then again as the three of them went swimming, and now subverting the manor's security circuits.

Guilt added itself to the shame she was already feeling from spying on the lovers. She'd been appallingly selfish, allowing a juvenile infatuation to distract her. Betraying Grandpa's trust.

Access HighSteal.

Sight, sound, and sensation fell away, isolating her at the center of a null void. Numbers filled her mind, nothing like a cube display, no colored numerals; this was elemental math, raw digits. The processor nodes obediently slotted them into a logic matrix, a three-dimensional lattice with data packages on top, filtering through a dizzy topography of interactive channels that correlated and cross-indexed. Hopefully the answer should pop out of the bottom.

She thought for a moment, defining the parameters of the matrix channels, allowing ideas to form, merge. Any ideas, however wild. Some fruiting, some withering. Irrational. Assume the monitors are unbreakable: how would I go about concealing the loss? An inverted problem, outside normal computer logic, its factors too random. Her processor nodes loaded the results into the channel structures.

The columns of numbers started to flow. She began to inject tracer programs, adding modifications as she went, probing for weak points.

Some deep level of her brain admitted that the metaphysical matrix frightened her, an eerie sense of trepidation at its inhuman nature. She feared herself, what she'd become. Was that why people kept their distance? Could they tell she was different somehow? An instinctive phobia.

She cursed the bioware.

* * *

Philip Evans's scowling face filled her bedside phone screen. "Juliet?" The scowl faded. "For God's sake, girl, it's past midnight."

He looked so terribly fragile, she thought, worse than ever. She kept her roguish smile firmly in place—school discipline, thank heavens. "So what are you doing up, then?"

"You bloody well know what I'm doing, girl."

"Yeah, me, too. Listen, I think I've managed to clear security over the monitor programs."

He leaned in toward the screen, eyes questing. "How?"

"Well, the top rankers anyway," she conceded. "We make eighteen different products up at Zanthus, and each of the microgee production modules squirts its data to the control center in the dormitory. Now the control-center 'ware processes the data before it enters the company data net so that the relevant divisions only get the data they need—maintenance requirements to procurement, consumables to logistics, and performance figures to finance. But the security monitoring is actually done up at Zanthus, with the raw data. And that's where the monitor programs have been circumvented; they haven't been altered at all."

"Circumvented how?"

"By destreaming the data squirts from the microgee modules, lumping them all together. The monitors are programmed to trip when production losses rise above fourteen percent; anything below that is considered a maintenance problem. At the moment the total loss of our combined orbital production is thirteen point two percent, so no alarm."

Julia watched her grandpa run a hand across his brow. "Juliet, you're an angel."

She said nothing, grinning stupidly into the screen, feeling just great.

"I mean it," he said.

Embarrassed in the best possible way, she shrugged. "Just a question of programming, all that expensive education you gave me. Anybody else could've done it. What will you do now?"

"Do you know who authorized the destreaming?"

"No, sorry. It began nine months ago, listed as part of one of our famous simplification-economy drives."

"Can you find out?"

"Tricky. However, I checked with personnel, and none of the Zanthus managers have left in the last year, so whoever the culprit is, they're still with us. Three options. I can try and worm my way into Zanthus's 'ware and see if they left any traces, like which ter-minal it was loaded from, whose access card was used, that kind of thing. Or I could go up to Zanthus and freeze their records."

"No way, Juliet," he said tenderly. "Sorry."

"Thought so. The last resort would be to use our executive code to dump Zanthus's entire data core into the security division's stor-age facility and run through the records there. The trouble with that is that everyone would know it's been done."

"And the culprit would do a bunk," he concluded for her. "Yes. So that leaves us with breaking into Zanthus. Bloody wonderful, cracking my own 'ware. So tell me why this absolves the top rankers?"

"It doesn't remove them from suspicion altogether; it just means they aren't the prime suspects anymore, now we know the monitor codes weren't compromised. Whether security personnel are involved or not depends on how good the original vetting system is. Certainly someone intimate with our data-handling procedures is guilty."

"That doesn't surprise me. There's always rotten apples, Juliet, re-member that. All you can ever do is hope to exclude them from achieving top-rank positions."

"What will you do now?"

The hand massaged his brow again. "Tell Walshaw, for a start. If we can't trust him, then we may as well pack up today. After that I'll bring in an independent, get him to check this mess out for me—se-curity, Zanthus management, the memox-furnace operators, the whole bloody lot of them."

"What sort of independent?"

He grinned. "Work that out for yourself, Juliet. Management ex-ercise."

"How many guesses?" she shot back, delighted. He was always challenging her like this. Testing.

"Three."

"Cruel."

"Good night, Juliet. Sweet dreams."

"Love you, Grandee."

He kissed two fingers, transferring the kiss to the screen. Her fin-gers pressed urgently against his, the touch of cold glass, hard. His face faded to slate gray.

Julia pulled the sheet over herself, turning off the brass swan wall lights. She hugged her chest in the warm darkness, elated, far too alert for sleep to calm her.

Access Surveillance Camera: West Wing, Guest Suite Seven.

3

ELEANOR HAD BEEN LIVING WITH Greg for exactly two weeks to the day when the Rolls-Royce crunched slowly down the dirt track into the Berrybut time-share estate.

It was two o'clock in the afternoon, and the sky was a cloudless turquoise desert. Eleanor and Greg shifted towels, cushions, and drinks out onto the chalet's tiny patio to take advantage of the unseasonable break in the weather. March was usually a regular procession of hot hard downfalls accompanying a punishing humidity. Greg could remember his parents reminiscing about flurries of snow and hail, but his own childhood memories were of miserable damp days stretching into May. Fortunately, typhoons hadn't progressed north of Gibraltar yet. Give it ten years, said the doomsayer meteorologists.

Eleanor stripped down to scarlet polka-dot bikini briefs, a present from Greg when he found she couldn't swim, promising to teach her. He rubbed screening oil over her bare back. Pleasantly erotic, although the heat stopped them from carrying it any further. They settled down to spy on the birds wading along the softly steaming mudflats at the foot of the sloping clearing. Most months saw some new exotic species arriving at the reservoir, fleeing the chaos storms raging ever more violently around the equatorial zones. The year had already seen several spoonbills and purple herons, even a cattle egret had put in a couple of appearances.

Greg lay on the towel, eyes drooping, letting the sun's warmth soak his limbs, slowly banishing the stiffness with a sensuousness that no massage could possibly match. Eleanor stretched out beside him on her belly and loaded a memox of Tolkien's *Lord of the Rings* into her cybofax. Every now and then she'd take a sip of orange from a glass filled with crushed ice and scan the shoreline for any additions.

Usually the girls he went with would drift away after a couple of days, maybe a week, unable to cope with his mood changes. But this time there hadn't been any: he had nothing to get depressed about; her body kept the blues at bay. And her humor, too, he admitted to himself. She rarely found fault. Probably a relic of her claustrophobic kibbutz upbringing—you *had* to learn tolerance there.

He wasn't quite sure who was corrupting whom. She was sensual and enthusiastic in bed; they screwed like rutty teenagers on speed each night. And he hadn't bothered to see any of his old mates since she moved in, not that he was pushing them out of his life. But her company seemed to be just as satisfying. It would be nice to think—dream really—that he could cut himself loose from the pain and obligations that came out of the past.

The rest of the country was in an electric state of flux, one he could see stabilizing in a year or two. He had wondered on odd occasions if he could manage the transition, too. Start to make a permanent home, stick to ordinary cases, earn regular money. There was just so much of the past that would have to be laid to rest first.

Whistles and shouts floated down from the back of the chalet row, the estate kids' twenty-four-hour football game in full swing. Up toward Edith Weston, bright, colorful sails of windsurfers whizzed about energetically. The county canoe team was out in force, enthusiastically working themselves into a collective heatstroke as their podgy coach screamed abuse at them through a bullhorn. Hireboats full of amateur fishermen and their expensive tackle drifted idly in the breeze.

Greg hadn't quite nodded off when he heard the car approaching. Eleanor raised herself on to her elbows and pushed her sunglasses up, frowning.

"Now that is unreal," she murmured.

Greg agreed. The car was old, a 1950s vintage Silver Shadow, its classic, fabulously stylish lines inspiring instant envy. The kind of fanatical devotion invested in both its design and assembly were long-faded memories now, a lost heritage.

Astonishingly, it still used the original combustion engine with a recombiner cell grafted on, allowing it to burn petrol. Two pressure spheres stored its exhaust gas below the chassis, ready for converting back into liquid hydrocarbon when the cell was plugged into a power source. The system was ludicrously expensive.

He watched in bemused silence as it drew up outside the chalet, shaming his two-door electric Fiat Austin Duo. Out of the corner of his eye he could see his neighbors staring in silence at the majestic apparition. Even the football game had stopped.

Given the car, the driver came as no surprise; he was decked out in a stiff gray-brown chauffeur's uniform, complete with peaked cap.

He didn't bother with the front door, walking around Greg's vegetable patch to the patio, scattering scrawny chickens in his wake. The way he walked gave him the authority. Easy powerful strides, backed up by wide powerful shoulders and a deep chest. He was young, mid-twenties, confident and alert.

He looked around curiously as he approached. Greg sympathized; the little estate had begun to resemble a sort of upmarket hippie commune. Shambolic.

Eleanor wrapped a towel around her breasts, knotting it at the side. Greg climbed to his feet, wearily.

The chauffeur gave Eleanor a courteous little half-bow, eyes lingering. He caught himself and turned self-consciously to Greg. "Mr. Mandel?"

"Yes."

"My employer would like to interview you for a job."

"I have a phone."

"He would like to do it in person, and today."

"What sort of job?"

"I have no idea." The chauffeur reached inside his jacket and pulled out an envelope. "This is for your time." It was two thousand pounds New Sterling, in brand-new fifties.

Greg handed it down to Eleanor, who riffled the crisp plastic notes, staring incredulously.

"Who is your employer?" he asked the chauffeur.

"He wishes to introduce himself."

Greg shrugged, not that impatient for details. People with money had learned to become circumspect in advertising the fact. Furtiveness was a national habit now; not even the Second Restoration had changed that. The PSP's local committees had become well versed at diverting private resources to benefit the community. And they'd made some pretty individualistic interpretations on what constituted "community."

Greg tried to get a feel from his intuition. Nothing, it was playing coy. And then there was the money. Two thousand just for an interview. Crazy. Eleanor was waiting, her wide eyes slightly troubled. He glanced down at the frayed edges of his cut-off jeans. "Have I got time to change first?"

The Rolls-Royce's dinosaur mechanics made even less noise than an electric car—sublime engineering. There was a glass screen between Greg and the chauffeur, frosty roses etched around the edges. It stayed up for the whole drive, leaving questions stillborn. He sank into the generous leather cushioning of the rear seat and watched the world go by through somber smoked windows. Chilly air-conditioning made him glad of the light suit he was wearing.

They drove through Edith Weston and onto the A1, heading south. The big car's wheelbase bridged the minor roads completely. Over a decade of neglect by the PSP had allowed grass and speedwells to spread out from the curbs; spongy moss formed a continuous emerald strip where the white lines used to be. It was only thanks to farm traffic and bicycles that the roads had been kept open at all during the depth of the dark years.

Horses and cyclists pulled onto the verge to let them pass, curious faces gaping at the outlandish relic. The impulse to give a royal wave was virtually irresistible.

There was some traffic on the dual-carriageway A1—horse-drawn drays, electric cars, and small methane-fueled vans. The Rolls-Royce outpaced them effortlessly, its suspension gliding evenly over the deep ruts of crumbling tarmac.

The northbound side of the Welland bridge had collapsed, leaving behind a row of crumbling concrete pillars leaning at a precarious angle out of the fast-moving muddy water, pregnant from five weeks of heavy rains. The bridge had been swept away four years ago in the annual flooding that had long since scoured the valley clean of all its villages and farms. During the dry season the river shrank back to its usual level, exposing a livid gash of gray-blue clay speckled with bricks and shattered roofing timbers, the seam of a serpentine swamp stretching from the fringe of the Fens basin right back to Barrowden.

The chauffeur turned off the A1 at Wansford, heading west, inland, away from the bleak salt marshes that festered across the floor of the Nene valley below the bridge.

Greg hated the waste, President Armstrong's legacy. It was all so unnecessary; levees were among the oldest types of civil engineering.

The Rolls turned off onto a dirt track. It looked like an ordinary farm path across the fields of baby sugarcane, leading to a small wood of Spanish oaks about three-quarters of a kilometer away. There wasn't even a gate, simply a wide cattle grid and a weather-beaten sign warning would-be trespassers of dire consequences.

The chauffeur stopped before the grid and flicked a switch on the dash before driving on. There was nothing between the metal strips: no weeds, puddles, only a drowning blackness.

They drove through an opening in the trees, under a big stone arch with wrought-iron gates, kept in excellent condition. Stone griffins looked down at the Rolls with lichen-pocked eyes.

There was a long gravel drive beyond the gates, leading up to a magnificent early-eighteenth-century manor house. Silver windows flashed fractured sunbeams. A tangle of pink and yellow roses boiled over the stonework, tendrils lapping the second-story windowsills.

Five dove-gray geodesic globes lurked among the forest of tall chimney stacks. Very heavy-duty satellite antennas.

The Rolls pulled to a smooth halt level with the gray stone portico. "Wilholm Manor," the chauffeur announced, gravel-voiced, as he opened the door.

A couple of gardeners were tending the regimented flower beds along the edge of the gravel, stopping to watch as Greg stepped out.

Something was moving in the thick shrubbery at the foot of the lawn, dark, indistinct, bigger than a dog, slipping through the flower-laden plumbago clumps with serpentine grace. Spooky. Greg reached out with his espersense, detecting a single thread of thought, diamond hard. He placed it straight away, an identification loaded with associated memories he'd prefer to forgo. He was focused on a gene-tailored sentinel panther. It padded along its patrol pattern with robotic precision, bioware archsenses alert for any transgressors.

He sucked in his breath, stomach muscles clenched. The Jihad legions had used similar animals in Turkey, a quantum leap upward from modified Rottweilers. He'd seen a sentinel take out a fully armored squaddie after the animal had been blown half to bits, jaws cutting clean through the boy's combat suit. They were fucking lethal. The manor's elegant façade suddenly seemed dimmer, fogbound.

He was shown through the double doors into the hall by an old man in a butler's tailcoat. The interior was as immaculate as he'd expected. Large dark oil landscapes hung on the walls; the antique furniture was delicate to the point of effete, chandeliers like miniature galaxies illuminated a vaulting ceiling: a decor that blended perfectly with the building. But it was all new, superimposed on the ancient shell by a stage dresser with an unlimited budget. The paint was glossy bright, the green and gold wallpaper fresh, the carpets unworn.

Greg hadn't known this kind of opulence existed in England any more. Yes, his usual clients were well off. But at most that meant a detached house with maybe three or four bedrooms, or some overseas-financed condominium apartment loaded with pieces of family heritage saved from the magpie acquisition fever of tax-office apparatchiks.

Given normal circumstances, the local PSP committee would've turned the manor into accommodation modules for about forty families who'd then work the surrounding land in some sort of communal farm arrangement, either a co-op or a full-fledged kibbutz. Wilholm's renovation was recent, post–Second Restoration.

The butler led Greg up a broad, curving stair to the landing, and he caught a glimpse of the formal gardens at the back. Bushes clipped into animal shapes sentried wide paths. A statue of Venus in the middle of the lily pond sent a white plume of water shooting high into the air. Spherical rainbows shimmered inside the cloud of descending spray.

The inevitable swimming pool was a large oval affair, a good twenty meters long. A tall tower of diving boards stood guard over the deep end, and there was a convoluted slide zigzagging along one side. A couple of big inflatable balls were floating on the surface. Three teenagers cavorted about in the clear water: two girls, one boy.

They seemed out of place, interlopers, their lively shrieks and splashes discordant with the funereal solemnity that hung through the rest of the manor.

He was shown into Wilholm's oak-paneled study, and the day finally began to pull together into some sort of sense. Philip Evans was waiting for him.

There had been this girl, Greg couldn't remember her name now, but the two of them had got rapturously drunk watching the coronation together. The triumph of the Second Restoration remained forever buried in that alcoholic netherland, but he distinctly remembered Philip Evans sitting in the abbey's congregation. The cameras couldn't keep off him. A small man in his mid-seventies, stiff-backed, using a stick to assist his slow walk but managing to smile brightly nonetheless.

Philip Evans was the PSP's bête noire; their Whitehall media department set him up as a hate figure, a campaign of vilification that left Orwell's Emmanuel Goldstein standing. It'd backfired on them badly. Evans became a romantic pirate to the rest of the country. A living legend.

Perhaps he deserved the notoriety. His Event Horizon company had been used, quite deliberately, as a weapon against the PSP's lumbering economic program. And Evans had wielded it with consummate skill. A number of prominent commentators credited him with hastening Armstrong's demise.

Event Horizon's cybernetic factories floated with blissful impunity in international waters right through the PSP decade, churning out millions of counterfeit gear systems each year.

His fleet of Stealth transports made nightly flights over England, distributing their wares to a country-wide network of spivs like demonic Santas. They proved unstoppable. One of the PSP's first acts on reaching office had been to disband most of the RAF.

The black-market gear hurt the economy badly, undermining indigenous industries, turning more people to the spivs. A nasty downward spiral, picking up speed.

Evans had changed for the worse in the intervening two years since the coronation. The flesh sagged on his face, becoming pasty white, highlighting dark panda circles around his eyes. His hair had nearly gone; the few wisps remaining were a pale silver. And not even the baggy sleeves of his silk dressing gown could disguise how disturbingly thin his arms were.

He was sitting at the head of a long oak table. Two holo cubes flanked him, multicolored reflections from their swirling graphics rippling like S-bend rainbows off the highly polished wood.

Greg sniffed the cool dry air; there was a tart smell in the study, peppery. Philip Evans was badly ill.

The aging billionaire dismissed his butler with an impatient flick of his hand. "Come in, Mandel. Can't see you properly from here, boy; my bastard eyes are going along with the rest of me."

There was another man in the study, standing staring out of the window, hands clasped behind his back. He didn't look around.

Walking down the length of the table, Greg saw that Evans was only whole above the waist. His legs and hips had been swallowed by the seamless cylindrical base of a pearl-white powerchair, torso fusing into an elastic chrome collar. It was a mobile life-support unit, analogue bioware organs sustaining the faltering body. But the mind was still fully active, burning hot and bright.

Greg shook his hand. It was like holding a glove filled with hot water.

"What do they call you, boy? Greg, isn't it?" The accent was pure Lincolnshire, blunt, as much an attitude as a speech pattern.

"Yes, sir."

"Well, I'm Philip, Greg. Now sit down; it ricks my neck craning up at you."

Greg sat, one chair down from Evans.

"This is my security chief, Morgan Walshaw."

The man turned, looking at Greg. He was in his late fifties, with close-cropped gray hair, wearing a blue office suit, plain fuchsia tie. Shoulders squared. Definitely ex-military. The recognition was instantaneous. A mirror.

Eyeing each other up like prize fighters, Greg thought. Stupid.

"Mr. Walshaw doesn't approve of my asking you here," Evans explained.

"I don't disapprove," Walshaw said quickly. "I just consider this an internal affair; sorry, nothing personal."

Greg looked to Evans, politeness software loaded and running. Showing respect. "May I ask why you chose me in particular for a job? Random selection is, frankly, unbelievable."

"Haven't decided whether you are going to do a job for me, yet, boy. You'll have to prove you're what I'm looking for first. I believe you cleared up a problem for Simon White last year? Delicate, a real ball crusher. That right?"

"I know Mr. White, yes."

"All right, don't go all starchy on me. I do business with Simon; he recommended you. Said you only work for the top man, keep your mouth shut afterward. Right?"

"That's correct," Greg said. "Naturally I offer confidentiality. But in taking on corporate cases I do so only for the board or chairman. Office politics are a complication I can do without."

"You mean I couldn't hire you?" Walshaw asked.

"Only if the chairman approved."

"You're ex-Army?" the security chief persisted. "Mindstar?"

"Yes."

"So it was the Army that gave you your gland," Evans said. "How come you didn't sign on with a *kombinate* security division after you were demobbed, or even turn tekmerc?"

"I had other things to do, sir."

"You could've earned a fortune."

"Not really," Greg said. "The idea that gland psychics are some kind of superbreed is pure tabloid. If you want someone who can see through brick walls, then I'm not your man. Glands are not an exact science. I tested out psi-positive with top marks on ESP, so the Army volunteered me for an implant, thinking I would develop a sixth sense that could pinpoint enemy locations, index their weapons and ammunition stocks. But the workings of the mind don't follow a straight logical course. I was one of the disappointments, along with several hundred others. People like me were one of the major factors in the decision to abandon the Mindstar program, and that was long before the PSP obliterated the defense budget."

"So what can you do?" Evans asked.

"Basically, I can tell if you're lying. It's a kind of super empathy, or intuition—a little mix of the two. Not much call for that on the battlefield. Bullets rarely lie."

"Don't run yourself down, boy. Sounds like you've got the kind of thing I'm looking for. So tell me, did I enjoy my breakfast orange?"

Greg saw the gland, glistening ebony, pumping. Physically, it was a horrendously complex patchwork of neurosecretory cells; the original matrix had taken the American DARPA office over a decade to develop. An endocrine node implanted in the cortex, raiding the bloodstream for chemicals and disgorging a witches' brew of neurohormones in return.

The answer was intuitive: "You didn't have orange for breakfast."

Morgan Walshaw blinked, interest awakened.

Evans grunted gruff approval. "The last quarter profits from my orbital memox-crystal furnaces have been bad. True or false?"

"They've been awful."

"You ain't bloody kidding, boy." The chair backed out from the table and trundled over to a window. Gazing mournfully across the splendid lawns, the billionaire said, "This job isn't for my benefit. I suppose you know I'm dying?"

"I guessed it was pretty serious."

"Lymph disorder, boy, aggravated by using the old devil deal hormone to keep my skin thick and my hair growing. So much for vanity; serves me right. This *thing* I've got, very rare, so they tell me. After all, it would never do for me to die of something common." He snorted contemptuously at his own bitterness. "Everything will go to my granddaughter, Julia. She's the one out there in the pool, the brunette. The lovely one."

"What about her parents? Don't they stand to inherit?"

"Ha! Call 'em parents? Because like buggery I do. If I hadn't paid off her mother, she'd still be in that Midwest cult commune, smoking pot and screwing its leaders for Jesus. And that son of mine is incapable of taking on Event Horizon. Couldn't anyway, even if he wanted. Legally incompetent.

"Best detox clinics in the world have tried to straighten his kinks. Too late. He's been on syntho so long—and I'm talking decades—the dependence is unbreakable. You cold-turkey his body and the lights go out. They shoved him through the whole routine—counseling, group analysis, deprivation motivation, work therapy—it amounted to one great big zero. The only time he even knows there's an outside world is when he's tripping." The anger rose again. "It's fucking humiliating. I was prepared for some rebellion, a bit of antagonism between us. That's the way it always is between father and son. But him! We had nothing, no love, not even hate. It was like everything I was achieving didn't even register with him. He walked out the door on his twentieth birthday, and that was it, not another word for twenty-five years. The only reason I found out I had a granddaughter was because that freako cult he wound up with tried to leech me for donations.

"That's why I've got to safeguard the company. For her. I'm not going to last for much longer, and she doesn't have the experience to take it on right away."

"But surely you'll be leaving Event Horizon in the hands of trustees?" Greg asked. "People you know can manage it properly."

"Damn right." There was a fierce spark of elation in Philip Evans's mind. "Event Horizon has the potential to become a global leader in gear manufacture. While Armstrong's PSP let all the other English companies rot away back here, I was buying top-grade Korean cyber-production systems for my factory ships, I kept my overseas research people well funded, made distribution deals with the biggest American net softmalls. And that was in the middle of the global recession. Well, now I'm moving it all back home, consolidating. That's going to be my last gift to this country, better than all the rest. The factories I'm bringing ashore have got a phenomenal growth potential; they'll create jobs, foreign exchange, encourage a whole pack of subcontractor companies. Event Horizon'll stop us sliding back into an agrarian economy. We can match those bloody German *kombinates*, and even the American conglomerates. The Pacific Rim isn't going to be the only economic superpower to emerge from this bloody Warming, my boy, you see. I'm going to show the whole world England ain't dead yet."

"Sounds good. So why do you need me?"

Evans scowled. "Sorry, I run on. Old man's disease. By the time you accumulate the resources to accomplish something worthwhile, time's up.

"The problem, boy, is my orbital operation up at Zanthus. Someone is running a spoiler against the company. They've turned the operators of my microgee furnaces up at Zanthus; thirty-seven percent of my memox crystals are being deliberately ruined. That adds up to seven million Eurofrancs a month."

Greg let out an involuntary whistle. He hadn't known Event Horizon was that big.

"Yeah, right," Philip Evans said. "I can't sustain that kind of loss for much longer. Lucky I caught it when I did." And there was a hint of pride at the accomplishment. Still on the ball, still the *man*. "The organizer circumvented some pretty elaborate security safeguards, too. Means whoever they are, they're smart and organized."

"They're clever all right," Walshaw conceded. He pulled out a black wood chair opposite Greg and sat down.

"And even the security division is under suspicion," Evans said. "Including Morgan here, which is why he's so pissed off with me."

Greg sneaked a glance at Walshaw, meeting impenetrable urbanity. The man had not—and never would—sell out. Greg knew him, the type, his motivation; he'd no grand visions of his own, the perfect lieutenant. And in Event Horizon and Philip Evans he'd found an ideal liege. The old billionaire must've understood that, too.

Walshaw nodded an extremely reluctant acknowledgment. "The nature of the circumvention does imply a degree of internal complicity, certainly knowledge of the security monitor procedures was compromised."

"He means the buggers are on the take, that's what," Evans grumbled. "And I want you to root 'em out for me, boy. You're about the nearest thing to independent in this brain-wrecked world. Trustworthy, as far as we can satisfy ourselves. So then, four hundred New Sterling a day, and all the expenses you can spend. How does that sound?"

"Do I have to sign the contract in blood?"

"Just don't screw me about, boy. I've spent close on twenty years fighting that shit President Armstrong and his leftie storm troops; now that he's gone I'm not going to lose by default. Event Horizon is going to be my memorial. The trailblazer of England's industrial Renaissance."

Greg felt a twinge of admiration for the old man; he was dying yet he was still making plans, dreaming. Not many could do that. "Where do you want me to start?" he asked.

"You and I will go down to Stanstead," Morgan Walshaw said. "Assuming I'm trustworthy."

"Don't be so bloody sarcastic," Evans barked.

"Stanstead is Event Horizon's main air-freight terminal in England," Walshaw explained, quietly amused. "All our flights out to Listoel originate there."

"Listoel?" Greg asked.

"That's the anchorage for my cyber-factory ships out in the Atlantic," Philip Evans said. "A lot of Event Horizon's domestic gear is still built out there, and it's where my spaceline, Dragonflight, is based. Anyone going up to Zanthus starts at Listoel.'

"Calling in the management personnel and memox-furnace operators who are currently on leave won't be regarded as particularly unusual," Walshaw said. "Once they arrive, you can use your gland ability to determine which of them have been turned. After that, you and a small security team will go up to Zanthus and pull whoever circumvented the security monitors, along with the guilty furnace operators working up there. We'll fly up replacements from the batch you've vetted."

"You want me to go up to Zanthus?" Greg asked. There was a sensation in his gut as if he'd just knocked back a few brandies in rapid-fire succession.

"That's right, boy. Why, that a problem?"

"No." Greg grinned. "No problem at all."

"It's not a bloody holiday," Evans snapped. "You get your arse up there, and you stop them, Greg. Hard and fast. I've got to have something concrete to show my backing consortium. They're due for the figures in another six weeks. I've got to have something positive for them. They'll understand a spoiler—God knows enough of the *kombinates* are trying to throttle each other rather than do an honest day's work. What they won't stand for is me dallying about whinging instead of stomping on it." Philip Evans subsided, resting on the powerchair's tall back. "That just leaves this evening."

"What's happening this evening?" Greg asked.

"I'm throwing a small dinner party—some close friends and associates, one or two glams, plus Julia's house guests. There's a couple of people I want you to screen for me. I've invited Dr. Ranasfari. He's leading one of Event Horizon's research teams, a genuine genius. I've got him working on a project I consider absolutely crucial to my plans for the company's future. So you handle with care." Evans stopped, looking as uncomfortable as Greg had yet seen him. For a moment he thought it was the illness. But the old man's mind was flush with an emotion verging on guilt. Walshaw had turned away, uninterested. Diplomatic.

"The second . . ." Philip Evans nodded vaguely at the window. "That lad out there . . . Adrian, I think his name is. Julia seems quite taken with him. Leastways, she doesn't talk of hardly anything else. Don't get me wrong; I don't object to him, not if he makes her happy. Nothing I want more than to see her smiling. She's my world. It's just that I don't want her hurt. Now, I know you can't expect eternal commitment, not at that age, and he seems pleasant enough. But make sure she's not just another tick in his stud diary. Life's going to be tough enough for her, being my heir; she surely doesn't deserve bad-news boyfriends as well."

4

THERE WAS A DINNER JACKET waiting for Greg in the guest suite after he'd finished bathing. It fit perfectly. He put it on, feeling foolish, then went out to find his host. At least he had remembered how to do up his bow tie.

The lights throughout the majority of Wilholm's rooms were old-fashioned electric bulbs, drawing their power from solar panels clipped over the splendid Collyweston slates. He had to admit that biolums' pink-white glow wouldn't have done the classical decor justice. Evans had obviously gone to a lot of trouble recreating the old building's original glory.

The aging billionaire chortled at the sight of Greg as he waited for his powerchair on the east wing's landing, flushed and fingering his starched collar. "Almost respectable looking, boy." The powerchair stopped in front of him. Evans cocked his head, taking stock. "I hope you know which knives to use. I can hardly pass you off as my aide if you start savaging your avocado with a soup spoon, now can I?"

Greg wasn't sure if the old man was mocking him or the marvelously doltish niceties of table etiquette, so religiously adhered to by England's upper-middle classes—what was left of them. Probably both.

"I was an officer," Greg countered. Not that he'd graduated from Sandhurst, nothing so formal. It was what the Army had called a necessity promotion—all the Mindstar candidates were captains— some obscure intelligence division commission. A week of learning how to accept salutes and three months' solid slog of data interpretation and correlation exercises.

"Course you were, m'boy; and a gentleman, too, no doubt."

"Well, I always took my socks off before, if that's what you mean," Greg said.

Evans laughed approvingly. "Wish I had you on my permanent staff. So many bloody woofter yes-men—"

The chair took off toward the main stairs at a fast walking pace. The old man looked much improved since the afternoon. Greg wondered how he'd pay for that later.

The three teenagers were heading for the stairs from the manor's west wing. Evans waited at the top for them. The taller girl bent over and gave his cheek a soft kiss, studying his face carefully. There was genuine concern written on her features.

"Now, you're not going to stay up late," she said primly. It wasn't a question.

"No." Evans was trying hard to make it come out grumpy but fell miserably short. Her presence resembled a fission reaction, kindling a fierce glow of pride in his mind. "Greg, this is Julia, that wayward grandchild I've been telling you about."

Julia Evans nodded politely but didn't offer her hand. Apparently her grandfather's employees didn't rate anything more than fleeting acknowledgment. In silent retaliation Greg tagged her as a standard-issue spoiled brat.

Actually, he acknowledged she was quite a nice-looking girl. Tall and slender, with a modest bust, and her fine, unfashionably long hair arranged in an attractive wavy style that complemented a pleasant oval face. She wore a slim plain silver tiara on her brow and a small gold Saint Christopher dangling from a chain around her neck. He thought her choice of a strapless royal purple silk dress was sagacious; she had the kind of confident poise necessary to carry it well, and not many her age could claim the same.

The boys would look twice, sure enough. Because she was sparky in that way that all teenage girls were sparky. It was just that she hadn't developed any striking characteristics to lift her out of the ordinary. And right now that was her major problem. She was a satellite deep into an eclipse. Her primary, the girl she stood beside, was an absolutely dazzling seraph.

Her name was Katerina Cawthorp, introduced as Julia's friend from their Swiss boarding school. A true golden girl, with richly tanned satin-smooth skin and a thick mane of honey-blond hair that cascaded over wide, strong shoulders. Her figure was an ensemble of superbly molded curves, accentuated by a dress of some glittering bronze fabric that hugged tight. A deliciously low-cut front displayed a great deal of firm shapely cleavage, while a high tight hem did the same for long elegant legs. Her face was foxy: bee-stung lips, pert nose, and clear Nordic-blue eyes that regarded Greg with faint condescension. He'd been staring.

Katerina must have been used to it. That sly almost-smile let the whole world know that butter would most definitely melt in her mouth.

Julia wheeled her grandfather's chair onto a small platform that ran down a set of rails at the side of the stairs.

"That father of yours, is he coming down?" Evans asked her sourly.

"Now, don't you two start quarreling tonight."

"Probably skulking in his room getting stoned."

She slapped his wrist, quite sharply. "Behave. This is a party."

Evans grunted irritably, and the platform began to slide down. Julia kept up with it, skipping lightly.

Naturally, Katerina's descent was far more dignified. She glided effortlessly, an old-style film star making her grand entrance at a blockbuster premiere.

It left Greg free to talk to the boy, Adrian Marler. He didn't have to ask anything; Adrian turned out to be one of nature's gushers. He launched into conversation by telling Greg how he'd just begun to study medicine at Cambridge, hoped to make the rugby team as a winger, complained about the New Conservative government's pitifully inadequate student grant, confided that his family was comfortably off but nowhere near as rich as the Evans dynasty.

Adrian was six foot tall with surf-king muscles, short curly blond hair, chiseled cheekbones, and a roguish grin that would send young—and not so young—female hearts racing; he was also intelligent, humorous, and respectful. Greg felt a flash of envious dislike for a kind of adolescence he'd never had, dismissing it quickly.

"So how did you meet Julia?" he inquired.

"Katey introduced us," Adrian said. "Hey listen, no way was I going to turn down the chance to crash out at this palace for a few days, meet the great Philip Evans. Then there's gourmet food, as much booze as you want, clean sheets every day, valet service." He leaned over and gave Greg a significant between-us-men look before murmuring, "And our rooms are fortuitously close together."

"She seems a nice girl," Greg ventured.

Adrian's eyes tracked the slow-moving, foil-wrapped backside in front of them with radar precision. "You have no idea how truly you speak." His mind was awhirl with hot elation.

"Are we talking about Julia or Katerina?"

Adrian broke off his admiring stare with obvious reluctance. "Katey, of course. I mean, Julia's decent enough, despite her old man being a complete arsehole. But she couldn't possibly match up to Katey, nobody could." He dropped his voice, taking Greg into his confidence. "If I had the money, I'd marry Katey straight off. I know it sounds stupid, considering her age. But her parents just don't care about her. It's a scandal; if they were poor, the social services would've taken her into care. But they're rich; they sit in their Austrian tax haven and treat her as a style accessory. To their set it's fashionable to have a child, the more precocious the better. That's probably why she and Julia are such closeheads. Near-identical backgrounds, both of them ignored from an early age."

Greg suddenly experienced a pang of sympathy, prompted by his intuition. Adrian was a regular lad, one of the boys, likable. He deserved better than Katerina. Although he didn't know it, his infatuation was doomed to a terminal crash landing. His rugged good looks and lack of hard cash marked him down as a passing fancy. Naïveté preventing him from realizing that the teeny-vamp sex goddess whose footsteps he worshiped was going to chew him up then spit him out the second a tastier morsel caught her wandering, lascivious eye.

Still, at least it meant Greg could start the evening by giving Evans one piece of news that he wanted to hear. Though whether it was good news was debatable. To Greg's mind, Julia would be hard pushed to find a better prospect for prince consort.

Philip Evans received his guests in the manor's drawing room. Its arching windows looked out onto the immaculately mown lawns where peacocks strutted around the horticultural menagerie along the paths. Maids in black-and-white French-style uniforms circulated with silver trays of tall champagne glasses and fattening cheesy snacks. A string quartet played a soft melody in the background. Greg felt as if he'd time-warped into some Mayfair club circa 1930.

The men were all dressed in immaculately tailored dinner jackets, while the women wore long gowns of subdued colors and modest cut. It made Katerina stand out from the crowd, not that she needed sartorial assistance for that. A stunning case of overkill.

Greg saw that despite his blunt Lincolnshire-boy attitude, Philip Evans made a good host. He slipped into the role easily. A lifetime immersed in PR had taught him how.

Julia stuck by his side, officially the hostess, being the senior lady of the family. The guests treated her with a formal respect not usually directed at teenagers. They must know she was the protégée, Greg realized. She accepted her due without a hint of pretension.

Greg hovered behind the pair of them, maintaining a lifeless professional smile as he was introduced as Philip Evans's new personal secretary. The old billionaire had assembled an impressive collection of top rankers for his party—a couple of New Conservative cabinet ministers and the deputy prime minister, five ambassadors, financiers, a sprinkling of the aristocracy, and some flash showbiz types, presumably for Julia's benefit.

Lady Adelaide and Lord Justin Windsor, Princess Beatrice's children, were also mingling with the guests, two tight knots of people swirling gently around them the whole time. Greg had managed to exchange a few words with Lady Adelaide; she was in her early twenties and as politely informal as only royalty could be, given the circumstances. He gave way to the press of social mountaineers well pleased; Eleanor would love hearing the details.

As he left, he saw Katerina moving with the tenacity of an icebreaker through the people around Lord Justin. She wriggled around an elderly matron with gymnastic agility to deliver herself in front of him, blue eyes hot with sultry promise. For one moment, watching Lord Justin's quickly hidden guilty smile, Greg allowed his cynicism to get the better of him. Could the young royal be the reason Philip Evans was unhappy about Adrian? Lord Justin was only five years older than Julia; a union between them was the kind of note an ultra-English traditionalist like Philip Evans would adore going out on. He eventually decided the thought was unworthy. Philip Evans might be devious, but he wasn't grubby.

The new arrivals seemed endless. Greg wanted to undo his iron collar; he wasn't used to it. But all he could do was smile at the blur of faces, sticking to form. The guests weren't a nightstalker crowd, he realized grimly, not the ones who cruised the shebeens searching for pickups and left-handed action. This was class, the real and the posed. Their conversation revolved around currency fluctuations, investment potential, and the latest Fernando production at the National Theater. Nobody here would be looking for a quiet moment to slip upstairs with someone else's escort. Greg steeled himself for hours of excruciating boredom.

There was one guest for whom Julia abandoned all her decorum, rushing up and flinging her arms around an overloud American. "Uncle Horace, you came!" She smiled happily as he patted her back, collecting an overgenerous kiss. The man was in his late fifties, red-faced and fleshy, his smile seemingly permanent.

The name enabled Greg to place him: Horace Jepson, the channel magnate. He was the president of Globecast, a satellite broadcasting company that had multiple channel franchises in nearly every country in the world, screening everything from trash soaps and rock videos to wildlife documentaries and twenty-four-hour news coverage. The PSP had refused Globecast a license while they were in power, although the company's Pan-Europe channels could always be picked up by Event Horizon's black-market flatscreens, complete with a dedicated English-language soundband. The PSP raged about imperialist electronic piracy; Globecast calmly referred to it as footprint overspill and kept on beaming it down. Greg had never watched anything else in the PSP decade.

Horace Jepson gave Philip Evans a hearty greeting while Julia clung to his side. Then she steered him adroitly away from a cluster of the celebrities who'd begun to eye him greedily, introducing him to one of the New Conservative ministers instead.

It was an interesting maneuver: if those manic self-advancing celebrities had sunk their varnished claws into Jepson, he would've had little chance of escaping all evening. So Julia Evans wasn't quite the airhead he'd so swiftly written her off as, after all. In fact, her thoughts seemed extraordinarily well focused, fast-flowing. He couldn't ever remember encountering a mind quite like hers before.

She returned and took her grandfather's hand. They shared a sly private smile.

It was a rapport that was quickly broken when Philip Evans spotted a couple making their way toward him and muttered, "Oh crap," under his breath. Julia glanced up anxiously and gave her grandfather's hand a quick, reassuring squeeze.

He studied the advancing couple with interest to see what had aroused the sudden concern and antipathy in both Julia and Philip. They were a handsome pair. She was in her mid-twenties, draped in at least half a million pounds' worth of diamond jewelry, and wearing a loose lavender gown that showed almost as much cleavage and thigh as Katerina. The man, Greg guessed, was forty; he had a dark Mediterranean complexion and obviously worked hard to keep himself fit. Each strand of his thick raven-black hair was locked into place.

Greg's espersense sent a cold, distinctly prickly sensation dancing along his spine as they approached. Beneath those perfect shells something disquietingly unpleasant lurked.

"Philip. Wonderful party," the man said, his accent faintly continental. "Thanks so much for the invite."

Philip returned the smile, although Greg knew him well enough by now to see how labored it was without resorting to his espersense.

"Kendric, glad you could come," he said. "I'd like you to meet my new secretary. Greg, this is Kendric di Girolamo, my good friend and business colleague."

Kendric smiled with reptilian snobbery. "Ah, the English. Always so eager to do down the foreign devil. Actually, Greg, I am Philip's financial partner. Without me Event Horizon would be a fifth-rate clothing sweatshop on some squalid North Sea trawler."

"Don't flatter yourself," Evans said in a tight flat voice. "I can find twenty money men bobbing about any time I look into a sewer."

"You see," Kendric appealed to Greg, "a socialist at heart. He has the true Red's loathing of bankers."

The knuckles on Julia's hand were blanched as she gripped her grandfather's shoulder, holding back the tiger.

The sight of someone as ill as Evans being deliberately provoked was infuriating. Greg allowed the neurohormones to flood out from the gland and focused his mind on ice—hard, sharp, helium cold. A slim blade of this, needle-sharp tip resting lightly on Kendric's brow, directly above his nose. "Don't let's spoil the party atmosphere," he said gently.

Kendric appeared momentarily annoyed by a mere pawn inter-rupting his grand game.

Greg thrust his eidolon knife forward. Penetration, root pattern of frost blossoming, congealing the brain to a blue-black rock of iron.

It felt so right, so easy. The power was there, fueled by that kilo-watt pulse of anger.

Kendric blinked in alarmed confusion, swaying as if caught by a sudden squall. The hauteur that had been swirling triumphantly across his thoughts flash-evaporated. His knees nearly buckled; he took an unsteady step backward before he regained his balance.

Greg's own unexpected flame withered, sucked back to whatever secret recess it originated from. Its departure left a copper taste film-ing his suddenly arid throat. He turned to the woman. "I don't be-lieve we've been introduced."

"My wife, Hermione," Kendric said warily, and she held her gloved hand out, the jewels of her rings sparkling brightly.

Her eyes swept Greg up and down with adulterous interest. She seemed mildly disappointed when all he did was shake her long-fingered hand.

He found himself comparing her to Eleanor. Only a few years sep-arated them, and put in a dress like that Eleanor would be equally awesome. Except Eleanor would laugh herself silly at the notion of haute couture, and she'd never be able to mix at this kind of party—Ashamed, he jammed that progression of thoughts to a rapid halt.

"Married, Mr. Mandel?" Hermione inquired. Her voice was the audio equivalent of Katerina's dress, husky and full of forbidden promise. Now, why did he keep associating those two?

"No."

"Pity. Married men are so much more fun."

Temptation had never beckoned so strongly before. She was one hell of a woman, but there was something bloody creepy scratching away behind that beautiful facade.

"We will talk later," Kendric said to Philip in a toneless voice. "Scotland needs to be finalized. Yes?"

"Yes," Philip conceded.

Satisfied with this minor victory, he moved on to give Julia a light kiss. Hermione followed suit, then wafted away with a final airy, "Ciao." But not before she winked at Greg.

Julia stood rigidly still for the embrace. Greg's espersense informed him she was squirming inside. She had good reason: there was a burst of unclean excitement in Hermione's mind as their cheeks touched.

"Who the hell are they?" Greg asked as soon as they were out of earshot.

Julia was kneeling anxiously by her grandfather's powerchair. The old man had sagged physically. His mind was gray.

She looked up at Greg with shrewdly questioning eyes. "Thank you for making Kendric back off," she said.

He detected her thoughts flying at lightspeed, never losing coherence. Odd. Unique, in fact.

"You have a gland," she said after a few seconds.

Philip's low chuckle was malicious. "Too late, Juliet; you've had your three."

"Oh, you," she poked him with a finger in mock exasperation. But there was an underlying current of annoyance.

"Di Girolamo is moneyed European aristocracy," he explained. "And he's right about us having financial ties, although being my partner is a complete load of balls. Did you ever buy any of my gear when the PSP was in power?"

"Yeah. A flatscreen, and a microwave, too, I think. Who didn't?"

"And how did you pay for 'em?"

"Fish mainly, some vegetables."

"Okay. The point is this: at the local level it was all done by barter. There was no hard cash involved. I would fly the gear in, and my spivs would distribute it, sometimes through the black market, sometimes through the Party Allocation Bureau. So far a normal company production/delivery setup, right? But none of your fruit and veg is any use to me; I can't pay the bankers with ten ton of oranges. So that's where Kendric and his team of spivs comes in; he makes sure

I get paid in hard currency. His spivs take the barter goods and exchange them for gold or silver or diamonds, some sort of precious commodity acceptable internationally—New Sterling was no good; it was a restricted currency under the PSP. They lift them out of the country, and Kendric converts them into Eurofrancs for me. It was a huge operation at the end, nearly two hundred thousand people, which is partly why the PSP never shut us down; you'd need a hundred new prisons to cope. Since the Second Restoration I've been busy turning my spivs into a legitimate commercial retail network—they're entitled to it, the loyalty they showed me. But now that New Sterling has been opened, there's no need for Kendric's people any more, not in this country."

"Kendric also used to make himself a tidy profit while he was arranging the exchange," Julia put in coldly.

"I would've thought you could have arranged the exchange by yourself without any trouble," Greg said.

"Nothing is ever simple, Greg," Philip replied. "Kendric's management of the exchange was part of my original arrangement with my backing consortium. I needed a hell of a lot of cash to fund Listoel, and I didn't have the necessary contacts with the broker cartels back in those days, not for something that dodgy. Kendric did. His family finance house is old and respectable, well established in the money market. And he offered me the lowest rates, a point below the usual interest charges in fact. We got on quite well back then. Despite his faults, he is an excellent money man. The trouble is, he's been getting a mite uppity of late, thinks he should have a say in running Event Horizon. Involve the consortium with the managerial decision process. Bollocks. I'm not having a hundred vice presidents sticking their bloody oars in."

"So why are you still tied in with him? You're legitimate now."

"Scotland," Julia said bitterly.

" 'Fraid so," Philip confirmed. "The PSP is still in power north of the border, so my arrangement with Kendric is still operating up there. Our respective spivs are virtually one group now, they've worked together for so long. It'd be very difficult to disentangle the two, not worth the effort and expense, especially as the Scottish card carriers aren't going to last another twenty months.

"And of course the di Girolamo house has an eight percent stake in Event Horizon's backing consortium. And guess who their representative on the board is."

"I still don't get it," Greg complained. "Why should a legitimate banker offer an illegal operation like yours a low rate in the first place? At the very least he should've asked for the standard commercial rate. And there are enough solid ventures in the Pacific Rim Market without having to go out on a limb here."

"It's the way he is, boy," Philip said quietly. "He doesn't actually need to get involved in anything at all. The family trust provides him with more money than he could ever possibly spend. But he's sharp. He sees what happens to others of his kind—they party; they ski, power glide, race cars and boats, take nine-month yachting holidays; they get loaded or stoned every night; and at age thirty-five the police are pulling them out of the marina. Half of the time it's suicide, the rest it's burnout. So instead of pursuing cheap thrills, Kendric gets his buzz by going right out on the edge. He plays the master-class game, backing smugglers like me, leveraged buyouts, corrupting politicians, software piracy, design piracy—I bought the Sony flatscreen templates Event Horizon uses from him. It's money versus money. His ingenuity and determination are taxed to the extreme, but he can't actually get hurt. I might not like him personally, but I admit he's been mighty useful. And he's exploited that position to grab his family house a big interest in Event Horizon. Clever. I like to think I'd have done the same."

"I'll get rid of him," Julia whispered fiercely. Her tawny eyes were burning holes in Kendric's back as he chatted up a brace of glossy starlets.

Philip patted her hand tenderly. "You be very careful around him, Juliet. He eats little girls like you for breakfast, both ways."

Greg could sense her raw hostility, barely held in check by her grandfather's cautionary tones.

He sat next to Dr. Ranasfari for the meal, an exercise in tedium; the man seemed to be a sense of humor–free zone. Ranasfari's doctorate was in solid-state physics, and his conversation was mostly of a professional nature; it all flew way over Greg's head. Although, curiously enough, Ranasfari loosened up most when he was talking to the ever-jovial Horace Jepson.

In the event, dogged perseverance finally enabled Greg to check him out as clean. He couldn't believe Ranasfari even knew what duplicitous meant. The doctor had a very rarefied personality, perfectly content within the confines of his own synthetic universe. A genuine specimen of a head-in-the-clouds professor. Whatever project Philip Evans had him working on, it was completely safe.

5

WILHOLM'S LIBRARY WAS A LONG, airy room on the ground floor, its arched ceiling painted with quasi-religious murals in rich, dark reds, greens, blues, and browns. Below this un-Christian pantheon, glass-fronted shelves ran the length of the walls, illuminated from within by tiny biolum strips; there were matching marble fireplaces at each end of the room, an oriel window giving a view out across the rear lawns. Three tables spaced down the center had genuine nine-teenth-century reading lamps at each seat. The air-conditioning was set to keep it degrees cooler than the rest of the manor. It was the room Julia preferred to work in: bringing Event Horizon data into her bedroom always seemed intrusive somehow. There had to be some distinction between private and working life, especially as she had so little of the former.

She sat in a plain admiral's chair behind a polished rosewood table, wearing a hyacinth cardigan over a peach chambray button-through dress, watching interviews on a big wall-mounted flatscreen. The image was coming over the company datanet from Stanstead.

Morgan Walshaw had commandeered a whole floor in the com-pany's airport administration block, using it to keep the furnace op-erators in isolation while they were processed.

He and Greg were doing the interviews in a modern office with a window wall overlooking the giant new freight hangar that Event Horizon used. Both of them sitting behind a chrome and glass desk, Morgan Walshaw in his usual suit, Greg in a red-and-white-striped shirt with braiding down the placket, a black-and-white mosaic tie.

It was a tedious way to spend the day, but she persevered. A penance for her earlier misdemeanor, that and a refuge, occupying her mind so that memories of Adrian couldn't encroach in that sneakily persistent way they did whenever she had a spare moment. He'd left this morning, together with Kats, the pair of them driving off on his Vickers bike, holographic flame transfers sparkling along the chrome gear-mounting. Julia had watched them go, kicking up a cloud of dust and gravel as they zoomed off down the drive, hard rock blaring from the speakers. It looked like a lot of fun.

Now monotony and responsibility had closed in on her again. Alone in a room with a thousand leather-bound books, not one of which she would ever read. Neither would Grandpa, come to that. They were just part of the ritual of being rich. Put into warehouse storage abroad while the PSP ruled and brought back here for glass-shelf storage. The tangibility of money. Stupid.

Greg and Morgan Walshaw were stretching in their swivel chairs as they waited for the next furnace operator to come in. Julia poured herself another cup of tea from the silver service on the table and munched a Cadbury's orange cream from the plate of biscuits. She'd never really paid much attention to Event Horizon's security division before; it was an alien subculture with its own language and etiquette and violence. Too much like an elaborate lethal game, freelance tekmercs and company operatives playing against each other at the expense of their employers. One of her bodyguards, Steven, had told her that once you were in security you never came out.

She'd secretly hoped to see a bit of action, a few sparks fly, in addition to learning more about the investigation procedures Morgan Walshaw used. But the interviews Greg had been running seemed to be fairly straightforward:—Name—Sorry to interrupt your furlough, but it is urgent—We're reviewing the contamination losses of memox crystals—Do you have any idea why it should be so high?—Have you ever been approached by anyone who wanted you to act against the company? Seven or eight questions, then he'd say okay and Morgan Walshaw would dismiss them. So far they hadn't uncovered anyone involved with the spoiler operation.

The impression Julia got from the screen was remoteness. Greg never smiled, never frowned; his tone was scrupulously impartial; he hardly appeared to be aware of the interviewees. She wondered what she'd feel if she were sitting there in the office with him. A tingling in her head as his espersense teased apart her emotions for examination? Her grandfather had said he couldn't read individual thoughts. Julia wasn't sure—he seemed so judgmental.

Julia sipped her tea as the next furnace operator came in. The woman was the fifteenth to be interviewed, a forty-three-year-old called Angie Kirkpatrick, wearing a khaki sports shirt and Cambridge-blue tracksuit trousers; medium height, fit-looking, self-assured—but then all of them were.

Angie Kirkpatrick sat on the other side of the desk from Greg and Morgan Walshaw, her expression of polite expectation carefully composed. Julia knew something was wrong straight away. Kirkpatrick probably wasn't aware of it; she had nothing to compare her interview to. But Julia could see Greg was sitting straighter, more attentive. Morgan Walshaw had picked up on Greg's state, too. Julia studied Kirkpatrick closely, still unable to see any evidence of culpability.

"We're investigating the high contamination level of memox crystals coming out of Zanthus," Greg said. "But then you guessed that, didn't you?"

"The contamination has been quite high," Angie said.

"Wrong answer," said Greg. "How long have you been working the spoiler?"

"What?"

"The whole eight months?"

"I don't know—"

"Seven months?"

"Listen!"

"Six?"

"Hey, you can't just—"

"Five?"

"Start accusing me—"

Greg leaned back in his chair and smiled. Julia was very glad she wasn't receiving that smile. It was predatory.

"Five months," said Greg, a simple statement of fact.

"This . . . What is this?" Angie demanded. She was looking straight at Morgan Walshaw.

"It's word association," Greg said. "I say a word, and I watch to see how your mind reacts. Is there stress and guilt, or is there merely innocent confusion? It doesn't matter what your verbal answer is: your thoughts don't lie."

Julia almost felt a pang of sympathy for the woman. Betrayed by her own soul. Greg's ability was eerie, silent, unfelt, and devastatingly accurate. A whole heritage of fear was built around people who could divine thoughts. Quite rightly—surely everyone was entitled to some core of privacy. She pulled her cardigan tighter over her shoulders.

"Stress and guilt, that's what peaked at five months," Greg said.

"You've got a gland," Angie said. Her defiance had gone.

"That's right."

She flushed hard. "I . . . I hadn't got any choice. They knew. Things. About me. Christ, I don't know how they found out."

"Just give us the details," said Walshaw, sounding bored, or perhaps weary.

"What'll happen?" Angie asked.

"To you? We probably won't prosecute, if you're being truthful about them blackmailing you. But you won't ever work in orbit again, not for anyone; we'll make quite sure of that."

"I didn't have any choice!"

"You could've come to us. We could've set a countertrap."

"I don't know. There's no difference between you, any of you. People like me, well, it's not fair."

"Never is," Walshaw muttered.

Watching Angie hunching in on herself, Julia realized the woman had already submitted; the fight had gone out of her. She was going to do exactly what Walshaw told her to. What an awesome reputation psychics had, that even their presence could sap the will like that. No wonder the PSP had been so troubled about the animosity of the Mindstar Brigade veterans.

"How did they turn you?" Greg asked.

Angie flinched when he spoke. "Are you still looking into my mind?"

"Yes."

She nodded reluctantly. "Okay. I was doing some uppers. Zanthus, it gets to you, you know? Four months in a dormitory can, everyone crammed together at night, recycled piss to wash with, can't taste your food. It just gets to you. It's no High Frontier dream, only sounds that way from down here. Anyway, it gets to the stage where you've really got to force yourself to turn up at Stanstead at the end of your furlough. I've got two daughters, see. They're beautiful kids, really—smart, happy. I take care of them when I'm on furlough; my ex has them when I'm up there. I hate the idea of him having them at all, but some choice, right? So seven years of this shit is too much; my eldest, she's fifteen; she's got a boyfriend; she's got exams this year. I should be there. Saying good-bye, it hurts like hell. So six months ago I've got to take something to ease the pain."

"What about your preflight medical?" Walshaw asked. "You must've known the drugs would show up."

"Maybe I wanted it to," Angie said. "Deep down. You know how strict Event Horizon is about narcotics abuse. Give Philip Evans that; he wants us healthy. Others have been caught; they got transferred, they were given therapy, kept their pay grade. We get a good medical cover deal, you know? But they found me before the furlough ended."

"Names?" Greg asked.

"Kurt Schimel. But he didn't talk with a German accent."

"That's all?"

"No, there were a couple more with him, a man and a woman. No names." She began to describe them.

Access Company Personnel File: Kirkpatrick, Angie. Zanthus Microgee Furnace Operator.

Julia stopped listening: Angie's file was unfolding in her mind. A data profile of names, dates, figures, promotions, training grades, personal biography, medical reports, biannual security reviews, her ex-husband. Her daughters were called Jennifer and Diana; there were even pictures. Ordinary, she was so ordinary. That was what struck Julia most. It was a big disappointment; she'd wanted to understand the woman, her motivations. Knowing the enemy. But now she didn't know whether to hate the she-demon who'd tried to wreck everything her grandfather had built or pity the pathetic woman who'd screwed her own life beyond redemption.

"They offered to flush my blood system clean," she was saying. "There'd be no trace of the drugs left when I went for the medical. They also smoothed out my bank account so the balance wouldn't show all those cash purchases when security ran its six-month review. And I'd only have to fox the crystal furnace 'ware for a year; their money would've been enough to let me get *out* afterwards. Just me and the girls, go and live quietly somewhere. God, you don't know what kind of deal that was to me."

"I do," Greg said.

Angie shuddered, hugging her arms across her chest.

Greg was staring into space above her head. "You said fox the furnace 'ware. I get some interesting implications from that. Would you elaborate on that for me, please."

Julia returned her attention to the interview. She would never have picked up on that detail. What kind of an impression had Greg seen? She wanted to ask him, "What do minds look like?" Didn't think she'd ever have the courage.

"Nothing much to it," Angie said. "Schimel gave me a program to load into the furnace's 'ware; it adjusts the quality inspection sensor records."

"The memox crystals weren't actually contaminated, then," Greg said thoughtfully.

"No. That wouldn't have worked. The security monitors would trip if more than thirty-seven percent came out bad, see? No way could we ever be allowed to go over the magic figure—that'd blow the whole gaff, right. Reconfiguring the injector mechanism each time you wanted to ruin a batch wasn't on, you'd never get a fine enough control over the output. It's not like flicking on a switch, you know. It takes time to make the blend perfect again, and the time varies. Some of those furnaces are a bitch to run. Then you've got the genuine duff batches to consider. What Schimel's program did was start with the genuine percentage of failures, then forge the rest."

Julia sat bolt upright, her tea forgotten. Frustration manifested itself as a surge of hot blood. She wanted to take Angie by the throat and shake the stupid tart till she rattled. Forty-eight million Eurofrancs' worth of perfectly good memox crystals deliberately dumped into the atmosphere to burn up. It was an appalling thought. Event Horizon's cash reserve reduced to incendiary molecules in the ionosphere.

Walshaw was giving Angie an entomologist's stare, deciding exactly how worthless she was. And it took a lot to get the coldly civil security chief riled.

Greg was shaking his head in bemusement. "You mean you just chuck away good crystals?"

"Yes," she whispered dully.

Walshaw opened his cybofax. "I want the names of all the other furnace operators you know that are involved."

"Do I have to?" she asked. "I mean you'll find them anyway, won't you?"

"Don't piss me off any further," Walshaw said in a tired voice. "Names."

Julia heard a metallic scrape behind her and turned in the chair. The manor staff were supposed to leave her alone when she was in here. But it was her father, Dillan, who was opening the library door.

She watched the wrecked man move dazedly into the room, hating herself for the pain she felt at the sight of him. He was wearing jeans and a bright yellow sweatshirt, with elasticated plimsolls on his feet. At least he'd remembered to shave, or someone had reminded him. There were a couple of male nurses on permanent call at the manor for when he got difficult and when he had nightmares. He wasn't much trouble, not physically, spending most of his days in a small brick-walled garden that backed onto the kitchen wing. There was a bench by the fishpond for him when the weather was fine and a Victorian summerhouse for when it rained. He would read poetry for hours or tend to the densely packed flower borders, throw crumbs to the goldfish.

And that was it, she thought, holding her face into that well-practiced expressionless mask. All he was capable of, reading and weeding. The nurses gave him three shots of syntho a day.

If we were poor, she thought, they'd lock us all away as crazy, the whole Evans family, all three of us, three generations. A dying man with grandiose aspirations for the future, a syntho addict, and a girl with an extra brain who can't make friends with anybody. We probably deserve it.

Dillan Evans smiled as he caught sight of his daughter. "Julie, there you are."

She rose smoothly from the admiral's chair, switching off the flatscreen and its images of treachery. Her father walked toward her, taking his time over each step. He was trying to hide a bunch of flowers behind his back.

She couldn't despise him; all she ever felt was a kind of bewilderment mingling with heartbreaking shame. For all his total syntho dependency, she was his one focal point on the outside world, his last grip on reality. He'd come with her to Europe, not caring about the location, not even caring about having to live in the same house as his father again, just so long as he was with her. Even the First Salvation Church had been glad to get him off their hands, and they recruited new bodies with the fervor of medieval navies.

"For you," Dillan Evans said, and produced the flowers. They were fist-size carnations—mauve, scarlet, and salmon pink.

Julia smelled them carefully, enjoying the fresh scent. Then she kissed him gently on the cheek. "Thank you, Daddy. I'll put them in a vase on the table—here, look—so I can see them while I'm working."

"Oh, Julie, you shouldn't be working, not you, not when it's a bright sunny day. Don't get yourself tangled up in the old bastard's schemes. They'll leech the life out of you. Dry dusty creatures, they are. There's no life in what he pursues, Julie. Only suffering."

"Hush," she said, and took his hand. "Have you had lunch yet?"

Dillan Evans blinked, concentrating hard. "I don't remember. Oh, God, Julie, I don't remember." His eyes began to water.

"It's all right," she said quickly. "It's all right, Daddy, really it is. I'm going to have my lunch in a little while. You can sit with me."

"I can?" His smile returned.

"Yeah, I'd like you to." She held the flowers up. "Did you grow these?"

"Yes. Yes I did, up from tiny seeds. Like you, Julie; I grew you, too. My very own snowflower. The one stem of beauty in the frozen wilderness of my life."

She put her arm in his, and steered him toward the library door.

"I was looking for your friend," Dillan Evans said. "The pretty one. I had some flowers for her as well." He began to look around, his face tragic.

"Katerina?"

"Was that her name? She had hair that shone so bright in the sun. I showed her 'round my garden. And we talked and talked. There's so few who do that. Did you know she can charm butterflies onto her finger?"

Julia winced at the thought of Kats talking to her father. Had Adrian been there as well?

She closed the library door behind her, blocking out the worries of the present. But only so she could suffer in a different way, she thought bleakly. Typical.

"Like an angel," her father said in a wistful tone. "Radiant and golden."

6

GREG HAD NEVER BEEN IN an airship before. In fact, the last time he'd been airborne in anything other than the ghost wing was in the Northern European Alliance's retreat from Turkey. The experience had left him with unsavory memories of air travel.

As with all retreats it was chaos bordering on utter shambles. Only the RAF emerged with any credit, commandeering anything with wings that didn't flap in one last ball-busting effort to get the squaddies out before the fall of eternal night. Greg wound up jammed between two blood-soaked medevac cases in a severely overloaded Antonov-74M, watching pinpoint nova flares floating serenely through the air in a desperate bid to lure the Jihad legion's Kukri missiles from the jet exhausts.

There was a universe of difference. The *Alabama Spirit* was a *Lakehurst*-class ship on the Atlantic run, a leviathan: first class passengers had individual cabins, three lounges, their own dining room, a casino, and twenty-four-hour steward service.

He'd taken a Dornier tilt-fan shuttle up from Stanstead the previous evening, after he'd finished interviewing the furnace operators and the Zanthus managers. It had been dark when they embarked above the English Channel; all he'd seen through the Dornier's cabin window was an oval of blackness blotting out the wisps of pale moonlit cloud. The airship's outer skin was one giant solar collector, providing electricity for the internal systems. Hydrogen-burning MHD generators powered a pair of large fans at the rear. He was looking forward to reaching Listoel in daylight and seeing the *Alabama Spirit* unmasked.

Morgan Walshaw had sent six security personnel along with him. Five hardliners, Bruce Parwez, Evan Hains, Jerry Masefield, Isabel Curtis, and Glen Ditchett, to handle the arrests. They'd all had duty tours up at Zanthus before, knew how to handle themselves in freefall. He'd checked them out, satisfied with what he'd found: tough, well-trained professionals. The staff lieutenant was Victor Tyo, a twenty-five-year-old Eurasian who looked so fresh-faced he could've passed himself off as a teenager without much trouble. It was his third field assignment, first in an executive capacity, and he was determined to make it a success.

Greg watched the approach to Listoel from the gondola's Pullman observation lounge, right up at the prow. Two kilometers below the lounge's curving transparent walls the deep blue Atlantic rollers stretched away to merge with the sky at some indefinable distance. The ride was unbelievably smooth.

"Have you ever been up to Zanthus before?" he asked Victor Tyo.

"Yes, I went up last year. The company launched a new microgee module, a vaccine lab. I helped interface our security monitor programs with its supervisor gear. It's my familiarity with the monitor programs which got me assigned to the case. Part of my brief is to upgrade them."

"That and the fact you've been cleared yourself. I'm supposed to vet the security staff out at Listoel and Zanthus, too. Until then, they're on the suspect list along with the furnace operators and managers."

Victor Tyo shifted uncomfortably. "That's some pretty powerful voodoo you've got there. Did you actually read my mind to clear me?"

"Relax, I can't read minds direct. I sense moods readily enough, but that's not quite good enough. For instance, I can see guilt, but most people have something to be guilty about. Petty criminals are the worst for that—the bloke fiddling his lunch expenses, accepting payola. Simply because they are so petty it gnaws at them, becoming a dominant obsession."

Victor's mind began to unwind, relieved he wasn't an open book for Greg to flick through at leisure. "Do I have much guilt?"

"More like anxiety," Greg reassured him. "That's perfectly normal, premission nerves. You must lead a commendably sinless life." He turned back to the window; the ocean below was turning green.

Most of the *Alabama Spirit*'s first class passenger complement had been drifting into the Pullman lounge for the last few minutes. A flock of stewards descended, offering complimentary drinks to the adults and explaining the docking procedure to the excitable children.

The sickly green tint of the water was darkening, reminding Greg of overcooked pea soup. Even the foam of the white horses was a putrid emerald color.

Listoel was straight ahead, a stationary flotilla of some forty-odd cyber-factory ships safely outside territorial waters, where hard-core ideological rhetoric wasn't worth hard-copying and there were no politicians demanding kickbacks. They were big, mostly converted oil tankers by the look of them, forming a cluster twenty kilometers across, with the spaceplane runway at their center, a concrete strip three and a half kilometers long. Approach strobes bobbed in the water, firing a convergent series of red and white pulses at the end of the concrete. Four large barges, supporting cathedral-size hangars, were docked at the other end. Another thirteen floated near by. Greg spotted five with the Event Horizon logo, a blue concave triangle sliced with a jet-black flying V, painted on their super-structure.

Each of the cyber-factory ships was venting a torrent of coffee-colored water from pipes at their stern. They were the outflows of the thermal-exchange generators. Every ship dangled an intake pipe right down to the ocean bed, where the water was ice cold and thick with sediment nutrients. The generators' working fluid was heated to a vapor by the ocean's warm surface water, passed through turbines, then chilled and condensed by the water from the bottom. The system would function with a temperature difference over fifteen degrees, although the efficiency increased proportionally as the difference rose.

The nutrient-rich water between the cyber-factory ships churned with activity; nearly a hundred breeder and harvester ships followed each other in endless circular progression. Fish were hatched; they gorged themselves on the rich bloom of algae; they were killed—the complete cycle of life embedded between two rusting hulls. Pirate miners were docked with some of the cyber-factories, distinguishable from ordinary cargo ships by the spiderwork crane gantries that lowered their remote grabs onto the ocean bed to collect the abundant ore nodules lying there.

Riding high above the anchorage was a squadron of tethered blimps, reminding Greg of pictures of London during World War II. He stood up at the front of the gondola in the midst of a silently fascinated crowd of children and their equally intrigued parents, watching a long probe telescoping out of the *Alabama Spirit*'s tapering nose. The increasingly frantic whine of the small directional thrust fans was penetrating the gondola as they maneuvered the bulbous probe tip into the docking collar mounted on the rear of the stationary blimp.

They were close enough now for Greg to make out the blimp's slender monolattice tether cables. A clear flexible pipe ran up one of them, refracting rainbow shimmers along its entire length. Hydrogen electrolyzed from seawater by the thermal-exchange generators would be pumped up it, refilling the *Alabama Spirit*'s MHD gas cells.

The probe shuddered into the collar, which closed about it with a loud clang, reverberating through the *Alabama Spirit*'s fuselage struts. Greg had seen those struts when he embarked, arranged in a geodesic grid, no wider than his little finger. The fibers were one of the superstrength monolattice composites extruded in microgee modules up at Zanthus or one of the other orbital industry parks. It was only after those kind of materials had been introduced that airships became a viable proposition once again.

Greg and Victor Tyo took a lift up to the *Alabama Spirit*'s flight deck, a recessed circle in the middle of the upper fuselage. The other five members of the security team were waiting for them, along with a cluster of Event Horizon personnel who were beginning their three-month duty tour at Listoel.

A handling crew were loading a matte black environment-stasis capsule into the cargo hold of the tilt-fan standing in the center of the flight deck. Greg could see radiation-warning emblems all over the cylinder. He knew it contained a Merlin, a small multisensor space probe riding a nuclear ion-drive unit, designed to prospect the asteroids. Philip Evans had been launching them at a rate of one a month for the last three years. Greg had listened to him explaining the program at his dinner party, clearly in his element, with an audience that hung on every word.

"Investing in the future," the old billionaire had said over after-dinner brandy. "I'll never see a penny back from them, but young Juliet here will. I envy her generation, you know. We're poised on the brink of great times. Our technology base is finally sophisticated enough to begin the real exploitation of space. My generation missed out on that; we were hopelessly stalled by the crises at the turn of the century—the Energy Crunch, the Credit Crash, the Warming, the disaster of the PSP. They all put paid to anything but the immediate. But now things are stabilizing again; we can plan further ahead than next week, set long-range goals, the ones with real payoffs. Unlimited raw materials and energy—they're both out there waiting for her. Just think what can be achieved with such treasure. The wealth it'll create, spreading down to benefit even the humblest. Fantastic times."

Philip Evans's corporate strategy had Event Horizon flourishing into one of the leaders in deep-space industry. And the Merlins were an important part of his preliminary preparations, prospecting the Apollo Amor asteroids for him, a class of rocks well inside the main belt and the most easily accessible from Earth. The Merlins sent back a steady stream of securely coded information on their mineral and ore content.

When the consortium of German, American, and Japanese aerospace companies finally rolled their scramjet-powered spaceplane out, launch costs would take a quantum leap downward. The single-stage launcher would open up a whole panoply of previously uneconomical operations. One of which was asteroid missions.

And with its carefully accumulated knowledge of extraterrestrial resources Event Horizon would be in the vanguard of the mining projects, so Philip Evans said. In a prime position to feed refined chemicals back to the constellations of microgee material-processing modules projected to spring up in Earth orbit.

Greg had been aware of an undercurrent of dry humor in the old man's mind as he expanded his dream, as though he was having some giant joke on his guests. But the Merlin was real enough. It was just that the whole enterprise seemed whimsical, or at best premature. There had been rumors about the spaceplane, now eleven years behind schedule; some said scramjet technology just couldn't be made to work, and even if it could, the cost savings would be minimal.

Greg's status earned him a seat at the front of the tilt-fan's cramped cabin, looking over the pilot's shoulder. She lifted them straight up for fifty meters, then rotated the fans to horizontal and banked sharply to starboard.

He'd been right. In the light of day the *Alabama Spirit* was spectacular. A huge jet-black ellipse framed by the dreaming sky, like a hole sliced directly into intergalactic night. It was four hundred meters long, eighty deep, sixty broad. Two contra-rotating fans were spinning slowly on the tail, keeping its nose pressed firmly into the refueling blimp.

Their descent in the tilt-fan was a long spiraling glide. Even here, where energy shortage was a totally redundant phrase, the pilot was reluctant to burn fuel. She must've been a European, Greg thought; obsessive conservation was drilled into EC citizens from birth.

They flattened out at the bottom of the glide and lined up on one of the big cyber-factory ships, swinging over the bow and pitching nose-up as the fans returned to the vertical. Greg read the name *Oscot* painted on the rusting bow in big white lettering.

The Dornier settled amidships with minimum fuss, its landing struts absorbing any jolts.

Greg tapped the pilot's shoulder. "Smooth ride. Thanks."

She gave him a blank look.

He shrugged and climbed out.

Sean Francis, *Oscot*'s manager, nominally captain, was waiting at the foot of the airstairs. He was tall and lean, dressed in a khaki shirt and shorts, with canvas-top sneakers, broad sunglasses covering his eyes.

Greg dredged his name up from Morgan Walshaw's briefing file. Thirty-two years old, joined Event Horizon straight out of university, some sort of engineering administration degree, fully cleared for company confidential material up to grade eleven, risen fast, unblemished reputation for competence.

He reminded Greg of Victor Tyo; the resemblance wasn't physical, but both of them had that same hard knot of urgency, polite and determined.

The security team spilled out of the tilt-fan to stand behind Greg, waiting impassively. Sean Francis looked at them with a growing frown.

"My office was told you're here to check on our spaceflight operations, yes?" Sean Francis said. "I'm afraid I don't understand; the Sangers are a mature system. I rather doubt their flight procedures can be improved after all this time."

Greg produced the card Walshaw had provided, which Francis promptly waved away. "It's not your identity I'm questioning," he said, "merely your purpose. Okay?"

"This is not the place," Greg said quietly. "Now would you please verify my card."

Francis held out his cybofax, and Greg showed his card to the key. There was an almost subliminal flash of ruby light as the two swapped polarized photons.

He took his time checking the authorization before nodding sadly. "I see. Perhaps my office would be a more suitable venue. Yes?"

The seven of them started down the length of the deck toward the superstructure, drawing curious glances from *Oscot*'s crew.

Instinct made Greg look up toward the southwest. There was a black dot expanding rapidly out of the featureless sky, losing height fast. It was a returning Sanger orbiter, curving in a long shallow arc, pitched up to profile its sable-black heat shield belly. Greg tracked its descent, working out that it would reach zero altitude right at the end of the floating runway. He held his breath.

The orbiter straightened out three hundred meters from the runway, wings leveling. It smacked down on the concrete, blue-white plumes of smoke spurting up from the undercarriage. Small rockets fired in the nose, slowing its speed.

"What if it missed?" Greg asked. The orbiters didn't have a jet engine; they couldn't go around.

"They don't," Sean Francis said.

I T'S IMPRESSIVE," MORGAN WALSHAW ADMITTED. "One of the
biggest tekmerc deals for quite some time. We estimate thirty to
thirty-five of them were assembled to turn our memox-crystal furnace operators. As far as we can tell, they started last June, and they
were still recruiting until November. That kind of involvement
would take *kombinate*-level resources." There was a grudging note in
his voice that implied respect, or even admiration.

Julia didn't like that; the security chief was supposed to be guarding her and Grandpa, not paying compliments to their enemies. It
was that bloody dividing line between the legal and illegal again, too
thin, far too thin.

"So it's impressive," Philip Evans grunted. "So is your division's
budget, Morgan. Question is: what are you doing about it?" He was
sitting at the head of the table in the study with Julia and Morgan
Walshaw on either side, facing each other.

Julia would've liked to voice her own criticism, but didn't quite
have the nerve. Morgan Walshaw was a forbidding figure; he'd always been stern around her, as if she didn't match up to his expec-
tations.

"My priority at the moment is to halt the spoiler," Walshaw said.
"Thanks to Greg Mandel we've rounded up all the guilty furnace operators who were on their furlough. Unfortunately none of the Zanthus management personnel he interviewed were responsible for cir-
cumventing the security monitors. We have to conclude the culprit
is up there now. Mandel should be able to find him without any trouble."

"Told you that boy was just what we needed," Philip Evans said.

Walshaw remained unperturbed by the implied criticism, his composure mechanical. "Yes. We shall have to give serious consideration to employing gland psychics in security after this. The tekmercs
seem to be making good use of them."

Julia pulled a face. Her grandfather caught it and squeezed her hand
softly.

"Certainly, I believe the tekmerc team who ran the spoiler used them quite extensively on this occasion," Walshaw went on. "We've been running some deep analysis on our furnace operators, and there is overwhelming evidence that the tekmerc team assembled a comprehensive profile on every one of them. Bank accounts, medical records, past employers' personnel files—they were all sampled by the team's hot rods. I think we'd be correct in assuming that the likely candidates were also scanned by a psychic to see if they would be susceptible in the final instance. It's very significant that not one of the furnace operators they approached ever came to us."

"How many did they turn?" Philip Evans asked.

"So far, we've nabbed fourteen, out of a total of eighty-three on furlough. Greg Mandel and Victor Tyo are due up at Zanthus tonight. Probability suggests there are between four and six furnace operators currently in orbit who've been turned. We've done our best to make sure no news of the roundup has leaked. Not that they can run, but there is the prospect of sabotage to consider. Out of the fourteen we've already got, two had consented to kamikaze if they were cornered up at Zanthus."

"Bloody hell!" Philip shouted. "What kind of people do we employ? That's damn near twenty percent of them willing to sell us out at the drop of a hat!"

"It's over now, Grandee," Julia said in a small voice. "Please." She bowed her head so he wouldn't see how upset she was. It'd been a good morning for him, he'd eaten well, and he wasn't sweating like he usually did; even his color was almost normal. But now she could see the pink spots burning on his cheeks, showing just how badly worked up he was, which wouldn't do his heart any good.

There were some days when she wanted it all to be over, this pain-drenched clinging to life. And that wish only brought more guilt. Psychics would be able to see that clearly. Perhaps Walshaw would hold off using them until afterward. She ought to have a word with him about that.

When she looked up, the security chief was staring candidly out of the window.

"All right, Juliet," her grandfather said in a calmer voice. "I'll be good."

She gave him a tentative smile.

"I don't believe the crystal-furnace operatives are representative of Event Horizon personnel as a whole, nor any of the other Zanthus workers for that matter," Walshaw said. "Theirs is an extraordinarily high-stress situation. There is an average of three fatalities a year, a significant chance of radiation poisoning, and the psychological pres-

sures from living in such a closed environment are way above normal. Those factors came out time and again from all the interviewees."

"Yeah, okay," Philip Evans said grumpily. "I'm a no-good mill
owner, exploiting his downtrodden workers. What else is new? You
got any good news for me?"

"Greg Mandel should've pulled the last of the furnace operators
by this time tomorrow. We'll be sending up the replacements on an
afternoon flight, so from tomorrow evening the spoiler will be over.
Plus, the memox crystals tagged as contaminated last week haven't
been dumped yet. That's nearly two million Eurofrancs we'll recover."

"Jesus, chucking away perfectly good crystals like a crap dump.
That's a bugger, that is." He gave Julia a forlorn smile.

Walshaw shrugged. "Only way to do it."

"What about the people who organized this?" Julia asked. Walshaw hadn't said anything about them, as if they didn't matter. He
lived for the game, not the players; she felt sure of it.

"Difficult," he said.

"Why?" She made it come out flat and cold, and never mind if he
disapproved.

"This is what we call a finale deal. It's all cutoffs, understand? The
tekmercs who made the moves, turned our people, they'd be assembled by an old pro, someone with a reputation. This leader, he's
the only point of contact between the team and the backers, the
ones who want Event Horizon spoiled. Now, first we'd have to find
one of the tekmercs. Okay, maybe we could do that; they've all gone
to ground right now, but a deal this size is going to leave traces, and
we've got some pretty accurate descriptions. Once we get a tekmerc,
we extract the team leader's name."

"How?" she blurted, cursing herself instantly. This was why she'd
never probed security before. The secret horror, and fascination.
Right down at the bottom of all the smart moves were people who
deliberately inflicted pain on each other, who chose to do that.

"Not as bad as you might imagine," Morgan Walshaw said
placidly. "Not these days. There are drugs, sense overload techniques, gland psychics. Greg Mandel would just read out a list of
names to the tekmerc and see which chimed a mental bell. But even
if we obtain the name, it still doesn't do us any good. That team
leader, he'll already have vanished off the face of the Earth. Finale,
remember? He won't put this deal together for anything less than a
platinum handshake. New identity, a *plastique* reworking from head

to toe—hell, even a complete sex change—it's been known. You see, it's not only us he's hiding from now. His ex-employers, they know he's the only link back to them and that I'm going to be hunting him. They want him zapped."

"So why would he do the job in the first place?" Julia asked.

Morgan Walshaw smiled gently. "Kudos. A finale is the top of the tree, Julia. If you've come far enough to be asked, you're good enough to survive. No tekmerc ever turns down a finale. Take this one: for the rest of time, he's going to be the one who burned Event Horizon for forty-eight million Eurofrancs. He beat me; he beat your grandfather. And even if I catch him, or they catch him, nobody's ever going to know. His reputation has made it clean."

"Bugger of a world, isn't it, Juliet?"

She turned to her grandfather, surprised by his level questing stare.

"You approve," she accused.

"No, Juliet, I don't approve. I regard tekmercs as pure vermin, dangerous and perennial. Doesn't matter how many you stomp on, there's always more. All I hope is that you've learned something from this sorry little episode. Don't ever lower your guard, Juliet, not for an instant."

She dropped her eyes to the table. "You will try, won't you?" she asked Walshaw.

"Yes, Julia, I'll try."

"Me, too." She pressed her lips together in a thin determined line.

"You'll do nothing, girl," Philip said.

"They nearly ruined us, Grandpa! Everything you've built. We've got to know who. I've got to know who. If I'm going to stand any chance, I need the name."

"Doesn't mean you go gallivanting about chasing will-o'-the-wisps."

"I'll do whatever I can," Julia said with stubborn dignity. She subsided into a sulk, certain that Walshaw would be silently censuring her outburst. Well, *let* him, she thought. Anger was an improvement on boredom. If only she didn't feel so apprehensive with it.

8

THE LASER GRID SCANNED SLOWLY down Greg's body, a net of fine
blue light that flowed around curves and filled hollows. He was quietly thankful he kept in trim: this kind of clinical catechism was humbling enough; suppose he'd got a beer gut?

He'd spent an hour in the Dragonflight crew center, out on one of
the spaceplane barges. An annex of the payload facility room, com-
posite-walled cells filled with gear-module stacks, most of them medical. The medical staff had been anxious to test him for exceptional
susceptibility to motion sickness; space-adaptation syndrome, they
called it.

"If you do suffer, we have drugs that can suppress it for a couple
of days," the doctor in charge had said. "But no more than a week."

"I'll be up there a day at the most," Greg told him. He was confident enough about that. The interviews at Stanstead had gone well.
After Angie Kirkpatrick had cracked it'd been a simple matter of
cross-referencing names.

The laser grid sank to his feet, then shut off. Greg stepped out of
the tailor booth, and a smiling Bruce Parwez handed him his clothes.
A long-faced man with bright black eyes. Dark hair cut close, just
beginning to recede from the temples. His broad-shouldered build
was a giveaway, marking him down as a hardliner.

"Your flightsuit will be ready this afternoon," the technician behind the booth's console said, not even looking up.

Greg thanked him and left, glad to be free of the ordeal.

Sean Francis was waiting for them outside. "The medics have
given you a green light," he said. "But I don't think we've ever sent
up anyone with so little free-fall training before." Francis had been
markedly relieved when Greg had cleared his ship's modest security
team, taking it upon himself to see him through his preflight procedures. He had been grateful for the assistance but found the man ir-
ritating after a while. He supposed it was culture clash. In age they
were contemporaries. But after that, there was nothing. Francis was
a dedicated straight arrow, high achiever. It made Greg pause for
what might've been.

"I've got several hundred hours' microlight flight time," Greg said.

"That'll have to do then, yes?"

"We'll take care of you," Bruce Parwez said. "Just move slowly and you'll be all right."

"You had many tours up at Zanthus?" Greg asked.

"I've logged sixteen months now."

"Is there ever much trouble up there?"

"Tempers get a bit frayed. Bound to happen in those conditions. Mostly we just separate people and keep them apart until they cool off. There's no real violence, which is just as well. We're only allowed stunsticks, no projectile or beam weapons—they'd punch clean through the can's skin."

They walked along a corridor made of the same off-white composite as the crew center, bright biolums glaring, rectangular cable channels along both walls. Then they were out into a sealed glass-fronted gallery running the length of the hangar's high bay, halfway up the wall.

Greg looked down at the Sanger booster stage being flight-prepped below. It was a sleek twin-fin delta-wing craft, eighty-four meters long with a forty-one-meter wingspan. The fuselage skin was a metallo-ceramic composite, an all-over blue-gray except for the big scarlet dragon escutcheons on the wings. Power came from a pair of hydrogen-fueled turbo-expander-ramjets that accelerated it up to Mach six for staging. Greg had only seen the spaceplane on the channels before; up close it was a monster, an amalgamation of stream-lined beauty and naked energy. Fantastic.

"How many Sangers does Dragonflight operate?" Greg inquired as the three of them moved down the gallery to see the orbiter stage being prepped in its big clean room behind the high bay.

"Four booster stages, and seven orbiters," Francis said. "And they're working at full stretch right now. The old man has ordered another booster and two more orbiters from MBB; they ought to arrive before the end of the year. Which will be a big help. Strictly speaking, we can't afford to take an orbiter out of the commercial schedules for a Merlin launch, although I appreciate his reasoning behind the exploration program. I just regard it as somewhat quixotic, that's all. Still, it's his money, yes?"

The orbiter, which rode the booster piggyback until staging, was a smaller, blunter version of its big brother: thirty-five meters long, rocket-powered, and capable of lifting four and a half tons into orbit, along with ten passengers.

Clean-room technicians dressed in baggy white smocks were riding mobile platforms around the open upper-fuselage doors. The Merlin had been removed from its environment-stasis capsule overnight. Now it was being lowered millimeter by millimeter into the orbiter's payload bay.

The probe was surprisingly compact; cylindrical, a meter and a half wide, four long. Its front quarter housed the sensor clusters, their extendable booms retracted for launch; two communication dishes were folded back alongside, like membranous golden wings. The propulsion section was made up of three subdivisions: a large cadmium tank; the isotope power source; shielded by a thick carbon shell; and six ion thrusters at the rear. It was all wrapped in a crinkly silver-white thermal protection blanket.

Greg let his gland start its secretion again, beginning to get a feedback from the technicians' emotional clamor. It was the first time he'd ever encountered the space industry. These people were devoted. It went far beyond job satisfaction. They shared an enormous sense of pride; it was bloody close to being a religious kick.

The Merlin had finally settled on its cradle inside the orbiter's payload bay. As the overhead hoist withdrew, the mobile platforms converged, allowing the huddles of white-suited technicians to begin the interface procedure. The pallet that would deploy the spacecraft in orbit was primed, attachment struts clamped to load points, power and datalink umbilicals plugged in. Monitor consoles were hive cores of intense activity.

Greg nodded down at the little robot probe and its posse of devotees. "What happens next?"

"We mate the orbiter to the top of the booster. After that the barge will dock with the airstrip. Your launch window opens at half past eight, lasting six minutes."

The payload bay doors hinged shut, bringing Greg one step closer to Zanthus. And it still didn't seem real.

From *Oscot*'s deck the western horizon was a pastel-pink wash flecked with gold, the east a gash into infinity, not black but dark, insubstantial, defying resolution, a chasm you could fall down forever. Greg watched the crescent of darkness expanding as the Atlantic rolled deeper into the penumbra, occlusion slipping over the sky, giving birth to the stars. There was no air movement at all, dusk bringing its own brand of stasis. The world holding its breath as it slid across the gap between its two states.

Greg was wearing a baggy coverall over his new flightsuit. The coppery-colored garment fit him *perfectly*, a one-piece of some glossy silk-smooth fabric, knees and elbows heavily padded. It had a multitude of pockets, all with Velcro tags. Small gear modules adhered to Velcro strips on his chest—atmosphere pressure/composition sensor, medical monitor, Geiger counter, communicator set. He'd even been given a new company cybofax, capable of interfacing with Zanthus's 'ware, which was in the big pocket at the side of his leg. There was also a lightweight helmet, which he felt too self-conscious to put on before getting into the Sanger.

The first real stirrings of excitement rose as he led the security team toward the waiting tilt-fan at the prow, the realization that he was actually going into space finally gripping. *Oscot*'s deck was a bustle of tautly controlled activity. The ever-present grumble of the thermal generators' coolant water was being complemented by the lighter braying of mobile service units. Five Lockheed YC-55 Prowlers were already on the deck: ex-military stealth troop/cargo transports. Their shape was the cousin of the original B2 bomber, a stumpy, swept bat wing with an ellipsoid lifting-body fuselage, the entire surface coated in some radar-nullifying matte black material. There were no roundels visible, not even serial numbers. True smugglers' craft.

How Philip Evans had ever got hold of them would undoubtedly be one of the multitude of stories forever lost in the fog of governmental turmoil that followed the Warming, Greg assumed. Some unnamed country's defense ministry cutbacks mothballing a squadron, an independent arms dealer who wasn't quite that independent, an end-user export certificate that no one queried, easy credit terms. And another operation suddenly had the means to corrupt and weaken the Red menace. Add enough such subtle, and nonattributable, assaults together . . .

The emergence of several European authoritarian/socialist administrations during the Warming had alarmed the American State Department to a considerable degree; multinationalism and open markets had supposedly put an end to such regimes long ago. But with transport industries faltering and the recession destroying markets on every continent, up they rose again.

Intelligence agency funding had been the one section of the budget that Capitol Hill had never cut, not even during the depth of the recession. For the agencies it was almost like the good old Cold War days. Certainly the Trinities had never lacked for weapons or ammunition.

Now try proving it, Greg thought wryly as he watched the sixth Prowler rise silently up out of its daytime sanctuary, an old oil tank converted into a split-level hangar. The big elevator platform halted at deck level with dull metallic clangs that rumbled away into the gloaming. The stealth transporters seemed to draw a thick veil of cloying shadow around themselves, eerily otherworldly.

Sean Francis caught Greg staring. "Neat machines. Yes?"

"I didn't know you still used them,' Greg said.

"Sure. Ninety percent of our gear output is scheduled for legitimate markets nowadays; we're even winding down our counterfeiting operation now that we're pushing the Event Horizon brand name. But the Prowlers make regular nightly runs into Scotland. Their PSP is pretty shaky right now. It'll only take a small push and they'll fall. Philip Evans is determined to keep the pressure on.'

Greg eyed the large pallets of kelpboard boxes being loaded through the Prowler's rear cargo doors. According to the labels on the boxes, it was all domestic gear systems. Corrupting the wicked commies with capitalist consumer goodies. He shook his head in bemusement; never anything new in the world. "You build all of that stuff out here?"

"Yes. It's a pretty broad range—crystal players, home terminals, microwaves, fridges, bootleg memox albums—that kind of thing. Our sister ship, *Parnell*, churns out more of the same, along with a whole host of specialist chemicals for our microgee modules up at Zanthus."

"So Event Horizon only has the two cyber-factory ships left out here now?" Greg asked.

"That's right. There used to be nine of us out here a couple of years back, but the rest have left now. They're docked in the Wash outside Peterborough. Their cyber-systems are being stripped out and reinstalled in factories on land. All part of the Event Horizon legitimization policy. They were all gear factories, except for *Kenton* and *Costellow*: those two used to specialize in producing the actual cyber-systems themselves. Real top-of-the-range stuff; all our own designs, too. The old man kept research teams going ashore in Austria. They provided us with the templates, good enough to match any of the Pacific Rim gear. Bloody clever that."

"Oh?"

"Don't you see? Philip Evans has built up a capability to expand the company at an exponential rate. The cyber-systems are *that* sophisticated. All he needs is raw material and financial backing. The factories will multiply like amoebas, yes?"

"You sound like you're happy with Event Horizon."

"Christ, I mean totally. Philip Evans is a genius. Event Horizon has so much potential, you know? A real crest-rider. And I've done my penance out here, ten years' bloody hard graft. When *Oscot* docks I'm going to be in line for a divisional manager's slot."

The integrated Sanger was sitting at the end of the runway, white vapor steaming gently out of vent points on both orbiter and booster, glowing pink in the fast-fading light. Greg's intuition made itself felt as he walked down the gantry arm toward the orbiter's hatch. It wasn't much, a ghost's beckoning finger, distracting rather than alarming.

For a moment he was worried that it might be the orbiter. That'd happened before—an Mi-24 Hind G in Turkey that was going to take him and his squad on a snatch mission behind the legion lines. He'd balked as he was climbing in. It was a mindscent: the chopper smelled wrong. The Russian pilot had bitched like hell until a maintenance sergeant had noticed the gearbox temperature sensor was out. When they broke the unit open, it turned out the main transmission bearings were running so hot they'd melted the sensor.

But this touch of uncertainty was different. There was no intimation of physical danger. He knew that feeling, clear and strong, experiencing it time and again in Turkey.

He hesitated, getting an inquiring glance from Sean Francis.

"We've only had eight fatalities in twelve years of operations," the *Oscot*'s captain said helpfully.

"It's not the spaceplane," Greg answered. Precisely how much his intuition was gland derived was debatable, but when he did get a hunch this strong it usually squared out in the end. Even before he'd received the gland, Greg had believed in intuition. Every squaddie did to some degree, right back to Caesar's foot soldiers. And now he had the stubborn rationale of neurohormones to back the belief, giving it near total credibility.

The rest of the security team were watching him. He gave them a weak grin and began walking again.

The orbiter's circular hatch was a meter wide, with a complicated-looking locking system around the rim. Bright orange rescue instructions were painted on to the fuselage all around it. Greg shrugged out of his coverall and put his helmet on before he was helped through by the launch crew.

It was cramped inside, but he was expecting that, low ceiling, slightly curving walls, two biolum strips turned down to a glimmer. Another circular hatch in the center of the rear bulkhead opened into the docking air lock.

"You the first-timer?" asked the pilot. He was twisted around in his seat, a retinal interface disk stuck over one eye, like a silver monocle. The name patch on his flightsuit said Jeff Graham.

"Yes," Greg said as he sat in the seat directly behind the pilot. Puffy cushioning slithered under his buttocks like thick jelly.

"Okay, only one thing to remember. That's your vomit lolly." Jeff Graham pointed to a flexible ribbed tube clipped to the forward bulkhead in front of Greg. Its nozzle was a couple of centimeters wide, a detachable plastic cylinder with REPLACE AFTER USE embossed in black. "You even feel a wet burp coming on, then you suck on that. Got it? The pump comes on automatically."

"Thank you."

The rest of the security team were strapping themselves in; they were the only ones in the cabin. Greg fastened his own straps.

Jeff Graham returned his attention to the horseshoe-shaped flight console. The hatch swung shut, making insect clicking noises as the seal engaged.

"Is there a countdown?" Greg asked Isabel Curtis, who was sitting across the aisle.

She gave him a brief acknowledging smile. A wiry, attractive thirty-year-old woman with bobbed blond hair. He could make out the mottled pink flesh of an old scar, beginning below her right ear and disappearing under the collar of her blue flightsuit. "No. You want to hear flight control, it's channel four. Give you some idea."

Greg peered down at his communicator set, fathoming its unfamiliar controls, and switched it to channel four. The voices murmuring in the headset were professionally bland, reassuringly so.

He followed the procedure: gantry-arm retracting, the switch to internal power, umbilicals disconnecting, fuel-pressure building, APU ignition. Half-remembered phrases from current-affairs programs.

The takeoff run was a steady climb of acceleration, turboexpander ramjets felt rather than heard, an uncomfortable juddering in his sternum. The build through the Mach numbers, night sky devoid of reference points, floor tilted up at an easy angle.

"Go for staging," flight control said.

The orbiter rockets lit with a low roar; vibration blurred Greg's vision. There was a hint of white light around the edges of the windscreen. Acceleration jumped up, pushing him farther down into the cushioning. The stars grew brighter, sharper.

The Merlin was deployed 130 minutes after takeoff, on the second orbit. The Sanger was 550 kilometers above Mexico. Greg had spent the whole time staring out of the windscreen, mesmerized by the globe below, the dazzle of daylit oceans, the sprinkle of light from Europe's nighttime cities, green and brown land that seemed to be in pristine condition, the muddy stain in the sea that marred every coastline. There were none of the physical symptoms he'd been told to look out for, just the strangeness of arms that waved about like seaweed: a whirling sensation, like a fairground ride, if he turned his head too fast.

A small screen on Jeff Graham's console showed the Sanger's payload doors hinging open. The little probe nosed out of its cradle, umbilical lines winding back onto their spools, loose ends flapping about. It seemed to hover above the Sanger as its communication dishes unfolded.

"We stick with it until Cambridge finishes the systems check," Jeff Graham told his passengers. "Never know, we might wind up taking it back."

But the babbling background voices confirmed the Merlin's integrity somewhere over the Mediterranean, and Jeff Graham fired the orbital maneuvering rockets, raising the Sanger's orbit. The last Greg saw of the Merlin was a dwindling gray outline over pale moonwashed water.

They caught up with Zanthus over Fiji, an orbit ten kilometers lower, closing fast. The terminator was a brilliant blue-and-white crescent six hundred kilometers below, expanding rapidly as they raced toward the dawn.

Zanthus rose out of the penumbra into direct sunlight. Greg saw a globular cluster of diamonds materialize out of nowhere. Occasional silent lightning flares stabbed out from it as the sun bounced off flat silvered surfaces.

"That's something, isn't it?" Jeff Graham asked.

"No messing," Greg said hoarsely. It was the biggest of the eight space-industry parks in Earth orbit.

The sun lifted above the Pacific, shining straight into the Sanger's cabin. Electrochromic filters cut in, turning down the glare.

Greg watched in silent respect as the Sanger slowly slid underneath Zanthus. Jeff Graham began to fire the Sanger's orbital maneuvering rockets, raising altitude, their trajectory a slow arc up to the space-industry park that would end in synchronized orbits.

Zanthus began to resolve, individual light points growing, assuming definite silhouettes. The largest was the dormitory, right at the heart. Ten cans, habitation cylinders fifty meters long, eight wide, locked together at one end of a five-hundred-meter boom; at the other end a vast array of solar panels tracked the sun. The whole arrangement was gravity-gradient stabilized, the cans pointing permanently Earthward.

Floating around the dormitory were the microgee modules, 156 materials-processing factories arranged in five concentric spheres. The formation was a loose one, a shoal of strange geometric insects guarding their metallic queen. There was no standardization to the modules; they ranged from small boxy vapour-deposition mesh molds brought up by the Sangers up to the fifty-meter-long, two-hundred-ton cylinders launched by Energia-5. All of them flaunted a collection of solar panels, thermal-dump radiators, and communication dishes, and some had large collector mirrors, silver flowers faithfully following the sun. Red and green navigation lights twinkled from every surface. Abstruse company logos bloomed across thermal blankets, as if a fastidious graffiti artist had been let loose; Greg hadn't known so many different companies used Zanthus.

Three assembly platforms hung on the outer edge of the cluster, rectangles of cross truss beams, with geostationary antenna farms taking shape below long spidery robot arms. Greg saw the Globecast logo on the side of one gossamer dish.

Personnel commuters, manipulator pods, and cargo tugs wove around the modules, slow-gliding three-dimensional streams that curled and twisted around each other, white and orange strobes pulsing, marking out their progress. There were spaceplanes moving in the traffic flows, rendezvousing with the five servicing docks, big triple-keel structures that acted as fuel depots, maintenance stations, and cargo storage centers. The spaceplanes unloaded their pods of raw materials, receiving the finished products from the microgee modules in exchange. Greg counted nine Sangers attached to one dock, staggered by how much their cargos would be worth. Philip Evans had mentioned how much Zanthus's daily output came to, but the figures hadn't registered at the time, silly money.

Greg watched Zanthus expand around them as Jeff Graham eased the Sanger into one of the traffic lines. An errant image of his gland discharging milky fluids. Neurohormones chased around his brain, and he deliberately focused inward, on himself, letting his mind wander where it would. It was a different state from the one he used to tease apart the strands of other people's emotions. Introspective. He was isolated from the security team's thoughts, alone and strangely serene.

If that peak of intuition he'd experienced hadn't concerned the Sanger, then, he reasoned, Zanthus itself must be the cause. He reached right down to the bottom of his mind and found the sense of wrongness again. It was too small, too flimsy to represent any danger, but it remained. Obstinate, and ultimately unyielding.

Frustrated, he let it go. Something wrong, but not life-threatening. The situation irked him. He knew he must be overlooking something, some part of the spoiler that wasn't what it seemed. Yet the operation was so clear-cut.

As if shamed by its failure, his gland dried up.

The Sanger was creeping up to the dormitory, its big cans dominating the view through the windscreen. Event Horizon used three of them for its 120-strong workforce, a third of Zanthus's total population.

Greg saw a Swearingen commuter back away from one of the Event Horizon cans, a windowless cylinder with spherical tanks strapped around both ends. Tiny stabs of white fire flickered from its thruster clusters.

Jeff Graham rolled the Sanger with a drumfire burst from the RCS thrusters. A huge Event Horizon logo slid past the windscreen; the peak of the flying V was missing, patched over with a rough square of hoary thermal foam. The RCS was firing almost continually. A screen on the flight console showed an image of the payload bay, with the air-lock tube extended. A matching tube jutted out of the dormitory can, the two barely half a meter apart.

Contact was a small tremble, the whirring of electrohydrostatic actuators clamping the two air-lock tubes together.

Jerry Masefield released his belt and drifted up out of his seat, using the ceiling handholds to crawl down to the rear bulkhead. Greg pressed his belt's release and cautiously pushed down with his palms. Victor Tyo and Isabel Curtis watched closely. He grinned at them and grasped one of the ceiling handholds. His legs developed a momentum all their own, pulling his torso along until he was lying flat against the ceiling.

Stomach muscles were the key, Greg decided, keep the body straight and rely on his arms to pull him about. He hauled himself toward the rear bulkhead, remembering to take inertia into account as he stopped.

There was a ripple of applause. The rest of the team were swimming out of their seats. Jerry Masefield had opened the air-lock hatch and disappeared inside. Greg swung slowly around the rim and followed him into the can.

*   *   *

Greg couldn't quite figure out the section of the dormitory can he'd emerged into, a tunnel with a hexagonal cross-section, three and a half meters wide, bright biolum strips every five meters, hoops protruding everywhere. Logically, it ought to have been a connecting corridor, except it was full of people. They lingered near the walls, aligned with their feet toward him, a foot or hand hooked casually around the hoops, all of them wearing flightsuits and helmets. A large proportion were eating; their food resembled pizza sandwiches, the same pale spongy dough, tacky fillings. No crumbs, Greg realized, and no need for plates and cutlery. Twenty meters away, four exercise bikes were fixed to the walls, riders pedaling away furiously. There was a sign opposite the air lock, an old London Underground station strip: Piccadilly Circus.

It was the noise that got to him first. Conversations were shouted, air-conditioning was a steady buzz, cybofax alarm bleepers were going off continuously, the PA kept up a steady stream of directions. Then there was the air—warm, damp, and stale. He began to appreciate Angie Kirkpatrick's point of view.

The dormitory commander, Lewis Pelham, and Event Horizon's Zanthus security captain, Don Howarth, were waiting for him. Lewis Pelham didn't attempt to shake hands, holding on firmly to one of the hoops as the rest of the security team boiled out of the air lock. "My orders are to afford you full cooperation," he said.

He had that same flat professionalism as Victor Tyo and Sean Francis, Greg noted. Did Philip Evans have a clone vat churning them out? "Somewhere private," he suggested, raising his voice above the din.

Pelham smiled, big lips peeling back, a round face. "Sure."

"It's shift change," Howarth said. "Not like this all the time; don't worry." His face was fluid-filled, too, a ruddy complexion.

They slapped the hoops, moving off up the tunnel, skimming along effortlessly. Greg climbed after them doggedly, one hoop at a time. A few cheers and jeers pursuing his progress.

"Five days," Howarth said, "and you'll be outflying a hummingbird." He was waiting by an open hatch. "Through here."

It was a toroidal compartment, wrapped around the central tunnel. A space station as Greg understood it, consoles with flatscreens and cubes flashing graphics and data columns, bulky machinery bolted onto the walls, lockers with transparent doors. Five beds were staggered round what Greg thought of as the floor, assuming the entrance hatch was in the ceiling. Lewis Pelham had oriented himself the same way as Greg, holding the edge of a bed to maintain his position. The security team followed suit as they came in.

"This is the sick bay," Pelham said. "Nobody in today. Will it do?"

"Do you have a brig?" Greg asked.

Pelham and Howarth exchanged a glance. "We can clear the suit-storage cabin if it's really urgent," said the security captain.

"Good enough." His gland began its secretions. "Close the hatch, Bruce," he said.

Bruce Parwez elevated himself and spun the lock handle.

Lewis Pelham regarded Greg without humor.

Greg closed his eyes as the compartment became insubstantial. Minds crept out of the shadow veils bordering his perception, a swarm of pale translucent pearls, compositional emotions woven tautly into penumbra nuclei. He focused on the two strangers before him. "Now, to start with, do either of you know anything about the excessive memox-crystal contamination?"

9

JULIA FLUNG HERSELF AT THE problem as she took her horse Tobias on their morning ride. There was a strong sense of urgency pushing her to find a solution now, almost one of despair. Greg Mandel had located the person who'd circumvented the security monitors and the five guilty memox-furnace operators up at Zanthus. The replacement operators were flying up today, their Sanger bringing the security team and the prisoners down. It would be over soon, congratulations all around, and a small security office left intact to track down one of the tekmercs. A vague hope, even less of finding the team leader and through him the backers.

Julia didn't even bother to open her eyes in the saddle. Tobias knew their route, down the edge of the manor's rear garden, past the spinney at the end of the trout lake, and into the meadows beyond. The horse's lumbering rhythm was soothing, rocking her gently back and forth on his back.

Normally she enjoyed Wilholm's grounds. The landscape crew hadn't been given much time after the communal farmers moved out, but they'd managed to re-create quite a reasonable approximation of a traditional English country-house garden. The flat lawns were clipped low, showing broad cricket-pitch stripes, young staked trees poked up at regular intervals, moated with colorful begonia borders. There was a citrus grove in the old walled orchard where apples and pears used to grow. Long winding rose-covered walks. Ancient-seeming statues.

Even her grandfather had been impressed. "The plants aren't the same, of course," he'd told her on their first inspection. He'd been in fine form that day, she remembered, genial and outgoing. It was a day or two after they'd moved in, a small treasured hiatus before the illness really took hold. He never spoke to anyone else as he did to her, never opened himself. "You wouldn't find any of these in Victorian gardens, not outside the conservatories. That was the zenith of the art, Juliet. But it's a damn good copy for all that; I can almost believe I'm back in my youth. I wish you'd seen England as it was, girl. We all said we hated it, the wet and the cold. Pure bollocks. You could no more hate the country than you could your own mother. Weather made Englishmen.''

The way he painted the land before the Warming had made her envious of his memories. Try as she might she just couldn't visualize Wilholm under a meter of snow.

But he seemed reasonably content with the facsimile. And he always had the roses and honeysuckle, immortal.

Now she ignored both varieties of the fragrant flowering plants while whirlpools of data rotated lazily in the open-ended logic matrix her augmented mind had assembled.

It was a simulacrum of Event Horizon's Zanthus operations, a vast web of data channels incorporating every activity, programmed to review the entire previous twelve months, the first three giving her a baseline for comparison. Byte packages slid smoothly along the matrix channels, interacting at the nodes, dividing, recombining.

The convoluted phantasm reminded her of a brass clock she'd seen in London once, sitting on a pedestal in the window of a Fulham Road antique shop. A real clock in a glass dome, every working part visible. She'd stood for ten minutes watching the little cogs clicking around, superbly balanced ratchet arms rocking fluidly, fascinated by the delicate intricacy. Then the minute hand had reached the hour, and it began to make twanging sounds, like a broken spring uncoiling; cogs on the outside of the mechanism shot out on telescoping axles gyrating wildly. The whole thing had looked like it was exploding. Julia had clapped her hands and laughed delightedly as it folded itself back together, ready for the quarter-hour strike. There was the same elegance and effortless precision in the matrix function.

She needed the knowledge it would produce. The fact that someone could wound Event Horizon so badly had frightened her more than she liked to acknowledge. It went deeper than mere corporate damage; what little control she had over her life was being manipulated, cut away. Her future was being decided right now by how well other people could defend her and Grandpa from unseen enemies. Fighting shadows.

It was the claustrophobic sense of not being able to do anything that was the worst. If she just *knew*.

The simulacrum was intended to give her some part in the struggle, to make the reliance less than absolute. She was going to start at the beginning, the furnaces, then work right back through the company, cross-reference every connection, examine every link, however tenuous. Somewhere, in all that hellishly convoluted maze of data, there would be anomalies, a mistake, a clue to the origin of the spoiler. Nobody was perfect enough to cover their tracks entirely. She'd find it. Data was her medium, a universe where she reigned. Processing power cost nothing; there was only time challenging her now.

New channels began to branch from the bottom of the matrix: how the microgee products were used, sales, maintenance, personnel, finance arrangements, tie-ins with other companies. The Zanthus matrix became the tip of a rapidly growing pyramid.

Queries began to surface.

A memox-furnace operator who'd left suddenly around the time the spoiler started. Julia plugged into Event Horizon's datanet, squirting a tracer program into the company's data cores. The woman had been four months pregnant, skipped her contraceptive in orbit. Doctors were worried about the baby's bone structure; it'd spent two months developing in free fall.

Faulty ionizer grids in the memox furnaces three months ago had slowed production. But the batch had affected other companies as well. Boeing Marietta had paid compensation.

There was a small but regular fluctuation in monolattice filament output, starting nine months ago. A 3 percent shortfall every month, and always in one batch. According to production records the filament extrusion ratio was incorrect, each time.

Julia cross-referenced it with the memox data. It fit like a jigsaw. Whenever the monolattice filament output dipped, the memox crystal output rose to compensate, maintaining total production losses at a level 13.2 percent.

She'd found it. Though what the hell it was, she hadn't got a clue.

End HighSteal#Two. Her processor nodes sucked the data mirage back into nothingness. There was a brief impression of free fall, dropping back into the world of primary sensations. The clammy late March heat, blouse sticking to her back, tight sweaty Levi's, smell of horse breath, birds trilling, red pressure on her eyelids.

Julia blinked, focusing slowly. A cloud of midges were orbiting the brim of her tatty boater.

She was in what she called the crater field. Two acres of small steep-sided hummocks and hollows, like the earth had been bombed or something. Buttercups smothered the rich emerald-colored grass all across the slopes.

A twitch on Tobias's reins, and he plodded toward the derelict tea plantation.

The communal farmers had tried to grow it on a PSP grant. Tea was fetching a good price after the Sri Lankan famine reduced the global harvest by a third, and England's new climate provided near ideal conditions for cultivation. But these were gene-tailored trees, and some nameless state lab had screwed up the DNA modification. The shoots were fast-growing all right, but the leaves ruptured into bulbous cherry blisters before they were ripe enough for picking. The plantation had gone the way of most PSP initiatives, abandoned and left to rot.

Julia dismounted, letting Tobias nuzzle around in the clover. The shire horse was becoming unfortunately flatulent in his old age. Poor dear.

He was another legacy of the communal farm, too old for plow work any more. The laborers had left him behind for Philip Evans to knacker, a trifling expense for a multibillionaire.

Julia had found him alone in the stables as she explored Wilholm the day they moved in. She'd fallen for the great shaggy animal at first sight. He was woefully thin, his coat caked in mud, covered in sores from the plow harness. And he'd looked at her so mournfully, as if he knew what the future held. That had been the last time anyone at Wilholm, including Grandpa, had dared to mention the knackers. She refused to ride anything else and ignored the snickers and winks of the staff when they saw her on the back of the huge plodding beast.

"You'll have to lose that sentiment of yours, girl," Philip Evans had scolded. "Can't run Event Horizon on sentiment."

Except she knew damn well he would have done the same thing.

The tea trees had been laid out in unerringly straight rows. Nearly a third of them had died, but the remainder, left untended, had spread wildly, swamping the gaps, rising up to merge overhead.

Julia left Tobias behind, walking a little way down one of the long tunnels of black branches. Her trainers crushed the crisp dead leaves littering the ground, making sharp popping sounds. For one moment she almost believed they heralded the long-lost autumn, an end to England's eternal Indian summer, when frost would fall and pull down white-fringed leaves. She missed the snow. It had been such a long time since a flake had fallen on her outstretched palm. In Switzerland even the Alps had occasionally been denuded of their sparkling white caps.

She sat with her back to the smooth bole of one of the living trees. The temperature had dropped appreciably in the orange-hued shade. She fanned he face with the boater and pulled out her cybofax.

When Greg's face formed on the little screen it didn't match her memory of him. Free fall had swollen his cheeks, his eyes seemed enlarged, but even through the slightly distorted features he looked dispirited. Something she would never have imagined. She'd been a little bit afraid of him the other night. Physically he wasn't exceptionally big, the same height as Adrian, but there'd been an impression of strength: the way he moved, clean and unhurried, knowing nothing would be in his way. And he'd never smiled, not meaning it anyway. Like he was only playacting civilized. He'd seemed a very cold fish, hard. Which, on reflection, was an interesting kind of challenge. What would make him take notice of someone, respond with kindness? And if he did, how safe that person would feel with such a guardian angel.

"Miss Evans," he said, expectant.

Julia wedged the cybofax into a fork on the gnarled branch in front of her and put her boater back on. "Julia, please."

"Julia. What can I do for you?"

"I called about the spoiler operation."

"You can tell your grandfather I've got all the guilty furnace operators under custody, and the person who destreamed the microgee module squirts."

Tell Grandpa, indeed. Like she was some sort of second-rate office messenger. "Oh, yeah. Is Norman Knowles under sedation yet? Mr. Tyo's report said he put up quite a struggle."

"How the bloody hell did you know that?"

"My executive code gives me access to all the security division communications." She regretted saying it instantly, flinching inwardly at how pompous she must've sounded.

"Oh. Well anyway, Knowles isn't going to be any more trouble. It's finished now; we're due down in another six hours."

"It isn't finished, Greg."

He frowned, inviting explanation.

She began to reel off her research findings, praying he wouldn't think she was talking down to him. The girls at school always said she talked as though she were delivering a lecture. But he listened intently, not interrupting like most people.

"You discovered this yourself?" he asked when she'd finished, and there was definitely a tone of respect in his voice.

"Yeah. The data was all there; it's just a question of running the right search program." Julia knew her cheeks would be red but didn't care.

"How much is the monolattice filament worth?" he asked.

"That's what doesn't make sense," she admitted. "The total loss is only nine hundred thousand Eurofrancs."

"And that bothers you?"

"Yeah! It's ridiculous. Why go to all that trouble? The memox spoiler works perfectly; there's no need to add the monolattice filament to it."

Greg didn't exactly smile, but she could sense his tension easing. "Tell you," he said, "I knew something about this spoiler operation was funny. You believe in intuition?" The question was sharp, as though the answer really mattered to him.

Julia forgot the tea plantation, the bark pressing into her back, muggy air. She felt real good talking to him like this, treated as an equal, not the patronized boss's granddaughter, not a scatty teenage rich girl. Right now she was a real person, for the first time in a long time. Maybe the moment would stretch and stretch.

Commit GregTime. To sip and savor whenever she felt down.

"I had to keep working on the Zanthus data," she said carefully. "Like it wouldn't let me go."

He nodded, satisfied with her response. "It's up here. I can feel it, no messing."

Which sounded pretty strange. Was that what he'd meant by intuition? "What's up there?"

"The twist. We're overlooking something, Julia." He paused, eyes closed, an impression of effort. "What was the monolattice filament intended for, anything important? Are you going to get clobbered with penalty clauses for nondelivery?"

Julia used the nodes to plug into the company datanet, remonstrating with herself. It was an obvious question. She traced the monolattice-filament contracts, running a quick analysis. "Not that I can find," she said. "But I'll have the lawyer's office double-check to be on the safe side."

"Right. In the meantime, I'll start interviewing the monolattice-filament module people." He let out a long breath, rubbing his nose. "Lord, how many of them are there?"

"Seven. We don't make much monolattice filament."

"That's something. You'd better call Morgan Walshaw. Bring him up to date, and have him round up those on their furlough. I'll have to vet them once I get down."

"Right."

"That was a terrific piece of work, Julia. Exactly the sort of proof I needed."

Julia watched his image intently. His camouflage of emotional detachment had slipped fractionally; he was keen now, animated. He looked much nicer this way, she decided. "What proof?"

"That the spoiler doesn't conform."

"But how does knowing it's odd help? That just makes it more confusing to me."

He winked. "Have faith. Now that I know, I'll keep looking. And I can look in the weirdest places."

"Where?" she demanded eagerly.

"Right in my own heart. Now you'll have to excuse me; I've got to get Victor Tyo organized."

"Right, sure." Granting him a favor.

End GregTime.

His image winked out, what might have been a smile tantalizing her. She reached out and plucked the cybofax from the tree. Grinning stupidly, feeling wonderful.

One of Wilholm's sentinel panthers was looking at her five meters away, violet saucer eyes unblinking. She clicked her fingers and it padded over. Warm damp breath fell on her cheek.

"Good girl." She stroked it behind pointed flattened ears. It yawned lazily at the affection, pink tongue licking its double row of shark-heritage teeth. Tobias snorted disapproval, shaking his thick neck, then went back to foraging the grass.

Right in his own heart?

10

Aʟᴇxɪᴜs McNᴀᴍᴀʀᴀ ᴅʀᴏᴘᴘᴇᴅ ᴛʜʀᴏᴜɢʜ ᴛʜᴇ sick bay's hatch, dressed in the sky-blue flightsuit that all the microgee module workers wore. His jowls overflowed his helmet strap, fingers resembled sausages. It was the last week of his shift.

"Grab him," Greg said simply. He'd soon learned to speak in a half shout; sound didn't carry far in free fall.

Victor Tyo and Isabel Curtis were already anchored to the chamber's walls on either side of the hatch. They clamped him between them with the efficiency of a tag-wrestling team, his legs and arms immobilized. Don Howarth jabbed a shockrod into his neck.

Greg had recognized the mental genotype as soon as he appeared: fissures of lassitude, leprous self-loathing. One of the kamikazes. He wasn't taking chances with them any more. His interview with Normal Knowles, one of the five managers, had finished badly. Greg had sensed Knowles was the one who'd circumvented the security monitors at the same time as Knowles worked out he had a gland. Unfortunately, Greg hadn't sensed Knowles was one of the kamikazes in time. Jerry Masefield had taken the brunt of the attack before he had been subdued. There was something uniquely disquieting about small globules of blood spraying about in free fall.

"Fuck you!" McNamara shouted.

The shockrod dug deeper. Don Howarth was a man worried for his position and pension. McNamara snarled.

Greg pushed off the wall and stopped himself ten centimeters from him. They were inverted, and Greg sensed how that irritated the man. The Zanthus crew put a lot of stock in orienting themselves to a universal visual horizon.

"Spit at me, and I'll shove that shockrod up your arse, no messing," Greg said calmly.

McNamara gave a start, thought about it, and swallowed.

"That's right. They sent me up here because I have a gland."

Frightened eyes peered at Greg from within wells of flaccid flesh.

"You've been screwing around with the monolattice-filament extruder 'ware, McNamara. Writing off perfectly good fibers. How long have you been doing it?"

"Hey, psycho freak, your gland gives you cancer, know that? You'll die rotting."

"Don't," said Greg. "The whole nine months? Eight? Seven?" He sighed. "Seven it is."

"Bastard."

"How did they get a lever on you?"

"Eat shit and die, boy-lover."

"We have this sweep going between us, you see. A fiver each, so you can understand we're anxious to know. With a lot it's sex. Drugs are quite popular. Then there's the geegees. Some are just cracking apart, can't take the stress. But I think you're a straight money man, McNamara. Greed, that's your bang, isn't it? Pure greed." Greg could smell breath heavy with herb seasoning. "Did they tell you why?"

"What?" McNamara was clenching his muscles rigid, trembling, his face hot.

"Why they only wanted that three percent taken out? Why not go for the jackpot like the memox furnaces?"

There was nothing in his mind, no indication that he knew an answer. Even the reference to the memox furnaces had surprised him. The tekmerc team had been good, Greg acknowledged, textbook. The furnace operators didn't know who'd circumvented the security monitors; McNamara hadn't known about the furnace operators. Tight thinking all the way down the line.

He stopped his gland secretion and turned wearily to Bruce Parwez. "Okay, I'm through with him. Stash him in the suit cabin."

"Right." He began to truss McNamara with nylon restrainer bands, arms, ankles, knees. The seething man was eventually hauled out of the sick bay by Isabel Curtis and Lewis Pelham.

"It must be getting crowded in that cabin—five furnace operators, now two from the filament modules," Greg said to Victor Tyo.

"Tough."

"Yeah. How many more?"

"McNamara was the last. Unless you want to work through the other microgee products."

"Christ, don't. Morgan Walshaw or Julia Evans would've been in contact if any other products were involved with the spoil."

"Yes, the last word I got from Walshaw was that he'd got up a team to analyze the output of every module." Victor fought against a smile. "I don't think he was too happy that Julia Evans had found another security breach."

Greg wedged his foot under one of the beds. His first impulse was to sit down, but the position made his stomach muscles ache. Everything about free fall was unnatural. There was a fish bowl on the wall beside the bed, a sealed meter-wide globe with a complicated-looking water filter grafted onto one side. Ten guppies were swimming slowly around. Even they were all keeping their bellies toward the wall, though the angle made it look as if they were standing on their broad rainbow tails.

"What was bothering him?" Greg asked. "That it was another breach, or that Julia Evans found it?"

"Both, I think."

"What's wrong with Julia?"

"Nothing. I met her once, nice kid." Victor popped a mint out of a tube with his thumb, snagging the spinning white disk in midair with his tongue. "Except we're all a bit worried about her grandfather. She's sort of young to be taking over a company like this. There are eighty thousand of us, you know. Most have dependents. That's a lot of responsibility for a teenage girl."

"Yet she's quicker off the mark than the whole of the security division."

Victor smiled boyishly. His face seemed almost unaffected by free fall. "There is that."

The sick bay suddenly rang as if it'd been hit by a hammer. Greg winced; he knew that was something he'd never get used to. The thermal stabilization went on for fifteen minutes every time the dormitory crossed the terminator, the can's metal skin expanding or contracting, protesting the adjustments with loud groans and shrieks.

"Shall I tell the pilot we're still okay for our original departure time?" Victor asked.

"Yes. We'll get the first flight off anyway and make sure McNamara is included. He's not the type I want up here a moment longer than necessary. You and I will go down in the second flight."

"McNamara's that bad?"

"Total nutcase, no messing."

"Right, I'll assign all our hardliners to go down on that flight, five of them, five of us; Knowles can go down with them as well. We can borrow a couple of hardliners from Howarth to come with us."

"How long can we delay the second flight?"

"You're the boss; as long as you want. Physically the Sanger can stay up here for thirty-six hours, but it'd be cheaper to send it down and wait for another."

"Plan for that, then. If anyone objects, tell them to contact Walshaw. And if he wants to know what the deal is, tell him to call me."

"Do you think there are some more tekmerc plants up here?"

"Unlikely."

"Why are we staying, then?"

"To find out why the monolattice-filament output was being tampered with." Greg wasn't too keen on having to explain his instinct to Victor. The security lieutenant was a programmer, confined to the physical universe where everything was precisely arrayed and answers were logical, black and white. Perhaps he was being unfair. But empathy was the tangible half of his gland-enhanced psi ability. Intuition, on the other hand, was a track leading down the black-ice slope to the hinterlands of magic, witchery. The province of prophets and demons.

Julia Evans was young enough to be impressionable. Victor, he suspected, would be a mite skeptical.

"I thought the tekmercs were holding the filament extruders in reserve," Victor said. "Then after we pulled the furnace operators, they just bring them into line."

"No. The tekmercs would know we'd check the other microgee modules eventually. And you've toughened up the security monitors yourself; there won't be a recurrence. There's no way they could ever hope to pull the same stunt twice in a row. They're too professional for that."

"Right." Victor thumbed his communication set and began talking to the Sanger pilot docked to the can.

The guppies were chasing tiny grains of food that the filter unit was pumping into their globe. Greg rubbed his eyes, yawning, a faint throbbing of a neurohormone hangover making itself felt at the back of his head. The last decent sleep he'd had was on the *Alabama Spirit*. Two—no, three nights ago. But the idea of sleep was foreign; he knew his body well enough to tell when he needed to bunk down. Ever since they'd arrived at Zanthus he'd been on the verge. Time stretched up here, knocking biorhythms along with the rest of normality. It was his mind that needed to wind down, a whole stack of accumulated Zanthus-time memories pressing in on him.

Voices percolated through the sick-bay hatch, interspaced by a salvo of plangent creaks from the can shell. Piccadilly Circus was filling up, the shifts changing over again.

Greg realized his gland was active again, though he couldn't remember a conscious decision to use it. The secretions brought on an unaccustomed dreamy sensation; it felt good, warmth and confidence washing through him, lifting the depression Alexius McNamara had left behind. The answer was close now, a surety.

He heard a protracted clanging as one of the Swearingen commuters docked with the can; hums and whines took over. Another
wave of voices broke, the high, restless kind people used when they'd
just come off work.

The answer clicked.

11

JULIA RACED OUT OF THE bathroom just as Adela was about to pick up her cybofax. "I'll get it," she called over the shrill bleeping. She tightened the belt on her robe and threw away the big yellow towel she'd been drying her hair with. Adela shrugged and began to close the curtains. Torrential rain was beating against the thick windows.

Julia dropped onto the bed and picked up the cybofax. Greg's face appeared on the screen. She flushed scarlet. "Give me a moment, Adela, please."

Adela picked the towel off the carpet, giving her a meaningful look before closing the bathroom door behind her.

"Are we secure?" Greg asked.

Julia pushed back some of her hair; it was all rat tails. Why did he have to call when she looked like this? "Yeah."

"Great. I know what the twist is."

Julia stared at him numbly. "And you called me first?"

"Yeah. You see, I need it confirmed before I go to Walshaw or your grandfather. So I thought you could do some research for me."

"Me?"

"You uncovered the monolattice filament discrepancy. It's as much your discovery as mine. I thought you'd want to see it through."

"I do," she said quickly.

Commit GregTime#Two.

"Right then," Greg said. "It's a Luxembourg-registered company that has to be checked out. Can you do that for me?"

"Of course. But, Greg, what's the twist?"

He smiled, and she noticed how drawn he looked.

"I think the memox crystals are being shipped down to Earth."

"Oh," was all she said because the jolt sent her thoughts racing. "Greg, the Sanger flights are well documented. Their cargo manifests are finalized weeks in advance. It'd be awfully difficult to sneak anything on board, certainly on a regular basis." She didn't like puncturing his idea like that; he seemed so keen about it.

But Greg's smile just broadened. "Forty-eight million Eurofrancs, Julia. When I took the case, we thought the crystals were being contaminated, dumped. But they're not contaminated, are they? They're perfect. For forty-eight million, it's worth trying to bring them down, even if you couldn't get away with it. Tell you, I'd try. If it's possible, those tekmercs will've done it; maybe they've found a psychic who can teleport the stuff back to Earth for them."

"Teleport?" she squawked in alarm.

"Old Mindstar joke, sorry."

"Ah." The goosebumps on Julia's forearms began to settle.

"The thing is, to find the flights the crystals went down on, Event Horizon would have to run a computer search through past spaceplane flights up to Zanthus. Say, over the period of a couple of months."

"God, Greg, do you know how many spaceplane flights rendezvous with Zanthus in one day, let alone a month?"

"Today there were twenty-three. That's where my problem lies. I'm convinced it's happening, but getting Morgan Walshaw to mount an investigation on that scale, with just my intangible hearsay to go on, would be difficult. That's even if the spacelines would cooperate and open their data cores to you, which is doubtful, and assuming the tekmercs haven't wiped the records anyway."

"So what's this company you want me to check out?"

"The weak link. There's always one."

"I know," she whispered fervently.

"Yes? Well, anyway, memox crystals, good or bad, are taken from the furnace modules to the servicing docks. From there, they're either loaded into a Dragonflight Sanger or included in a waste-dump stack, depending on how the batch was coded. Ample scope there for hanky-panky."

Access HighSteal#Two.

She fired off a tracer program as soon as the simulacrum materialized. "It's a contractor!" she shouted excitedly.

"Right. Event Horizon doesn't own any interorbit craft. There are three specialist transport companies based up at Zanthus to serve the manufacturers. You pay High Shunt to move your cargo around and to perform your waste dumps."

"It's got to be them."

"No messing. Now if you'd just care to prove it for me." He was grinning at her.

She beamed right back; it was like they had some sort of affinity bond or something. And she'd been the one he'd come straight to. Not Morgan Walshaw, not Grandpa. Her. "Coming up," she said.

It wasn't even difficult. Event Horizon's commercial intelligence division compiled a survey of every company they did business with. Large or small, each of them was scrutinized before the contract was finalized.

Julia's executive code plugged her right in. High Shunt's daedal aspects expanded in her mind, a comprehensive listing of its history, management structure, performance, assets, personnel. It was a respectable company, formed eight years ago, good safety record, developing as Zanthus grew.

List Ownership.

A stream of banks, pension schemes, trust funds, and individuals flooded through her, giving percentages and acquisition dates. One of them leaped out at her as if it were haloed in flashing red neon. Thirty-two percent of High Shunt was owned by the di Girolamo family house.

"Gotcha, Kendric," she whispered.

12

STANSTEAD AIRPORT WAS SUBTLY DEPRESSING. New developments were erupting like shiny volcanic cancers in the middle of abandoned jet-age structures, vibrant young challengers. But the chances for inspiration that new materials and energy technologies provided, the opportunities to learn from the past and build a commercial enterprise that complemented the local environment, had all been lost; the steel and composite structures worshiped scale, not Gaia. They had neither grace nor art, simply history repeating itself. Stanstead had originally been built on the promise of the postwar dream, only to find itself betrayed like the rest of the country.

Greg looked down on the architectural shambles from an office on the top floor of Event Horizon's glass-cube administration block and wondered how many times that cycle would turn down the centuries. Hopes and aspirations of each new age lost under the weight of human frailties and plain bloody-mindedness.

The airport's ancient hangars were dilapidated monstrosities, corrugated panels flapping dangerously as they awaited the reclamation crews. Next to them were six modern cargo terminals made from pearl-white composite; a constant flow of Dornier tilt-fans came and went from the pads outside. Black oval airships drifted high overhead.

He could see an old An-225 Mriya at the end of the barely serviceable runway. The Sanger orbiter he'd returned in yesterday had been hoisted on top by a couple of big cranes. The configuration was undergoing a final inspection before flying back to Listoel.

He heard Philip Evans's querulous voice behind him and closed the gray-silver louver blinds that ran along the window wall, shutting out the sight of the tilt-fans hovering outside. The glass was sound-deadened, blocking the incessant high-frequency whine of their turbines.

Only Morgan Walshaw and Victor Tyo were in the office, sitting in hotel lobby silicon-composite chairs at a big oval conference table. There was a large flatscreen on the wall at the head of the table, showing Julia and Philip Evans in the study at Wilholm. Julia's hair was tied back severely, and she was wearing a double-breasted purple suit-jacket over a cream blouse. Going for an executive image. It didn't quite come off; her face, despite its current solemnity, was far too young. People would underestimate her because of that, he knew. He had.

But it was Philip who worried him. The old man looked just awful; a heavy woollen shawl wrapped around his thin frail shoulders, eyes that were yellow and glazed. His deterioration even over the five short days since the dinner party was quite obvious. He seemed to be having a great deal of trouble following the proceedings, his attention intermittent.

Julia shared Greg's opinion, judging by her expression. Her pretty oval face was pale and drawn, crestfallen. It looked as though she hadn't slept for days, her big tawny eyes were red-rimmed, never leaving her grandfather. He wondered if he'd asked too much from her, especially at this time.

"It was Kendric di Girolamo who organized the spoiler operation," Greg said. "The evidence which Julia has unearthed for us puts it beyond doubt."

The corners of her lips lifted in acknowledgment.

"My girl," Philip rumbled.

"We had two problems arise out of what we discovered," said Greg, "which when taken together cancel each other out. We already knew that with his control of High Shunt, Kendric could divert the memox crystals from the waste dump. But that left us with the question of how he could get hold of a Sanger to bring them back down to Earth. At five hundred million Eurofrancs each, it's too expensive for him to buy one; besides we'd know if the di Girolamo family house owned a spaceplane. And to hire one from a legitimate spaceline he would've had to list the cargo manifest, both for the operator and the spaceport authority. It would've been impossible for him to explain where the memox crystals originated from. Oh, he might've been able to do it once, or even twice. But not on a regular basis. The space industry is close-knit, it knows itself. If he was bringing down three flights of memox crystals a month, the pilots and payload handlers would've started to ask questions.

"Then we have the second problem: why did he bother with the monolattice filament when he'd already corrupted the memox-furnace operators? Julia found the answer to that."

"After I found High Shunt was owned by the di Girolamo house, I took a closer look at all the other companies working up at Zanthus," she said, reading from her cube. Her voice was like a construct, level and droning. "The clincher was a company called Siebruk Orbital. It's the smallest one up at Zanthus, consisting of a single standard microgee module staffed by two technicians. They're listed as a research team investigating new vacuum-fabrication techniques."

"So?" Philip asked.

"*Fabrication* techniques," Greg said. "I think they're turning the monolattice filament into small reentry capsules inside that module. Then they fill them with memox crystals and hand them back to High Shunt for a waste dump, retroburning them so they fall into the atmosphere."

"Siebruk Orbital belongs to Kendric?"

"Siebruk Orbital is registered in Zurich, which gives total anonymity for the owner," said Julia. "But the Sanger which launched the module was a Lufthansa charter. It was put up ten months ago, which, incidentally, fits the timing perfectly. Payment for the flight came from Siebruk Orbital's company account at the Credit Corato bank in Italy. All perfectly legal and above board. However, the di Girolamo family finance house has a thirty-five percent stake in Credit Corato. It's supposition, of course.'

"Has to be," Philip said softly. He was looking at something off-screen, wistful.

Victor Tyo activated the terminal on the table in front of him, the cubes lit. "After Greg came to me with this, I ordered a review of data from our Earth Resources platforms, specifically the oceans under Zanthus's orbital track. There are three designated areas for waste dumps, all over water in case burn-up isn't complete. Two over the Pacific, one over the Atlantic." An image formed in one of the cubes, a white dot on a blue background. The dot began to move, trailing a white line behind it. After a minute the center of the image was a near-solid blob of white. "What you're seeing is a movement record built up over the last two months of a ship in the Atlantic, two hundred kilometers east of the waste dump area. As you can see, it stays within a patch of ocean about fifty kilometers in diameter. We did a computer simulation of a nonlifting body profiled descent trajectory; two hundred kilometers is well within the established criteria. I believe the ship is Mr. di Girolamo's recovery vessel." The cube display changed, showing an overhead view of a ship at sea. "This was taken at first light this morning with a platform's high-definition photon amp." The angle of the cube image shifted in increments until the ship appeared to be leaning over at forty-five degrees. The name *Weslin* was visible on the side.

"According to Lloyd's data core, *Weslin* is owned by MDL Maritime," Julia said. "MDL Maritime is another Zurich-registered company. Credit Corato handles its account."

"Bingo," Morgan Walshaw said quietly.

Philip's eyes found the camera, looking down at Greg. Confusion distorted his enervated features. "Why?" he asked. "Kendric di Girolamo has a large legitimate financial interest in Event Horizon through his family finance house. He was hurting himself with the spoiler."

"The spoiler made him forty-eight million Eurofrancs, and as to Event Horizon's suffering, he wouldn't lose a thing, not in the long run," Greg said. "You see, he wasn't looking to make a killing from the crystals directly; they were a means. With Event Horizon's declining profits on top of your health situation he would have gained enough leverage with the other members of the backing consortium to have himself appointed to the board of trustees you've arranged to run Event Horizon until Julia comes of age."

"It's a reasonable enough request," Julia put in reluctantly. "The consortium is entitled to a representative. I doubt we could keep their nominee off. Not legally."

Philip nodded slowly. "The consortium has mentioned it . . . Someone . . . to oversee their interests." His voice sounded terribly weak. Julia was looking at him, almost in pain with what she saw. His head turned from the camera again. Greg thought he was looking out of the study window. "Then what?" he whispered.

"This is just theory, you understand, based on what you told me about Kendric trying to muscle in on the management side of Event Horizon. But after Kendric landed his boardroom seat I'd say that he simply planned to close down the spoiler, bringing Event Horizon's accounts back to their usual profit level. He'd disguise the link of course, make it an issue—shuffle personnel, target resources at the furnace maintenance division—but that kind of high-profile result would guarantee him the chairmanship. Now, because Event Horizon is a family company, he can never own it. But as chairman he could oversee a massive asset-stripping raid, presumably by his own front companies. That sort of money he is most definitely interested in. Julia and the consortium would be left with nothing."

Julia had listened raptly the night before, after she'd pulled the information about Siebruk Orbital for him. "So simple," she'd said, when he'd finished explaining. "I had all the pieces before you and I didn't put them together. If you hadn't had your suspicions that the memox crystals were being brought down, we would never have uncovered Kendric's involvement."

It was his intuition, of course. A foresight equal to everyone else's hindsight. He hadn't told her that. Let her go on thinking he was a magician. Event Horizon might have a few more jobs coming up, and they paid bloody well.

"I see," said Philip. "Either way, Kendric wins. How typical."

"What are we going to do about di Girolamo?" Victor asked.

"The options are regrettably limited," said Walshaw. "Our respective Scottish operations are almost fully integrated. We can hardly untangle them now, certainly not with the Scottish PSP so close to falling. A replacement for Kendric would be hard to find."

Julia cleared her throat. "The ship in the Atlantic."

"Yes," Walshaw said. "I can arrange a hardliner assault. We might even retrieve some more of our memox crystals."

"See to it," said Philip. "You've done some good work for me here, Greg. I won't forget. You, too, boy."

Victor ducked his head.

Julia took her grandfather's hand, steadying the shaking fingers. "That's enough, Grandee."

"I'll get back to you later," Walshaw said.

Julia gave him a vaguely remorseful nod before the image blanked out.

Greg spent another ten minutes filling in details for Walshaw before saying good-bye. He'd been away from Eleanor for too long.

"There's a permanent job for you at Event Horizon if you want it," the security chief said as Greg reached the door.

"Thanks, but no thanks," Greg said. He didn't even have to think about it. Office hours, suit, tie, the same people day after day. He had wanted something regular but not regimented. "I'm not ready for that yet."

The 1950s Rolls-Royce was waiting for him on Stanstead's buckling gray concrete as he came out of the administration block, chauffeur already opening the door.

Philip Evans died two days later. His funeral was the biggest civic event to be held in Peterborough for two generations. The prime minister and two senior royals were in respectful attendance.

His will named Julia Hazel Snowflower Evans as his sole beneficiary.

13

JULIA WATCHED THE CRACKLING LIFE of the nighttime city through the Rolls-Royce's tinted windows, impatient for the ride to be over, the drama she'd conceived to unfold. She could almost believe they were driving through some German metropolis. Peterborough's New Eastfield district possessed the same frantic pace and power, the strut that came from being number one.

Its buildings were post-Warming, laid out in a precise geometrical array, like Manhattan before the Anarchy March. They were foreign funded, a thorn in the side of the PSP, physical evidence the Party couldn't fulfill its promises. All of them followed the same palaeo-Spanish theme, six-story, marble or cut stone, with long balconies that sported a profusion of greenery and flowers. Smart-uniformed doormen stood outside the gingery smoked-glass lobbies.

Wealth was everywhere, in clothes, jewelry, salon beauty, in the absence of bicycles and graffiti.

The road was clogged with traffic: gas-electric hybrid BMWs and Mercs cruised up and down, their headlights and taillights two contrasting severed ribbons of light. The folksy tables of pavement cafés were spread out under brightly striped awnings, alternating with arched entrances into small arcades of exclusive shops. Brightly lit windows full of designer-label clothes and esoteric gear silhouetted the fast-moving pedestrians, painting their faces in cool neon tones. Soft warm rain had fallen earlier in the evening, its residual sheen reflecting gaudy biolum ads in long wavering flames from walls and paving slabs.

But the prosperity was only a few blocks across. A ghetto of the rich. She remembered Grandpa saying that New Eastfield was a seed, that in a proper economy this kind of lifestyle would spread out like a microbe culture, consuming and changing its surrounding neighborhoods, right out to the city boundaries. He'd wanted the New Conservatives to build cores like it in every English city, showcases for a top-led society, the acceptable face of capitalism.

Good old Grandpa. An eternal optimist. But there were a *lot* of people enjoying the balmy evening street life.

"Are you sure Bil will be there?" Katerina asked.

Julia turned away from the window, back to the subdued oyster shade inside the car. Her friend was wearing a skintight black tube dress; a slash down the front was loosely laced up, showing the deep cleft between her breasts. Brazen, but Julia was forced to admit she looked wonderful. Her hair was a fluffy gold cloud.

"He was invited," Julia said tonelessly. Bil Yi Somanzer: the hottest, meanest rock and roller in the history of the world, ever. Even Kats would look ordinary around his groupies. She smiled in the shadows; Kats had only agreed to come after she'd promised her Bil would be there.

"Well, Julie, dear, anyone can *invite* him. Having him turn up is different."

"He'll be there. Stars and the media, they need each other. Feed off each other. And media doesn't come any bigger than Uncle Horace."

Kats wasn't convinced, fuchsia lips screwing up petulantly, but Adrian nudged her quiet. He was wearing a white jacket, black bow tie, a red rose tucked into his buttonhole. Stunningly handsome. And he'd silenced Kats from spouting off inanely because he knew she was still supposed to be shaken over Grandpa's death. Her feelings mattered to him.

The Rolls dipped down into the giant Castlewood condominium's underground garage. Horace Jepson had his own private park on the second level. Thick metal doors swung open as the chauffeur showed his card to the lock.

Steven Welbourn and Rachel Griffith, Julia's two bodyguards, hurried out of the trail car as the little convoy came to a halt. Both of them were wearing formal evening dress, Steven in a dinner jacket, Rachel in a long navy blue gown. Their alert faces scanned the stark, brightly lit concrete cave. They needn't have bothered; two of Horace's own security staff were waiting for them.

There was a distinct air of farce about the entire scene. But Julia was careful not to show disapproval. Steven and Rachel were just doing their job, and she got on quite well with them. Steven had been with her for years, almost since she came to Europe, a twenty-seven-year-old with sandy hair that she teased him was already thinning. He was sympathetic about her circumstances, and his discretion had been demonstrated time and again, considering the schoolgirl truancies that he could have told her grandfather about. Rachel had been with her for about a year; a twenty-two-year-old with neat close-cut mousy hair, she came across as a mix of big sister and maiden aunt.

Courteous, but an absolute stickler for security protocol, always checking the toilet cubicle first, which could get embarrassing. Of course, one day she might be very glad of them. Besides, any complaints would find their way back to Morgan Walshaw. And then there'd be another bloody lecture.

The five of them squeezed into the penthouse lift. Kats and Adrian didn't notice the press, lost in a private world of furtive smirks and hungry looks. Julia gritted her teeth.

The lift opened straight into the vestibule of Horace Jepson's suite. Music and conversation hit them as the doors slid apart.

On her previous visits, the center of the penthouse had been divided up into various function areas by hand-painted Japanese silk screens depicting scenes from mythological battles, samurai and improbable creatures. Now the screens had all been folded back against the walls leaving one big open space. Colored jelly blobs of hologram light swam through the air, wobbling in time to a loud acid-thrash version of "Brown Sugar." Bodies packed the black-tiled dance floor, a rainbow riot of frantic movement, older sweating men with younger energetic girls. More people lined the vestibule walls under the umbrella of fern fronds, drinking, chattering excitedly. She recognized a lot of faces from the channels.

Trust Uncle Horace. There was nothing refined about this party: it was deliberate Dionysian overload without a refuge, forcing you to enjoy. She wondered if he'd have a topless model bursting out of a cake at some point. More than likely.

Horace Jepson broke free of the crowd, shooing away a girl who had the glossy vibrancy and dazzling pout of a Playmate. He was smiling warmly at Julia. A genuine smile, she thought. Then it flickered slightly as he took her in, as though she'd come in the wrong sort of dress or something. But she'd chosen a five-thousand-pound Dermani gown, pale pink silk with a mermaid-tail skirt, nothing like as tarty as the rest of the girls she could see, so that couldn't be it.

His smile had mellowed by the time he reached her. He took both her hands and gave her a demure peck on the cheek.

It was almost saddening. He used to give her big bear hugs and a huge slobbery kiss. Funny, she'd always hated them at the time. Now they were a part of an old familiar world, lost and gone for good.

"I was afraid you weren't going to come," he said.

"Try keeping me from a party."

"That's my gal. Say, look, I'm real sorry about Phil. One of the best, you know?"

Behavioral Response: Sorrow.

She'd loaded the program in the processor node to remind her, keyed by any mention of Grandpa. For her to giggle at his name, at people's earnest sympathy, would never do.

"Thank you. Do something for me, Uncle Horace?"

"Sure, honey."

"Don't treat me like glass. I won't break. And it only makes it worse."

"Right." He grinned at Katerina and Adrian. "Come on in, you guys. We're just getting warmed up. Plenty of action here tonight."

Julia thought his glance hovered around Kats's cleavage. Then he was looking over her shoulder at Steven and Rachel, a faintly puzzled expression on his face as Kats dragged Adrian past him into the throng.

"No escort, Julia?"

" 'Fraid not."

"Hell, gal, why didn't you let me know? Cindy could've fixed something up for you. That girl's got a list of boys bigger than a census bureau."

"Maybe next time."

"Damn, Clifford won't be over before the weekend. He would've done just fine. You met Cliff before? My boy? From my first marriage."

"You've mentioned him," she said dryly. Had the two of them walking down the aisle in his mind.

"Oh well, let me introduce you to a few people. Hey, maybe I can have one dance. Make an old man happy."

"I think your friend would scratch my eyes out first." She nodded at the Playmate girl.

"Ouch, Julia. There's a lot of Philip in you," he said admiringly.

She quashed the laugh while it was still in her gullet.

Sorrow.

"Good. Because I'd like to do some business with you."

Horace Jepson suddenly became wary. "Most of Globecast's contracts with Event Horizon are pretty much cut-and-dried."

"Well, not formal business. More a favor."

"Go on."

"There's a program I might want broadcasting. It's important to me, Uncle Horace."

"What sort of program?" he asked cautiously.

"A planet-wide exposé. Every current-affairs channel Globecast owns."

Now his face really fell. "Julia, honey, do you know the kind of legal angles on this? I mean, if you're really hot on rubbishing someone, then hearsay ain't no use."

"I've got the proof. All we need."

"Damn, but I wish you didn't grow up so fast."

Kendric di Girolamo was at the party, and Hermione. Julia didn't know when they'd arrived. Kendric was his usual oily suave self, dancing with a girl who made the Playmate look like a hag.

Their eyes met and held. She gave him a cool, level gaze. Quietly satisfied at the startled light in his eyes. Quickly hidden.

He knew full well she couldn't stand the sight of him; expected a girlish glare, a tossed head, flouncing off in a huff. Instead he got a dispassionate assessment from a multibillionairess. Small wonder he was surprised. Hopefully concerned.

Squirm, she wished him silently. Her eyes moved on sedately, showing him how little he mattered. Fighting the impulse to whoop for joy. It'd begun.

Horace Jepson had hired a five-piece rock band for the evening, the Fifth Horseman, their axmen tooled up with reasonable copies of Fenders. They were dressed in torn T-shirts, studded leathers, and thigh-length boots. Clean, though, Julia noticed. But they were a tight outfit for all their synthetic attitude, the rhythm pumping out of their Gorilla stacks hot and fast. The singer had a Ziggy Stardust stripe across his face, 3-D paint opening into middle-distance.

She danced with Bil Yi Somanzer to a number that could've been "Five Years." Uncle Horace had introduced them, interest in her name and wealth finally penetrating the megastar's syntho stupor. Basking in the jealousy that lashed out in tangible waves from the other girls. His skin was smooth and shiny from *plastique*, his voice slurred. He groped her backside and asked if she fancied a quick trip to one of the bedrooms. The band finished their stuff, and they parted. His reputation upheld.

Seeing Kats standing on a table trying to Bunter down a long glass of champagne to the boisterous cheers of an admiring audience of young blades. The hologram blobs congregated around her legs in a silent red-and-green swarm, floating up inside her skirt. Adrian hovering on the sidelines, tolerant, fixed smile.

* * *

Talking to a young French finance manager who was helping Uncle Horace to expand Globecast into Europe. He was nervous about her, stammering, telling her about the investment ratios of various gilt stocks and the new junk-bond markets opening in South America. She turned down his invitation to dance. Boring.

Kendric offering a gentlemanly hand to Kats as she climbed down off the table, face flushed. He handed her a drink. Hermione joined them, palpably excited. Laser fans swept across the trio, sparkling off jewels, teeth, lips, fluorescing Kats's cloud of hair into an electric-pink halo.

A dance with Adrian. Doing his duty. A smoochy number, so he'd have to hold her close. Swaying rhythmically with the feel of his hard body pressed against hers, his hands on her back.
"You dance well," she told him.
"Oh, yeah, thanks." Distracted.
She shivered beneath his hands.

Kendric and Kats dancing. She was hanging on to every word he uttered, both laughing ebulliently, plainly delighted with each other's company. Her body flowed with the music, lost to the beat, wild and sensual.

Half a dance with Uncle Horace. His face red and puffing as he gave up, leading her over to the seafood buffet. Picking out their food together, Horace with something to say about every dish, urging her to sample. His own plate piled high. Divine crabs.

A cocktail that took the bartender an elaborate three minutes to prepare. Only it tasted like orange juice that someone had spilled vinegar into. She flashed him a smile saying how wonderful it was and poured it into the punch bowl when no one was looking, green ice-swan sculpture and all.

Kendric and Kats nearly alone on the dance floor. Doing the lambada. Adoration in her eyes.

She chatted to the Playmate girl, whose name was Cindy, and was actually a data-compression expert. So much for first impressions. Cindy was raucous and worldly wise and had lots of funny stories about men in general. A life lived in the fast lane, with no regrets. She hung on to every word; Cindy gave her a window on the kind of world she so rarely glimpsed.

Cindy was well into a completely unbelievable recital of her recent Spanish holiday when both of them became aware of the shouting. The Fifth Horseman ground to a halt in a dissonant metallic skirl.

Adrian, Kendric, and Kats stood in the middle of the dance floor, two against one. Kats stood beside Kendric, breathing heavily, sweat-darkened tassel ends of her hair sticking to her shoulders. Hologram blobs orbited the trio slowly.

"Enough!" Adrian yelled.

Kendric raised a warning finger. "Go home, little boy, you're making a fool of yourself."

"I'll go all right. You people make me want to puke. And you're coming with me." He tried to grab Katerina, but she dodged nimbly behind Kendric.

"No way," she shrilled. "I'm having some real fun. First time in bloody ages, too."

Julia knew Kats well enough to see how she was loving the scene, milking it. The center of attention. All the glitzy people she worshiped were focusing on her, asking who she was, a girl so desirable she was worth fighting over in public.

Kendric grinned. "That seems pretty plain, little boy. Go play somewhere else."

"Come on," Adrian entreated. His fists were clenched, face beaming hatred at his rival.

Kendric's arm snaked protectively around Katerina, his hand squeezing her breast. "I do so detest these revolting peasants. Why don't you and I go somewhere quieter? My yacht is anchored in the marina."

Katerina's face was flushed with triumph. She tossed her head. "Sounds good. Better than anything Mr. Ten Centimeters here ever offered me."

Kendric roared with laughter. There were snickers from the guests. Adrian paled, staring at Katerina in complete and abject incomprehension.

There was a voice inside Julia's skull pleading at her to rush over and throw her arms round Adrian. He was too honest, too decent for this to be happening to him.

Somehow she managed to keep her feet in place, clinging magnetically to the black tiles.

Kendric and Katerina turned as one. Walking away. Adrian stared at their departing backs, his hands had fallen limply to his side.

"Katey," he called after her.

She let out a playful squeal as Kendric pinched her rump, giggling. Never looking around.

"Katey!"

Julia closed damp eyes.

The music boomed again.

Julia waited for five days after the party before she sat in the chair at the head of the study table and called Kendric. The arrangements with Globecast had taken a while to finalize, but Uncle Horace had come through in the end, God bless him. And then there was her nerve to screw up.

When the phone's flatscreen activated, Kendric was sitting on the aft deck of his yacht, the marina forming a bright enticing backdrop, slightly out of focus. The sight of him stiffened her own resolution. He was wearing a lemon-yellow silk shirt, open at the neck, looking supremely relaxed, impenetrably black glasses covering his eyes, just the right amount of stubble shading his chin, emphasizing masculinity. It was a calculated pose, she thought, intended to demonstrate the ease with which he moved through life, his authority and influence. The epitome of an international wheeler-dealer.

It was working, too, the effect seeping out through the screen to abrade her own confidence. She gripped the armrests on her chair against the impulse to smooth down her hair. Wishing she'd taken some time to straighten out her own appearance. Her blouse was nothing special, a hundred-and-fifty-pound Malkham; she'd already worn it a couple of times before. She should've worn a Chanel suit.

"Hermione was only saying the other day we don't see enough of you, Julia," Kendric said. "It's such a pity. We're having a party here on the *Mirriam* tomorrow night, nothing formal. Why don't you come along? A lovely young girl like you ought to involve herself socially. Katerina tells me you don't have many friends. That makes me so sad."

Julia didn't trust herself to speak for a moment. That little cow Kats had told him that! How he and that dyke Hermione must've laughed. God, what else had she told them?

"I'm afraid I'm a very busy person nowadays, Mr. di Girolamo. I'm in industry, you see, not finance. It means I have to work for a living."

"Julia, please. What is all this Mr. di Girolamo? I am Kendric, your friend, your grandfather's friend."

"Bullshit. Grandpa tolerated you. I won't. Don't think I don't know what you're after."

"After, Julia?"

"Ranasfari's project. That's what it was all about, right?"

He smiled a wounded smile. "So much of your late grandfather you have inherited. You are a straight talker. I respect that, Julia. It is a rare commodity. Pleasing in this world of deceit. So in return I, too, will be a straight talker. You have to tolerate me, or at least my family house. It's in our contract. Unbreakable." The smile hardened. "A profitable arrangement all round."

"I've had my financial division draw up a buyout agreement; your house will be well compensated."

"And you expected our house to agree to this? Julia, you are more naive than I thought. Multibillion Eurofranc contracts are not torn up because of schoolgirl temper tantrums."

"You are the house's representative in the consortium. Your family will accept your judgment in this matter."

"And my judgment is no."

"You won't like the alternative."

"Threats, Julia? Has it come to this? And with what will you threaten me?"

"A scandal." She was disappointed by how hollow it sounded. A whole complex of doubts was rising. She'd banked so much on forcing Kendric to accept the buyout. Never even considered he would refuse. There was no way now she could mitigate failure.

Kendric chortled delightedly. "A scandal. In this world? In this day and age? Scandal is dependent on perspective, Julia. You smuggle three and a half million Eurofrancs' worth of gear into Scotland every night. Isn't that a scandal? Everyone knows I am a lovable rogue. Certainly your dear grandfather did. After all, Event Horizon bought all those templates from me."

"The memox-crystal spoiler."

"Ah yes, I heard your orbiting furnaces were producing a depressing amount of contaminated crystals. How unfortunate for you."

"The rest of the consortium would be very upset to hear that you planned to steal Event Horizon's assets, don't you think? It might be difficult for the di Girolamo house to find partners after that."

"Fantasy," he said. But there was no smile anymore.

She let go of the armrests and placed her hands on the table, pleased by how steady they were. "The onus is on proof, of course. Even if I could prove your involvement, the family would simply disown you, claim they weren't involved, which they possibly weren't. The house could survive your fall. What the house would not tolerate is for you to drag them down with you."

"An admirable summary," he mocked. "So where is this alleged proof?"

She played the terminal keys, squirting data over to the yacht's gear cubes. "First understand I am not bluffing. See this? It's Globecast's Pan-Europe channel schedule for next Tuesday; the *Investigator Chronicle* documentary is going to be given over to you, Kendric. I'm going to make you a star. All the data my security people turned up on your crystal-spoiler operation was passed on to the program's researchers. We even found them a reentry capsule to show; it was bobbing about amongst *Weslin*'s wreckage. You know about those capsules, Kendric; they're the sort Siebruk Orbital assembled up at Zanthus."

"No, Julia, I do not know."

"Wrong." She called up her ace from the terminal's memory core. "Take a good look, Kendric. That's a transfer order for eight million Eurofrancs to be paid into the account of the newly formed Siebruk Orbital company from your family house, eleven months ago. And, Kendric, it's your authority code on the order. You own Siebruk Orbital. And the di Girolamo house funded it." She requested the terminal to show the second transfer order. "Then five months later you went and repaid the money, without any interest. Money you recovered from selling the memox crystals. My money, Kendric. Did they know? Did you tell them you were borrowing family money to finance your own schemes?"

He was hunched over his terminal cube, studying the two transfer orders without a trace of humor left. "Where did you get these?" he demanded. A crow's-feet wrinkle indented the skin on either side of his mouth as his lips compressed.

"The Credit Corato bank, of course."

"Impossible. They are forgeries."

Julia felt the tension drain out of her. She leaned back into the chair and grinned wickedly at the screen. "No forging involved. Accessing the bank's records is the president's prerogative. So is waiving client confidentiality, though I don't intend to make it a habit."

"President?" Shock raised his voice an octave.

"I bought it. Well, fifty-three percent, anyway. Quite a good investment actually, according to my accountants. I'm the di Girolamo finance house's new partner. How does that grab you?"

"Bitch," he breathed.

"Careful, Kendric. I might just lower my offer. Schoolgirl temperament, you see."

"You bought the bank?" He sounded incredulous.

"Yeah."

"You bought the bank just to make me authorize the buyout?"

"Yeah."

He looked from the cube to the phone screen and back again, bewildered. "How much did all this cost you?"

"Plenty, but it was worth it."

"I don't believe this. Do you hate me that much?"

"What do you think, Kendric?" she asked, her voice dangerously shaky.

"I think you are impulsive, dear Julia. If you go on frittering Event Horizon away like this there will be nothing left in a few years. What would your grandfather think of that?"

Behavioral Response: Sorrow.

But she didn't need the reminder, not anymore. "He shared my opinion of you," she murmured.

"Indeed? And if I don't authorize your buyout offer?"

She shrugged. "The *Chronicle* people get a copy of the transfer orders. They'll go ahead and broadcast then. Without them, the program would be one big libel case."

Kendric squared his shoulders, clearing his throat, salvaging what dignity he could. "Very well, Julia. If that's the way you want it."

His capitulation left her feeling omnipotent. As soon as his image vanished she called Adrian. It was a formality. She knew she was on a winning streak.

Get a grip on yourself, girl, she told herself sternly; you must look barmy with this grin plastered across your face. People would cross the street to avoid you. But the grin remained.

Then Adrian appeared on the screen, and all the wonder blew away in a blast of trepidation, chilling her heart. He'd lost his verve, the chirpy smile and devilish glint were gone. Brokenhearted. Just how hung up on Kats had he been?

"Hello, Julia, nice to see you." The words said it, but not the voice; that was funereal. Had she called too soon?

"Sorry to bother you, Adrian. I can call back if it's not convenient."

"No, please, I'm deep into cell composition right now. God, it's dull."

"Oh, well, that's something. At least I'm more interesting than an amoeba."

He looked blank for a second, then smiled sheepishly. "That did come out wrong, didn't it?"

"Not to worry. Look, I wouldn't have called, but I need this truly enormous favor, and I don't know who else to turn to."

"What?" There was a flicker of interest.

"Well, there's this publishing company which is throwing a big book-launch party next weekend. And I've got to go; it's a social obligation. Event Horizon won the contract to supply them with memoxes, you see. Only the embarrassing thing is, I haven't got anyone to go with. The business keeps me so busy right now, I don't get to meet people my age."

He scratched the back of his neck, staring at the floor, looking very unhappy. "I dunno, Julia—"

"I've got to find someone, Adrian. People will think I'm funny if I just keep turning up to these events by myself all the time. It'll only be for the weekend. I could have the car pick you up. You wouldn't miss any lectures."

"Oh, I see." A grin plucked at his mouth. "Well, we can't have people thinking that, now can we? I'd be honored."

They sorted out details, and she signed off glowing. Yes. He'd said yes! *Honored.*

G REG HAD SETTLED COMFORTABLY INTO his morning regimen when the phone shrilled. He was straddling the wooden bench in the lounge, back flat against the chalet wall, lifting the bar smoothly, letting it fall, push again. The exercise was mindless, easing him into a near dream state. Push. Relax. Nothing to it. He'd rigged the pulley up to a pump that filled the chalet's rafter tank. Twenty minutes each morning was enough to top it up. It supplied the toilet and shower in the bathroom. The Jacuzzi didn't work anymore; there weren't enough solar cells on the roof to heat that much water. He didn't mind. Showers with Eleanor were more than enough compensation.

She'd blossomed beautifully over the last six weeks, independence giving her a seasoned self-assurance. There was very little left of the timid, uncertain girl he'd seduced that night in the Wheatsheaf. Easy youthful enthusiasms had given way to measured assessments. Eleanor voiced her own opinions now instead of quiescently accepting other people's, and she no longer watched over her shoulder, fearful of past shadows. If her father ever showed up again, he would be in for the shock of his life. Greg almost wished he would come.

The real foundation of their relationship was the level of trust, which was total. That was unique to Greg. He'd never escaped the habit of letting his espersense sniff out the faults and insecurities of anyone in his presence. It was a behavioral reflex, one of the psychologists assigned to the Mindstar Brigade had told him, establishing your superiority over everyone to your own satisfaction. Don't worry about it; we'd all do it if we could.

With Eleanor it wasn't necessary. He knew her too well.

The phone jarred his mind away from introspection. He ignored it. Push. Relax. Perhaps the caller would give up. Push, slop of water overhead. Relax. His belly was like steel now, flat and hard; legs solid, arms powerful. He'd never been fitter, not even as a squaddie. It made him feel good, confident, capable of tackling anything.

The phone kept on shrilling. There was a dump facility in the terminal for messages, but the caller wasn't using it. Push. Relax. Someone must want him urgently.

He let the bar fall and walked over to the new Event Horizon terminal. The chalet was all kitted out with Event Horizon gear now. And he'd left a whole lot more in the delivery van. There simply hadn't been room for all the stuff that Julia had sent. Eleanor had had a ball picking out what they could use.

The fee money had been good as well. He'd paid off the outstanding installments on the Duo, then went to town refurbishing the chalet—new carpets, curtains, restoring the furniture; stripped the roof down and replaced the tiles; tacked on a second solar panel to power the new air conditioner. There hadn't quite been enough cash to replace the shaky walls, but the money ordinary cases brought in should see to that before the end of the year. He'd already worked on a couple since the memox skim, both corporate, sniffing out dodgy personnel.

The phonescreen swirled and Philip Evans's face appeared. "Hello, Greg. I need your help again, boy. Someone is trying to kill me."

Greg suppressed a smile. Ten years in the business, and nobody had ever phoned in a cliché before. "Bodyguard services aren't really my field, sir, wouldn't your own security . . ." He trailed off and stared at the screen, stared and stared. Small muscles at the back of his knees began to twitch, threatening to topple him.

When he looked back on it, he blamed his exercise-induced lethargy for putting his mind on a ten-second delay to reality, that and intuition. It wasn't just the voice and image that convinced him; any animation synthesizer could mimic Philip to perfection. But this *was* Philip Evans, grinning away at the other end of the connection. Both the natural and neurohormone-boosted faculties squatting in his brain forced him to accept it at a fundamental level.

The black-clad funeral procession wending its way through Peterborough's rain-slicked streets occluded his vision.

"You're dead," he told the image.

"Gone but not forgotten."

That malicious chuckle. Perfect. *Him.*

"Sorry to give you a shock, m'boy, but I'd never have called unless it was absolutely vital. Can you come out to Wilholm? I really can't discuss too much over the phone. I'm sure you appreciate that."

The tone mocked.

Greg's skittish nerves began to flutter down toward some kind of equilibrium. Shock numbness, probably. "I . . . I think I can manage that. When?"

"Soon as possible, Greg, please."

The image wasn't perfect, he realized. This was a Philip Evans he hadn't seen before, flesh firmer, skin-color salubrious. Stronger. Younger by about a decade.

"Okay. Are you in any danger right now?" At some aloof level, he marveled at his own reaction. Treating it as just another prosaic problem. Spoke volumes for Army training.

"Not from anything physical. The manor is well protected."

Physical. So what was a ghost afraid of anyway, being exorcized? Should he stop off to buy a clove of garlic, a crucifix, a *grimoire*? "I'm on my way."

He pulled on his one decent suit, barking a shin on that idiotically oversize bed in the scramble to shove his feet into a pair of black leather shoes. Thought about taking the Walther and decided against.

The Duo bounced along the estate's gravel track and lurched onto the road. He set off toward Wilhelm Manor coaxing a full fifty-five kilometers per hour from the engine, rocking slowly in the seat. The Duo had thick balloon-type tires, made out of a hard-wearing silicon rubber. They were designed to cope with the country's shambolic road surfaces without being torn to ribbons. A typical PSP fix, he thought, adapting the cars to cope with their failure to maintain the roads.

There was a white watchman pillar standing outside Wilhelm's odd cattle grid. He wound the side window down and showed his card to it.

"Your visit has been authorized, Mr. Mandel," a construct voice said. "Please do not deviate from the road. Thank you."

The manor's spread of ornate flora was in full bloom, a spectacular moiré patchwork of sharp primary colors. Big jets of water were spurting across the parched lawns. He could see the two gardeners working away among the rose beds. They leaned on their hoes to watch him walk up to the front doors. However did that idle pair manage to keep the grounds in such a trim condition?

The butler opened the door. Morgan Walshaw stood behind him, his face drawn. A quick check of his mind showed Greg he was laboring under a prodigious quantity of anxiety.

"Mandel." Morgan Walshaw greeted him with a curt nod. "This way." A stiff finger beckoned. Greg followed him up the big curving staircase. The butler shut the doors silently behind them as they ascended.

"What the fuck is going on?" he asked the security chief in a low tone. "Did he fake his death or what?"

Walshaw's face twisted into a grimace. "Explanations in a moment. Just ride it out, okay?"

They arrived at the study and Walshaw opened the door, giving Greg a semi-apologetic shrug as they went in.

The interior was almost the same as it had been on his last visit. Big table running down the middle, stone fireplace, dark paneling, warm sunlight streaming through small lead-lined panes of glass, dust motes sparkling in the beams.

In the middle of the table was a circular black column: seamless, a meter tall, seventy-five centimeters wide. It rested on a narrow plinth that radiated bundles of fiber-optic cables like wheel spokes. They fell over the edge of the table and snaked en masse across the Persian carpet to a compact bank of communication consoles standing by the wall.

Julia was seated at the head of the table where her grandfather used to sit, wearing a rusty-orange-colored cotton summer dress, with a slim red leather band around her brow holding back her long hair. One of the two gear cubes in front of her was showing tiny editions of himself and Walshaw walking up the stairs together; the other had his Duo driving up to the manor.

Her mind was beautifully composed. Greg recognized the state; the kind of tranquility that follows a severe emotional jolt.

His skin crawled with rigor, an animal caution awakened. There was something deeply unsettling about walking into the study.

Her tawny eyes never left him.

He looked at the column, ghoulish images creeping into his mind. Frankenstein, zombies, the undead, brains in glass tanks . . .

"Thank you for coming," said Philip Evans's voice, all around, directionless.

Greg's eyes remained fixed on the column. "Stop fucking about. Where are you?"

"Good question. Unfortunately philosophy was never my strong point. I've thrown off my mortal coil sure enough, but my mind has been saved. You're looking right at me, boy. It's a neural-network bioware core. A real special one, custom grown, you might say. The lab team spliced my sequencing RNA into the ferredoxin nodes, replicating my neuronic structure. Then when I was dying they used a neurocoupling to translocate my memories. Not a copy, not some clever Turing personality-responses program, but my actual thought processes. Axon stimulators literally squeezed me out of my skull and into the NN core. Continuity was unbroken, my faculties are intact—enhanced if anything. Memory retrieval is instantaneous, there's none of that scratching around forgetting people's names and faces. I have access to all Event Horizon's data, too. Locating that memox-crystal skim took me four days when I was flesh and blood. It wouldn't take me ten seconds now. And there's no pain, Greg. I'm free of it. Not just death and illness but all those aches which mount up over the years, the ones you learn to ignore, only you never can, of course. They've gone."

Greg pulled out one of the solid wooden chairs and sat heavily. "Jesus Christ." The column must be solid bioware. He tried to work out how much that would cost. Fifteen, twenty million? Bioware was horrifically expensive. Immortality for billionaires. He wasn't sure whether he was fascinated or utterly disgusted. The concept didn't sink in readily.

"I can create the image of myself in a cube again, if that would be easier for you to talk to, boy."

Greg shuddered. "No, thank you."

Morgan Walshaw sat next to him, resting his hands on the table, face blank.

"Why am I here?" Greg asked stoically.

"Because we have a problem," said Julia. "Someone is trying to wreck Event Horizon's future."

He received the distinct impression she was enjoying his discomfiture.

"You see, Greg," she said, "Dr. Ranasfari has succeeded in developing a viable room-temperature gigaconductor for us."

Greg looked at her sharply. "You're kidding!"

He remembered some Royal Engineering Corps officers he'd been stationed with once had talked about the stuff. A panacea, they'd called it. The answer to the energy shortage, to carbon dioxide pollution. Every university and *kombinate* in the world had its own research team working on gigaconductors before the Credit Crash. Then there were innumerable megabudget military programs; a gigaconductor would have produced a whole new generation of weapons.

"Told you he was a genius, boy. Edison of the age. Dedicated, too; it took him over a decade of solid grind to crack."

"Quiet, please, Grandpa. It's a tremendous breakthrough, Greg; its energy storage density is phenomenal. It will replace every other form of power-storage system in existence: gear, cars, ships, planes, airships, spaceplanes; they'll all use it. And it's cheap, clean, and relatively easy to produce. Our whole way of life will be altered. It's a revolution equal to the introduction of the steam engine."

"And Event Horizon holds the patent," Philip chuckled savagely. "We're going to wipe the floor with the opposition. A Custer and the Indians massacre. I'll make damn sure of that when I introduce the stuff on the market."

Greg took another look at the mass of fiber-optic cables leading out of the plinth, trying to work out the NN core's bit rate. "You're still running Event Horizon," he said. All Philip Evans's talk about arranging for trustees he had confidence in, and the flash of cunning at the time, came flooding back to him.

"Damn right I am, boy. There are no trustees, never were; the nominees are all Zurich fronts. Event Horizon is my life. No individual in the world can run a company better than me. I'm talking fifty years' worth of accumulated experience. There's no substitute for that. It's the efficiency of dictatorship. A group of trustees would be worse than useless, lawyers and airhead accountants; they'd never push the gigaconductor with the kind of vigor necessary to effect a complete domination of the market. Discussion groups, reports, delays for consultation. What a load of crap. Event Horizon run by a committee would shrivel up and die an ignominious death. This is the perfect solution.

"Before now, when a family company grew too big for one person to pay attention to every detail it used to stall. It was inevitable. Responsibilities had to be delegated, the initial individual-led drive was diluted. But the NN core solves even that. I can devote myself one hundred percent to each problem, no matter the size, coordinate every policy, supervise every division. No *kombinate* will be able to match a company run along these lines."

"You were doing pretty well before," Julia said acidly. "One ordinary person, and an ill one at that. With the right people in key posts Event Horizon will prosper. All that's needed is direction, a firmness of purpose, the big decisions made quickly and implemented without delay."

"And you can do that, Juliet, can you?"

"Yeah."

"Rubbish. You don't have anything like the experience."

She was angry now, straight-backed rigid, gripping the arms of her seat. "I do."

"Node implants don't give you experience, girl, just theory. All that money you spent getting rid of Kendric—pure bloody folly."

Greg flicked a glance at Julia, intrigued. Her cheeks were burning red, embarrassed rather than angered. Implanted nodes had been banned in England by the PSP for the usual heinous crime of elitism.

The New Conservatives had yet to repeal the act. But at least he could finally explain away her remarkably smooth thought currents and that marvelous ability to fish obscure data out of memory cores.

"It's like chess," Philip Evans explained gently. "You know how each piece should move, but you don't know the rules, the strategy. You'll learn, Juliet, really you will. It just takes time. And I'm here to bridge the gap for you."

"But the NN core is untried," she said, fighting to keep her voice level. "How do we know all your memories translocated? Suppose these miraculous thought processes of yours are incorrect? And you're basing judgments about the company's entire future on them."

Finally Greg understood her terror. She was afraid of losing everything; that wonderful edifice that was Event Horizon collapsing to rubble because it was balanced on a single assumption. And she had no way of checking the NN core's integrity. No control.

"If I could bring us back to our current problem," said Morgan Walshaw. "Unless something is done to solve it, we may lose the core anyway."

"You told me someone tried to kill you," Greg said.

"Damn right, boy. Yesterday evening the NN core's inputs were blitzed, saturated with override-priority data squirts. Every channel simultaneously, ground links and satellite circuits. It was clever; the attacker was attempting to force me out of the NN core with the sheer quantity of input. With all the data being given a priority code, the core-function management program would have to assign it storage space, eventually displacing my memories. I would've been erased, for God's sake! That's attempted murder in my book."

"So what went wrong?"

"I'm not a rational, neatly mathematical program. I fought back, began wiping their data as it came in, changed the priority codes, shut down the Event Horizon datanet—and you wouldn't believe how much that's going to cost us. They bloody nearly succeeded, though. If I'd been a Turing personality-responses program it would've been all over."

Greg was fast getting out of his depth. He remembered questioning a legion cleric his squad had captured in Turkey, a fanatical fundamentalist so devout he didn't even acknowledge the infidel's existence: his associative-word trick had been useless. The sense of displacement was familiar. He tried to sort out some sort of priority list in his mind.

"Have you safeguarded yourself from that attack method being employed again?"

"Yes. It's a question of code encryption. I've altered my acceptance filters so that only half of my input circuits will accept priority squirts. Of course, there's nothing to stop them from thinking up new methods."

"So the problem is now centered around tracking down the source of the attack, right?"

"And eliminating it," said Walshaw.

Greg opened his eyes. "Your department."

Walshaw gave him a brief nod.

"So where did the data squirt originate from?" Greg asked.

Walshaw ran his hand through what was left of his hair. "We've no leads on that, I'm afraid. There were at least eight separate hot rods who hacked into the Event Horizon datanet, probably more, but with the shutdown we lost a lot of data. The blitz was well organized. All eight violators used multiple cutouts to prevent us from tracing them."

"I'm surprised they got in so easily."

"Entry is no problem," said Philip Evans. "It's when you try to get our main account to transfer a million Eurofrancs to your Zurich bank or peek into research-team memory files that you run into trouble. Nobody has ever had a requirement to fend off this type of infiltration before. Its own crudity was what made it so successful."

"Crude?"

"Well, relatively."

"I'm trying to eliminate possibilities," Greg said. "It wasn't a blanket attack, was it? What I mean is, it was purposefully directed at you. They knew you were here?"

"Yes. I would say it's got to be one of those bastard *kombinates*. They've discovered Ranasfari cracked the gigaconductor, and they're badly worried. Anyone with a gram of sense can see the upheaval it's going to cause. Trouble is, they can't destroy it; there's no turning the clock back. Instead they've settled for the next best thing, which is yours truly. Without me Event Horizon won't be nearly as successful in marketing the stuff. They'd only have Julia and the nonexistent trustees to deal with."

"So that rules out joyburners," Greg said. "They don't work in packs, anyway. How well guarded is the knowledge of your continued existence?"

"Only twelve people in the world knew," said Morgan Walshaw.

"Thirteen counting yourself. That's myself, Julia, Ranasfari, and the team which grew the NN core."

"Just nine of them?" Greg asked incredulously.

"There's nothing complicated about the process," said Philip. "We've had neurocoupling for eight years now, and the RNA splice is a standard procedure. It's only the cost of this much bioware which prevents it from becoming widespread."

"Okay, next question. Would the hot-rod team which launched the blitz have to be told you were here, or could they find out by analyzing the data flow through Event Horizon's network?"

"They'd know the NN core was an important part of the network from observing the data flow, but that's all. Unless they were specifically told what the NN core was, the best they could guess is that it was an ordinary bioware number cruncher loaded with a Turing personality-responses program."

"In other words, they know about you."

"Looks that way, boy."

"With only twelve people knowing about the core, I can pin down that mole for you, no messing," Greg said. "So where is the other leak liable to have come from?"

"Ministry of Defense, I hope," said Walshaw.

"Most likely," Philip Evans admitted. "Morgan here kept a tight security cordon around the gigaconductor project, but we had to cooperate with the MOD. It was on a confidential basis, of course, but leaks are inevitable on a project this big. You just have to balance the risk against the payoff."

"Two separate leaks," Morgan said. "It's an appalling lapse. One I could accept, but compromising the NN core and the gigaconductor as well, that hurts."

Greg paused, worried about what Walshaw had said, his intuition producing that annoying tingle again. Two separate, simultaneous, high-level leaks was stretching coincidence a long way. "Did you ever find out how Kendric's tekmerc team acquired their data on Zanthus's security monitor parameters in the first place? They must have had copies to work out that destreaming maneuver."

Walshaw frowned, glancing at the black column. "We are still tracking down the actual tekmercs. They've taken a lot of trouble to cover their tracks."

"So nobody I found passed the data over?"

"No."

"Could it have been a hot-rod burn which pulled the data?"

Julia cleared her throat, giving Walshaw an inquiring look. The security chief nodded reluctantly.

"To get at the monitor programs you would have to either burn straight into the security division's data core or copy the programs direct from Zanthus's 'ware," she said. "Zanthus would probably be the easiest option, but you would need to be up there to do it."

"If it was a hot-rod burn," Greg mused.

"Bloody hell, boy; you're not telling me we've still got a Judas in the company?"

"There is no such thing as coincidence," Greg said soberly. "Two leaks on the two greatest ultrahush projects Event Horizon is running, plus a loose end over the security monitor programs. Make up your own mind."

"I said that it had to be someone familiar with our security data procedures," Julia said.

"So you did, Juliet, so you did."

Walshaw shook his head in dismay, lips drawn taut. "This means we're going to have to open the field of inquiry to include the whole security division headquarters staff, two hundred and eighty personnel." He cocked an eyebrow at Greg. "Exactly how many interviews can you handle?"

"Tell you, not that many, not in the time frame we'd need. Remember, if this mole exists, he'll know we're gunning for him now; he'll be watching for us. At the first sign of any security operation geared to pinpointing him he'll vanish—if he hasn't already. My advice is work from the other end, that way we can keep the operation at a manageable level, track down the blitz hot rods and the people who paid them, and then we'll find out if there is a mole in your senior staff."

"You just said there was!" Philip sounded irritated.

"Covering my options."

"Bloody hell."

"If it is just one person, then it's going to be a very senior staff member," Walshaw said. "The security around the NN core was rock solid, damn it."

"A staff member or an executive assistant," Greg said. "Someone who had access to financial records and saw how much money was being spent on an ultrahush bioware project."

Walshaw took a stiff breath. "Possible," he said.

Greg's espersense registered exactly how much the admission cost him. "Okay, back to the hot rods," he said. "Is the Ministry of Defense the only outside institution you've informed about the giga-conductor?"

"Yeah," said Julia. "Bringing them in was an integral part of Grandpa's campaign."

"Oldest dodge in the book," Philip said. "Offer the military a worthwhile new technology, and they fund its development from shaky prototype right the way through to fully functional operational status; then you tack civil applications on the back at minimum cost. The production-facility pump has already been primed by good old taxpayers' cash."

"They leapt at it," Julia confirmed. "This country's entire armed services have got to be rebuilt from the ground up after the PSP virtually dismantled them. And what's more, until we offered the New Conservatives the gigaconductor option, most of the hardware would have to be imported. Our defense industry was a major casualty under Armstrong's rule. As a result, for the last couple of years Whitehall's been swarming with lobbyists representing foreign arms teams. It looked like the cabinet was going to have to buy American fighters and German tactical zone air defense equipment, along with half a dozen other modern systems that the military can't do without. Authorizing that kind of expenditure would be a political nightmare. Oh, the suppliers would give us poor local companies licensed production and favorable offset deals, but we'd still be lagging way behind in the actual technology. Now, though, we've got a chance to clear the pitch and start fresh, compete with our rivals on level terms. Every kind of hardware, from fighters to laser pistols, is going to have to be redesigned because a gigaconductor-powered version is always going to be more powerful than its conventional equivalent. You double the range of beam weapons. Gigaconductor fighters will operate quite easily above Mach seven. And what's the point in even having a navy any more when hypersonic transports have a global range?

"The gigaconductor can provide the New Conservatives with a viable military force equipped with a new generation of sophisticated high-energy, global-range weapons, all of which are produced indigenously. Or at the very least in collaboration with overseas partners. They'll get their modern army without having to compromise their nationalist ideals. And on top of that we'll be in an excellent position to win export orders."

"The whole world is going to be hammering on our door," Philip Evans said gleefully. "The fees from license production will rake in a couple of billion Eurofrancs each year alone, minimum; then there's our own profits. Think of how Event Horizon will grow with that kind of annual investment in its infrastructure."

"The Ministry of Defense will conduct their own inquiry, of course," said Morgan Walshaw. "See if any of their personnel were the source of the leak. And if they were, who the data was channeled to. We've told them that the blitz was aimed at the lightware crunchers we use in the gigaconductor project. There's no need for them to know about the NN core."

"Bloody right, boy. Something like this would bring the fruitcakes pouring out of the woodwork. Everyone and his grandmother would want to be loaded into an NN core."

"Somebody outside Event Horizon already knows, though, Grandpa."

"Don't remind me, girl. At least they've not made it public, for whatever reason. Probably afraid of losing whatever advantage they've got over the other *kombinates*. That'll be something for you to watch for, Juliet, if they do get me. Whichever bastard is the first to put the pressure on you for a low licensing fee, they're the ones."

"Don't talk like that," she said, quietly insistent. "Nobody's going to get you."

"Are your security programmers trying to backtrack the hot rods behind the blitz?" Greg asked Walshaw.

"Yes, although I don't hold out much hope of success. The hacker community is a hard one to crack; our best chance is if a rumor escapes. Someone bragging, stoned, or drunk."

"I'll see what I can do. I have a contact in that area."

"Who?" asked Philip.

"Tell you, you pay me for results, and that's what you'll get. But your money doesn't entitle you to know my sources. Without confidentiality I'd never be able to hang on to them."

"Oh, pardon me." Philip shoveled on the sarcasm, thick and dripping.

"Sounds like a reporter," Julia muttered tartly.

"I'm reassembling the team which built the NN core for you to interview," Walshaw told Greg. "We disbanded them after Mr. Evans was successfully translocated. Shouldn't take more than a day or two. They're all still employed by us."

"Right then, in the meantime I'll get started on Ranasfari's research team," Greg said briskly. "Oh, by the way, Julia?"

She looked up, half smiling, expectant.

"Who've you told that your grandpa's still intact?"

"No one!" It emerged as an indignant squawk. Her mind flamed like a solar flare from high-energy outrage. No guilt, no subterfuge.

"How dare you!"

"Sorry, just checking that . . ."

"He's my grandpa!"

"Juliet, shush. Greg's doing exactly what I asked him here for."

She shut up but spiked Greg with an evil glare.

He swiveled around to look inquiringly at Walshaw.

"I have never told anybody that Philip Evans's memories are intact, nor that Event Horizon has perfected a gigaconductor," the security chief said formally. True.

"Aren't you going to ask me, boy?"

Julia was suddenly very alert, giving Greg an intent stare, her mind colored by a strange mix of curiosity and trepidation.

The hairs along the back of Greg's neck pricked up. He concentrated. Right at the edge of perception was a faint nebulous glow. Details were nonexistent. Half-life? Half-death? Not a mind as he knew minds. And yet, and yet . . .

"No," he said eventually.

"Ah well, worth a try." The disembodied voice was utterly devoid of emotional content.

The study window showed green grass and blue sky. Reality. Greg focused on that. A flock of dark birds flew by. Infinitely reassuring in their normality. "We've got four lines of investigation," he summarized. "The hot-rod pack which launched the blitz, the team which built the NN core, Ranasfari's gigaconductor research team, and a possible executive-level mole: that's a lot of ground for me to cover. I'm going to need money, not to mention help. There's a colleague I'd like to bring in, spread the load a little."

Walshaw produced a card from his pocket, embossed with the company's triangle and flying V emblem. "This will give you unlimited access to any Event Horizon facility. It also provides you a credit line direct to the company's central account. Please try not to spend more than half a million."

The little oblong of active plastic sat in Greg's palm, innocuous. Half a million. Eurofrancs or New Sterling? He didn't ask. These people were *serious*.

"Who's your colleague?" Julia asked, her face lifted with interest.

"Another psychic, a Mindstar veteran like myself."

"What's his speciality?"

"Her. Her speciality. She can see into the future."

She didn't call him a liar to his face, but his espersense told him it was a close-run thing.

15

JULIA CLOSED THE STUDY DOOR behind her, looking around in sudden desperation. She couldn't let Greg go without at least trying to explain. Damn Grandpa for blabbing like that. When he was alive in the flesh he would never have said anything to hurt her.

He was walking down the stairs, head just visible bobbing above the railing.

"Greg! Wait."

He turned around, paused. She ran along the landing, ankle-length skirt flapping around her legs.

Standing in front of him, her resolution wavered. What did he actually think of her? There'd never been any thank-you card for the van of gear she'd sent to his home. But would someone like Greg even think about thank-you cards? Damn that bloody Swiss snob school. It'd distorted her perspective on real life. As if anyone else ever bothered about *Debrett's Etiquette* in this day and age, let alone treated it as a bible.

He was watching her with quizzical respect. But was it *bought* respect? Oh hell. She searched his face for a hint of sympathy, any sign of that brilliant moment when they seemed to think as one. "They didn't alter me, you know." There, she'd gone and said it, betrayed her insecurities. Would he laugh?

"What didn't?" Greg asked.

She blinked; that wasn't the response she'd been expecting.

"The bioware nodes. People think they turn you into some kind of mental freak. But it's just like having an encyclopedia on permanent call, that's all. I'm a total whiz at general-knowledge questions." She flashed a bright entreating smile.

"Of all the people in the world, I'm the least likely to be prejudiced against you."

"Oh . . . yeah." She knew her cheeks would be reddening. God, how stupid. She was making a complete fool of herself. Why couldn't conversation flow from her lips? Kats never had the slightest trouble talking to men; no matter what she said they'd smile and agree. "What's it like? I wanted a gland. But Grandpa said no."

"I'm glad he did," Greg said gently. "The price is far too high. Take my case. I have to steel myself against people, build a high wall to shut them out. Every mind is awash with fears and intolerance and fright, all the human failings. We school ourselves to hide them from showing in our voices and expressions, but to me it's an open book. I'd drown in it if I let my guard down. And there's the pain, too, actual physical pain from the neurohormones. It can cripple me if I don't keep a firm control over the secretion levels."

Commit GregTime#Three. Nobody else was ever this honest with her about themselves. It must mean he felt something, even if it was only a variant of parental concern. "Why don't you have it taken out if it's that bad?"

"I'm a psi-junkie, Julia. I couldn't give up the gland any more than you could give up eyes. Once it's in, you're hooked. But if I was living my life again I'd run a million miles rather than have a gland."

She nodded with earnest sympathy. "I didn't realize. I thought one might help me run Event Horizon, show me who was disloyal. I took the assessment tests and came out ESP positive. Grandpa was furious."

"You'd be spreading yourself too thin. Run with what you've got, Julia. Event Horizon is going to demand every scrap of your attention. You can always hire specialists like me to combat specific problems."

"But how do I know who to trust?" she whispered insistently.

His fingers found her chin, tilting her head up. "That's everybody's problem, Julia, not just yours. It's an unending question. People change; someone who you could entrust with the crown jewels one day will sell out for a pound the next. You want my advice? Put your faith in Morgan Walshaw. Strange as it may sound, people like that need someone to work for. So long as you don't evolve into some kind of irresponsible playgirl he'll remain loyal."

She pulled a face. "Morgan? God!"

"Just remember, loyalty doesn't mean slavish obedience. If he disagrees with you on some issue, he won't be doing it simply to spite you. Ask him to explain his reasons, and *listen* to the answer."

"You're worse than Grandpa," she moaned.

"Life's a bitch, then you die. No messing." He grinned and started down the stairs again.

She walked in silence with him until they reached the hall. The air was cooler in the big vaulting chamber, its black-and-white marble tiles drawing away April's dry heat.

"Greg . . . there's something else."

"Hey, what am I, your confessor?"

"No, this is about the blitz." She knew he'd changed, hardening somehow. It was like she'd spoken a code word, switching his mind from levity to total attention.

She started to tell him about Kendric, the buyout, her threat, speaking rationally, without rancor. And doing it that way made her mortified by how petty she sounded. What was it Kendric had said? Schoolgirl temper tantrum.

"I couldn't let him go unpunished," she said. "He set out to destroy everything Grandpa spent fifty years of his life building, not to mention my future."

Greg looked troubled, staring at one of the Turner landscapes without seeing it.

"Do you think I was right?" she asked nervously.

"Yeah, probably. I'd have done the same, I think."

"So the blitz might have been Kendric's vendetta against Grandpa and me? Nothing to do with the gigaconductor."

"Could be. But I think it's reasonable to assume Kendric is involved up to his neck; he's certainly my first choice. This possible mole implicates him directly."

"You keep calling him 'possible'."

"Yeah. It's almost too easy to write everything off onto one master spy. But the evidence is pretty strong. Who knows? And now that I think about it, this whole gigaconductor thing adds a new dimension to the memox-spoiler operation. Kendric was more than likely after the patent the whole while; that was the asset he really wanted to strip."

"That's what I thought. But I couldn't tell you at the time. Sorry."

"No problem. I didn't need to know. Tell me, exactly when did Dr. Ranasfari crack the gigaconductor?"

"Tenth of November." She didn't have to query the nodes; the date was ingrained. The last time she'd seen Grandpa really happy.

He sat slowly on an old monk's bench, thinking hard. She hovered, agitated. Wanting to know what he was mulling over, unwilling to interrupt. The hall's silence amplified every sound as she fidgeted.

"Halfway through the memox spoiler," Greg mused. "So it had already been working for a few months. The thing is, if the mole, or whoever, had already breached the security cordon around Ranasfari, then it's odds on that it was Kendric, or Kendric got word of it. Pirate data traffic is his speciality, after all. Tell me, would he have known in advance that Ranasfari was going to crack the gigaconductor? What I mean is, was the breakthrough sudden?"

"Not really. Ranasfari has been working on the project for a decade. He was confident of a positive result for almost a year beforehand. Then he produced a cryogenic gigaconductor last May. A room-temperature version was only a matter of time after that; a lightware cruncher problem, solving the chemical makeup, rather than any revelation in fundamental physics."

"Yeah, I figured something along those lines. You see, ten years is a hell of a long time to keep something hushed up. If the mole informed Kendric about the cryogenic prototype, then he would have had time to organize the memox crystal spoiler. The dates certainly fit."

"But you don't think so?"

"Not sure."

"Why?"

"If Kendric knew about the gigaconductor, why did he authorize your buyout of the di Girolamo house?"

"I told you: I blackmailed him."

"A couple of billion Eurofrancs each year, that's what your grandfather said the gigaconductor royalty license would bring in, is that right?"

"Yeah, in fact it's a conservative estimate."

"So answer me this: with an eight percent stake in Event Horizon, which you could never legally make him give up, why should Kendric worry about his family house being dragged through the mud? In fact, you would've looked pretty bloody silly if he hadn't knuckled under; exposing one of your own financial backers as a shark, then still having to cut them in on a share of your gigaconductor profits."

The nodes turned the problem into neat packages of equations for her. Greg and the hall slipped away as she pushed them through a logic matrix. They began to develop a life of their own, the channels unable to confine them, twisting out of alignment. The instability began to absorb more and more of the nodes' processing power. She scrambled to maintain cohesion, loosening the parameters, adding additional channels. But her mind originated nothing ingenious enough to halt the imminent collapse. She observed helplessly as the channels wound in on themselves, constricting in ever-tighter curves, sealing the data packages in closed loops.

The bioware-generated edifice crumpled beyond salvation. Her imagination invested the scene with sound. From a vast distance she could hear a cathedral of glass slowly toppling over.

"Kendric couldn't have known about the gigaconductor," she said finally.

"You reckon?"

"Yeah. No. Not really. It's a paradox, you see; he must've known, yet he couldn't have."

"That's the way I see it." He seemed ridiculously cheerful. "Know what we're going to do about it, Julia?"

"What?"

"Put Kendric at the top of the suspect list, then forget about him. Concentrate on tracking down the source of the leaks. When I've done that I'll see where they lead. Then we might begin to understand the game he's playing."

She wasn't certain anymore. Problems should be logical, solutions readily available. The pride she'd possessed in her own ability was dented: the nodes had always been a bulwark in her defense against other people, elevating her soul. No matter appearances and social awkwardness, she knew she was superior. Now this. Unable to provide her with an answer for the first time. And it was an answer that was utterly critical.

But Greg didn't seem unduly bothered, which gave her a certain degree of confidence. The guilt that this might have been all her fault was dissipating. What more had she been expecting from him?

He rose from the black-polished bench. "Couple of days, week at the most, and it'll all be over, no messing. You can look back and laugh."

"Thank you, Greg."

"You haven't seen the bill yet. Walk me to the car? I might get lost otherwise; normally when I'm in buildings this size there are hordes of other people queuing to catch their trains."

She laughed. A joke. He was joking with her. Then her father came into the hall, and the sudden bud of joy was crushed as though it'd never been.

Dillan Evans was wearing jeans and a baggy brown sweater that was fraying at the end of the sleeves. He was walking with a drunkard's hesitancy, taking care that his feet trod only on the black tiles.

"Hello, Daddy," Julia said quietly.

He nodded absently at her and looked Greg up and down with bleary eyes.

Julia felt like weeping. It was bad enough witnessing her father's state in private; having it exposed like this only exacerbated the pain.

She watched in dismay as he straightened up ponderously. "Bit old for her, aren't you?" he said to Greg.

"Daddy, don't, please." Her voice had become high, strained. She caught Greg's eye, a tiny motion of her head telling him to say nothing. Please. He inclined his head discreetly, thank God.

Dillan grunted roughly. "Out of the way, don't embarrass us, keep out of sight, keep your mouth shut, never know what might come out. Want me to shut up, Julie? Is that it? Want your father to keep his dirty mouth closed. Afraid of what the old fool will say? I'm only looking after your welfare. I've got a right to meet my little girl's men friends."

"Greg is not a boyfriend, Daddy. He's someone who works for us."

"Work, eh?" A crafty expression twisted his vacant face. "Been up to see the old bastard, have you?"

"What?" Julia blurted, alarmed.

"The old bastard. Up there in the study."

"Grandpa's dead, Daddy. You watched the funeral on the channel," she enunciated with slow deliberation, as though she were explaining a particularly difficult fact to a small child.

"Oh, Julie, Julie. How you hate me, a disgrace, a failure as a father. Beneath contempt. Written off. Well I'm an Evans, too, don't forget. A mighty Evans. I see things; I listen to what's going on. I know." He started up the stairs, clinging tightly to the banister rail. His foot slipped, nearly sending him tumbling. He looked around at her mute face staring up at him. "I could have done it. If he'd given me the chance, I could've run the company. Bastard never gave me the chance. He did this to me, his own son! Not you, though, Julie; everybody loves you. He does, I do. Everybody does." The words spluttered into incoherence. He glanced around nervously, suddenly confused as to where he was, what he'd been saying. His hand pulled hard at the banister, starting him off on the climb again. He began muttering fractured words as he went.

Julia buried her face in her hands. After a while she felt Greg's arm around her shoulder. Misery compounded as she found she was quivering silently.

"Sorry," she mumbled, lowering her hands to wipe at her eyes. Absolutely refusing to cry. Then the implications of what her father had said penetrated. "Oh, God, do you think he was the one?"

"Not deliberately, if that's what you mean," said Greg. "Maybe he let something slip. But it wouldn't do any good asking him. I doubt he'd remember. And I couldn't tell whether or not he was telling the truth."

She considered that if Greg couldn't make sense of her father with his ability—"His mind has gone, hasn't it? I mean, really gone, destroyed."

"Julia." He held her firmly, a hand on each shoulder. "Isn't it about time you booked him into a clinic?"

"He's my father," she insisted plaintively. "He needs me."

"He's hurting you, Julia. Far too much. You can't hide that from me, remember? A clinic will care for him properly. You can visit. Hell, you can afford to build a clinic. Put it in a house like this one; he won't even realize the difference."

She studied something away to the side of his head, swallowing hard. "Maybe," she whispered.

"You should get out," he expanded blithely, changing tone, breaking the mood. "A girl like you ought to be beating off the boys with a stick. Stay up till the wee hours at disreputable parties. That sort of thing. Do you the world of good. Wilholm is grand to look at, but it isn't exactly jumping and jiving, now is it?"

"No," she smiled meekly. "I'm going away next weekend, actually. A book launch."

"A what?"

"A book launch. It's a big PR event, lasts for two days, truly swish. Naturally the Evans heir was invited."

"Good. It's a start. Now, what about a boy?"

"I know someone," she said defensively. And the thought lit that idyllic warming core of delight.

They walked out into the furnace heat of a cloudless day. The sun's glare yellowed half of the sky.

"Good-bye, Greg, and thanks again." She stood very close as he blipped the Duo's lock. Would he kiss her?

He tugged the Duo's door open and smiled affectionately, like a doting uncle. "Anytime."

Oh well.

She waved at the car until the curve of the drive took it from view.

End Greg Time#Three.

She'd have to edit her father out, though.

16

Scorching April sunlight metamorphosed the A1 into a bubbling ribbon of tar, for once reversing the rampant greenery's encroachment. Nettles and grass were sucked below the surface by sluggish eddies, consumed and fossilized within the black brimstone.

The Duo moved along the northbound carriageway with one continuous ripping sound. Greg drove automatically, trying to make sense of the case. He hadn't admitted it to Julia, but Kendric di Girolamo had him badly worried. A paradox, she'd said. And she was right. Intuition convinced him Kendric was involved with the blitz attack somewhere along the line, no faint tickle either. But why had the man allowed her to buy him out? Maybe Gabriel would know.

He drove straight through Edith Weston, on to Manton, and turned right, freewheeling down the hill toward Oakham, saving the batteries. A dense strip of rhododendron bushes planted along the side of the railway line running parallel to the road was in full bloom, tissue-thin scarlet flowers throwing off a pink haze as they basked in the rich sunlight. Greg barely registered them; he was worried by the idea of a high-placed mole hidden somewhere among Event Horizon's staff. The last thing he needed was an opposition that was being fed his own progress reports. Maybe it would be best not to keep Walshaw a hundred percent up to date. More subterfuge, more complexity.

Dillan Evans disturbed him as well. Not so much his state but the fact that he could piece together his father's particular bid for immortality from the snippets of conversation he'd picked up around the manor. If Dillan Evans could, anyone could. That definitely meant interviewing all of Wilholm's staff. Another neurohormone hangover to anticipate. Or had Dillan Evans realized because he knew exactly how avaricious and egotistic his father was? That, given that the bioware's capability existed, he would inevitably spend a fortune bringing it to fruition and constructing an NN core. Either way, it left Dillan as a real monster of a loose end. No messing.

Greg had been surprised how bravely Julia handled her father. Her mind's peppy sparkle had dimmed severely in his presence, but her outward composure had been beautifully maintained. He admired that kind of dignity.

He even felt a degree of pity for Dillan. It would've been so easy to condemn him, but he couldn't find the scorn. He deserved compassion more than anything; a lost ruined man, cowering in the double shadow of his parent and child.

His sorry state made Julia all the more remarkable—or perhaps not. The best roses grew out of manure heaps. And despite being the end product of a decidedly screwed-up family, she shone like the sun. Embarrassingly so in his presence.

Sighing resignedly at the memory, he drove into Oakham, reducing speed as the cycle traffic built up around him. When Greg was a teenager it'd been a sleepy rural market town, home to nine thousand people. Then the Warming melted the Antarctic ice, and Oakham received a spate of refugees from the drowned Fens. Its population rose to well over the fifteen thousand mark, and all without a single new house being authorized by the PSP county committee. The town became a microcosm of English life, compressed, confined, and frantically scrabbling to adapt to the environmental and social revolutions of the new century.

Greg slowed to a crawl by the library at the end of the High Street. People were dismounting from their bicycles, wheeling them forward into the dense crowd ahead. The High Street was packed with market stalls, but there was just enough space left for the Duo between them and the waist-high piles of slowly degenerating kelpboard boxes that swamped the pavement. Greg grated into the gap with a broadside of horn blasts and followed a shepherd driving his small flock of rotund beasts, gene-tailored for meat heaviness. The Duo's wheels squelched softly on the carpet of gray-brown turds they laid on the pitted tarmac.

The buildings on this side of the street were mostly old estate agents and building societies. They'd all closed down in the Credit Crash, and the PSP had requisitioned the empty premises under the one-home law, converting them into accommodation modules. Even now there was little improvement in the housing pressure; council and government were locked in a squabble over funds for a new estate on the southern edge of the town. Entire families had crammed into the makeshift facilities behind the shops' broad plate-glass windows, the oldest relatives sitting among the bleached displays like flesh-sculpture buddhas watching the world go by.

Not all of the old retail businesses had gone under: there was still a hotel, a couple of butchers, a recently denationalized bank, and a century-old family gear business that had survived, but most of the town's trade had been usurped by the thriving High Street market. The stalls were crude wooden trestle affairs, keeping the sun at bay with awnings of heavy cloth, patterned in brightly colored stripes or loud checks. Animals bleated mournfully in their pens, birds squawked inside cramped wicker cages. Pyramid mounds of fruit were stacked high, every color of the rainbow. Ranks of skinned rabbits hung from poles, stall owners languidly flicking leafy switches at them to keep the flies off. There were clothing stalls, cobblers, tinkers, gear repairers, distillers with an astonishing array of liqueurs, carpenters, potters, the whole repertoire of manual crafts clamoring for attention.

Three hundred meters and ten minutes later Greg cleared the market and turned right into Church Street, parking outside a little bakery shop.

On the other side of the road was a head-high stone wall, rapidly disappearing under an avalanche of dark waxy-leafed ivy. There was a raised garden behind it, enclosed by buildings on two sides and a chapel on the third. He went through the open wooden gate and took the steps two at a time.

The garden and buildings used to be part of the Oakham School campus, but private education hadn't lasted six months after the PSP came to power, swept away in the card carriers' Equalization crusade. And after that the refugees had hit town demanding somewhere to live. The campus was requisitioned as fast as the shops, playing fields given over to allotments.

The school's Round House was a plain circular building sitting on the south side of the raised garden, three stories high, and built from pale Stamford brick. Its door was closed and locked. Greg stood in front of it, motionless, waiting. It was a game he and Gabriel played. After half a minute he admitted defeat once again and turned to the small touch panel set into the brick. He started pecking out the six-digit code for room seventeen.

"Come on up," Gabriel's voice chimed out of the intercom before he'd finished. The lock buzzed like an enraged hornet.

Gabriel Thompson had been a major in the Mindstar Brigade, possessed of the most reliable precognition faculty ever recorded. She was thirty-nine, only two years older than Greg, but judging from physical appearance alone he would've said it was closer to twenty. Her fair hair had already faded to a maidenly pearl white; flab was accumulating all over her body. She wore a fawn-colored woolen cardigan and tweed skirt, making her broad and shapeless, a half-hearted attempt to disguise her physical deterioration.

It pained him to see her this way, a prematurely middle-aged spinster. Especially as his mind insisted on remembering her as that neat, efficient young officer in Turkey. A fine-looking woman in her day, idolized like an elder sister.

He was given a moody stare as he entered her room on the second floor; it was one of thirty in the Round House, originally intended to sleep two girl boarders. As a permanent bedsit it was terribly cramped.

"Typical," she said. "Only ever visit when you want something." Badly applied dabs of makeup made her face shine in the golden afternoon sunlight filtering through the net curtain.

"Not true. Oh, Eleanor says hello."

"I doubt it." Gabriel began pouring tea from a silver pot into two bone china cups, all neatly laid out.

Rock music from one of the other rooms thumped out a soft bass rhythm in the background, echoing down the stairwell.

"So, what have you come for this time?" she asked.

"Philip Evans."

"He's dead." She paused for a moment, then her eyes widened in surprise. "Christ!"

All she needed was a word, a phrase, extrapolating the future from there. Events closest to her came across strongest. There would be no point in him asking her what was going to happen to someone on the other side of the world; she wouldn't be able to see them.

She'd described the probabilities to him once, explaining her limits after he'd asked her for some impossible piece of intelligence information when they were fighting the Jihad legion.

I'm standing at the mouth of a very large river, she'd said, *at the moment when the future becomes the present, and I'm looking across the land where the water originated, seeing the first fork, and beyond that the tributaries branching away, and then the tributaries' tributaries, splitting, multiplying, ad infinitum. The far horizon gives birth to a trillion rills, all converging to the mouth, each one the source of a possible destiny. They are the Tau lines, future history. On their way toward me they clash and merge, building in strength, in probability, eradicating the wilder fringes of feasibility as they approach confluence, until they reach the mouth: the point of irrevocable certainty.*

She could send her mind floating back along those streams, questing, probing for what would come. The prospect terrified her, he knew. She'd hidden that from the Army, but of course he'd seen it at once. The knowledge cost him; as the one person whose empathy allowed him to see the true extent of that dread, he felt protective toward her. He was her involuntary confessor, obligated.

Way ahead of her, at the farthest extremity of each of those streams, where the flow was little more than a trickle in the dust, her death waited for her. She refused to let her mind roam far into any of the possible futures, but even that self-imposed proscription meant she lived with the mortal fear of the streams drying up, one by one, the drought inching toward her; a reality so blatant she'd never be able to shield her eldritch sight against it.

Greg thought of himself sitting in a plane as it began its long fall out of the sky, standing paralyzed by fear in the middle of the road as some huge lorry bore down, brakes squealing, unable to stop in time. She had to live with the prospect of seeing that eventuality raising its head every minute of every day. Knowing that it was inevitably going to happen.

So he forgave her for going to seed. His espersense was a heavy cross. He would never have the strength to carry hers.

"Exactly," he said. "Philip Evans made it back from the grave. Can you see who's behind the blitz on his NN core?"

"Hmm." Her mind betrayed how intrigued she was. "I'll have a look." She cut a slice of almond cake and began munching, staring up at the ceiling, eyes unfocused.

He sipped his tea, trying to identify the herbs. Rosemary, possibly. The market stalls weren't particularly choosy what they ground up.

"Not a thing," Gabriel said.

He didn't show any disappointment. (Was there some alternative-universe Greg Mandel currently raging at her failure?) The answer did exist. Down one of those Tau lines was a future where he and Gabriel teamed up and successfully tracked down whoever had attacked Philip Evans. But for the moment the distance was too great. She wouldn't stretch herself that far, not even for friendship's sake.

"Will you help?" he asked.

She looked dreadfully unhappy.

"No big visions," he reassured her. "Just cross out probabilities for me, eliminate suspects and dead ends. That kind of thing. I've got to interview Event Horizon's gigaconductor team tomorrow; that's over two hundred people. Then I'll probably wind up having to go through the security division's headquarters staff for the mole. My espersense can't last out that long. Twenty's my limit. And that hurts bad enough."

"All right," she whispered.

He held up the card Morgan Walshaw had given him. Gabriel stared at it, mesmerized. He could sense the trepidation mounting in her mind. She wanted to soar into the future and find out what it meant. The larger, ever-present dread held her back.

"Afterwards," he said, "succeed or fail, I'm going to pay for your operation. That's your fee, Gabriel; that gland is coming out."

She looked at him incredulously, her mind spilling out hope. Her eyes watered. "I can't," she moaned.

"Bullshit," he said softly. "I'm the one who can't; I can keep my demons at bay. You can't. You think I'm blind to what the gland has done to you? You're getting out, Gabriel. No more living under the pendulum."

Tears began to roll down her cheeks, smearing the makeup. She twisted around to avoid his eyes, looking out of the window.

He put his hands on the nape of her neck, feeling the solid knots of muscle, massaging gently. "I hate seeing you like this. You don't live; you crawl from day to day. It's a miserable existence. Too timid to walk under the open sky in case a lightning bolt hits you. It's got to stop, Gabriel. No messing."

"You bastard, Mandel. I'd be nothing without the gland, nothing."

Outside, the sun shone down on the school's old chapel on the other side of the garden, its pale stone gleaming like burnished yellow topaz.

"You'd be human."

"Bastard. Prize bastard."

"Truthful bastard."

He turned her to face him. She was suddenly busy with a lace handkerchief, wiping away tears, making an even worse hash of the makeup.

"Tomorrow," he said. "We'll start with the Event Horizon Astronautics Institute, okay?"

She looked confused for a moment, then gathered her thoughts, entering into that familiar trance for a few seconds. "Yes, that's a good start."

"Right, then. I'll pick you up at nine o'clock."

"Fine." She sniffed hard, then blew into the handkerchief.

Greg leaned forward and kissed her brow.

A PAIR OF DOLPHINS SPIRALED around Eleanor, silver bubbles streaming out from their flashing tails, wrapping her at the center of an ephemeral DNA helix. Playful scamps. She'd come to love the freedom of the water over the last few weeks. Down here, surrounded by quiet pastel light, tranquility reigned; life's ordinary worries simply didn't exist below the surface. Sometimes she spent hours swimming along the bottom of Rutland Water, one small part of her mind checking the long rows of water-fruit rooted in the silt, while her memories and imagination roamed free. Daydreaming really, but this gentle universe understood and forgave.

The marine-adepts had warned her about the state. "Blue lost", they called it. But she couldn't believe it was that dangerous. Besides, the reservoir was finite, not like the oceans they talked of, where some of their kind never returned. Swimming away to the edge of the world.

She helped tend their crops three or four days each week; with inflation the way it was, the water-fruit money came in useful. And she could spend the time thinking about life, the world, and Greg, weaving the strands in fanciful convolutions, so that when she left the water behind her mind was spring fresh and eager for the sights, sounds, and sensations of land again. Mental batteries recharged. The world outside that ever-damned kibbutz was too big to endure in one unbroken passage.

She felt a dolphin snout poking her legs, upsetting her balance. It was Rusty, the big old male. She knew him pretty well by now, though some of the others were hard to distinguish. Rusty had a regular ridge of scar tissue running from just behind his eyes down to his dorsal fin. The marine-adepts never talked about it, so she never asked. But something had been grafted onto him at one time. She didn't like to think what.

They'd brought eight dolphins with them to the reservoir to help harvest their water-fruit. The dolphins' long, powerful snouts could snip clean through a water-fruit's ropy root. All of them were ex-Navy fish, their biochemistry subtly adjusted, enabling them to live comfortably in fresh water as well as salt. Greg said that was so they could be sent on missions up rivers. But whatever Rusty had been made to do back then hadn't affected his personality; he could be a mischievous devil when he wanted to be.

Like now.

She suddenly found herself flipped upside down, whirl currents from his thrashing tail tumbling her further. The remains of Middle Hambleton spun past her eyes. Shady rectangular outlines of razed buildings rising from the dark gray-green alluvial muck. One day she was determined she'd explore those sad ruins properly.

She stretched her arms out, slowing herself, then bent her legs, altering her center of gravity, righting herself. A shadow passed over her, Rusty streaking away, beyond retribution. She let herself float upward.

At the back of her mind she was marveling at her own enjoyment. She, a girl who couldn't even swim six weeks ago, even though the kibbutz at Egleton was right beside the reservoir. The marine-adepts had thought that hilarious.

For the first few weeks after she'd moved into Greg's chalet she'd had a sense of being divorced from selected sections of his life. Apart from the Edith Weston villagers everyone he knew was ex-military; the marine-adepts, Gabriel, that mysterious bunch of people in Peterborough he'd referred to obliquely a couple of times, even the dolphins. They were a hard-shelled clique, one that'd formed out of shared combat experiences. She could never possibly be admitted to that. And the marine-adepts were naturally reticent around other people; it wasn't quite a racial thing, but they did look unusual until you were used to them. The only time they left the reservoir was to drive their water-fruit crop to Oakham's railway station.

Breaking through their mistrust had been hard going. The turning point had come when Nicole had finally taken over her swimming lessons, more out of exasperation than kindness, she'd thought at the time. But a bond had formed once she realized how keen Eleanor was, and the rest of the floating village's residents had gradually come to accept her. A triumph she considered equal to walking out on the kibbutz in the first place.

She could never hope to match the marine-adepts in the water. They had webbed feet that enabled them to move through the water with a grace rivaling the dolphins', and their boosted hemoglobin allowed them to stay submerged for up to a quarter of an hour at a time. But with flippers and a bioware mirror-lung recycling her breath she was quite capable of helping them in the laborious nurturing of the water-fruit. Planting the kernels deep in the silt, watching out for fungal decay in the young shoots, clearing away tendrils of the reservoir's ubiquitous fibrous weed that could choke the mushy pumpkinlike globes. The marine-adepts had staked out eight separate fields in the reservoir and earned quite a decent living from them.

Her only real failure among Greg's friends had been Gabriel Thompson. The woman was so stuck-up and short-tempered Eleanor had wound up simply ignoring her. She suspected Gabriel had a jealousy problem. Always mothering Greg.

She broke surface five hundred meters off shore, about a kilometer away from the Berrybut time-share estate. The sun was low in the sky, and she could see flames rising from the estate's bonfire.

Rusty's chitter tore the air ten meters behind her. She slapped the water three times and he vanished again. Some Navy dolphins had been fitted with bioware processor nodes to make them totally obedient to human orders. But Nicole said the Navy had left Rusty's brain alone. The marine-adepts used a hand-signal language to talk with the reservoir dolphins. Eleanor had mastered most of it, and Rusty nearly always did as she asked. That little edge of irrepressible uncertainty in his behavior was what made him such fun.

She felt the change in water pressure as he rose underneath her; then she was straddling him, clutching desperately at his dorsal fin as he began to surge forward. Homeward-bound fishermen in their white hireboats stared with open-mouthed astonishment as she sped past, slicing out an arc of creamy foam in her wake.

Rusty let her off fifteen meters from the shore, where the bottom started to shelve. A flock of panicky flamingos took flight, pumping wings creaking the air above her. She gave her steed an affectionate slap and waded ashore, arms aching from hanging on against the buffeting water.

The familiar claimed her as she walked up the slope to chalet six. Meat roasting on the bonfire, pork by the smell of it. Dusty whirlwind of the football game, rampaging along the side of the spinney. Swapping easy greetings with the few adults milling about. Dogs underfoot, Labradors, who made the best rabbiters. A couple of wolf-whistles following her progress. She smiled at that. Something else she wouldn't have been able to cope with before.

She wore a one-piece costume whenever she went into the water now. The polka-dot bikini that Greg had bought her was far too skimpy for any serious diving—typical lecherous male. Not that she wanted to change him. Nighttime with Greg was one continuous orgy: hot, strenuous, sweaty, and tremendously exciting, another fruit forbidden to her at the kibbutz.

The Duo was parked in its usual spot. She was looking forward to hearing what he'd been called away to, the message he'd left on the terminal had been oddly brief.

She shrugged out of the mirror-lung and plugged its nutrient coupling into the support gear on the veranda.

Greg was inside, dressed in an old purple sweatshirt and shorts, fooling around with the kitchen gear. Whatever he was cooking smelled good.

"My savior." She gave him a radiant smile. "After your message I wasn't sure if you'd be back, and I haven't got the energy left to cook."

He slurped a spoonful of the sauce he was simmering. "Béarnaise, it's nice, try some." He held up the spoon.

She took a sip as his other arm slipped around her waist, hand coming to rest on her buttock. "You're right, not bad." For a moment she thought he was going to dump the meal and urge her into the bedroom. He always got turned on by the sight of her in a wet swimming costume. And there was plenty of time before she was due behind the bar at the Wheatsheaf. But then she looked closely at his face and wrinkled her nose up. "God, you look awful."

"Thank you."

"Sorry . . . but, what have you been up to?"

"Do me one favor," he implored.

"What?"

"Just don't tell me I look like I've seen a ghost."

"I don't like it," Eleanor murmured.

It was long past midnight, the time for honest talk. They were lying on top of the big bed, the duvet crumpled up somewhere on the floor. The heat from making love beneath it would have been intolerable. As it was, they'd left the window full open, curtains wide to let the balmy night air flow around their bodies.

A quarter-moon was riding high in the sky, bathing the room with a spectral phosphorescence. She stretched out on her side beside him, her hands pillowing her head.

"Why not?" There was a certain tenseness in his voice.

"Just don't," she said.

"Female intuition?"

"Something like that."

He wet the tip of his forefinger and began to trace a line from her shoulder to the flare of her hips, innocently curious. "I'm supposed to be the one with the hypersenses."

"You want logic? Okay. It's too big. You're a one-man band; they're warring armies. They're out to kill each other, Greg. That security man, Walshaw, said as much. This gigaconductor stuff, it pushes the stakes too high. You don't know who the other side is; you don't know who to watch out for. There are an awful lot of *kombinates* who will suffer because of the gigaconductor. Any one of them could decide they don't want you interfering."

"Firstly, I share Julia's conviction that Kendric di Girolamo is involved somewhere, the mole is his plant. So at least I know one direction of attack which I should be guarding myself from. And secondly, I'm not convinced that it is the gigaconductor which is the root cause of the blitz. Erasing Philip Evans's memories wouldn't halt its introduction, not with the Ministry of Defense pushing it. He's important, but not that important, no matter what he likes to think. I suppose it's partially conceit. By maintaining that Event Horizon can't do without him, he's justifying the expense of the NN core. I'm not so sure. Julia has inherited his drive, more if anything, and she's bright, she learns fast. She's just very young, that's all. No crime. The company won't fail with her in charge."

"A personal vendetta extended to wiping a Turing personality program? Come on, nobody's that obsessive."

"Don't you believe it. Philip Evans trod hard on a *lot* of toes to build up Event Horizon. In any case . . ."

"What?" She looked at him intently, seeing the confusion on his moonlit face.

"Philip Evans's memories aren't just a simple Turing program; there's more to it. He's not alive, I'll grant you that. But neither is he wholly dead. I saw something with my espersense."

Eleanor stroked his abdominal muscles lightly, fingers dancing as she considered what he'd said. She never quite knew how to interpret his psi ability—it all sounded so vague and mystical, like tarot cards and reading tea leaves. Yet he did have the talent, no denying that. Her father's horror and fright still returned to her occasionally.

"All right," she said, "if it is di Girolamo, or someone else, looking for vengeance, they are even less likely to appreciate you coming between them and the Evans family."

"All I shall be doing is interviewing Event Horizon personnel to find their mole and seeing if my own contacts know anything about the blitz. There's no danger in that." He took her hand and brought it up to his lips, kissing her knuckles. "Look, this is what I've been

wanting to break into for years. It's a regular case, just interviews and
data correlation, and it pays regular money. I'm not going to touch
the hardline side."

"What do you mean, break into? I thought this is what you did."

"Part-time," he said. "But this is the second time in a few months
that Event Horizon has called me in to sort out their problems. No
amount of advertising and PR work can generate that kind of reputation. This could be what I need to make the switch. I could maybe
put myself on a business footing, get an office, a secretary, some assistants—hell, pay taxes, too. I think I'd like that."

She moved closer, resting against him, feeling hot sweaty skin
pressing into her belly. It was a funny mood he was in, indecisive,
which wasn't like him at all. "I don't want to change you, Greg."

He grinned and patted her backside lightly. "Too late, you already
have. Don't you want me to have a regular job?"

"I'd like that, yes. But I don't want you getting hurt trying to build
some kind of impossible reputation."

"Tell you, there's no worry on that score. I'll be perfectly safe;
Gabriel's coming with me."

"I see." It would have to be Gabriel he took along. Eleanor reckoned her psi ability was completely tabloid. But if she started protesting now he'd think she was just being childishly petulant. And she
could hardly see the two of them running off together. Gabriel had
to be at least ten years older than Greg. Whatever bond they had between them was locked safely in the past.

"I'm only being practical," he said. "Gabriel can spot trouble long
before it starts. And whilst we're on the subject of practical, you
might care to look at the chalet walls some time. We're providing a
home for more insects than you'll find at a natural history museum."

"Money," she said in disgust. "It always boils down to money."

"The way the world's built. Nothing to do with me."

She rested her head on his chest, listening to his heartbeat. "I
know. I wasn't angry at you."

"There's something else wrong, too," he said. "I simply cannot believe a mole, no matter how highly placed, could breach a security
cordon which Morgan Walshaw set up, certainly not a security cordon around something as ultrahush as the gigaconductor. The stuff
is Event Horizon's entire future. You haven't met him, but take it
from me, he's as good as they come. Reliable, smart, experienced,
he just doesn't make elementary mistakes. If it had been breached at
any time in the last ten years, he'd know."

Eleanor thought he was saying it mechanically, as though he was trying to convince himself with repetition. "So the mole isn't an executive; he's on the inside of the cordon."

He shifted his shoulders, restless. "Doubtful. Walshaw would arrange to have every one of Ranasfari's research team vetted and constantly reviewed. And if the mole was on the inside, how come he knew of Philip Evans's NN core?"

"Oh, yes. Hey, what about a psychic? Surely someone with a gland could peer in on both the gigaconductor laboratory and the clinic where they spliced the NN core together?"

"Unlikely, although I admit it's possible. There aren't many of us, not even worldwide. And the premier-grades, the ones whose ESP is powerful enough to reach into Event Horizon's research facilities from a distance, you can count them on one hand. Not that they're used for anything so mundane as trawling in any case. It's like this: to bring in a premier-grade psychic you have to know there's something worthwhile for them to peek. Almost a catch twenty-two scenario. Normally, premier-grades are brought in to acquire specific items, like a formula or template. And as Event Horizon has already patented the gigaconductor that would seem to preclude their involvement. If a kombinate had acquired the gigaconductor's molecular structure they would've slapped down the patent before Event Horizon. The blitz would never have happened."

"A prescient like Gabriel, then. One of them looked into the future, saw Event Horizon churning out the gigaconductor, and sold the information to a kombinate."

"Gabriel is the best prescient there is, and she didn't know, not even with her own future interwoven with the gigaconductor."

Eleanor nearly said that it could've been a prescient who wasn't so totally neurotic as Gabriel but held her peace. Greg could get quite unreasonably defensive when it came to the silly woman. It was the military clique thing again. She knew she would never be able to appreciate the kind of combat traumas that they had been through together in Turkey.

"So what are you trying to say?" she asked.

"Just that it doesn't ring straight. Blitzing the core out of spite isn't kombinate behavior."

"It was a vendetta, then."

He let out a long wistful sigh, frowning. "Wish I knew."

"Poor Greg."

She snuggled closer, brushing her breasts provocatively against his torso as she slid on top of him. Greg had a thing about big breasts, which she exploited ruthlessly when they were having sex. He glanced down owlishly, frown fading.

"I was thinking," he said. "Why don't you come with me when I visit my contacts? There's one in Peterborough I'll probably visit."

She tried not to show any surprise. Nicole had dropped the occasional hint that he'd taken an active part in the events leading up to the Second Restoration, and she'd guessed that was tied up somewhere with his old Army mates in Peterborough. But he'd never offered to introduce them before.

"I'd like that." Short pause. "Will Gabriel be coming?"

"Er, no. The contact I'm thinking of doesn't like too many visitors. We can go the day after tomorrow; I fixed up to take Gabriel to Duxford in the morning, interview Ranasfari's people. Shouldn't take long."

"Right." She thought it was about time to lighten the atmosphere, take him away from intrigue and human failings. She tapped a hard fingernail on his sternum. "Now what about this Julia? She sounds a bit of a handful to me."

"She is. You'll never guess what she wanted me to do."

"What?" She couldn't help the note of bright curiosity that bubbled into her voice.

"I'll show you."

18

LESS CHOICE LESS PRICE

THE CRUDE PLACARDS LINED THE M11 for kilometers on either side of Cambridge. Large kelpboard squares, sprayed with fluoro-pink lettering that dribbled like a window's condensation. They flapped beneath sturdy sun-blistered road signs, themselves so old the few legible names had distances in miles.

CAKE AND EAT IT NOW!

"What's the matter with them?" Gabriel exclaimed irritably as the Duo passed Little Shelford. "Do they want those bloody card carriers back in power?"

KRILL DON'T HAVE BOLLOCKS
THEY JUST TASTE LIKE THEM

"You are deep into student country," Greg told her, amused by her reaction. "What did you expect? They just don't like governments, full stop. Any sort of government. Never have, never will. They think demonstrating political awareness is exciting. You should encourage questing young minds."

DIGNITY NOT ECONOMIC THEORY

The Duo's cooler was going full blast, grinding out uncomfortable gusts of frigid air. Gabriel's grunt was lost in the noise of the fans.

"They can't have it both ways," she said. "Two years ago there wasn't any food at all. Inflation is the price you pay for a free-market economy. Wages rise to cope; it's cyclic."

"But do student grants rise as well?"

"Christ, whose side are you on? If they're so bloody aware, they should know freedom isn't perfect. If they'd tried protesting when Armstrong was running the country, they would've become nonpeople before you could say community responsibility."

"So put up your own banners. Tell them, not me."

The motorway was in surprisingly good condition. Dead sycamores with peeling bark and bleached wood rose out of the scrub tangle at the edge of the hard shoulder. Greg toed the brake as they approached a large densely packed patch of scarlet flowers shining with livid intensity under the Sahara-bright sun. He thought they were poppies at first, except they were too big. A single palm-size petal, waxy; thousands of them waving in the breeze.

"Someone agrees with you," he said dryly, inclining his head.

Two young men in somberros and dirty jeans were ripping down one of the kelpboard placards. Their bicycles lay on the fringe of the flamingo flower carpet. He spotted badges with the deep-blue crown of the New Conservative party emblem pinned on their T-shirts.

Gabriel nodded with tight approval at this vandalism of graffiti. Greg returned to the tarmac ahead. Crazy world.

He turned off the nearly deserted road at junction ten, onto the A505. There was a new brightly painted green and gold sign at the side of the sliproad.

DUXFORD
EVENT HORIZON ASTRONAUTICS INSTITUTE

Freshly torn scraps of kelpboard littered the grass below it, flapping like broken butterflies in the hot dry breeze.

The Astronautics Institute was an all-new construction that'd sprung up out of the ruins of the Imperial War Museum. Armstrong's extremist followers had gleefully set about eradicating the museum's exhibitions and aircraft collection after they'd come to power, calling it a war pornography monument. The cabinet declared that Duxford was to become the National Resource Reclamation Center, intended as the prestigious mainstay of the PSP's self-sufficiency policy. They said it would dismantle the war machines scrapped under their demilitarization program and turn them into useful raw material for industry.

Greg remembered the hundreds of APVs and Challenger IV tanks parked in the Chunnel marshaling yards after he got back from Turkey. All earmarked for Duxford and ignominy.

But all Duxford had ever achieved was to smash up the beautifully restored aircraft displays and the first few trainloads of redundant Army vehicles. The promised smelleders had never materialized, and the dole-labor conscripts had rioted. For eight years the aban-

doned hammer-mangled wrecks on the runway had snowed rust
flakes onto the concrete, oil and hydraulic fluid seeping through the
cracks, poisoning the soil. Then after the PSP fell, Philip Evans chose
the site to be the foundation of his dream.

The Astronautics Institute had been visible as a gleaming blister
on the horizon ever since the Duo passed junction eleven outside
Cambridge. After that Greg found himself constantly readjusting his
perspective to accommodate the size of the thing. It was *huge*.

He'd spent a few minutes the previous evening reviewing the data
that he'd been given at Wilholm. But it'd completely failed to prepare him for what he was seeing now.

The main building was a five-story ring of offices, research labs,
and engineering shops, eight hundred meters in diameter, present-
ing a blank wall of green-silvered glass to the outside world. The area
it enclosed had been capped by a solar-collector roof, giving the staff
a voluminous hangarlike assembly hall for space hardware.

Construction crews were still finishing it off; two motionless
cranes stood on opposite sides; piles of scaffolding littered the raw
packed limestone surround; ranks of silent contractor vehicles were
drawn up across the parking yards. Standard transit containers full
of Event Horizon's own cybernetics were stacked outside the assembly hall's sliding doors, waiting to be installed. A saucer-shaped
McDonnell Douglas helistat hovered overhead, its five rotors generating an aggressive downdraft as it struggled to maintain its position against the light northeasterly wind. A container was being
winched down out of its belly hold, swaying like a pendulum in the
gusts. Two more helistats waited high overhead.

Greg could see machinery and gear being moved from their temporary accommodation in patched-up museum buildings into the institute. With the bulk of the structure complete, Event Horizon's research, design, and management teams were starting to take up
permanent residence.

A ragtag army of scrap merchants had been let loose on the old
airport, piling vans and horse-drawn carts high with the twisted
shards of metal which were still strewn across the runway and taxi
lanes. One of the merchants had modified an old street-cleaning
lorry to sweep up the thick stratum of rust, and a dense cloud of orange dust foamed up from its bald tires as it thundered up and down
the concrete strip.

Philip Evans had built his mindchild with an eye to the future. Its
proximity to the university colleges had proved subversively addictive, offering finance and top-range research facilities to budget-

starved faculties. A move that put the cream of the country's intellect at his disposal.

Physically, the institute was a totally self-contained complex, taking the concept of centralization right to its extreme. It could design and fabricate mission hardware ranging from torque-neutralizing screwdrivers for orbital riggers right up to the refineries that would latch on to asteroids and leech out the ores, minerals, and metals. Independent and efficient. And with the money the gigaconductor royalties would bring in, Greg realized, quite capable of achieving the space-activist dream: exploiting the solar system's wealth.

It also housed the team that had cracked the gigaconductor. Philip Evans had brought Dr. Ranasfari back to England after the Second Restoration, wanting to keep a tight rein on his company's resident genius. Setting him up at the Astronautics Institute had been Morgan Walshaw's idea.

With so many recently assembled research and design groups scattered throughout the old museum buildings while they waited for their new facilities to be completed, the place was in a constant state of flux. Ranasfari's team could establish themselves in an office and laboratory unit at the center and remain unnoticed among the flustered crowd. The lost in plain view concept had worked for two years.

"No wonder Evans was so upset when the memox spoiler began to affect Event Horizon's profit margin," Greg said as they drew close to the institute's gates. "How much did this lunatic conceit cost him, for Christ's sake?" The data squirted from Philip Evans's NN core into his cybofax concerning the institute had only given him generalities, PR gloss. No hard financial facts.

Gabriel answered with a shrug. He sensed a cold trickle of intimidation damping her thought currents.

The institute was circled by a mushroom ring of ten geodesic spheres housing the satellite uplinks. On the eastern side was a peculiar horn-shaped antenna, unprotected from the elements. It had a temporary look to it. People were walking among the dove-gray Portacabins at its base, ant size. The damn thing must've been thirty meters high. Scale here was something else again.

Greg had a shrewd idea that that was the source of Gabriel's dismay. She'd grasped the institute at once. With him, the ego-ablating effect was taking time, a slow dawning of his own utter insignificance.

A four-meter chain fence topped by razor-wire marked out the perimeter. There was a smaller fence inside, fine granite chippings between the two. A guard-dog run, or at least some form of hunt animal.

The entrance road was split into five channels, each with a pole barrier. Greg chose number one. The Duo had to pass over ratchet spikes before they got to the red-and-white striped barrier.

"What does he keep in here?" Gabriel muttered. "Crown jewels?"

"Oh no, something far more valuable than that. Knowledge."

A company bus drew up in lane two, full of sanitized young technical types, all of them wearing pale shirts and neat ties. Greg showed his new card to the white watchman pillar, and the barrier raised itself obediently.

"But can we get out so easily?" Gabriel asked.

"Your department."

There were three parking yards. He found a space in the first, in the shadow of a big JCB. Gabriel climbed out, twisting her pearls self-consciously. The air was stifling, so Greg slung his leather jacket over his shoulder.

"We don't belong here," Gabriel declared. She'd turned a complete circle, taking in the strange conflation of creaky old buildings, chaotically jumbled wreckage, and new megastructure with a child-like expression of awe. "You and I. It's not our world." Her mind state verged on depression.

"Don't be such a Luddite," he said.

She gave him a soft, pitying smile. "You don't understand. This place, it has destiny. I can feel it, portent after portent, the weight of them pressing down, suffocating. Future history, eager to be enacted, glories waiting to be born."

Her words triggered his own instinct, a feedback reinforcing misgivings. Another reason Gabriel lived alone; even he had to take her in small doses. What she saw, rambled about, there was no escape from knowing it was all true. Suppose she was to hint the approach of his own death?

There was a work crew laying the last stretch of paving slabs between the yard and the main building. A clump of bedraggled and confused daffodils were sprouting in one of the concrete troughs beside the entrance.

"Ready?" he asked just before they went in. "Shouldn't take long."

"You're telling me this?"

He grinned at the old reliably cranky Gabriel and waved the magic card at the door pillar.

Ten minutes later Greg was standing beside the front rank of seats in a deserted ten-tier press gallery, looking out into the institute's Merlin mission control. It was the final humbling; he was a small bewildered child permitted a privileged glimpse of adults playing some marvelously intricate game, understanding nothing.

On the other side of the tinted glass, concentric semicircles of consoles faced big wall-mounted flatscreens showing pictures of alien worlds. Young shirtsleeved controllers sat behind them, studying cubes full of undulating graphics, muttering instructions into throat mikes. The central display was a map of the inner solar system, a snarl of colored vector lines showing the disposition of the Merlin fleet.

The scene should've been generating a flood of urgency and excitement. Greg hadn't forgotten the emotion of the Sanger crew out at Listoel. Instead he received an impression of tension, his espersense confirming the mass anxiety.

Nervous knots of the controllers were forming at random amid the gear consoles, talking in low, concerned tones, breaking up to reform with different members, human Brownian motion.

"Bit of a flap on at the moment, I'm afraid," said Martin Wallace. He was an institute security officer who'd been summoned in a hurry by the authority vested in Greg's card. A stocky Afro-Caribbean in his late thirties, uncomfortable with Greg and Gabriel's appearance and what it implied. "Trouble in orbit. One of the Merlins has packed up for no apparent reason. The flight management teams are shitting bricks." He stopped and flinched. "Sorry, ma'am."

Gabriel bit back a smile.

Greg peered through the glass, recognizing one of the figures in conference around the flight chief's desk. "How long before we can see Dr. Ranasfari?" he asked as he rapped his knuckles on the thick glass.

"Shouldn't be long." Wallace stood at attention, upset by Greg's breach of etiquette.

Greg rapped again, harder.

Irked faces turned to look. Greg beckoned to Sean Francis. The young executive started, then nodded and headed for the door to the press gallery, brushing off protests from the cluster of senior controllers he was in deep conversation with.

"This is as good a place as any," Greg said. "We'll do our interviews here. You see that we're not disturbed."

"Right." Wallace backed out, not exactly bowing, but coming close.

"Macho," Gabriel drawled. "Any orders for me, Captain?"

"Yeah, now that you mention it, Major, start skipping through the gigaconductor team. All the possible interviews I could have with them, see which of them, if any, leaked the information."

Her good humor darkened. "Don't want much, do you?"

"I'm not asking you to stretch. Just find what you can. I'll be satisfied with anything, even a string of negatives."

"All right."

Sean Francis bustled in. Completely unchanged, still pleasant, firm, capable, eager. Annoying.

"What brings you here?" he asked after Greg introduced him to Gabriel.

"I'm investigating the hackers' assault on Event Horizon's data network."

"Really? You believe someone here is involved, yes?"

"Could be. What are you doing here? I thought you were bound for greater things. Julia told me you'd made the management board."

Greg's first-name terms with his boss didn't escape Sean Francis's notice; a sharp spike of interest rose in his mind at the mention of her name. Outwardly, his positive cheeriness expanded. "Ah, but this *is* greater things. Miss Evans appointed me as an independent management examiner after *Oscot* anchored in the Wash for decommissioning. I travel 'round company installations and report back directly to the trustees. This way I build up a working knowledge of Event Horizon second to none. Means I'm going to be on line for a top-rank management position in a couple of years, yes? Opportunities like that only happen once in a lifetime. I grasped it. And, well, here I am."

"Doing?"

"Troubleshooting. Miss Evans has given the Merlin project a high-priority rating. I'm here to hustle them along."

"So what's the problem?" Greg asked. His gland began the neurohormone infusion. Sean's mind swam into a sharper focus.

"Merlin malfunction. Number eighteen: it's the first series-four model. Lot of high hopes riding on it. But the bitch is stalled in Earth orbit, three and a half thousand kilometers up. Absolutely dead in the water. Disaster time. We're talking reputations on the line here."

"Ranasfari's?" Gabriel asked sharply.

Francis cocked his head to one side to look at her. "Why do you ask?"

"Humor us, Sean," Greg said, and showed him his new Event Horizon card.

The sight didn't flummox him quite like it had Wallace, but his mind tightened appreciatively. "So? I'm impressed. This attack on the datanet is being taken seriously, yes?"

"The Trustees attach a certain importance to it," Greg said. "Now, what about Ranasfari?"

"Do you know what he's been working on?" Sean Francis asked cautiously.

"Room-temperature gigaconductor."

"Fine, okay, had to be sure. You understand? Can't just shout my mouth off, yes?"

"We understand," said Gabriel.

Francis caught the undertone of irony. "The series-four Merlin is fitted with gigaconductor power cells. Thing is, Event Horizon has put in a bid to fit the RAF's Matador AGM-404 exospheric interceptors with the same marque of cells. If it is the gigaconductor which has screwed up, then we're really up the old creek, yes?"

"And is it?" Greg asked.

"Too soon to say. They're still running the fault analysis." Sean Francis's mind betrayed a lot of apprehension. Greg wrote it off as the pressure. Failure this soon after his promotion would send him tumbling right back down to the obscurity he'd clawed his way up from.

"Why do you need gigaconductor power cells on a nuclear-powered space probe?" Greg asked.

"The isotopes only power the thrusters during the flight phase, lifting the Merlin out of Earth orbit and boosting it along its interception trajectory. Once it's matched velocities with its target asteroid they're jettisoned along with the shielding, which reduces the total mass to just over a ton. Maneuvering becomes a lot simpler and faster without all that surplus mass to shift around. The gigaconductor cells charge off the solar panels and provide power to the thrusters for the final approach phase as well as moving the Merlin around the surface after rendezvous. Some of these Apollo Amor rocks are quite large; we need forty or fifty sample points to build up an accurate picture of the ore composition."

Greg could see the little group of flight controllers around the chief's desk craning their necks in his direction, impatience registering in their surface thoughts.

"You'd better be getting back," he told Sean Francis. "Glad to see you're getting ahead. One last thing: did you know Philip Evans is still alive?"

From an academic viewpoint Francis's reaction was a fascinating emotional evolution. His initial stare was pure disgust; from there Greg's espersense read him progressing through disbelief and into contempt, then back into worry, and finishing up plain confused.

"I saw the body," he said eventually.

"Right, well, thanks for your time."

"I hope you're not going to be so tasteless with Miss Evans. She was very close to her grandfather."

"Of course not. I'll tell you why I had to ask you that, one day," he said, projecting as much bonhomie as he could muster, which simply served to deepen Francis's confusion.

He flicked an uncertain glance at Gabriel and departed, a much puzzled man.

"Congratulations," Gabriel said archly. "You've just ruined his entire day. He can't concentrate on anything, he's so mixed up by that last crack of yours."

"Tough. Life at the top isn't all roses. The sooner he learns, the better off he'll be."

"Do you have to be so bloody rude to everyone?"

"We don't have the time to piss about. Whether that arriviste likes me or not isn't something I'll lose any sleep over. I'm doing my job the only way I know how." He caught the antagonism rising in her. "Besides," he said resignedly, "it's Philip Evans who's tweaked me."

"Philip Evans?"

"Yeah. That NN core of his is fucking weird, unsettling. For a start I can't stop wondering if I'd translocate my thoughts if I was given the opportunity; I mean, it's a sort of immortality, isn't it?"

"And suppose some smart hacker breaks in—every dark secret you ever had will be wide open to them. Blockbuster stuff, if they publish it."

"Yeah, you're right. Forget it. What did you see in Mr. Dynamism Francis's future?"

"Nothing much, a lot of frenetic activity here for the next few days, several consultations with young Julia Evans about the Merlin. In fact he seems to have taken rather a shine to our Miss Evans."

"Sean Francis?" Greg couldn't keep the reproach from showing in his voice. Cursed himself silently. "But he's years older than her."

Gabriel's grin was wicked. "He's three years younger than you. And she doesn't regard you as out of reach, now does she?"

Years of experience prevented him from showing the slightest ire. "The girl's got a silly crush, that's all. I can handle that. But Sean Francis, marrying the boss's granddaughter, well, that's . . ."

"Shocking? But Julia isn't the heir anymore; she *is* the boss now." Gabriel put her hand over her heart, sighing fulsomely. "I think it's romantic, myself."

"Does he? No, don't answer that, I don't want to know."

"Julia's really got you in a tizz, hasn't she?"

"Can we get back to the case, please?"

She chuckled. "Certainly, Gregory. You can forget about Sean Francis; he really is a clean-cut square. His only failing is his ambition. He looks at every problem to see how he can benefit from it."

"That's no crime."

There was a knock on the door. Martin Wallace poked his head around. "Dr. Ranasfari's here."

"Show him in," Greg said, and mouthed *kid gloves* to Gabriel, suddenly wishing he'd thought to warn her in advance.

Dr. Ranasfari was in a foul mood. He looked like he hadn't slept for days. His eyes were red-rimmed; his hair was hanging limply; small flakes of dandruff dusted his collar. Creases crisscrossed his white shirt. There was no tie. Even the institute's regulation security tag was missing.

His mind reflected his physical appearance: dull, shot through with frissons of agitation. The prospect that his creation had failed, coupled with the blitz against his patron, had come as a severe shock, Greg guessed. Jolting the secure academic world through which he moved. And now he had to answer impertinent questions. He wore hostility like a hedgehog coat.

"I'll be as quick as I can," Greg said. "I'm sure you have to get back to the Merlin."

No response.

"Have you ever told anyone about Philip Evans's NN core?"

"Certainly not."

"What about the gigaconductor?"

"No." Ranasfari sounded uninterested.

"Unintentionally perhaps, a slip of the tongue? One mistake would be all it'd take. People place a lot of weight on your words."

"Please, Mr. Mandel. Ask your questions, reassure yourself. But don't attempt to ingratiate yourself. I fully appreciate the emphasis Philip Evans places on your investigation. I have already discussed it with him. That is why I agreed to see you. Your conclusions from a minimum data source during your earlier instance of employment indicate your professional competence. Although, I personally suspect a degree of intuition was involved on your part."

"It was."

"Interesting. Is that part of your psi-enhancement?"

"It seems to be, although it's very much a secondary facet. Now, a loose word?"

"No. I don't make that sort of mistake."

"You of all people must appreciate the logic that there has been a serious leak within Event Horizon. Knowing about both the giga-conductor and the core logically makes you a suspect. However, now that I'm satisfied you are not the origin of any leak"—Ranasfari smiled thinly—"that leaves the team which grew the core and your own gigaconductor researchers."

The physicist's thin lips compressed dolefully. "I realize this. It . . . is difficult to accept that one of my people is responsible. I hope you are not asking me to point an accusatory finger?"

"No. But I'd appreciate any other leads from your department. For instance, the lightware cruncher you used to design the original cryogenic gigaconductor with, could that have been hacked?"

"No, it is isolated from the Event Horizon datanet."

Greg paused for a moment, waiting for any ideas to surface from his subconscious. He was aware of a background ache behind his temple. Options were converging at an alarming rate; he had a growing sense of conviction that the assistants weren't going to be the leak origin. Perhaps he'd picked the assumption off Gabriel. She was sitting on the bottom tier of seats, eyes closed, lost among the Tau multiplicities.

"Exactly how serious is this Merlin failure?" Greg asked, intuition prompting.

"Unless the cause can be determined precisely it will be a major setback to both programs," Ranasfari answered.

"Both?"

"Yes, the Merlin prospecting missions and the commercial production of the gigaconductor."

"When did the Merlin actually fail?"

Ranasfari picked up on the flash of excitement in his voice. "I think I see what you are driving at. Yes. The Merlin failed yesterday morning, eight twenty-four, to be precise."

"After the blitz."

"Correct: approximately ten hours. Do you believe the two events are connected?"

Greg was certain of the connection. But there was a fragment of bedlam jarring what would otherwise have been an immaculate fusion of disjointed thoughts. The implication that it wasn't an obvious union. Yet it seemed straightforward. He almost let out a groan; this was as bad as the memox spoiler.

"The attack against Philip Evans could've been a blind," Greg ventured. "Remember the blitz was perpetrated against the whole Event Horizon network; one of the hackers could easily have tampered with the Merlin control programs while it was going on."

"But why the delay?"

"An attempt at disassociating the events? No, wait a minute; how much altitude could the Merlin add in ten hours? Would it make recovery more difficult?"

"Altitude increase over ten hours would be approximately one thousand five hundred kilometers; you have to remember that at the start of the flight the Merlin masses four times as much as it will when it rendezvouses with its target asteroid. That means a low initial acceleration. But certainly that additional fifteen hundred kilometers would add considerably to the cost of recovery. Its current three-and-a-half-thousand-kilometer orbit is way above the Sanger ceiling. An interorbit tug would have to be chartered specially, which is a totally uneconomic prospect. Physical recovery was well down our option list. In fact, given normal circumstances, it wouldn't be considered unless a second Merlin suffered a similar failure. There are a great many conceivable reasons for the shutdown; the gigaconductor cell is not the only new component in series-four models. Few components are common to every Merlin; its development is a continual process of evolution. And, of course, the gigaconductor cells performed perfectly in the space environment simulation tests; they were most extensive."

"But in the meantime a question mark hangs over introducing the gigaconductor cell."

"Yes, unfortunately. A Ministry of Defense team from Boscombe Down has already arrived to review our fault-analysis data."

"What has happened to the Merlin? Is it a total breakdown?" Greg asked.

"It looks like it. The propulsion system has shut down, and the communication link has been severed. It won't even respond to signals directed at its omnidirectional antenna."

"Could its state have occurred by transmitting a rogue set of instructions, ordering it to shut down?"

"Indeed," Ranasfari agreed. "Providing you had the correct codes."

"Which, presumably, are stored here in the institute's memory cores."

"Yes."

"And are they isolated from the Event Horizon datanet?"

"No."

"So the attack could be an attempt to discredit Event Horizon's gigaconductor, which at the very least would delay military funding of your production lines, giving your rivals an opportunity to make up lost ground."

"That is certainly a theoretical possibility." The shadowy over-
tones of worry were lifting from Dr. Ranasfari's mind. "I congratu-
late you, Mr. Mandel."

Greg felt a weight of relief lifting. "I'd like to be kept informed of
your progress on analyzing the Merlin failure."

"Certainly."

"And if you can't find anything concrete, may I suggest charter-
ing an interorbit tug to recover it."

"I doubt the expense would be authorized."

"Mission planning will cost nothing. And if I don't come up with
any positive leads, I'll press Philip Evans to cough up the money."

"I'm sure someone as persuasive as yourself will have no trouble.
Good day, Mr. Mandel." Dr. Ranasfari exited with what might have
been the ghost of a smile on his mouth.

Gabriel gave him a slow laconic clap, the sound echoing hollowly
in the empty gallery. Her eyes were still closed. "I am impressed. That
was one of the slickest pieces of seduction I've seen for many a year.
Poor Eleanor couldn't have stood a chance."

Greg ignored the crack. "Simple logic. You want wholehearted cooperation, get them on your side. And empathy does have its uses.
Like charm, some of us have it."

He slouched on the journalist's seats next to her, letting the foam
below the black imitation leather mold itself to his buttocks, and
stretched his legs out. Beyond the glass, dismay seemed to be tightening its grip.

"How goes it with Ranasfari's team?"

"Total washout." Her eyes fluttered open. "If you interviewed
every one of them, all you'd find is a couple who've got a nice racket
flogging off Event Horizon equipment and five synthoheads. You
were right: Morgan Walshaw knows how to handle security."

"Has to be either the Ministry of Defense or a mole, then."

"Shaping up that way," she agreed. "So, what now?"

"Elimination. My intuition says the Merlin failure and the blitz are
related in some way. At the moment the only way I can reconcile the
two is if the attack on Philip Evans was intended to divert his attention while the Merlin was hashed up to discredit the gigaconductor."

"That's pretty tenuous, Greg. A few gigaconductor cells which
may or may not have failed aren't going to bring the whole enterprise
to a grinding halt. The breakdown could've been some kind of freak
overspill from the attack on the NN core. That would be a connection of sorts."

"No, the Merlin breakdown wasn't an accident."

Gabriel didn't respond. At least she never questioned his intuition.

"Can you see the result of the failure analysis?" he asked.

"Sorry. Too far in the future from where we are."

"Well, not to worry. We'll find out in due course. It might all turn out to be empty hypothesis; Lord knows psi intuition isn't stone-scripted. But I'd put a great deal of money on that connection. I'll decide for sure after we've interviewed the NN core team. Walshaw should have reeled them in by the day after tomorrow. By the way, what can you see of Ranasfari?"

"Oh, God." She let out a long contemptuous breath. "Definitely a contender for the world's most boring human being. He just doesn't have any interests outside his professional work. I'm sure it can't be healthy."

"Leaves him open to blackmail?"

"I shouldn't think so. What could you possibly corrupt him with? In any case, he doesn't do anything remotely incriminating for the next few days, make that a week. And you've already cleared him."

"True." He pushed all the suspicions emanating from intuition out of his mind, canceling the gland secretions, trying to sketch in a wholly logical course on the resultant virgin whiteness. "I want to take you to Wilholm and meet Philip Evans sometime."

"What for this time?"

"Two things. Give the staff the once-over to see if they knew about the NN core. And see if there's going to be another attack on him. If there is, it would mean I'm wrong about the opposition aiming at the gigaconductor. We'd be back to vengeance, Kendric di Girolamo, and the mole."

"Makes sense. When?"

"Tomorrow afternoon. I'm busy in the morning."

"So you are."

He couldn't tell whether her carefully neutral tone was disguising anger or amusement. Her mind gave the impression of total indifference. A balance of the two, perhaps?

"Will Julia be at Wilholm in the afternoon?" he asked.

A broad smile spread across Gabriel's chubby face. "You know, I do believe she will."

19

NINETY PERCENT OF ENGLAND'S ROAD network had been abandoned in the PSP decade; the energy crunch put paid to most private travel, and the incendiary sun steadily deliquesced the tarmac to a worthless residue. A pre-Warming-style maintenance program was out of the question, economically unfeasible, environmentally unsound. Motorways and critical link roads were kept open, but the rest was left to waste away. People who could afford cars bought them configured to cope with the rough terrain. The A47 was one of the roads the PSP was forced to refurbish; it was an essential transport artery between Peterborough and the A1, and the PSP desperately needed the goods that the city manufactured. It meant that the A47's traffic levels were high, and most of the vehicles commercial. Driving down it was a new experience for Eleanor; she began to realize how different England's city life had become from the pastoral existence of the countryside and smaller market towns. It was almost as though the country were developing a split personality. Of course, the gulf was more pronounced here than anywhere else.

Peterborough struck her as a tripartite Babylon, the old, the new, and the waterbound condemned by adverse circumstances to live with each other, rival siblings cooped up in the same house. It sat on the shore of the gigantic salt quagmire that used to be the most fertile soil basin in all of Europe. The Lincolnshire Fens were originally marshes, drained over centuries to provide a rich black loam that could grow any crop imaginable. They were perfectly flat, like Holland; on clear days you could see for forty or fifty kilometers over them, so some of Oakham's refugees had told her. The trouble was, the Fens' average height above sea level was two meters; in some places, like the Isle of Ely, they were actually below sea level. When the Antarctic ice melted they never stood a chance.

Peterborough absorbed nearly two-thirds of the population displaced by the rising water. The city had no choice; it was hemmed in between the new sludge to the east and a shabby band of tent towns on the high ground to the west. None of the refugees were going to move; they had lost their homes, they had found a functioning urban administration, and they were through with running, so they sat and waited for government to get off its ass and do something. The three attempts the PSP mounted to disperse them ended in riots. So the Party was left with no choice. They poured money into permanent accommodation projects, as well as allowing in foreign investment to ease the load on the Treasury, and as a result it became one of the most prosperous cities in England. Huge housing estates mushroomed to serve vast industrial precincts, a crazy mismatch of developments sprawling venomously over the green belt. A deep-water port was built above the drowned cathedral; dredgers reopened the Nene, gouging out a new laser-straight channel directly into the Wash.

Trade links, determination, and money, lots of money: that was the giddy synergy brew. Peterborough became England's Hong Kong, a unique city-state of refugees determined to carve themselves a new life. High on that special energy that crackles around Fresh Start frontiers. Everybody was on the make, on the take. If you couldn't find it in Peterborough, it didn't exist. A philosophy completely out of phase with the rest of the country's lethargy. The PSP city hall apparatchiks just couldn't move fast enough to keep track of the construction chaos that boiled out from the suburbs. Half of the economy was underground, Eurofrancs only; smuggling was rife; spivs bought themselves penthouses in New Eastfield. A resurgent Gomorrah, her father had called it.

Eleanor followed a big methane-powered articulated lorry down the gentle slope toward the bloated Ferry Meadows estuary, née Park, the Duo's suspension thrumming smoothly on the tough thermo-cured cellulose surface. The A47 turned left at the bottom of the slope, running along the top of a small embankment above the filthy, swirling water. After the lorry rumbled around the bend, she could see a string of ten barges moored across the mile-wide estuary between the base of the embankment and Orton Winstow. Artificial islands of rock and concrete were rising beside each of them.

She watched a crane swinging its load of rock from a barge across to the center of an island, dropping it with a low rumbling sound. A cloud of dust billowed up. When it cleared, she could see a gang of men swarming over the pile, rolling rocks down onto flat-topped carts so they could be packed behind the encircling wall of concrete.

The idea for an eddy-turbine barrage had been started back when the PSP was in power. They were generators that looked like propeller blades, mounted in narrow nacelles and tethered between the islands where the current spun them as it ebbed and flowed.

Peterborough's post-Warming industrial base had been founded on light engineering and gear production, easily served by the city's electricity allocation from the National Commerce Grid and supplemented by solar panels. But the explosion of manufacturing had begun to attract heavier industries, pushing the power demand close to breaking point. Then after the Second Restoration the newly legitimized Event Horizon arrived. With its wholly modern industries, Peterborough was the obvious choice to supply the cyberfactories with components once Philip Evans brought them ashore. The already vigorous city went into overdrive. But its expanded fortunes brought it up against infrastructure capacity limits. The eddy-turbine barrage was intended to relieve the now chronic energy shortage, one of a dozen projects rushed into construction to cope with the excessive demands Event Horizon was placing.

The traffic was snarled up in front of the Duo. Eleanor slowed and saw a bus in front of the lorry had stopped to let out its passengers. They were all men in rough working clothes, carrying or wearing hard hats. They joined a group of about seventy waiting on the embankment below the road, level with the line of barges. There was a small jetty at the bottom of the embankment. A boat had just cast off, ferrying some of the men out to the islands. She could see a clump of men who'd been left behind on the jetty arguing hotly with a pair of foremen.

"They'll be lucky," Greg murmured as the Duo drove past the crowd milling aimlessly on the embankment.

"Why?"

"Tell you, the eddy-turbine barrage is a council project, right. Unless you're on the city council labor register, there's no way you'll get to work on it."

"Well, why don't they sign on with the council, then?" she asked.

"A lot of people on the dole right now are ex-apparatchiks. And the New Conservative Inquisitors have got their hands full purging the administration staff of any that got left behind after the PSP fell. The government is nervy about them; what with inflation and the housing shortage, a few well-placed PSP leftovers could cause serious grief. So the last thing the council wants is to take them back, especially not on a project as important as this one."

"Why don't you apply to join the Inquisitors?" she teased. "That'd be a regular job."

Greg grinned. "They couldn't afford me." He pointed ahead. "This is the turn. We'll park in Bretton and walk the rest of the way."

She took a left through the old Milton Park golf club entrance. The

Duo powered along the rough cinder tracks lined by hemispherical apartment blocks that'd sprung up to replace the greens, tees, and bunkers. The three-story buildings were self-contained Finnish prefabs, a burnished pewter for easy thermal control. Fast-growing maeosopsis trees dominated the estate, their long branches curved over the tracks, affording a decent amount of shade. There were small allotments ringing each of the silvery hemispheres, laid out with uniform precision.

"Tidy," she remarked, approvingly. "They've got a different attitude here."

"You're not being fair. Think what this'll be like in twenty years' time. Just the same as Berrybut."

"It might. Then again it might not. These people are more in tune with the future; they believe in it."

They drove by a clump of mango trees in full fruit. She saw children playing around the trunks, seemingly immune to the ripe temptation dangling above their heads. "Whatever happened to scrumping?"

"Do you want to move?" Greg asked.

"No." She grinned. "You couldn't live here."

They left the rustic eloquence of the Milton estate behind and slowed, slotting into the chain of vans and rickcarts trundling through the grid maze of the Park Farm industrial precinct. It was made up of bleakly functional sugar-cube factory units with coal-black solar-collector roofs. Nearly half of them sported the Event Horizon triangle and flying V emblem, she saw; most of the rest were overseas companies, some *kombinate* logos. The foreign factories were anathema to the PSP, economic imperialism, but they had to let them in to pay off the massive investment loans that the Tokyo and Zurich finance cartels had made in Peterborough's new housing.

"Do you mean you would move if it wasn't for me?" Greg asked.

"Don't be silly." She was still grinning. He looked like he had bitten something sickly.

"You don't have to come with me to see Royan, you know," he said. "It isn't exactly a picnic at the best of times. It'll only take me an hour or so."

"Oh no," she said loudly. "You don't get out of it that easily, Greg Mandel. Do you realize I know practically nothing about the time between you leaving the Army and meeting me? This is the first glimpse you've ever allowed me into this section of your life."

"You only had to ask."

She shot him a quick glance. "If you'd wanted me to know, you would've told me. And now you're starting to. I'm not sure what it means, but I'm bloody pleased."

"He takes some getting used to," Greg offered. She recognized the tone—regret for the impulse decision to invite her. Just how bad could his friend be?

"You said he was hurt?"

"Very badly. Completely disabled, and burnt. It's not pretty."

"I won't embarrass you, Greg."

"I didn't imagine you would; rather, the reverse. My past is not totally savory."

"Women?"

"No!"

"There were," she corrected demurely. "That sort of knowledge isn't exactly hereditary."

He gave her a weak smile and gave up. Happier, though, she thought. However badly disfigured this Royan turned out to be, she was determined Greg would never be disappointed he'd introduced them.

The narrow streets and iron-red bricks of Bretton were registering through the windscreen. She parked in an old school yard, next to an impressive New Conservative council banner proclaiming its incipient refurbishment as the community's cultural center. The classrooms were all boarded up, and someone had driven surveyor's stakes through the playground.

She got out and looked at him expectantly. He was wearing Levi's and his leather jacket over an olive green T-shirt. She'd dressed in a shapeless navy blue sweatshirt and black jeans; nondescript, as he'd told her. Now she was beginning to realize why; Bretton was a backwater, untouched by the vitality that roared through the rest of the city. The houses she could see all had heavy wooden shutters over the windows, and solid metal security doors.

Greg blipped the Duo's lock.

They were quickly surrounded by about fifteen kids, none of them in their teens yet. Silent, eyes shining bright out of grubby faces.

"Car watch, fella?" piped a prepubescent voice.

"Highway robbery," Greg protested.

The ritual was a relief in an obscure fashion, putting her back on solid ground. Bretton was still plugged into the rest of the city, during the day, at least.

"Five pounds," the lad said.

"I think we'll park in the next street," Greg retorted.

"Four."

"It's very dirty," Eleanor pointed out.

The kids put their heads together.

She exchanged an amused glance with Greg.

"Three," declared the summit. "And we wash it, too."

"Half now?"

"Two now," said the highly affronted ringleader.

He and Greg showed cards, both of them pictures of woe.

"Wonder what Walshaw will make of a three-pound transport expense item?" Greg mused whimsically as the kids moved in on the Duo, two racing away for water and sponges.

She let him guide her into the center of Bretton, pleased he was with her. The place looked rough. She would never have gone into it by herself.

The main street was roofed over by an erratic collage of plastic sheeting, solar cells, corrugated iron, even thatch, all supported by an equally bizarre collection of trusses like telegraph poles and rusting chunks of electricity pylons. It was a twilight world where relief from the sun's heat was tempered by the clouds of arid dust any motion kicked up. The stalls snaking along the pavements lacked the cramped clutter of Oakham's disarray; here the shops were coming back into use. There was a greater emphasis on material goods. Food was appearing in packages again. But no tins yet, she noticed.

They grazed the stalls for stuff Greg said Royan would want. Junk, Eleanor thought. He picked out circuit boards, electric motors, inexplicable mechanical gizmos that were parts of bigger machines, antique watches, the windup sort. Three plastic carrier-bags full, which came to thirty pounds. There was no logic behind it. He seemed delighted when he found a Sanyo VCR. It was lying among Mickey Mouse phones and kettles on a stall that was half lobster tanks, half broken gear. He haggled the owner down to a tenner and departed well pleased.

She began to wonder about Royan again. Strange gifts.

They walked out of Bretton and into the Mucklands Wood estate, and Eleanor decided that Bretton wasn't so bad after all, not compared to this. The fifteen high-rise blocks that had risen out of the dead forest were council-run low-cost housing. They represented the least successful aspect of the city's expansion program. A throw-back to the worst of the 1960s style of instant slums.

They were twenty stories high, identical in every respect right down to the cheap low-efficiency slate-gray solar cells clinging to every square centimeter of surface. Heat shimmer twisted the blocks' harsh geometry, blurring edges; it was as though nature were trying to distort the inhuman ugliness that their desolate lines delineated. The ground between them was a wasteland. Less than half of the estate's intended employment workshops had been built, and those that the council had completed were abandoned, either burned out or gutted. The Trinities gang symbol was scrawled everywhere, brash and sharp, a closed fist gripping a thorn cross, blood dripping. She'd heard of the Trinities, even in the kibbutz. Anti-PSP in a big way.

Mucklands Wood could've been deserted. Nothing moved; worse, there was no sound: there should've been something coming from those hundreds of grimed windows, music or shouting. Their footsteps crunched loudly on the badly rucked limestone path.

She stuck close to Greg's side, eyes darting about nervously. "Is this part of your past?" she asked.

"Briefly. I taught some of the people who live here."

"I never knew you were a teacher."

"Tell you, not your sort of teaching, school and such. I trained them in streetcraft."

"Streetcraft?"

"Techniques to break police ranks, ambush their snatch squads, how to counter the assault dogs. That kind of thing. It's a reversal of the counterinsurgency courses the Army gave me."

"Oh." You wanted to know, she told herself. Her eyes dropped to the crushed yellow stone fragments of the path.

"Stay calm," Greg said quietly.

She glanced at him, puzzled. His eyes had that distant look. He was using his gland.

Then the Trinities boy stepped out from his hiding place behind a crumbling employment workshop wall; he did it fast and smooth, simply *there*. And it was all she could do not to yelp in surprise. He fit her image of an urban predator perfectly, almost a stereotype. Asian, somewhere in his mid-twenties, with hair cropped close, wearing a filthy denim jacket with the arms torn off, slashed T-shirt, and tight leather trousers. Two bowie knives and a compact stun puncher were clipped on to his belt. There was some sort of gear plug in his left ear. A taut strap running round his neck held his throat mike. The Trinities emblem was painted on his jacket.

He leered at her, and she knew he could read her fright. "What the fuck are you arseholes? Hazard junkies?"

There were more Trinities spreading out of the ruins behind her and Greg, dressed in a grab bag of camouflage jackets, jeans, and T-shirts. Faces hard, carrying weapons ranging from knives up to things whose function she couldn't guess. They fanned out, forming a tight blockade.

"Cool it, mate," Greg said levelly and put a bag down, holding out his right hand, very slowly.

The youth's sneer faded when he saw the Trinities card Greg was holding. "Where you get that?"

"Same place as you."

"No shit?" He pulled out his own card and showed it to the one in Greg's open palm. Confusion twisted his features as his card acknowledged Greg's authenticity. "I don't know your face."

"I don't know yours," Greg said.

"Don't smartarse me!" he shouted.

"Greg's one of us, Des," a throaty female voice said from behind Eleanor. Out of the corner of her eye she saw a small figure with spiky mauve hair, wearing tourniquet-tight leopard-skin jeans and a sleeveless black singlet. The girl's age was indefinable; thin-faced, she could've been anywhere between fifteen and thirty. She was cradling a big gauss-pulse carbine casually across one arm. Bandolier straps crossed her flat chest, loaded with red-tipped slugs. Additional power magazines were clipped to her belt. Her face was one big smirk.

"Shut the fuck up, Suzi," shouted the boy confronting them. "Hear me? You could drive a fucking tank through that mouth of yours. This is my turf; I'm the Man here. These bastards could be Party."

Eleanor held on to Greg's forearm with her free hand, pinching. Suppose the card wasn't good enough?

Greg grinned faintly. "Hi, Suzi."

The mauve-haired girl gave him an impish thumbs-up.

Des's face darkened. "You know these?" His forefinger jabbed at Greg.

"Sure," said Suzi. "Greg's been Trinity from way back. Taught me all kindsa things." Her eyes met Eleanor. "Good, too, isn't he?"

Eleanor kept her face perfectly blank, emotions frozen, just as they'd been for all those years in the kibbutz. "Depends on the material he's got to work with, dear." Not the greatest comeback in the world, but pretty bloody good, considering. Even Greg seemed vaguely surprised; approving, too, she suspected. Suzi started laughing.

"So why the big reunion?" Des asked.

"I'm here to see Son," said Greg.

"Christ, Des, let the man through."

"Last fucking warning, Suzi. I'll rip you good if you don't shove it."

"Just ask Father," Greg said. "He'll tell you my credit is good."

"Yeah? So what about her?" Des pointed at Eleanor. "I don't see no card."

"She's with me."

"No shit?"

"Des, the man has our card; that makes him one of us."

The new voice was deep. It didn't seem loud, but it carried to everyone. Authoritative, Eleanor decided. The Trinities were suddenly still and attentive. There was a hint of irritation in the voice, which she was very grateful wasn't directed at her.

When she looked around she saw a tall black man picking his way over the cracked concrete footings of a stillborn employment workshop. She thought he looked about the same age as Greg, moved the same way, too: dangerous grace. Most of his two-meter frame was muscle. He was wearing combat fatigues, clean, with knife-edge creases, a blue beret sporting a single silver star; she recognized it as an old-style British Army regimental insignia. Greg's memory cores at the chalet were full of military trivia like that.

"Shit, yeah, Father. But—," Des began.

"But *nothing!* Man with a card is one of us, always. We don't all dress like crap. You got that?"

Des's head lolled about like a moody nodding doll. "Sure, okay, Father. I just didn't want to take no chances, y'know?"

The tension had evaporated from the other Trinities. Some of them grinned publicly at Des's squirming, led by Suzi.

"I know, boy. Now, is it going to happen again?"

"No, sir."

"I don't hear you so good." The big man's eyes flashed around the circle of Trinities.

"No, sir!" they yelled gleefully.

"Dismissed," he barked. Suzy flipped Greg a jaunty wave as the troop filtered away over the barren artificial moonscape.

Greg and the black man were bear-hugging each other.

Muscles slackened all over Eleanor's body in one convulsive shiver; she hadn't been aware how tightly wired she'd become. So many weapons, and not even Greg could've protected them if that animal Des had got it into his mind to shoot. Mucklands Wood was like nothing she'd heard of before, undiluted anarchy. The cold flush pricking her skin wouldn't abate now until she was back in the safe sanity of the Duo, heading out.

Greg and his friend released each other, both smiling broadly.

"Man, you've been AWOL a long time."

"That's the way it goes." Greg shrugged. "I can't afford to be seen with the likes of you nowadays. I'm a respectable professional now, legitimate."

"Legitimate, shit. Soft, that's what."

"Yeah. Teddy, meet Eleanor. Mate of mine."

Teddy's smile got wider as he swept her with an appraising gaze; then he pulled his beret off in a gesture of hopeless gallantry. "Christ, officers always did steal the best of everything." He offered his hand and drew her knuckles to his lips. The ultimate stamp of approval. It cleared the air marvelously.

"Bit jumpy, aren't they?" Greg said as the three of them walked toward the nearest tower.

"Yeah, sorry about that," Teddy growled. "We had us a chunk of extraparliamentary action against some Party hacks two days back. Couple of my troops got hit. They're just keeping alert. Can't blame 'em for that."

"You expecting some retaliation?" Greg asked.

Teddy shrugged. "Dunno. The war isn't nearly over, Greg. There are tens of thousands of card carriers out there. Smart, well organized, and tough with it. They'll do it to us all over again if we let 'em."

"Are the Blackshirts making any serious moves?"

"No bullshitting, Greg, they are screwing this city. Almost as bad as we did. Trouble most nights; police are stretched to the limit. Inquisitors can't seem to get on top of 'em. Blackshirts have got Walton sewn up tight and hard: nobody in, nobody out unless they say so. We sit and eyeball each other over the A15, and I keep pissing myself over what they're cooking up in there. Son watches what he can, of course, but even he's got limits. What I'd like is some Spiral-armed Mi-24s, go in and beach-head the place, flush the bastards out. Just like the good old days."

"This isn't the good old days, Teddy. We got rid of them, and they aren't coming back. The Blackshirts are just a bunch of zombies, don't know they're dead yet."

"I know how to tell 'em."

"How many of them are in there now?"

"Maybe two hundred regular Blackshirts, five if they called in the hardliners they've got scattered about the county. But it's the rest who give me sleepless nights. Half of 'em still work in city chambers. If they get their act together, they could cause a lotta pain. This inflation is stirring people up, man, lotsa grumbling about the New Conservatives. And you bet they've got it all planned out, fucking

Party always loved plans. I can't fight that, Greg. That ain't physical, man. Physical I can handle. I gotta leave 'em to the New Conservative Inquisitors. More fucking bureaucrats. I tell you, it plain drives me nuts."

"People won't fall for the PSP twice," Eleanor said. "They're not that daft."

Teddy smiled softly down at her. "Gal, I sure as shit hope you're right. Cos it ain't just here; every town in the country is the same. Party ain't got the power no more, but that don't mean they don't want it again. Bad. But whichever way it tilts we're ready for 'em, AKs loaded and Bibles to hand. You bet."

"So how is Goldfinch, anyway?" Greg asked.

Teddy rolled his eyes, sighing in despair. "Crazy as ever. Man, you should hear his sermons now. He's overloading on the vengeance routine, hot for it he is, and slick with it. Keeps the kids in line but good; they know they're fighting for what's right. Time just floats on by when he's in that pulpit. Even been getting civvies from Mucklands coming, too. You want to see him?"

"I'll pass. It's Royan I'm here for."

"Thought so. See you're loaded up with his rubbish."

Two Trinities stood guard at the doors into the tower. They saluted smartly as Teddy walked by, never even giving Eleanor the eye. The hall belied the appearance of the building's external decay, clean and tidy, if somewhat spartan.

She thought she saw Greg wink at a tiny camera lens peeking out of the top of the door frame.

"I won't come up," said Teddy. "Your rap's probably big hush anyway."

"Not from you," Greg said.

"Thanks, man. Anything you need the Trinities for?"

"It isn't shaping up that way. But if it does."

"We're here, Greg, always here. Ain't got no place else to go. You come in and say good-bye before you go."

"Right."

Teddy gave Eleanor another fast smile and disappeared into the old warden's flat. She got a blink of maps and screens on the wall, heavy-duty communication gear on boxy desks, and an enormous color print of Marilyn Monroe.

The lift doors opened, and Eleanor leaned heavily on the rear wall. She let out a hefty relieved breath and gave Greg a hard stare. "Perhaps you were right about me not coming," she said.

"Hey, I apologize about Des; I didn't know that was going to happen." He punched for the top floor, and the lift began to hum upward.

"Maybe you didn't, but I should've. This estate, it saps hope, breeds people like that."

"You're wrong there. Mucklands Wood is one of the safest places to live in Peterborough."

She snorted disbelief.

"Straight up. Providing you're a resident. The Trinities don't tolerate theft and violence against their own."

"Vigilantes."

"Call them what you like. Just don't forget those troops are the ones who stood against the PSP's Constables when the violence was at its worst."

"I'm sorry, Greg. I didn't mean to knock them; I see how deep your involvement goes. And I am glad I came. When my nerves calm down I'll be able to express it better."

"Tell you, you did all right out there. Lot of people would've run."

"Me, too, if I'd thought it would've done any good. Was Teddy being serious about the PSP still being active in Walton?"

"Sure."

"Well, why doesn't the government do something?"

"Like what? We're living under a judicial system now. The rule of law is paramount. Being a member of a political party isn't an offense in this new, fair England. Being in the Trinities, doing what they do, now that is a crime."

She shook her head in wonder. "It's all so wrong. Stupid."

"Yeah. I know."

20

T HE LIFT HALTED WITH KNEE-BENDING suddenness and chimed metallically as the door slid open. The corridor outside was narrow, its walls unpainted breeze blocks; a greening biolum strip ran down the length of the ceiling. Greg and Eleanor walked down to the end, and he knocked on the familiar panelboard door of 206. There was a brief flicker of guilt; he hadn't visited for weeks. Now he'd come because he wanted something.

Qoi opened the door. A thirteen-year-old Chinese girl dressed in a blue silk Mao suit with red and gold fantasy serpents embroidered on her sleeves. She bowed deeply. "He is expecting you," she said in a voice pitched as high as birdsong.

Two-oh-six was a dole family's accommodation module, three rooms and a cupboard-size hall. It was on the corner of the tower, which gave it two windows. Being a bachelor, Royan wasn't entitled to it, but as he wasn't listed on the council's occupancy register they were unlikely to insist he vacate it.

The door to Royan's room slid open and a gush of hot humid air, rich with the smell of humus, spilled out. The interior was a bastard offspring of a botanical garden and an experimental CAD-CAM shop.

Thirty blue-white solaris spots shone down on four rows of red clay troughs that grew clumps of orchids, fuchsias, cyclamen, African violets, gloxinias, and jasmine; tall standard hyacinths towered over them, giving off a thick cloying perfume.

A little wheeled robot scuttled along the alleys between the troughs. It was a patchwork of miscellaneous components, something a surrealist sculptor might've built in a fit of hallucinogenic dementia. A droopy flexible hose that ended in a copper watering-can spout hung out of one side, sprinkling milky water over the sphagnum moss that frothed across the surface of the troughs' loam.

One wall was covered from floor to ceiling in TV screens, not modern flatscreens but the antique glass vacuum tubes of the last century. They'd been taken out of their casings and stacked edge to edge, like bricks, in a metal frame. Some were showing channel programs, some relayed images from cameras dotted around the tower, others had reams of green script unfurling in a constant cascade from top to bottom.

An aluminum tripod stood in the middle of the floor, its camera silently tracking Greg as he ducked around the hanging baskets full of busy Lizzies and fleshy trailing nasturtiums. Twin fiber-optic cables fell from the back of the camera, snaking across the abraded brown lino to Royan's 1960s vintage dentist's chair; they terminated in the black modem balls filling his eye sockets.

Greg sensed the gag reflex of Eleanor's mind as she fought to control her revulsion and shock, barely managing to contain a phobic groan.

He forced himself to grin and nod at Royan's bloated, T-shirted torso. Royan didn't have any legs, and his arms ended just below the elbows, their stumps capped with gray plastic cups that sprouted fiber-optic cables, plugging him into various 'ware cabinets about the room.

All the screens went blank. Then words began to form, meter-high letters, phosphor green, strangely fragmented by the reticulation of black rims.

HELLO, GREG. WHO'S THE LADY?

Royan was fifteen that night six years ago, Greg's last street fight. Set up as a march on Peterborough's council hall protesting about the latest protein rationing. The Trinities were infiltrating the crowd, thirsting for aggro. It was a big crowd, ugly. The Party called out the People's Constables.

People's Constables: a replacement for Special Constables. Greg could just remember them from his youth: weekend policemen who used to dress up in their smart dark uniforms and make an enthusiastic cock-up of directing traffic at the Rutland county fair.

People's Constables were in a different league. A different fucking universe, as far as Greg was concerned. Recruited from the ranks of extreme-left shock troops and black-flag warriors who'd kicked police and beat up press photographers at rallies and marches, it was the biggest case of role reversal since Dracula turned vegan. The People's Constables came under the direct authority of local PSP committees, employed to smash heads whenever people complained about the latest drop in living standards. Basic Party militia.

Their favorite weapon was a bullwhip, with a lash of monolattice carbon. They were taught to go for the legs first.

Royan, flush with the élan of youth, was in the crowd's front rank. He was caught in the first charge. The crowd retreated, leaving their downed behind. People's Constables clustered like angry wasps about each of the inert bodies, slashing with hot fury.

It was the Trinities who retaliated, prepared by Teddy and him, driving the Constables back with a berserker bombardment of molotovs, lighting the night sky with a lethal fallout of fireballs.

Greg had dragged Royan out of the flames, far, far too late. He often wondered if he'd have done the boy a bigger favor by going for a beer instead.

"This is Eleanor," Greg said.

HI, ELEANOR. YOU ARE VERY PRETTY.

"Go ahead," Greg told her. "Just speak normally; he can hear."

Royan's ears were the only sensory input he had; lying in the hospital, his sole means of clinging to sanity. It was a month before he was given an optical modem and another fortnight before he got his forearm axon splice. The axon splice gave him the ability to communicate, the nerve impulses intended for his amputated hand feeding a computer input. Whenever he visited, Greg thought of ghostly transparent hands typing a keyboard in some incorporeal alien dimension.

Eleanor cleared her throat self-consciously. "Hello, Royan. Glad to meet you."

I LIKE YOU. YOU DIDN'T YELL OR ANYTHING.

"Hands off," Greg warned. "She's mine."

LUCKY. LUCKY. LUCKY. GREG IS VERY LUCKY.

"I know. Brought some junk for you."

EVERY LITTLE HELPS.

He directed Eleanor to tip out her bag of redundant gear onto a big flat-top workbench. Royan had fixed up two obsolete General Electric car-factory waldo arms beside the bench, their spot-welding tips replaced with multisegment talonlike grippers. Greg could never understand how the floor took the weight of the brutes.

They telescoped out with juddering clumsy motions and began sorting through the pile. He put the Sanyo VCR down next to the scuffed glass bubble that held Royan's microassembly rig.

JACKPOT. LOTS OF GOOD BITS IN THAT. THANKS TO BOTH OF YOU.

It never mattered what he brought; Royan would eventually find a way to use it. Patiently tinkering with nominally incompatible modules until they could be fused together and incorporated into his cybernetic grotto.

Another of the potpourri robots rolled up to Greg and Eleanor, a Pyrex jug full of steaming coffee balanced on its roof.

HELP YOURSELVES.

Greg sipped gingerly as the waldos whirred away industriously behind him. The coffee was excellent, as always. Royan fiddled it out of the inventory computer of a plush New Eastfield delicatessen, directing its delivery van to a Trinities safe house in Bretton. Eleanor's eyes widened in appreciation as she tasted the brew.

"Job for you," Greg said.

PARTY INVOLVED?

"Don't think so. But the person who's hired me hates them more than you do."

IMPOSSIBLE. WHO IS IT?

"Tell you in a minute. First part of your help is answering questions for me. I need to know the kind of information floating 'round the circuit at the moment. Will you do that?"

SHOOT.

"Have you heard about the blitz against the Event Horizon datanet?"

CHUCKLE CHUCKLE. THE CIRCUIT HAS BEEN BUZZING WITH NOTHING ELSE FOR THE LAST THREE DAYS. BIGGEST DEAL SINCE MINISTRY OF PUBLIC ORDER MAINFRAME WAS CRASHED.

"Who set it up?"

NO IDEA. BIG PUZZLE. RECRUITING NOT DONE THROUGH THE CIRCUIT. ODD ODD ODD.

"Could the hot-rod pack have been foreigners?"

NO. CIRCUIT KNEW ABOUT IT TOO SOON. HINTS DROPPED. NO NAMES, THOUGH. UNUSUAL. IF I'D TAKEN PART, I'D WANT PEOPLE TO KNOW MY HANDLE. THAT KIND OF BURN PUSHES THE GOING RATE UP, MAYBE EVEN DOUBLES IT. SILENCE WOULD HAVE TO BE BOUGHT. LOTS OF MONEY INVOLVED.

"So how would I go about recruiting without using the circuit?"

GOOD QUESTION. TEKMERC WHO HAS WORKED WITH SOLO HOT RODS BEFORE. **SHRUG.** THEY'D HAVE TO HAVE GOOD CONTACTS.

The little robot that'd been watering the troughs ran across the floor to a tap on a wall and eased itself underneath. Water poured into its tank. Greg watched the operation over the rim of his cup. "Tell me about Philip Evans."

HE WAS THE OWNER OF EVENT HORIZON. DIED A MONTH BACK. RICH RICH RICH.

"That's it?"

NO. THERE'S WHOLE MEMORY CORES LOADED WITH BIO-

GRAPHICAL DATA. YOU WANT A PRINTOUT?

"No, thanks. What I meant was, is there anything current?"

OPPOSITION MPS PROTESTED ABOUT COST OF HIS FUNERAL. THAT'S THE LAST ENTRY.

"Okay, I've got a big hush for you. Philip Evans's memories have been stored."

AH-HA.

"Tell me how you'd go about doing that."

BEST WAY WOULD BE IN A BIOWARE NEURAL NETWORK. FERREDOXIN HAS THE POTENTIAL. YOU'D HAVE TO SPLICE EVANS'S SEQUENCING RNA INTO THE NODES, DUPLICATE HIS BRAIN STRUCTURE, THEN SQUIRT HIS MEMORIES INTO THE CORE WITH A NEUROCOUPLING. THE COST WOULD BE UTTERLY LOONY. BUT I SUPPOSE PHILIP EVANS COULD AFFORD IT. AFTER ALL, THAT'S ONE WAY OF TAKING IT WITH YOU. RIGHT?

"Right." Greg thought for a moment. "So all you'd have to know to deduce the nature of Evans's core was that his memories had been translocated, nothing else?"

YES. IT'S BEEN RAPPED ABOUT FOR YEARS. HAMBURG UNIVERSITY LOADED A TURING PERSONALITY INTO THEIR BIOWARE CRUNCHER A FEW YEARS BACK; ITS RESPONSES REALLY WERE INDISTINGUISHABLE FROM A HUMAN'S. ALL IT LACKED WERE BACKGROUND MEMORIES. I RAPPED WITH IT ONCE. CREEPY CREEPY CREEPY.

"If you knew of a bioware core which housed some kind of sophisticated personality responses program, how would you set about disabling it?"

MACRO DATA SQUIRT. FORCE THE PERSONALITY PROGRAM OUT OF THE CORE.

"Did you think of that yourself, or was it something you picked off the circuit?"

ALL MINE, CROSS HEART. IT'S OBVIOUS SOLUTION.

"Does that mean it wasn't a personal attack against Evans?" Eleanor asked. Intense interest had resulted in her coffee going cold. She'd either forgotten, or had accommodated, Royan's state, acting perfectly naturally. There weren't many who could do that.

Royan would've noticed, too; he was an acute observer within his small kingdom. For some obscure reason Greg was delighted. He wanted them to be friends, to approve of each other. It meant a lot to him, although he couldn't say exactly why. The bloody quacks would have lots of psychobabble about resolving the past, no doubt.

He poured himself another coffee. "It's a possibility," he admitted.

"Any hacker observing the Event Horizon datanet would know a lot of management decisions were originating from that one core. Whether or not they knew it was Philip Evans himself, I'm not sure."

IF IT WASN'T FOR VENGEANCE, THEN IT WAS PROBABLY CONNECTED WITH EVENT HORIZON'S GIGACONDUCTOR. AM I RIGHT OR WHAT?

"You're right." Greg wasn't surprised; Royan kept himself well plugged into the circuit, trading data whenever it was to his advantage. "Philip Evans believes the blitz was an attempt at a spoiler, reducing Event Horizon's ability to market the gigaconductor by removing his managerial experience. So how did you find out about the gigaconductor?"

EVENT HORIZON HAVE A GIGACONDUCTOR DEVELOPMENT CONTRACT WITH THE MINISTRY OF DEFENSE.

"My God," said Eleanor. "Does everyone know about the country's military secrets?"

NOT NECESSARILY. BUT THE GIGACONDUCTOR IS SUCH A BIG DEAL, IT'S IMPOSSIBLE TO KEEP IT UNDER WRAPS. WEAPONS APPLICATION PROJECT DETAILS HAVE BEEN LOADED INTO THE MINISTRY OF DEFENSE MAINFRAME. THAT MAKES THEM AVAILABLE TO PEOPLE LIKE ME, AND THERE ARE A LOT OF PEOPLE LIKE ME. CHUCKLE CHUCKLE. WELL NOT QUITE.

Greg considered that; Event Horizon's gigaconductor wasn't half as secret as Morgan Walshaw had believed, yet the Ministry of Defense had been brought in only after the patent was filed. He still couldn't believe a *kombinate* would bother with a spoiler like the blitz, not after the chance of filing their own patent had been lost.

"When did you find out about the gigaconductor?"

THIRD WEEK IN DECEMBER. MINISTRY OF DEFENSE BEGAN A NEW ULTRASECURE FILE AT THE START OF THE MONTH. I WAS INTERESTED. TOOK A COUPLE OF DAYS TO BURN.

He used the teaspoon to lift the skin off his coffee, running the dates through his mind. If he assumed another hot rod had burned open the ministry file around the same time as Royan, then the blitz could well be a *kombinate* operation. But how had they discovered the NN core existed? He was back to the question of the mole's existence again. "Could you pull data from Event Horizon's security division memory cores without tripping any alarms?"

IF YOU ASKED ME TO, I MIGHT CHANCE IT. BUT I'D HATE TO HAVE TO TRY. WHAT DID YOU WANT PULLED?

"The Zanthus microgee-furnace production-monitor programs."

WOW! WEIRD WEIRD WEIRD. ANY MEMORY CORE CAN BE
BURNT OPEN, BUT SOME ARE MORE DIFFICULT THAN OTHERS.
EVENT HORIZON IS MOST EQUAL OF ALL.

"Do you know anyone else who could do it?"

THERE ARE ABOUT FOUR OR FIVE OF US WHO COULD WRITE
MELT PROGRAMS GOOD ENOUGH. BUT IF YOU WENT TO THE
CIRCUIT WITH THAT REQUEST, IT WOULD COST YOU TWENTY
THOUSAND NEW STERLING, MINIMUM.

Greg grunted; the answer was about what he expected. Kendric
could afford that, no messing, but would he have bothered to asset-
strip Event Horizon if he hadn't known about the gigaconductor?
There were still too many unknowns. "Does anyone on the circuit
know how the blitz ties in with the Merlin failure?"

WHAT MERLIN FAILURE?

"That answers that," he muttered in an undertone. He gave Royan
a quick outline of the space probe's breakdown. "Intuition tells me
they're connected. But I can't see how. I'm just not convinced about
the validity of the blitz. What could it hope to achieve?"

DUNNO. THE AMOUNT OF EFFORT EXPENDED MOUNTING THE
BLITZ IS COMPLETELY OUT OF PROPORTION TO THE DAMAGE IT
WOULD CAUSE. EVENT HORIZON LOST A LOT OF DATA IN THE
RESULTANT DATANET SHUTDOWN, BUT NOTHING CRITICAL.
THAT IMPLIES VENGEANCE.

The green letters with their subliminal flicker jolted him. He shook
his head at his own slowness. The blitz had exactly the kind of protective layers as the memox-crystal spoiler, each one a cover for the
one underneath, and progressively more complex, more subtle.
Kendric di Girolamo's method of operation. A bright sensation of
satisfaction rose up; identical patterns and intuition now both focused on Julia's nemesis. That coincidence was far too much to ignore. Except . . . Kendric was smart. He wouldn't use the same pattern twice. Unless that was what he wanted people to think.

Greg sipped the last of his coffee reflectively; there were limits to
paranoia. Go with your intuition, he told himself, at least you know
you trust that.

SO WHAT DO YOU RECKON, HOLMES?

"Insufficient data. You want to do me a huge favor?"

FIND OUT WHO WAS IN ON THE BLITZ?

"Got it in one."

GRIN. SILENCE IS GOLDEN AT THE MOMENT, SO IT'LL MEAN
HACKING HOT RODS, ACCESSING THEIR MEMORY CORES TO SEE
IF THERE'S ANY REFERENCE TO THE BURN. AND IT'LL HAVE TO BE

THE SOLO HOT RODS. THAT COTERIE WEREN'T VIRGINS. OOPS, PARDON MY FRENCH, ELEANOR.

She looked straight at the camera, brushing loose strands of titian hair from her face, and gave him a warm smile.

"If that's too big a deal for you, I can bring some help in from Event Horizon's security division," Greg said solemnly.

HOW SOON DO YOU WANT THE ANSWER, SMARTARSE?

Greg saluted the camera with his empty coffee mug. "Soon as possible, if not before."

Royan's mouth parted a slit, revealing bucked teeth yellowed by the pulped vegetable mush Qoi fed him. His version of a smile. THE HUNT IS ON.

A whole load of apprehension lifted from Greg. Nobody hunted better than Royan or had more practice. And he took it seriously, deadly serious. Royan had monitor programs stashed in every major public data core in the country, sleepers watching for key words and names. Out of the four hundred seventy People's Constables on duty the night of the riot there were less than two hundred left alive. The boy had been hunting them out ever since he plugged his axon splice into a gear terminal: seeking out their home addresses, tracking them through promotions, transfers, redundancies. Greg and the rest of the Trinities were told where to find them, what they looked like now, at what point in their daily routine they were most vulnerable.

Greg had personally taken out sixteen for him.

"Thanks," Greg said.

SNEAKY PRESENT FOR YOU, GREG. YOU MIGHT HAVE A USE FOR IT. GIVE ME YOUR CARD.

One of the waldos stretched out across the work top, claw opening. He fumbled in his Levi's pocket and fished out the Event Horizon card. The tarnished silver metal closed about it, and the arm retracted, rotating on its vertical axis, then slid out again, pushing the card into a slot on one of the gear consoles banked up behind the flat-top bench.

HEY, GREG, DO YOU KNOW HOW MUCH CREDIT THIS BUGGER CAN TRANSFER, QUESTION MARK, TRIPLE EXCLAMATION MARK.

"Yeah, so go careful."

TRUST TRUST TRUST. WHERE'S IT ALL GONE? PUT YOUR RIGHT HAND ON THE BLUE SQUARE.

He leaned across the bench as a square lit up on a gear module, and did as he'd been told, pressing with his fingertips. Nothing visible happened.

I'VE BEEN WRITING THIS FOR THE TRINITIES. THOUGHT THEY MIGHT BE ABLE TO USE IT TO GAIN UNLAWFUL ENTRY.

The card popped out of the slot like a slice of toast. Greg snagged it neatly.

THUMBPRINT WILL ACTIVATE CREDIT AND ID CONFIRMATION AS USUAL, LITTLE-FINGER PRINT WILL ACTIVATE DATA-CRASH CANCER. ITS SQUIRT SHOULD BOLLOCKS UP GEAR LOCKS AND TAKE OUT ENTIRE MEMORY CORES.

Greg looked at the card. Out of the two of them it was rapidly becoming the more useful.

YOU'LL BOTH COME BACK TO VISIT ME, WON'T YOU?

The screens blanked out, then PLEASE appeared in bright scarlet letters, fuzzy round the edges.

"Yes," Eleanor said quickly, and looked at Greg for confirmation.

"Yes," he echoed.

I'D LIKE THAT, said the letters, reverting to green.

One of the waldos slid out in front of Eleanor and opened its claw with the panache of a conjurer producing the coin that'd just been swallowed. There was a Trinities card resting in the mechanical palm. FOR YOU, MY NEW PRETTY LADY FRIEND. THE TROOPS OUTSIDE WON'T GIVE YOU ANY HASSLE IF YOU SHOW THEM THIS. SO YOU DON'T HAVE TO WAIT FOR HIM TO BRING YOU.

"You do know him well, don't you?" Eleanor said coyly, her eyes dancing with amusement.

The camera whined as the lens twisted around, zooming in for a close-up on Eleanor's face. She held her poise without flinching.

WE CAN HAVE A GOSSIP. IT'S BEEN YEARS SINCE I HAD A REALLY GOOD GOSSIP ABOUT SOMEONE BEHIND THEIR BACK. IT'LL BE FUN. THE STORIES I CAN TELL YOU ABOUT HIM.

"You've got a date."

"Hey," Greg protested.

YEAH. SNEER. YOU GOT A COMPLAINT?

He held his hands up. "I'll be back, too."

GOOD. MISS YOU, GREG. BAD.

"Promise," he mouthed to the camera.

Qoi materialized silently at their side and showed them out.

JULIA TOOK THE BROAD STAIRS of Wilholm Manor two at a time, her burst of speed nearly skidding her feet from under her when she reached the hall's polished marble tiles. She pushed up the heavy iron latch on the front door. Rachel came out of the old butler's pantry, looking miffed; it should have been Steven on duty, but he'd called in sick. The disapproving expression fell from her face to be replaced by her usual natural diligence.

Julia enjoyed the momentary lapse. So Rachel was human after all. Wonder who was in there with her?

She pushed the big oak door open and went outside. It was raining lightly, drops falling vertically from a high, almost nebulous cloud sheet. The air seemed solid with humidity. She stood under the portico, heart pumping strongly.

You in a hurry, girl?

Julia clamped down on her racing thoughts as the silent voice whispered into her brain, resenting the way her grandfather was interpreting her actions. He'd loaded a personality package, coded OtherEyes, into one of her processor nodes, digesting her body's senses in real time, feeding the formatted sensations back to his NN core.

I'd go crazy otherwise, he'd pleaded. *Camera images are no substitute, flat and insipid; I'm human, damn it. I need human touch and smell, heat and cold. Not all the time, just the occasional reminder. Keep in touch with the real world.*

So she'd acquiesced, and still wasn't sure if it was such a good idea. She'd carefully reviewed the processor node's basic management program, making sure its neural-interface flow was strictly one way. Acceptance only. None of her thoughts could seep in for him to examine. Not bloody likely. But despite the precautions, it meant having Grandpa chuntering away inside her mind the whole time OtherEyes was loaded. There were advantages—his insights could be illuminating—but he did *moan* so.

From her position she could see a pair of forlorn-looking wheelbarrows that'd been abandoned down at the far end of the garden, piled high with weeds. She didn't blame the gardeners for taking a break from the heat and damp. She was already perspiring under her white cotton summer dress. Her skin itched.

Too bloody hot it is, Juliet.

Show me your April, she asked, on some fey impulse.

For an instant the trees lost their leaves, their branches becoming thick black crockery cracks superimposed on a band of somber gray landscape. There were no flowers in the garden, though the shrubs were covered in a crop of glossy scarlet berries. Steam shifted to clammy mist, cold water droplets clinging to branches and grass. Icy air cut through her thin dress. Small bedraggled birds pecked for worms in the slushy gravel. A remote style of beauty, lonely.

The strange apparition withered. She was rubbing her bare arms against the lingering impression of chill.

Now those were the days, her grandfather said happily.

I suppose.

But she wouldn't want it to happen very often, say every five years.

The Duo rolled out of the warm drizzle and pulled up close to the portico. There was someone sitting in the passenger seat. Julia smiled a welcome.

Isn't he a bit old, Juliet?

Her smile locked.

Greg is a nice man, Grandpa. He doesn't patronize me like everyone else. You've no idea what a relief that is.

She was going to have to go back over the processor node's inputs; he was learning far too much of her private self, that aspect of personality that should remain secret. Her own body language was playing traitor.

Greg got out of the Duo, scurrying quickly around the rear of the car for the shelter of the portico. He shook out the collar of his leather jacket, nodded at Rachel. He wasn't bothering with suits any more, Julia noted. Levi's and T-shirts were more agreeable on him, anyway; he'd never looked quite right in a suit, caged. It was great to think he felt familiar enough around her to relax, let her see his real self. Most people were so guarded with her.

"Hello, Greg. Was it something important?" Or did you come just to see me? Unlikely, but . . .

Lovesick. Your knees have gone all watery, Juliet. Mental laughter.

Grandpa, if you don't stop that right now, I'll cancel the link. First and final warning, okay?

No bloody sense of humor, that's your trouble, m'girl.

Greg was looking at her strangely, head slightly cocked as though he were concentrating on a faint voice. "Could be," he said pleasantly. "Brought someone to see you and your grandfather."

The woman getting out of the Duo's passenger seat, with some difficulty, was about fifty, Julia thought as she sized her up. Dressed in a pleated maroon skirt and a flower-print blouse under a woolen jacket, a double string of pearls around her neck. Her fading fair hair had been given a light perm. Julia didn't quite know what to make of her. She certainly couldn't be Greg's girlfriend. Surely? Perhaps his aunt.

Now there's a candidate for a healthy diet if ever I saw one.

It took a great deal of willpower not to clench her fists. And what must Greg be seeing in her mind?

Shut! Up! Julia shouted into the node.

"This is Gabriel Thompson," Greg was saying. "My Mindstar colleague."

Julia forgot all about the exasperating intrusion in her mind, suddenly excited and fearful in a way she couldn't explain. She opened her mouth.

"Yes, I can," said Gabriel.

Julia gaped, elated, then suspicious. Recovering her composure. "You must know that is the first thing everyone is going to ask you by now," she countered.

"True." And there was a burst of humor in the woman's deep-set leathery eyes. Gone almost before it registered.

She looks so sad, Julia thought. Haunted.

If her ability is real, then she will be able to see her own death approaching. How would you feel about that, Julia?

"There must be an easy way of proving you can see the future," Julia persisted as the three of them walked up the stairs toward the study. Rachel had gone back to the butler's pantry, satisfied Greg and Gabriel posed no threat.

"I can give you a short-term localized prediction, but you must remember that you possess the ability to alter that future. Nothing is a certainty. For instance, I could tell you what I see you eating for dinner tonight, but it would be singularly pointless as you could order the cook to prepare something else just to prove the prediction wrong."

"So make it something I won't alter." She glanced at Greg to see if he approved of her badgering. He must've understood how intrigued people would be.

Eighth time you've looked at him.

Wipe OtherEyes.

The abrupt silence was like an empty hole, torn out. She felt a fragment of guilt; this was Grandpa she was punishing. But he shouldn't abuse the privilege. He *had* to learn that.

Gabriel's eyes had that distant focus, just like Greg's. As though the gland lifted them out of this universe for a while.

"This afternoon, four o'clock, you'll get a call from your precision cybernetics division in London. The manager will submit the last quarter returns, and he'll keep emphasizing the efficiency figures; they're up by five percent."

"All right," Julia said enthusiastically. Four o'clock, an hour and a half: she could wait that long. Typical of regional managers to fish for compliments.

"Unless you call him first and ask for the report," Gabriel pointed out.

"I won't. I think I believe anyway. You'd never be so bold if you weren't certain."

Greg and Gabriel both seemed content with her answer. She showed them into the study, walking straight to her seat at the head of the table.

"Look, Grandpa, Greg's come to visit us, and he's brought a friend."

Julia noticed Gabriel's reticence as she sat down. The woman's gaze never left the black column on the table as she perched on the front edge of the wooden seat. If she really could see the future, how could anything shock her?

Julia listened to her grandfather saying hello in a civil tone, giving away nothing. Then Greg started to report on his progress to date. Her eyes wandered while he was speaking, and she saw Gabriel was using the gland again.

"Bugger!" Philip Evans exclaimed when Greg had finished. "That fucking Ministry of Defense, more bloody trouble than it's worth. I never knew it leaked that badly. The whole hacker circuit, you say?"

" 'Fraid so. They all know you've cracked the gigaconductor and been awarded development contracts."

"So it could be any of the *kombinates*," Julia said. "You've no leads."

"A lot of negatives, which is cutting down the field considerably. At the moment my personal suspicion is Kendric di Girolamo and a highly placed mole. Place as much emphasis on that as you wish."

"Vengeance." Philip Evans sounded skeptical. "If he's that twisted, why not try to assassinate Juliet here? Got to be cheaper than buying eight hot-rod hackers and their silence. She's well protected, but no security is proof against a professional hardliner tekmerc, not when he's striking out of the blue."

She shrank a little inside, compressed by steely arctic fingers. It's only theory, she told herself. Don't let it bother you. But there was no need for him to say it quite so bluntly.

"I don't know," said Greg. "I still don't understand why Kendric allowed Julia to buy him out. Even if he didn't know about the gigaconductor when he started the memox-spoiler operation, he certainly did by the time she confronted him."

"I see what you mean," Julia said. "We filed the patent on November fifteenth and informed the Ministry of Defense on the seventeenth. Even assuming Kendric doesn't have a mole feeding him data, he ought to have known it existed by the end of the year at the latest, like your contact did, which would've given him months to work out the implications before I hit him with the buyout. He should've held on for all he was worth, risked family displeasure over Siebruk Orbital. For those stakes they would've forgiven him anything. In fact, now that he has withdrawn the di Girolamo house, they're going to be furious with him when I go public with the gigaconductor and they realize what they've lost out on." The idea of Kendric giving up bothered her deeply. Kendric was smart and crafty. That bastard would have something in reserve. She knew he would.

Gabriel stirred, blinking rapidly. "Wilholm's staff are clear," she announced.

"From what?" Julia asked.

"From knowing your grandfather is stored in this NN core. They hadn't put it together like your father."

Julia knew her cheeks were reddening at the reminder and didn't care, not any more. "How do you know?"

"I scanned the possible futures where Greg interviews each of them this afternoon; he wouldn't find any culpability. Oh, except that your gardeners are flogging ten percent of Wilholm's vegetables on the village market."

"Little buggers," Philip squawked.

"Oh, shush, Grandpa. I know all about that."

"How come?"

"I'm mistress of the manor, remember? It's my job to know." She turned back to Gabriel. "I thought you said nothing about the future was certain?"

"Not in the future, no," said Gabriel. "But if the staff had known about the NN core and passed on the data, that would mean they'd pieced the knowledge together in the past; it's already happened, an immutable fact."

"Yeah . . . right." It sounded kind of screwy, but the nodes confirmed the logic. Providing you believed in precognition in the first place.

"That just leaves Dillan, then," Philip said, and Julia knew that tone of voice well enough. They were heading for another blazing row once Greg and Gabriel left. She wondered if Gabriel had seen it already. The woman's alleged ability was disturbing. It might be a good idea to be out on Tobias at four o'clock.

"Not quite," Greg pointed out. "We still have the whole NN core team to interview tomorrow, as well as the security division headquarters staff."

"I know all the NN core team; they're good people, boy. No worries on that score. It'll be Dillan, or someone in security, or even this mole of yours. You'll see."

"The NN core team still have to be checked off," Greg said, polite but unyielding. "Process of elimination; old procedure, but it can't be improved on."

"Don't interfere with the experts, Grandpa. Isn't that what you always say?"

"Juliet, you're impossible!" Even with his construct voice he managed to convey affection.

A truce. She pulled a face at the NN core.

"What about you, Gabriel?" Philip asked. "Can't you see the results of these interviews Greg is going to hold?"

"Sorry. That's tomorrow morning, and several kilometers away. Can't stretch that far."

"Well, what about if Greg was to interview Dillan? Today, here?"

Gabriel stiffened. "Your son has no idea whether or not he told anybody. He is only aware of your translocation on odd occasions," she said reproachfully. The implication for responsibility hovered almost tangibly in the air.

Julia realized that Gabriel was more redoubtable than her appearance suggested. Like Greg, the gland gave her total access to a soul's weakness. Did Grandpa have a soul? That old-style-April chill closed around her.

Primate Marcus was preaching to her again, hand on Bible, scorning hubris and human greed. Temptations that would result in your ultimate downfall. Sweet Jesus had shown people the way by rejecting both.

And Grandpa certainly hadn't abandoned anything.

"What about the NN core?" Greg asked.

"Yes," said Gabriel. "Though it could go either way."

"What's that supposed to mean, m'dear?" Philip Evans asked.

"As I explained to Julia, the future is never definite," Gabriel said. "There are a multitude of alternate possibilities. The best indicator of certainty is when a lot of those futures hold a common theme. You understand? It's like gambling. If two-thirds of the possible futures which I see have it raining tomorrow, then it will most likely rain. But it isn't an absolute. The further into the future, the more hazy my predictions."

"So what's going to go both ways?" Julia asked raptly.

"A second attack on your grandfather's NN core. I'd say there was a sixty percent probability it will happen."

"Does this attack succeed?" Philip asked.

"Not if you take simple preventive measures," Gabriel said. "Forewarned is forearmed. Do you believe me?"

"Damn right I do, m'dear. What sort of attack, a data-squirt blitz like last time?"

Gabriel paused, frowning. Ice-maiden formidable. Julia had the impression a lot of it was theater, like a gypsy's crystal ball. Overawing the superstitious peasants.

"A Trojan program. It's indexed as an ordinary factory-quota update, but once inside your filters it multiplies like a hot rabbit, expanding to take up all the available memory capacity."

"When?"

"If it happens, it'll be sometime on Tuesday morning. Of course, the nearer we get to the event, the more specific I can get, and I can also give you more accurate odds."

"I want to know every change, m'dear. No matter what time of the day or night, you get in contact with me whenever those odds shift."

"Can't you tell us who sends the Trojan?" Julia asked plaintively.

"I'm sorry. Wherever the origin of the attack is, it's not close to Wilholm."

Julia sat back and sighed wanly.

"Whoever they are, they seem determined," Greg said thoughtfully.

"It has to be a personal vendetta," Julia said. "That means Kendric's behind it, and the mole exists, doesn't it?"

"Possibly," Greg said. He seemed strangely reluctant to commit himself. But she knew. It was Kendric. She'd always known. There was almost a feeling of contentment accompanying the conviction.

"I'd like you to get some of your security programmers hooked into the Event Horizon datanet," Greg said. "See if they can back-track the hot rods if this second attack does happen."

"Good idea, boy. I'll get Walshaw on it."

Greg and Gabriel rose. He gave Julia an encouraging smile. "Don't worry; it's just a question of waiting to see which lead takes us to the organizer. After tomorrow's interviews our options should be clear enough to start making some headway."

She couldn't draw as much comfort from his words as she would've liked. The promises were too vague. But at least he was trying to help her, some part of him cared.

The two of them departed, leaving her alone in the study with the feverishly active memories of a dead man and the hot rain swatting the window.

22

HALF PAST TWO IN THE morning found Greg lying on his back, hands behind his head, staring up at the blackness that hid the bedroom ceiling. He could hear the reservoir's wavelets swishing on the shore outside.

The deer had come to drink under cover of the night, venturing out of the new persimmon plantation at the back of Berrybut spinney. His fading espersense perceived their minds as small cool globes of violet light, timid and alert. Eleanor had been entranced with them for the first couple of weeks after she'd moved in, waiting up each night to see them slip furtively out of the trees.

The afternoon rain had lowered the temperature appreciably, but sleep was impossible. Intuition was running riot inside his cranium, even though he'd ended the gland's secretions. Swirling random thoughts clumped together, producing an image. It didn't matter how many times he told himself to forget it; the image just kept reforming. The same one, over and over.

Eleanor let out a soft hum and wriggled slightly. He hoped he featured in that dream.

No good. He wasn't going to sleep.

Greg went through the usual mincing motions as he slid gingerly out of bed, making far more noise than if he'd just done it properly. Eleanor sighed again. He pulled the duvet up round her bare shoulders, then put on his toweling robe and went into the lounge.

Through the chalet's front windows he could see the moonlight painting the checkerboard pattern of Hambleton peninsula's meadows and orange groves in mezzotint contrasts. Silent and serene. Strange how remote it seemed from the kind of global-class corporate battles fought only a few kilometers away in Peterborough. He sometimes wondered if a day would come when he wouldn't be able to leave, giving up on the external world and all its conflicts. And who would really be hurt if he did let go? Certainly not Eleanor.

Greg closed his eyes, but instead of Rutland Water's landscape there was only the taunting image.

Not this time, then.

He disconnected the Event Horizon terminal's voice input, opting for the silence of the touchpad keyboard so Eleanor wouldn't be wakened. That done, he began to set up a link to Gracious Services.

Even Royan wasn't clear on where the circuit's name originated, but under its auspices England's hackers would pull data from any 'ware memory core on the planet—for a price.

Greg logged into Leicester University's mainframe and entered a cutoff program that'd disengage the instant anyone tried to backtrack his call. Royan had written it for him years ago. He couldn't afford to be anything but ultracircumspect dealing with Gracious Services. He didn't want any of its members uncovering his own identity and selling the information in turn—the ultimate irony. The average hacker had a moral code that made an alley tomcat a paragon of virtue by comparison. After confirming the cutoff's validity he routed the link through another cutoff in the Ministry of Agriculture onto the Dessotbank in Switzerland, crediting it with a straight ten thousand pounds New Sterling direct from Event Horizon's central account.

After that it was just a question of establishing two more cutoffs, one in Bristol city council's finance mainframe, then on through the CAA flight control in Farnborough, and dialing the magic number.

Gracious Services had a nonsense number; there was no phone on the end of it. But every English Telecom exchange computer in the country had been infiltrated with a catchment program that would slot the caller directly into the circuit.

Never, not once, in all the years they were in power, did the PSP manage to tap the Gracious Services circuit or expunge the catchment program from Telecom's exchange computers. They tapped individual phones and caught people using Gracious Services that way, but that was all. Rumor had it the card carriers used the circuit themselves on occasion.

The terminal's flatscreen snowstormed for a second then printed:

WELCOME TO GRACIOUS SERVICES.
WE AIM TO PLEASE.
DATA FOUND OR MONEY RETURNED.
NO ACCESS TOO BIG OR TOO SMALL.
JUST REMEMBER OUR CARDINAL RULE: DO NOT ASK
FOR CREDIT!!!
PLEASE ENTER YOUR HANDLE.

Greg typed THUNDERCHILD, his old Army call sign.

GOOD MORNING, THUNDERCHILD. YOUR UMPIRE IS WILDACE. WHAT SERVICE DO YOU REQUIRE?

PHYSICAL LOCATION OF INDIVIDUAL.

OK, THUNDERCHILD. I'VE GOT SEVEN HOT RODS RARING TO BURN FOR YOU. IS THIS GOING TO BE A GLOBAL SEARCH?

I BELIEVE THE INDIVIDUAL TO BE IN EUROPE, QUITE POSSIBLY IN ENGLAND.

THIS IS THE WAY IT IS, THUNDERCHILD. A EUROPE-WIDE SEARCH WILL COST YOU FOUR THOUSAND FIVE HUNDRED NEW STERLING. IF WE GET A NEGATIVE RESULT, THAT MEANS YOUR TARGET ISN'T IN EUROPE. IT'LL ONLY COST YOU TWO THOU-SAND. IF YOU WANT US TO RUN A GLOBAL SEARCH, IT WILL COST YOU SEVEN THOUSAND. OK?

RUN A EUROPEAN SEARCH FOR ME, WILDACE.

YOU GOT IT. I HOLD THE MONEY. I DECIDE HOW IT'S SPLIT.

SOUNDS GOOD.

DEPOSIT FOUR THOUSAND FIVE HUNDRED POUNDS NEW STERLING INTO TIZZAMUND BANK, ZURICH, ACCOUNT NUMBER WRU2384ASE.

Greg entered Wildace's number, authorizing the transfer from his Dessotbank account.

OK, THUNDERCHILD, YOUR CREDIT IS GOLDEN. WHO IS THE TARGET?

The image coalesced in his brain, rock solid, grinning arrogantly, and he typed KENDRIC DI GIROLAMO.

Greg's imagination painted the picture for him; seven people scat-tered across England, dark anonymous figures hunched over their customized terminals, mumbling into throat mikes, touch-typing, watching data flash through cubes. It was a race: the first one who satisfied Wildace they had the correct answer would get the money, less Wildace's commission. Reputations were made on the circuit.

It took twenty or thirty runs, successful runs, before anyone could even think about going solo.

Royan had trained himself on the Gracious Services circuit. He could've gone solo, running data snatches against *kombinates* for the tekmercs. But, of course, he had a different set of priorities.

Greg sat back, wondering if he had time for a drink. He didn't have a clue how long the run was going to take. He didn't use the circuit often; the last time had been almost a year ago, tracing a money sink set up by Simon White's accountant.

Whatever he asked for, Gracious Services invariably produced an answer. Their only failure to date had been confirming whether or not Leopold Armstrong had died the day the PSP was overthrown. They weren't alone. New Conservative Inquisitors had drawn a blank. Even the combined ranks of the Mindstar Brigade vets had been stumped. Most people thought he was dead, including the surviving top-rank apparatchiks. Possibly trying to create a martyr, Greg thought. Two years was an impossibly long time to remain hidden if he was alive.

There had been very little of Downing Street left after the electron-compression warhead had detonated. The explosion created a deep glass-walled crater one hundred meters across, flattening every building for five hundred meters beyond its rim. Hundreds of silver rivulets scarred its slopes, molten metal that had solidified as it trickled downward. The only human remnants were individual carbon molecules, mingling with the oily black pall clotting the air overhead.

It was the first time an electron compression warhead had been used in anger. A technology capable of producing a megaton blast without the radiation and fallout of fission weapons. Rich man's nuke, the tabloid channels called it.

So far only two nations had demonstrated they had the capability to construct such devices: China and America. Both had denied involvement, naturally. Rumors of other nations conducting secret tests and having hidden capabilities Greg dismissed outright. In today's world, still jittery after the recession and a hundred small, nasty bush wars, if you had the means to defend yourself you made damn sure everyone knew about it, especially as electron compression meant you could use overwhelming force even within your own borders with no worry of radioactive contamination. New mutual defense organizations were being formed now, replacing the old twentieth-century groupings. Asia and Africa were still at the negotiating table, trying to thrash out a cohesive policy. China was busy signing up its smaller neighbors and putting immense pressure on Japan to join. And Japan would never agree to shelter under a Chinese umbrella if they had their own electron compression devices. The United States was leading the Pacific Treaty Nations, which was a big comment on shifting economic and geopolitical forces. Greater Europe was still America's single largest trading partner, but only by a few percentage points. The White House's attention was primarily focused to the west these days, desperate to bring a measure of stability to the Pacific basin. In reflex, Germany and the Russian Republic were frantically revitalizing and expanding the Northern European Alliance, the two of them pressing ahead with a joint high-priority electron compression development project. If they had it today, they'd trumpet the fact, and no messing. Two years ago they definitely didn't have it.

No, it had to be either America or China. Greg could never quite decide, not even with his intuition. America, with its multitude of dark agencies, was the obvious choice. He really couldn't see why China would give one to the urban predator gang that claimed to have smuggled it into Downing Street. Although, there again, in the fantasy land in which clandestine operations seemed to be conducted, who knew what motives fueled policy? Certainly the New Conservative–appointed inquiry team had never made much of an effort to find out the warhead's origin. Surprise surprise.

His intuition had also failed miserably when it came to the Armstrong question. Greg had made his own contribution to Mindstar's effort to confirm the president's death, drawing a complete blank. Perhaps his feelings impinged on his intuition too much. He wished Armstrong dead dead dead, burning in Dante's hell for evermore.

He gazed out of the chalet lounge's window while the unbidden reflections drifted past, bringing the associated emotions back with them, the elation and the suffering. Flames and laughter.

Seventeen minutes after Gracious Services began the search, his terminal's flatscreen came alive again.

GOT HIM FOR YOU, THUNDERCHILD. KENDRIC DI GIROLAMO CURRENTLY ON BOARD HIS YACHT *MIRRIAM,* DOCKED AT PE-TERBOROUGH'S NEW EASTFIELD MARINA, BERTH TWENTY-SEVEN.

THANK YOU, WILDACE, Greg typed.

NO PROBLEM. HOT ROD HANDLED BLUEPRINCE BURNED HIM FOR YOU. SAYS IF YOU WANT ANOTHER RUN HE'LL BE HAPPY TO OBLIGE, FEE NEGOTIABLE.

I'LL REMEMBER.

PLEASURE TO DO BUSINESS WITH YOU, THUNDERCHILD. WILDACE SIGNING OFF.

So Kendric was in Peterborough, was he? Close to the action. How convenient.

Greg made one final call, then headed back to the bedroom.

23

THE SHEER NUMBER OF EVENT Horizon facilities springing up in Peterborough after the Second Restoration, coupled with Wilholm's proximity, meant that the company had to establish a large finance division in the city. Julia used it as her de facto head office, so it was only natural that Morgan Walshaw should use it for his security division's command center as well. It was a temporary arrangement while both divisions waited for their respective custom-built headquarters to be completed. The building they had moved into for the interregnum was the old Thomas Cook office block, situated at the top of a small bluff overlooking the Ferry Meadows estuary, on the western side of the town. In doing so they'd ousted the PSP Minorities Enhancement Council staff who had occupied it ever since currency restrictions put an end to the glories of package holidays.

After Event Horizon had taken over, the company engineers immediately set about building a concrete embankment along the bluff to halt the erosion that was eating toward the foundations. At the base of it they planted three small lagoons of gene-tailored coral to house a set of tidal turbines that powered the finance division's gear. Seeing a building that wasn't plastered with the glossy black squares of solar cells came as something of a novelty.

The security office inside, which Greg and Gabriel had been loaned for interviewing the NN core team, was a cramped cell of a room with a metal table and three plastic chairs. It looked out toward Longthorpe, where gulls strutted about on the partially exposed mudflats.

Emily Chapman left the office without looking around, her rigid back conveying stark disapproval. She had every right to be upset, Greg acknowledged. He was actually doing the interviews with the NN core team. He'd thought it politic; Gabriel had dropped into one of her best prickly sulks at having to examine his possible interviews with over 250 of the security staff in the building and told him to take a share of the load himself for a change. But she could've timed it better.

The trouble was, Philip Evans had been right: the NN core team were all grade-A people—keen, loyal, honest, hardworking, churned out by Event Horizon's blandification program. They hadn't taken kindly to his accusations.

"Shit creek, and no messing." He could feel a neurohormone headache coming on. Thank God there had only been nine of them to question.

"Don't swear," Gabriel snapped primly.

"I've got a right. None of them leaked the information about the NN core. How are you doing with the security personnel?"

"You wouldn't find anything."

"What? None of them have any shameful secrets?"

"They might well have, but if so, they can certainly hide it from you."

His unwinding espersense caught her gelid mind tone. Eggshell-walking time. "Bugger, you know what that means."

"Dillan Evans."

"Yeah, unless we can produce this mole pronto. And I'm now having serious doubts he ever existed. Christ, how am I going to tell Philip? Maybe I'll tell Julia first; she's pretty protective when it comes to her father. Can't say I blame Dillan, though. The man is totally fucked. Not rational."

"Saved by the bell."

"What?" His cybofax bleeped. "Oh."

The call was a data squirt, a scramble code he knew by heart. Royan. His spirits lifted as the decrypted message rolled down the cybofax's little screen. Royan had found one of the hot rods involved in the blitz: Ade O'Donal, operating from Leicester under the handle Tentimes. Greg snapped the cybofax shut with a flourish; at last he could take some positive action, get out of dead company architecture and pull in hard information. When he glanced up Gabriel was already standing by the door, expectant. "Coming?" she asked.

Greg drove past the ranks of company buses in the car park and out on to the A47.

Getting under way didn't noticeably alter Gabriel's disposition. "Fascinating," she said. "The lovely Eleanor, a full-fledged Trinity urban predator. The mind boggles."

"I wish you'd make an effort. That girl's never said a single bad word about you. And God knows she's entitled."

"Greg, you can't just abandon all your old mates in her favor, however besotted you are with her gymnast legs and top-heavy chest."

He pulled his anger down to a tight incendiary ball. Anger never did any good, not against Gabriel. But it was fucking tempting to let fly once in a while. Not this time, though. He needed her. And she knew it. "Eleanor gets on perfectly well with the marine-adepts, and Royan has taken a shine to her."

"That was the first time you'd been to see Royan for two months. You know how much that boy worships you."

Fell into that one, he told himself. Just as she'd intended, guiding his conversation down the Tau line she'd selected.

Greg gunned the Duo along the A47 above the flooded remains of Ailsworth. Her words had kindled not so much guilt as a sense of melancholy.

Arguing with her when she was being this waspish was impossible. Whatever he said in his defense, she'd have a parry honed and ready, the best of all possible answers. Besides, truthfully, he had neglected Royan. Eleanor made it easy to forget. Life and the future, rather than Royan, a shackle to an emetic past. He just wished Gabriel didn't use a sledgehammer to ram home the point.

He was aware of her studying his face intently. She gave a tart nod and leaned back into the seat cushioning.

The last section of road leading into Leicester cut through a banana plantation. Methane-fueled tractors chugged between the rows of big glossy-leafed plants, hauling vast quantities of still-green fruit in their cage trailers. Cutter teams moved ahead of the tractors, machetes flashing in the sun.

Incorporated in the city boundary sign was the prominent declaration PSP FREE ZONE.

"Oh yeah?" said Gabriel.

Greg let the snipe ride, though he conceded she had a point. Leicester council had earned a reputation for sycophancy during Armstrong's presidency; it was one of the last to acknowledge the Party's perdition.

That obedience was the root of its downfall; a numbing historical repetition, those showing the most loyalty receiving the least. With such devotion assured, the PSP had no need to pump in bribe money. Leicester had declined as Peterborough had risen. Now the city's New Conservative–dominated council was striving hard to obliterate the image of the past in an attempt to attract hard-industry investment.

"Give them a chance," Greg said. "It's only been two years."

"Once a Trot, always a Trot."

"Exactly where would you be happy living?" he asked in exasperation.

"Mars, I expect. Turn left here."

"I know."

He turned off the Uppingham Road and nudged into the near-solid file of bicycle traffic along Spencefield Lane. The big old trees whose branches had once turned the road into a leafy tunnel were long dead. New sequoias had been planted to replace them. They were grand trees, but Greg couldn't help wondering whether they were a wise choice if the residents were aiming for permanency; give them a couple of centuries and the sequoias would be skyscraper high.

The original trees had been trimmed into near-identical pillars six meters high, supporting giant crossbeams over the road. Each arch was swathed in a different-colored climbing rose. The sun shone through the petals, creating a blazing sequence of coronal crescents. It was like driving under a solid rainbow.

Greg slowed the Duo to a walking pace as they passed the entrance to an old school. Cars were clustered along the verge ahead, sporty Renaults, several Mercs, one old Toyota GX4. Image cars.

"Shouldn't there be sailboards strapped on top of them?" Gabriel said under her breath.

Greg concentrated on house numbers, praying she'd snap out of it before long. Of course, he could always ask her when her mood was due to end. He clamped down on a grin. "That's the address."

The house was hidden behind a head-high brick wall that had a hurricane fence on top; a thick row of evergreen firs hid most of the building from the road. The gate was a sturdy metal-reinforced chain-link, painted white. Cameras were perched on each side, their casings weather-dulled.

"He's having a party," Gabriel said, with facetious humor disguising the tingle of nerves Greg knew would be there.

"How nice. A big one?"

"For him. It's enough to provide us with cover, anyway."

Greg parked the Duo beyond the last of the guests' cars. "Front or back?"

"Front, of course. Your card is good for it."

He felt a burn of anticipation warming his skin, heightening senses. Black liver-flesh of the gland throbbing enthusiastically.

They strolled back to the gate, unhurried, unconcerned. Greg showed his Event Horizon card to the post, using his little finger for activation. The gate's electric bolt thudded, and the servos swung it back.

It remained open behind them, its control circuitry bleached clean. He sent a mental note of thanks to Royan.

The mossy gravel drive crunched under their feet. O'Donal's house was a large one, three stories of dull russet brick with inset stone windows, the slates on the mansard roof a peculiar olive green. Nobody had bothered with the front garden for years: the grass was tangled and overgrown, and dead cherry trees were still standing. Some sort of stone ornament, a birdbath or a sundial, poked up through a tumble of cornflowers. A brand-new scarlet BMW convertible was parked in front of the triple garage.

"The man that answers the door is a minder; he'll make trouble if you let him," Gabriel said. "Take him out straightaway."

"Right." He rang the bell. Music and laughter wafted over the roof.

Greg saw him coming through the smoked glass pane set into the grimy hardwood door, an obscure blotch of brown motion, swelling to cloud the whole rectangle.

The door was pulled open.

"Hello, sorry we're late."

The man behind the door was street muscle in a suit: early twenties, tall, stringy, dark hair, broad forehead crinkling into a frown.

Greg stepped forward neatly, one foot on the mat, the other coming up, farther and farther. Fast. It was victory through surprise. A smiling man and a portly spinster eager to party just didn't register as a threat. Not until the carbon-mesh-reinforced toe of Greg's desert boot smashed into his kneecap.

His mouth opened to suck in air, eyes wide with shock. He was toppling forward, leg giving way, and bending to clutch desperately at his shattered knee.

Greg brought his fist straight up, catching the minder's chin as he was on his way down. The force of the blow snapped his head back, lifting him off his feet, back arching, arms and legs flung wide.

He crashed back onto the shiny blue ceramic tiling, skull making a nasty cracking sound, a thin stream of pea-green vomit sloshing from his slack mouth.

Greg took in the dark hall behind him with a quick glance, espersense wide for alarmed minds. Big tasteless urns holding willowy arrangements of dried pampas grass making the most impression. But the hall was empty. Nobody had witnessed their arrival.

"Jesus, Greg." Gabriel was kneeling beside the prone minder, feeling for a pulse.

Greg opened the cloakroom door. "In here." There was a wicker dog basket on the floor; jackets were piled high on a washbasin. It smelled of urine and detergent. "Come on!"

Gabriel shot him a filthy look but took hold of the minder's left arm as Greg grabbed the right. They pulled him across the tiles.

"If he was going to die, you'd have told me not to hit so hard."

"You know bloody well it doesn't work like that," Gabriel said. "There are a million ways you could've dealt with him."

"Well, is he going to be all right or not?"

"I don't bloody know; some futures have him dying."

Greg shoved the dog basket out of the way and left the minder with his head propped up against the toilet bowl. Gabriel rolled up one of the jackets and slipped it behind the minder's head. He was still breathing.

"How many futures?" Greg asked.

"Some."

Greg recognized the defensive tone and relaxed. The minder would survive.

"There's a rear belt holster," Gabriel said reluctantly.

Greg kneeled down and felt underneath the minder. Sure enough, he was carrying a Mulekick, a flattened ellipsoid in gray plastic, small enough to fit snugly into Greg's palm, with a single sensitive circle positioned for the thumb and a metal tip that discharged an electric shock strong enough to stun a victim senseless.

"We'll need it later," Gabriel said cryptically.

Greg dropped it into his jacket pocket and followed her back out into the hall.

The house would've given any halfway competent interior designer nightmares. To Greg it looked as though it'd been decorated by someone watching a home-shopping catalog channel and picking out all the furniture and fittings that had the brightest colors. There was no attempt to blend styles.

The lounge had two three-piece suites, one upholstered in overstuffed white leather, the other done in a bold lemon-and-purple zigzag print. A harlequin array of biolum spheres hung from the ceiling on long brass chains, imitating a planetarium's solar system display. Dark African shields hung on the wall, along with spears, tomahawks, broadswords, and longbows. The weapons were interspaced with antique rock-concert posters, mostly from Leicester's De Monfort hall—Bowie, Be Bop Deluxe, Blue Oyster Cult, David Hunter, The Stranglers, one for The Who at Granby Hall in 1974. If they were real, and they looked it, they must've cost a fortune.

The party was in full swing on the other side of the lounge's sliding patio doors. Thirty or so people were clustered around the back garden's baby swimming pool. Led Zeppelin was blasting out of tombstone-sized Samsung speakers.

A petite blond girl in a lime green one-piece swimsuit shoved the patio door open. Robert Plant's fearsome vocals slammed into Greg's eardrums. She came in dripping water all over the deep white pile carpet. He caught a whiff of bittersweet air. Quite a few of the partygoers around the pool were puffing away on fat Purple Rain reefers.

"Hi," the blond said when she saw Greg and Gabriel. "We're out of champagne again."

"Can I help?" Greg asked.

"S'all right, I know where it is." She looked at Gabriel. "You want a suit for the pool?"

"No, thank you."

"We'll get something to drink first," Greg said. "Have a rap with Ade. Is he out there?"

"Sure," said the blond. "Over there by the grill, in the lubes stupid hat. Hey, can you cook?"

"Sure."

"Try and get him to let you do the steaks, okay? He's half pissed already; we're gonna be eating coal if it's left to him."

"You got it. How do you want yours?"

She pulled long wet strands of hair from her face, uncovering a dense constellation of freckles. Hazel eyes sparkled at him. "Juicy," she purred.

"Already done."

She peeked surreptitiously at the people outside. "Catch you later," she promised. There was a corrupting wiggle in her walk as she headed for the kitchen.

"Would you like me to wait?" Gabriel inquired, oozing salaciousness.

"We have to stay in character."

"Nice for some. Let's get this over with."

"How do you want to play it?"

Gabriel stared thoughtfully out at the party. "Sucker him in here first. Then arm-twist him into taking us to his gear cache. We'll apply the real pressure there."

"Is that here in the house?"

"Yes. In the basement. Quite a setup. Our Tentimes is an ambitious lad."

They went out through the patio door into heat, noise, and a smell of charring meat. None of the guests paid them any attention; they were all concentrating on the pool.

Somebody had rigged a pole across the water. Two naked girls

were sitting astride it, facing each other: one was white with sun-
burned shoulders, the second was Indian. They were whacking each
other with big orange pillows. The crowd roared its approval as the
white girl began to slip. She fell in slow motion, abandoning the pillow and gripping frantically at the pole, sliding inexorably toward the
horizontal. A flurry of blows from the Indian girl speeded her
progress, aided and abetted by wild shouts of encouragement from
the side of the pool. At the last minute she let go of the pole and
grabbed the Indian girl. They both shrieked as they hit the water. The
white flower bloom of spray closed over them, sending up a plume
that soaked some of the spectators.

Groans and cheers went up. The girls surfaced, giggling and spluttering. Furious little knots of partygoers formed, passing money
back and forth.

"Jenna next," someone called.

"And Carrie."

"Two-to-one on Carrie."

"Bollocks, evens."

"I'll take that."

The two new girls began to edge toward each other along the pole.

Ade O'Donal stood on the cracked ocher flagstones at the shallow end of the pool, white chef's hat drooping miserably, a wooden
spatula in his hand. According to Royan's data squirt he was twenty-
four, but his sandy hair was already in retreat, both cheeks were sinking, becoming gaunt, his skin was pasty white, reddening from too
much sun. He wore an oversize azure cotton shirt speckled by sooty
oil spots from the barbecue, and his loud fruit-pattern Bermuda
shorts told Greg who had chosen the house's furniture.

O'Donal grinned gormlessly around the faces of his friends as the
girls poised, ready. Then his eyes met Greg's and froze.

The wooden spatula slashed downward. "Go," O'Donal shouted.
The girls began pummeling at each other, the blows from their saturated pillows sending out clouds of sparkling droplets. Partygoers
began cheering again. The blond in the lemon swimming suit was
walking round the pool filling glasses, a magnum clasped in each
hand.

The Indian girl clambered out of the pool, cinnamon skin glistening, and shook her long black dreadlocks. She pressed up against
O'Donal, her high conical breasts leaving damp imprints on his shirt
as she kissed him. He handed her his glass, which she tossed down
in one smooth gulp.

O'Donal pushed her away and walked around the pool toward Greg and Gabriel.

They retreated into the lounge. O'Donal followed.

"Are you with someone?" he asked; his voice was firm, ready to deal sternly with gatecrashers.

"We're here to see you, Ade," Greg said.

"This is a private party, pal. Guests only."

"Private party. Big house. Lots of expensive friends. You're coming up in the world, Tentimes," Gabriel said.

O'Donal's jaw muscles hardened. He slid the patio door shut, muting the music and catcalls. Greg sensed the cold apprehension rising in his mind. O'Donal's eyes kept straying to the door leading to the hall.

"Sorry, Tentimes," Greg said. "Your hard case couldn't make it. It's just you and us."

"Will you quit with that handle," O'Donal hissed edgily. "These people don't know who I am."

"What do they think you are?"

"Programmer on a commission to Hansworth Logic." He brightened. "Hey, I never expected you to show in person, y'know. I mean, I don't mind you coming, no way. I just didn't think it was the way you worked. So what is it—you want me to run another burn?"

"You're sweating, Tentimes," said Gabriel. "This is all new to you, isn't it? The high life, money, girls?"

"We'd never have guessed," Greg said, looking pointedly around the lounge.

"Hey, look, what the fuck is this?" O'Donal demanded. "And what have you done to Brune?"

"Don't know, didn't stop to check," said Greg. "What does it matter? Ace hot rod like you can afford plenty more like him."

O'Donal's apprehension now blossomed into outright worry. A little muscle spasm rippled across his bony shoulders.

The pillow fight outside had degenerated into a wrestling match. One girl ripped the bikini top off the other. The spectators whooped approval.

O'Donal licked his lips. "Hey, come on, who are you people?"

"We're from Event Horizon," said Greg.

O'Donal's already pale face blanched still further. "Oh, shit." He took a half step backward, ready to turn and bolt, then stopped at the sight of the Walther eightshot in Greg's hand.

"You're not used to this, are you, Tentimes?" Gabriel asked with silky insistence. "A solo hot rod, your combat is all mental. Well,

this time the feedback is physical. You want my advice? Play ball.
Don't annoy us. There are another seven who took part in the blitz.
We'll just work down the list until we get some cooperation."

"I didn't have any choice!"

"Tell us about it," Greg suggested. "Downstairs."

"Down? Where?"

"Your terminals," Gabriel said.

"Shit, how . . ." O'Donal clamped his mouth shut as Greg flicked
the Walther's nozzle toward the door.

Out in the hall O'Donal stopped and sniffed the air; then his eyes
found the smear of viscous liquid on the tiles. A small pulse of anger
colored his thoughts. "Through here," he said, pointing dully at a
recessed door.

"You open it," Gabriel ordered. "Seeing as how it's keyed to your
palmprint. I'd hate my colleague to receive that thousand-volt
charge."

O'Donal swallowed hard, almost a gulp. As he turned to the door
Greg slapped the back of his head, knocking his face against the flaking varnish. The cook's hat fell off.

"Shit!" There was real fear in O'Donal's voice and mind. He
looked at them to plead, a bead of blood seeping out of his left nos-
tril. "I wasn't gonna. Honest, shit. I wouldn't have. Shit, you've
gotta believe me!"

"Sure," Gabriel crooned.

Behind the hall door were fifteen steps leading down to another
door made of bronze-colored metal. It slid open at O'Donal's voice
command.

"Impressive," Gabriel murmured.

The basement had been built as a wine cellar; the scars where the
racks had been ripped out were still visible on the rough brick walls.
A metal air-conditioning duct that had ensured the bottles were kept
at a perfectly maintained temperature ran along the ceiling.

The basement was a hot rod's crypt now, smelling faintly of ace-
tone. There were five terminals sitting on a low pine table, all different makes, each hardwired with customized augmentation modules. Hundreds of memox crystals were stacked neatly on narrow oak
shelving. Four big cubes clung to the wall facing the table, two on either side of a long flatscreen that was lit up like a football stadium
scoreboard. The Gracious Services circuit, detailing burns in
progress, hackers on-line, requests, available umpires. Greg searched
and sure enough saw Wildace's name.

"Expensive, too," Greg said. "According to the circuit you've only been solo for six months. Means you've been scoring pretty good, Tentimes. How do you do it?"

"What . . . what are you going to do to me?"

Greg shoved the Mulekick against the matte black surface of the Hitachi terminal on the table. There was a flat crack as the power tubes discharged. A zillion precious delicate junctions were smelled into worthless cinders. The smell of scorched plastic filled the air.

O'Donal yelped as though he'd received the jolt. "Oh, *shitfire*, do you know how much that *cost* me?" He stared aghast at the ruined Hitachi.

"Don't know, don't care," Greg said indifferently. "Now, where's the money coming from?"

"They give me targets, pay good."

"They?"

"They, him, her, shit I don't know. We've never met."

"Got a name, a handle?"

"Wolf."

"How does Wolf get in touch? Through the circuit?"

O'Donal shook his head, eyes blinking rapidly. "No, that's the sting, man. Wolf calls over the phone. Direct! God, you've no idea how bad that trip was the first time. I mean, that's the whole point of the circuit, right? It protects us as individuals, no hassle, no danger. You pay your dues, and you're covered. It's worked that way for twenty goddamn years. Then Wolf comes along and blows it right out of the water. Why me? I mean, what did I do?"

"When did Wolf first contact you?" Greg asked patiently.

" 'Bout ten months ago."

"But not through the circuit?"

O'Donal glanced from Greg to Gabriel, face screwing up from anger and, strangely, outrage. "It was in a pub! I was having a drink with some mates and the fucking phone goes behind the bar, asking for me by name. Wolf knew who I was, where I was, knew about my burns. That is like the most heavy-duty shit a hot rod can get, y'know."

Greg whistled, intrigued in spite of himself. It'd take good organization to spring a net like that: money and expertise. And for what? A team of tame hot rods. Who would want that? And more to the point, why? "How does Wolf get in touch now?"

"Call box. I have to check in every three days. Dial a number, just like you do for Gracious Services. If there's a burn in the offing, I get run around town for an hour until Wolf's happy I'm not pulling a backtrack."

Gabriel was sitting in the black leather high-back chair behind the table, tenting her fingers and staring up at the pewter-colored duct, lost in thought. "The method of recruiting interests me," she said. "This Wolf definitely knew you were an active hacker?"

O'Donal nodded sullenly. "The bastard read out a whole list of my burns."

"How complete a list?"

"Dunno." He caught the look Greg gave him. "Yeah, all right. I didn't spot any missing."

"Going back for how long?" she asked.

"Couple of years, ever since I plugged into the circuit."

"Have you ever had a criminal record?"

"What? No."

"Don't lie," Greg said. The guilt had glinted in his mind.

"I'm not," O'Donal insisted hotly. "No record." He flushed hard, not looking at Gabriel. "Got pulled once, mind. Pigs said she was underage. Shit, I mean no way, not that size, melon city."

"When was this?" Gabriel asked keenly.

"Six, seven years back."

"The police, did they search your home?"

"For sure, tore it apart, bastards. They had to drop the charges after that." He sniggered at the memory. "My mates went and visited her for me. Straightened her out but good. She didn't want to talk to no one after that, least of all the pigs."

"Were you into gear then?"

"Yeah, a bit. Nothing serious though, not then."

"And where were you living?"

"Steve Biko tower."

Gabriel smiled acute satisfaction. "Your turn," she said to Greg, as if it were some kind of channel quiz show.

"I'd like a list of all the burns you've done for Wolf," he said.

O'Donal scowled sourly but began typing on the Mizzi terminal.

"Carefully," Gabriel warned. "Make sure the code is the right one. We don't want any mistakes like a call for help or anything equally tiresome. And believe me, I'll know if it isn't the right one."

The truth finally dawned. "Shit. You two, you're psychic, right?"

"Got it in one," Greg said. "How else did you think we found you?"

O'Donal's subconscious discharged a heavy rancorous stream of revulsion and dread, contaminating his conscious thoughts.

Greg showed his cybofax to the Mizzi, and O'Donal squirted the list of his burns over.

"How much do you get paid for a burn?" Greg asked.

"Depends, normally around five grand."

"And for the Event Horizon burn?"

"That was a real big deal; I got fifteen for that."

"No messing. So which half were you in on?"

"I don't follow you, man. What halves?"

"The attack was twofold, remember? The priority data-squirt blitz against the core, and the shutdown instructions beamed up to the Merlin. Which were you in on?"

"I don't know nothing about no Merlin shutdown. All Wolf told me to do was hack into the Event Horizon datanet and fire off a squirt at some bioware cruncher core. Man, you've never seen anything like that blitz memox, custom job." He lifted a glittering black sphere the size of a tennis ball from the table, multifaceted like an insect eye. "The multiplex compression in this lover is absolute genius. Hell, I can't even retro the bytes. Sure wish I could. I'd love to be able to write my own like this someday."

"Did this Wolf tell you what the core was?" Greg asked.

"Sure, it's some kind of fancy Turing personality responses program they've whizzed up to manage the company."

"Have you ever thought of backtracking the money transfers from Wolf? Find out who he is? Hit back, perhaps."

"Yeah. Big zero."

"How come?"

"I ain't up to that, man," O'Donal muttered quietly.

"Not up to much, are you, Tentimes?" Greg plucked one of the memox crystals from the shelves, reading the handwritten label. "This a core-code melt virus?"

"Yeah."

"Wolf supplied it, right? How many of them come from Wolf?"

"Some, 'bout half. I write my own, too, man!" O'Donal was stuffed with righteous indignation. "I see what you're getting at; I'm no cyborg, man. I've got my own scene outside that arsehole. I'd have made solo without Wolf. I would!"

"Give me your bank account number, the one your Event Horizon burn money was paid into."

O'Donal clutched at his hair with both hands, pulling hard. "Shit, no way, man. I've got everything stashed in there. I only burnt your fucking company once."

Greg jammed the Mulekick down on O'Donal's Akai terminal. Blue-white static tapeworms writhed across the heat-dump fins, snapping and popping like arid matchwood.

"All right!" O'Donal shouted. "Jesus." He looked down hopelessly at the tiny wisp of smoke rising from the back of the Akai.

The restraint of fear was wearing thin; anger was predominating again. Greg knew he'd have to do something about that. Soon.

O'Donal's fingers trembled softly as he squirted the information from the Mizzi to Greg's cybofax. "Hey, listen, you ain't going to like *do* anything to me, are you? I cooperated, man, really I did. You know it all now. God's honest truth, every last byte."

"That's right," Greg said, and straight-armed O'Donal with the Mulekick, punching the electrode deep into his small flacid beer gut.

O'Donal's cheeks inflated, eyes bulging. Alcohol-toxic breath rushed out of him, and he curled up, collapsing backward onto the terminals. Memox crystals went glissading over the cold brick floor.

"Did you enjoy that?" Gabriel asked.

"No. Come on, time for us to make our exit."

Greg sneaked a peek through the lounge door on the way out. The pool was filling up: people fully clothed, people half clothed, naked people, empty magnums and sodden burger baps were bobbing about among them. A cloud of thick blue-black smoke was mushrooming up from the barbecue grill; the steaks and sausages were burning fiercely. Led Zep was crashing out "Whole Lotta Love." Hell of a party.

Greg tugged the Duo away from the curb in a tight U-turn, ignoring the shrill clamor of incensed bicycle bells, and headed back toward Oakham.

Gabriel hunched down in the passenger seat and devoured the information O'Donal had squirted into his cybofax.

"Make any sense to you?" Greg asked.

"Nothing obvious leaps out. The targets are companies and finance houses. Most of the time Wolf wanted logic bombs crashed into their data cores, though there are some data snatches, too, mainly high-tech research."

"Doesn't tell us much. I'll squirt it over to Morgan Walshaw, get his economic intelligence team to run an analysis on it, see who benefits most."

"But you've got a pretty good guess. I know you. You're almost happy about finding this list."

"Yeah. What odds will you give me that our friend Kendric di Girolamo comes up top of the beneficiaries?"

"You really have got it in for him, haven't you?"

"Yep, logic and instinct both. All I need is proof, and darling Julia's avenging angel will take it from there."

"I'm not so sure," Gabriel said. "That entrapment gig this Wolf character snared O'Donal with, it's very long-term. Find a gear-crazy kid who's growing up in exactly the right sort of environment that'll turn him to hot-rodding, then tap his phone for seven years just to get the evidence to nail him with. Why? I mean what's he doing for Wolf that he wouldn't have done ordinarily on the Gracious Services circuit?"

"Let's see. How many burns are on that list?"

"Thirty-two, including the one against Event Horizon."

Greg slowed the Duo and turned on to the B6047 heading for Tilton. It was a terrible road, so overgrown in places that the tarmac had vanished under grass and thistles. He steered into the ruts left by the farm wagons to get some decent traction, hoping nothing was coming the other way.

"Thirty-two is one hell of a lot of burns for a ten-month period," he said. "And Wolf has a team of at least eight hackers running these burns for him. Gracious Services is normally pretty independent, but even their umpires might begin to wonder what was going down. They're smart; if there is a pattern to the burns they'd spot it. Wolf isn't the type to leave his flank exposed like that."

"Hence the need for privacy. Yes, I can buy that. Well, we'll just have to see what Walshaw's people come up with. By the way, what did you want O'Donal's account number for?"

"Wolf chose O'Donal because he isn't a true hot rod, not yet. He's a greenhouse product, force-grown, given viruses on a plate instead of developing his own talent to write them. That way he can't stray from Wolf's carefully ordained path. O'Donal doesn't have the ability to backtrack the credit transfers, but Royan sure as hell does."

"That still doesn't explain away the police complicity in O'Donal's entrapment."

"Kendric has more than enough money to bribe a squad or two of underpaid bobbies."

Gabriel groaned in dismay. "Christ, and Eleanor thinks I'm neurotic."

24

J ULIA CLOSED THE HEAVY PANELED door behind her, stepping into the understated elegance of the Princess of Wales suite. The room made her uncomfortably aware of just how uncouth her own bedroom was. Here she was surrounded by temperate shades and smooth curves; the brocade-covered furniture seemed to flow into the walls. Several antique pieces were dotted around, and instead of clashing with the modern setting they complemented it to perfection. Part of their appeal was in their placing, she'd decided. She was continually afraid she'd bump into one of the little Pope chairs and ruin the whole effect. She'd never be able to put it back in the exact spot.

Several huge bouquets of fresh flowers filled the air with their perfume. She breathed down the scent and headed for the bathroom. The evening had been an utter delight so far. She was determined not to lose the theme now.

"See you in a couple of months," was her grandfather's parting shot as she'd left Wilholm. He was paring down the sarcasm now but couldn't resist one last dig.

She'd brought eight suitcases with her to the Marlston Hotel for the book launch. Actually, it was the gala relaunch of the Alaka publishing company. They'd decided to promote their new catalog in grand style, no expense spared. A three-day junket for celebrities, financiers, aristocrats, and the media—even some of their authors were there. Three days, and more importantly, three nights.

Julia hadn't been quite sure what level the event was going to be pitched at, so she'd made some meticulous preparations. The first night dinner-dance had turned out to be a formal occasion, so, after much deliberation, and consulting Adela, she'd chosen a twelve-thousand-pound Salito gown. It was midnight black, because it was hard to look bad in black; scarlet and gold moiré patterns skipped across the fabric at every movement; the back was low, and the skintight front uplifting. For once she'd abandoned her Saint Christopher and worn a single diamond choker. Her hair had taken Adela and the hotel's in-house crimper three-quarters of an hour to arrange; they'd made it seem slightly ruffled, as though it weren't styled at all.

The most difficult thing to do with hair the length of hers.

And it'd worked a dream. A miracle. Walking slowly down the stairs to the reception with Adrian on her arm she'd felt like a queen on her way to her coronation. Every head in the hall had turned to watch her progress; seven channel cameras had focused on her.

Serene, the nodes had yelled to her mind; grinning or giving a thumbs-up like some crass ingenue would've wrecked everything. But she'd kept her composure, and Adrian had walked tall beside her.

Alaka's chairman had hurried to the bottom of the stairs to receive his guest of honor. The band had struck up, and she'd been offered champagne by a liveried waiter. All on camera.

She grinned oafishly at her reflection in the bathroom mirror, dignity gone, clapping her hands in celebration. The Salito split down its invisible seam and she wriggled out of it, kicking off her shoes. Choker and panties joined them on the mossy purple carpet.

Two minutes. The time since Adrian had said goodnight. A soft kiss that had lasted far longer than politeness dictated. His room was two doors down the corridor.

He'd stayed with her all evening, turning down offers to dance with anyone else. And there'd been a lot of good-looking girls who'd asked him. Most of them were the daughters of the rich and famous that Alaka had invited. Julia had enjoyed their company, girls her own age who weren't so self-conscious and hung up about money as most people. There had even been a couple of them she wouldn't mind meeting again, potential friends.

Yes, it had been the best evening for quite some time.

Three minutes. Naked, she looked at herself in the full-length mirror. Not totally displeased. Her figure was lanky, but elfin rather than skinny. Her breasts were nicely rounded, even if she didn't have Kats's milk-beast size, and they didn't sag at all. Reasonably broad feminine-looking hips, too. And an all-over tan that'd taken two days on her balcony to perfect.

An uncomfortable sensation of emptiness was plaguing her stomach. What had Adrian seen when he looked at her? Her figure or her money and name? She couldn't forget that Bil Yi Somanzer hadn't even noticed her before Uncle Horace told him who she was.

Four minutes. Her bedtime lingerie was laid out, ready. Adela hadn't been consulted in that department, not at all. Julia had bullied herself into making the decision. Kats wouldn't have had any second thoughts.

She drew a deep breath and pulled on the French knickers; they were sheer silk, a pale peach color, inset with lace. Her robe was white silk, ankle length. The combination was simple, sensual.

Impact was the most important thing. Overwhelm him, get him off balance and push. She studied the mirror critically, then retied the belt. It still wasn't right. Five more goes and the front of the robe was open to her navel, showing a long V of deeply tanned skin and a more than generous slice of breast.

Seven minutes. Julia went back out into the bedroom, dimming the biolums to a faint rose-tinted glow.

Rachel was on duty outside. When they'd arrived, Julia had told her that Adrian was to be allowed in At Any Time. Rachel's face had never flickered; the woman must be a cyborg.

How long to wait? That was the real twister. Give him say twenty minutes—no, fifteen ought to be enough. All he had to do was take off his dinner jacket.

Nine minutes. She stood by the bed. An antique four-poster. So romantic.

If he wasn't here after fifteen minutes, then she'd damn well go to his room. If she could find the nerve. What if his door was locked? What if he said no? What if one of those little vixens from the party was with him?

God, don't even think about it.

Ten minutes. There was a light rap on the door.

"Come in," she said, furious at the sudden quaver afflicting her voice. She almost let out a whimper of relief when she saw it was Adrian. He was wrapped in his burgundy toweling robe. Bare feet, no pajamas.

She blipped the lock. Sealing him in.

"Julia!" There was a note of surprised admiration in his voice and desire lighting his eyes as he drank down the sight of her.

She couldn't stand it anymore and ran at him. Swept up in strong warm arms. Spinning around and around. Both of them laughing jubilantly.

O N SATURDAY MORNING GREG PARKED the Duo on a side street just outside New Eastfield and handed over a fiver to the local teeny-bopper extortionists before walking out into the plush precinct's tranquil boulevards. He'd used the Event Horizon card to splash out on new light-gray slacks, blue canvas sneakers, and a jade green pure wool Stewart sweater. His usual jeans and T-shirt would've aggrieved the private police squad that New Eastfield's residents employed.

One major contributory factor to Peterborough's post-Warming prosperity had been its burgeoning maritime links. The Nene allowed cargo ships to sail right into the heart of the city. They docked at a new port and warehouse complex that had sprung up in place of the old shopping precinct and Queensgate mall.

In addition to the commercial shipping, an armada of nearly seven thousand small boats had set out from the Norfolk Broads as the Antarctic ice melted, converging on the city. They'd anchored around the island suburb of Stanground, their moorings evolving into a hugely complicated maze of jetties built out of timber scavenged from the roofs and floors of deluged buildings out in the Fens. The boats at the center were trapped there now, ten years' worth of rubbish clogging the water around them, embedding them in an artificial bog. He'd heard that around ten thousand people lived in the sprawling boat town. The actual figure was uncertain; Stanground's inherent chaos made council hall governance nigh on impossible, an aspect that the residents took full advantage of. The narrow twisting channels were Peterborough's main haven for smugglers, pumping hard currency Eurofrancs into the city's economy.

Finally, there was an impressive squadron of pleasure craft. The potential of the city's industrial vigor, coupled with the kind of seedy spice endemic to monstrous overcrowding, proved a powerful attraction to Europe's shipborne rich. People who ran their mini-empires of financial trusts and venture projects from floating gin palaces. They were a flock in eternal migration, never in one port long enough to qualify for the taxman's attention.

They had their own marina in New Eastfield, north of the Nene's main course. The quays were concrete, substantial, immaculately clean. Every requirement was catered for, from stores supplying five-star food and maritime gear to a not-so-small dry dock capable of providing complete refits.

Greg hit the marina itself around eleven: a whole community of clubs, sports complexes, shops, restaurants, and pubs along the waterfront, open to permit holders only. Royan had loaded his ID into the membership computer. The promenade was a kilometer long, built from huge granite cubes. Five quays stabbed out into the deep harbor that'd been dredged for the yachts of the megarich.

A gauzy layer of cumulus clouds diffused the sun into a sourceless light overhead. The humidity this close to the Fens basin approached steam-bath levels.

He found Angelica's, a single-story flat-roofed emporium opposite the center quay where the *Mirriam* was berthed. It was a food hall selling wholesale quantities of nouveau delicacies he didn't even know how to pronounce.

Greg walked down the cul-de-sac side alley and found the delivery bay's metal roller-door at the rear. Beside it, embedded in the bricks, was a series of metal rungs. He started to climb.

The uniformity of the solar-collector roof was broken by two satellite-dish weather domes and three big conditioning stacks, their fans spinning silently. Dead center was a box structure of slatted wooden panels that housed Angelica's water tanks. Greg crouched down and scuttled over to it. One of the slat panels was hanging loose. He pulled it aside and slipped in.

The panel opened into a narrow gap between two big water tanks, one and a half meters wide, three long. There wasn't enough headroom to stand up, and he had to hunch down with his hands brushing the floor. What space there was had nearly been used up.

At the far end, various photon-amp lenses were poking through the slats, their cables feeding a jumble of compact gear modules. Weird little halos of colored light cloaked five miniature flatscreens that flickered with the image of the good ship *Mirriam*, half covered with red digital readouts.

Right in front of the entrance panel was a pile of drink cans and food wrappers. Greg nearly put his foot in an adult-size potty that had been connected into Angelica's plumbing by a ribbed flexible pipe. There was only one smell: ripe human.

Between the rubbish and the gear was a thin yellow sponge mattress. Suzi was lying on it, wearing blue shorts, soaked a shade darker by sweat. Her mauve spikes had drooped in the torrid heat.

She peered at him out of the gloom. "Christ, 'bout time you showed. See what we've been suffering for you."

"All in a good cause." He stepped over the potty and squirmed onto the mattress beside her. One of the gear modules poked sharply into his back.

"Cozy," Suzi smirked spryly. "You wanna do it? There's enough room if you ain't into anything too kinky."

Greg was suddenly very aware of her tough little body pressing against him. "We'd die of heat exhaustion."

"Yeah, tits the size that new girl of yours was stacked with, can't say I blame you."

Greg nearly started to protest but thought better of it. "I hope you're not handling the observation all by yourself. This heat is bad for you. Seriously."

A growl rumbled up from the back of her throat. "Shit no. It's four-hour shifts only up here. The rest of the squad is spotted 'round the marina; some of them signed on with the company that's got the franchise to keep the promenade clean. And there are another two in hire cars for tailing Kendric's Jag when he goes runabout. We've been drawing up a habits and behavior profile. Just like you taught us, right? *Know* the man, get to understand him. No hassle in that; talk's pretty loose around here. One of us made barman at a pub the crews use. Nothing they like better than slagging off their owners."

"Sounds good so far. What have you got for me?"

Suzi wriggled a hand free and pointed at the screens. "This Kendric, he's a fucking martian. Not of this earth, y'know? The lives these yacht people lead. Un-be-lievable! Tell you something, though, no way is he a card carrier. I mean, the PSP's local chairpricks, they had it all, right? Eternal junket time. But they haven't got nothing compared to this geezer. The money he's got. He wouldn't last five minutes if they ever got back in power."

"Ah." He'd wondered about the peak of vexation in her mind. "No, Kendric's not Party. But my guess is that he's involved in a spoiler against Event Horizon. And with the economy all shaky with inflation right now, Event Horizon taking a tumble would be serious bad news. The only people who'll benefit are the PSP relics in legitimate opposition. That good enough for you?"

"What's the spoiler?"

"Ministry of Defense. Ultrahush."

"Figures," she agreed without much enthusiasm. "Son told us Kendric was plugged into big-league corporate operations."

Greg studied the various images on the five screens. *Mirriam* was the biggest yacht in the marina. Sixty-five meters long, gleaming silver-white, with jet-black ports. Crewmen stripped to the waist were visible, washing down the wide afterdeck. "Is Kendric on board right now?"

"Yeah, as always. Believe me, nothing at all happens in this marina before noon. They're all too busy sleeping off last night's orgies. Right now, it's business time for Kendric. He holds a couple of conference sessions in the middeck lounge each day. There's a whole bunch of squarearse lawyer types who turn up each morning to see him. Don't know what they rap about in the cabin, *Mirriam*'s ports are screened, but anything they say out on the deck we've got on a memox cartridge for you." Her eyebrows puckered up. "Isn't that Julia Evans girl in charge of Event Horizon now?"

"Yeah. She owns it."

"No shit? Heard Kendric on about her . . ." Suzi began typing on a keyboard. "Remember the file code," she muttered, and consulted a cybofax. "Here we go."

One of the small screens changed to a scene on the *Mirriam*'s broad afterdeck. Greg squinted down at it. Kendric was sitting on one of the plastic recliners, dressed in an open-neck shirt and tailored shorts, drinking from a tall cut-crystal glass. The man with him was in a suit, his collar undone, tie hanging loose. He looked to be in his late forties, a flat bulldog face with red skin.

"Here," said Suzi. She handed Greg an earpiece.

". . . missing out badly," the man in the suit was saying, in a faint Scottish brogue. "Our Party is damn near down, Kendric; it cannot last long. Terrible thing, food's short, there's no gear, no methane for the farms. People are going to the spivs like never before. There's a hell of a turnover in silver right now. If you could just have a wee word with young Julia Evans, come to an arrangement wi" her till the Party goes down. I can ship it out by the ton."

"Impossible," Kendric said flatly. His face was dangerously hard. "That frigid bitch and I have severed all our business contacts. There will be no resumption."

" 'Tis a lot o' money, Kendric."

"Ride it out. I'm closing some deals that will make the black currency market utterly trivial. And I certainly shall not forget your forbearance."

The man in the suit shook his head sadly and took a drink from his glass.

The image froze. "Didn't mean much at the time," said Suzi. She pecked at the keyboard again.

This time it was evening. A gauzy layer of cumulus clouds glowed copper above the *Mirriam*. There was a crowd of about fifteen people drinking on the afterdeck: the women in low-cut cocktail dresses, men in suits or blazers. Laughter, clamorous conversation, and the chink of glasses filled the earpiece.

Kendric was standing at the stern with two other men. One tall and slim with thinning blond hair, the second a handsome African in brightly colored northern tribal robes.

"You have got to provide the house with alternative investments, Kendric," said the blond-haired man. "And fast."

"I've acquired some options in a Pacific Rim portfolio," the African said earnestly. "They'll give you a sixteen to seventeen percent return, guaranteed minimum."

"No," Kendric said.

"You won't find anything better. Not short term."

"I'm sorry. I know how hard you worked to put them together. But no."

"You should've hung on, Kendric," said the blond man. "We could've squared it with the family over Siebruk."

Kendric's handsome features darkened. "That deranged little shit, Evans. Buying a fucking bank! I've never heard of anything so . . . so—" He clutched at the polished brass taffrail. "Goddamn that bitch!"

The blond man turned to look out over the marina.

"Look," said the African. "The family is going to insist on an equivalent viability from the money released by pulling out of the Event Horizon backing consortium."

Kendric didn't respond.

"The family—," began the blond man.

"Put them off," Kendric snapped. He caught himself and rested a companionable hand on the blond man's shoulder. "Six months, Clancy. If I haven't come through by then, I'll step down from the family board anyway. Okay?"

Greg considered the faces on the screen. The two financiers' obvious concern. Kendric's driving anger. And intuition was totally spurious. A cornered animal had no choice in the way it reacted. "Have you got a record of all the visitors?" he asked.

Suzi tapped the sensor array with possessive pride. "No sweat. Day or night, anyone on or off gets tagged. We've got infrared and low level, for night work. Not that we need them; that baby is lit up like a football pitch after dark. And we've got an antenna rigged to intercept *Mirriam*'s local calls. But there's nothing we can do about her satellite uplinks. Trouble is, the local calls have all been the big zero so far, social gabbing and ordering booze, that kind of crap."

Greg grunted and wiped some of the sweat off his forehead. "Good. If I know who he's been seeing, I might be able to get a clearer idea of exactly what he's planning."

"You figuring on doing an extraparliamentary number against him?"

"Insufficient data."

She bent back and dragged a koolcan of orange from the heap at her feet. "I'd like in if it happens." She twisted the tab ninety degrees.

Greg watched frost forming over the can with something akin to lust. "No promises. As I said, this is big-league. Black-hat spooks with viral wasps and funny midnight accidents."

Suzi pulled the tab and gulped down the icy stream of bubbling orange, burping loudly. "Figures."

"So, what happens in the afternoon?"

"She—Hermione, right?—goes shopping, maybe does lunch with a load of airhead cows just like her. Evening, they party, sometimes on one of the other yachts, mostly on theirs, 'bout twenty-five came to it last night. Then after midnight they take off for the Blue Ball. That's a casino in New Eastfield. Hottest spot in town, people say. We tailed them for you, but no fucking way could we get past the bouncers. They pack up around three or four and come straight back. Spoke to a couple of the casino's waitresses, though. They reckoned Kendric and Hermione usually pick up a girl at the Blue Ball, bring her back to *Mirriam* to provide themselves with some fun. These waitresses, a friend of theirs let herself get talked into going along with them once. Bad scene, Greg; no sadism, but she was really put through her paces. Kendric and Hermione screwed her brains out. Then she got kicked off the next morning. Apparently, they all do. One-nighters: fuck and forget."

"What about the crew?"

Suzi grinned knowingly. "Just in case you're thinking of visiting, right? There's nine real crew, sailor types, including the captain. On top of that you've got seven assorted staff—cooks, maids, and such. Then there's six bodyguards, mean-looking bastards. Oh, here," she leaned over him, tiny pointed breasts squashing against his cheek, damp and salty. He detected a glint of amusement in her mind. She scrabbled among the gear modules and came back with a memox crystal. "This has got all the visitors' faces and times they turned up. We managed to get names for a few of them."

One of the flatscreens switched to the *Mirriam*'s blueprints. "There are always at least four people left on board," Suzi said, pointing at it. "We think we've got their cabins assigned, but you can never be sure."

Names had been superimposed over the various cabins.

"Great. Where did you get the specs from?" Greg asked.

"Son snatched them. *Mirriam*'s hull was built in Finland, but she was fitted out up in Tyneside. Apparently the English are still unbeatable when it comes to quality handicrafts."

Greg squirted the memox crystal data into his cybofax and began skipping through the faces. The images were good, high definition, most seemed to be staring straight into the lens. Morgan Walshaw should be able to assemble profiles on them.

"Oh yeah," Suzy muttered. "They've got themselves a permanent doxy on board, too. She don't do much, too fucking stoned the whole time by the look of her. That Kendric, *ménage à quatre* every night. Some stud, huh?"

Greg flipped through the index until he came to the girl; she'd been given a number but no name. Her face appeared on the cybofax's little screen.

"That's some looker," Suzi said, craning over his shoulder. "Wouldn't mind her for myself."

"Has she been on board the whole time?"

"Yeah, since we've been watching, anyway. Why, you know her?"

"Yes. Her name is Katerina Cawthorp."

SO WHY I***FYRNST . . . +! IS JULIR'SSSS FRIEND SHCKED UUUUP WITH KENDRIC DE GIROLAMO???

"I don't know the specifics," Greg said, his voice raised, strained.

Royan was jittering about in his dentist's chair, shoulders jerking in an erratic pumping rhythm. Royan was having one of his bad days, and when Greg considered just how shitty even Royan's good days must be . . .

CONNNNECTED?

"There is no such thing as coincidence."

WAS I HE%%%%LPING YOU WITH 10TIIIIMES>>?

The catheter bag that dangled below the chair on a chrome coat hook was filling with an oily bilious liquid.

"Big help. He was a blackmail victim, not a proper hot rod. Someone has been feeding him sophisticated viruses to use on burns."

THINK HE WAS ODDDDDD. TOOOO QUICK TO GOOOO
SOLO. NOT EN***)£' SHITTTT END END END. NOT ENOUGH
CIRCIT SKORES TO HISSS HANDEL. HURTSSS GREEG. REALLLY
HURTS MEEEEE.

And how could he answer that? He smiled broadly, feeling a prize
turd. "Hey, you made a friend in Eleanor. She's planning on coming back."

BEAUTY AN>>>>## BEAAST. HORRRIBLENASTY FILTH!!!£
MEMEMEMEME. YOU SCREW BABIESBABIES MAKKK" MAKE BABIES
TOOOGETHER. . . . IIIIIIIII WANNT WANT SHITFILLTH.

£%::)) GOOOOOOO AWWWAY GGRE&

Greg couldn't move. Revolted and horrified. He wanted to get out,
out and never come back. Break free. The Trinities, the Constables,
Blackshirts, this tower, this room, Royan: they were all facets of his
ingrained guilt, soul-devouring.

DON'TTTTTT CRY.

He rubbed knuckles into his eyes, vision blurring.

QUUIK<<<< WHYCOME???

Qoi appeared in the kitchen door, concern marring her fragile, sensitive features. She flashed Greg a look he couldn't begin to interpret.

WHY

"I needed you to run a finance backtrack for me. I think it's the
missing link, the one that'll tie Kendric to the hot rods."

The screens exploded into an incoherent image-mash: channel
shows, himself seen through Royan's eye camera, sticky tears smearing his cheeks, mad computer graphics, starchy-neat data tables dissolving into tight vortices of green and blue alphanumerics. One of
the little trash robots trundled across the floor, gears grinding
harshly, and bumped into a plant trough. It backed off and hit the
trough again and again. Bewitched with a mindless insect sentience.

Qoi was at Royan's side, pinching his nose with one hand, trying
to push a feed bottle's nipple into his mouth. He flung his head from
side to side; a desperate thrumming sound rose in his throat.

DATA DATA DAT————————LEAVE IT IT IT"

A multitude of red and green LEDs lit up on one of Royan's
cranky gear consoles. Greg retrieved the memory O'Donal had given
him from his cybofax and showed it to the console. Squirting.

The screens were showing a giant still picture of Trafalgar Square.
Greg recognized it instantly. A euphoric classic. The day the PSP fell,
beamed out live by every channel in the world. The crowd singing
God Save the King, orange flames rising from a hundred PSP banners, ten thousand Union Jacks waving in joyful celebration, a

residue of smoke from Downing Street boiling through the air. The scene was swelling, individual pixels becoming golf-ball size, a nonsense mosaic.

Royan sounded as though he was choking. Qoi had got the nipple into his mouth; he was sucking frantically, treacly globs of mashed apple running down his chin, dribbling onto an already badly stained T-shirt.

Behind Greg the robot suddenly stopped its mad battering. There must've been something in the apple. Royan was visibly wilting.

"You go now, please," Qoi said, bowing from the waist.

The lunatic kaleidoscope shrank as the screens began to wink out one by one.

Qoi's small expressive eyes were filled with a sorrow that had no right inhabiting someone her age. "Nothing more you can do."

A FLOCK OF BLACK STORKS WERE flapping lazily overhead as Greg walked up the *Mirriam*'s gangplank. The bodyguard teleported out of nowhere to block his path, a hand holding both railings. He was wearing a red-and-green-striped rugby shirt and coffee-colored shorts. "You looking for something?" he asked in strongly accented English.

"Yes, Mr. di Girolamo."

"He's not expecting you."

Greg couldn't see the bodyguard's eyes; they were hidden behind wraparound Ferranti sunglasses. His neck was thickly muscled, displaying a vast network of protruding veins. Whatever steroids he was taking, they were playing hell with his blood pressure.

"Just tell him Greg Mandel is here to see him." He held up the Event Horizon card.

The bodyguard thought it over, then called over his shoulder. Another bodyguard appeared at the top of the gangplank: a black bear of a man, more than two meters tall, shoulders in proportion, sweat glinting on his broad forehead. The two of them exchanged a brief murmur; then the first stabbed a meaty forefinger at Greg. "You. Don't move." He disappeared below deck, leaving his replacement to fold his arms and look Greg up and down contemptuously.

Greg ignored the attempted intimidation. If Kendric was relying on people like this to protect him from a professional snatch posse, then he was in deep trouble. They looked tough and probably knew their combat routine, but put them up against a tekmerc hardliner team and they wouldn't last the opening second.

Muddy water lapped quietly against the yacht's hull.

Greg had deliberately waited until midday to give Kendric a chance to recover from his partying at the Blue Ball.

"You've cracked," Suzi had barked when he told her he was going on board.

"Tell you, I have to get near Kendric," he said.

"Why, for Christ's sake?"

"Ask him questions; see how he reacts."

"Crazy." She crossed herself, eyes rolling. But she helped organize the backup, positioning the Trinities around the marina. Greg couldn't find any fault in her method; Suzi had been one who listened.

Knowing the squad was providing covering fire gave him a degree of confidence walking into the lion's den. The orders Suzi had were simple enough: on no account was he to be taken into the yacht itself.

"Okay, you can come up." The first bodyguard had returned. The set of his jaw radiated severe disapproval.

Mirriam was sixty-five meters of sheer beauty. Whatever his other faults, Kendric certainly knew the difference between refined style and pretentious glitz. *Mirriam* was conceived as a shrine to the former. Her polished wooden decks gleamed with a rosy sheen under the desert-bright sun. Every immaculate brass fixture was mirror bright. The low-friction white paint was painful on the eyes.

Greg was led around to the afterdeck. It had integral couches with puffy leather upholstery forming an island in the center, several recliners dotted about. There was a clutch of chrome gym equipment on the starboard side, just outside the lounge-cabin doors.

Katerina was lying prone on the bench press, using its leg lift, a big LCD counter notching up each pull. She was dressed in tight black neoprene sprinter shorts, green stretch leggings, and the top of a loose mauve T-shirt that'd been slashed in half, its ragged hem barely covering her large breasts. Her mane of blond hair was held back with a broad white elastic toweling band. She was perspiring heavily, drawing breath through her nostrils, an expression of grim concentration on her perfect chiseled features.

"I do know you," she said through clenched teeth. The weight she was lifting was almost as much as he used in his own regimen. "You were at Julie's house."

"That's me," Greg said. "Nice party, wasn't it?"

"You can go now, Mark. Kendric will be out in a minute."

The bodyguard looked like he wanted to protest but didn't quite know how. Greg flashed him a sunny smile, receiving a dark scowl for his trouble.

Despite the Ferranti glasses, Greg could tell the man's eyes were on Katerina as he shuffled off forward. It was understandable, given the circumstances. His own gaze kept switching between her fantastic legs and her abdomen, hypnotized by the hard cords of muscle flexing below her smooth tanned skin. Ever hopeful her little scrap of T-shirt would ride up just that fraction higher.

"Ninety-seven, ninety-eight, ninety-nine, finish," she gasped.

"Is it worth it?"

Her head dropped back to rest on the bench's thin padding. "Kendric likes me to be fit," she said. Her voice was high, childlike, and remote. "He says that anyone blessed with a body as good as mine has a duty to keep it in tip-top shape. He wouldn't enjoy me so much otherwise."

"And what Kendric says and enjoys is important, is it?"

Her eyes closed. "Yes. Very. They do things to me, you see, such wonderful things. If I can't please them in turn, they might stop. I couldn't stand that."

The passive singsong lilt she used to recite her doctrine gave him a chill. He folded his espersense around her.

Katerina's mind was strange—unruffled, as though she'd been popping tranquilizers. There was little mental activity; she was taking only the minimum notice of her surroundings. It was almost a hibernatory state. But there was no sign of any posttrauma withdrawal or any of the jagged rents of chemical-induced damage he had been expecting. Greg went deeper.

Beneath the sluggish currents of her surface thoughts there was a treasured core of memory, a glowing center of delicious anticipation and joy. But for all its bright glory, it was a contaminant, tainting every thought.

"What wonderful things?" he asked softly.

Katerina's face became dreamy. "They love me," she said.

"How do they love you?"

"Sometimes gently. Sometimes so fiercely they make me cry. It doesn't matter which. It always ends wonderfully."

Greg felt his skin going slick with cold sweat. "How long has this been going on, Katerina?"

"Ever since I came here. Time doesn't really bother me now; I'm too happy. Adrian tried, of course, tried so hard, but it never came with him, not properly. I'm so lucky they took me away from him. I might never have known otherwise."

"When did they take you away?"

She looked out vacantly across the marina, her mind nearly losing the thread of thought. "At the party, Uncle Horace's party. Bil Yi was there; that's what Julie promised. So I went. Only they were there, too. He was funny and kind. It was exciting." She turned back to look at Greg. An angel's face vandalized by tears. "He's so strong. And I'm afraid."

Kendric di Girolamo slid open the cabin-lounge door and stepped onto the aft deck. Hermione followed a pace behind.

"Mr. Mandel." He took Greg's hand in a limp grip. "So nice of you to call. I trust Katerina has been entertaining you satisfactorily." He was wearing a navy blue blazer with bright brass buttons and a spotted silk handkerchief peeping out of his breast pocket, a dark green cravat filling the top of his open white shirt. White flannel trousers and dark blue sneakers completed the nautical image.

Hermione bestowed a gracious smile. A musky breath of orchid perfume stole around Greg, caressing, starting off that certain tingle. The weeks hadn't dimmed the memory of her beauty. Skin-deep, he warned himself, camouflage. She was dressed in a cerise off-the-shoulder gypsy top and blue knee-length skirt. He was reminded of a bird of prey waiting to pounce, mesmerically deadly.

Katerina rose from the padded bench, bare feet slapping on the wooden deck as she came to stand close beside Kendric. "I've done my routine," she said, looking up adoringly at his face. "All of it, everything you said."

Greg turned away from her desperate search for Kendric's approval. Studying the New Eastfield skyline.

Kendric gently wiped her tears with his forefinger, an act that resulted in an almost electric jolt firing through Katerina's mind. His touch was awakening her. An incredibly warped version of Sleeping Beauty and Prince Charming.

"Well done, my dear. I shall attend you in a little while. I have to have a few words with this gentleman first."

The desolation on her face was heart-wrenching.

"Come along, darling," Hermione said. "It's just silly man's talk. We'll go and get you ready. You're all smelly after that exercise. A nice shower is just what you need." She took Katerina's hand and led her back into the cabin.

Katerina looked back at Kendric, eyes round, imploring. "Hurry."

Kendric blew her a kiss.

The door closed. Through the blackened glass Greg could just make out Katerina pulling off her mauve T-shirt. Hermione's arm slipped possessively around the girl's narrow waist, leading her deeper into the *Mirriam*.

"Such an exquisite young girl," Kendric said, watching Greg's face with narrowed eyes. "I have always admired your English roses. After one has broken through that cool reserve, their adventurousness knows no bounds." There was a fragment of disappointment registering in his mind at Greg's refusal to show the slightest execration.

"I'm afraid I can't stop long, Mr. di Girolamo," Greg said. "My friends would worry about what'd happened to me."

"No," Kendric said. His thoughts were steely.

"I'm sorry?"

"No. You're not staying at all, Mandel. Katerina let you on board. My mistake; you should not have been allowed within a million kilometers of the *Mirriam*."

"But I was wondering if you could help me."

"I inquired about you after our first encounter. I know what you are. A gland psychic. A Mindstar veteran. You were not going to ask me anything; you were going to uncover. Event Horizon's truth-finder general, sent to pry by your whore-daughter mistress."

Greg held his dismay in check. "Any answers you give would be entirely voluntary. I can't read people's thoughts."

"So you claim, and other people fervently hope. It is a particular human weakness you pry on, Mandel; we want, need, to believe we are secure against you. But I have a vast repository of confidential commercial information in my brain. I choose not to believe the word of a repulsive grotesquery, a failed laboratory experiment."

Greg let the neurohormones discharge into his brain, desperately searching around with his intuition. There was guilt here, a strong scent; Kendric and Julia were tied together, hating each other, feeding off each other. With a shock he knew she was as guilty as Kendric. Both of them willfully stimulating the other's black obsession, a perverted symbiosis.

He was jerked out of his meditative analysis by hands like a pair of vises clamping round his upper arms. The bodyguards were standing on either side of him.

"Mark, Toby, throw him off," Kendric said.

"I'm going," Greg told them. He sensed rather than saw Mark's smirk.

"Too right," the bodyguard said.

Greg contracted his espersense, neglecting the other minds arrayed around the *Mirriam*, focusing on Kendric alone. "Wolf," he shouted.

There was no reaction. No guilt, fright, consternation, panic. The name hadn't registered. Instead, a band of mild puzzlement tapered through Kendric's mind. It was followed by a rising tide of wry satisfaction when he realized how shaken Greg was by the negative.

Toby and Mark frog-marched him off the aft deck and down the side of the superstructure, Kendric's laughter chasing him all the way.

He was dropped abruptly at the top of the gangplank, stumbling. Something with the force of a runaway train slammed into his backside. He tried to curl up into the trusty old paratroop landing crouch, but it didn't seem to work very well. He saw a fast, confusing snapshot sequence of yachts and water and sky at impossible angles, each black interstice punctuated by a new burst of pain that mercifully shut off almost as soon as it registered, leaving a patch of numbness. The bioware node spliced into his cortex that regulated his gland was also programmed to blank out nervous impulses above a predetermined pain level. Mindstar had included the limiter as an experiment to try and alleviate shock in combat injury cases, but the Army had never brought it into widespread use; there was too much danger of squaddies ignoring the damage they'd received and making it worse.

The unyielding concrete of the quay arrested his helter-skelter momentum with a sickeningly loud slap. His brain seemed to be floating at the center of a closed insensate universe. There was harsh laughter from afar followed by running feet. Hands grasped him, hauling him upright.

"Shit. You okay? Can you walk?"

Tactile sensation eased back, the cortical node reopening enough nerve channels for him to regain control over his limbs. Bruises throbbed sharply across his legs, arms, and back. His left leg was shaking. Both hands smarted from wide slashes of grazed skin, filming over with blood. Tunnel vision showed his suede desert boots at some vast distance. He couldn't breathe through his nose; it was full of warm sticky liquid.

"Come on, lean on us." That was Suzi.

Greg did so, gratefully.

"You want those pillocks taken out?" There was a note of hope coloring her voice.

"No." He shook his head. Big mistake. The world reeled alarmingly; acid bile rose, scouring his throat.

"Green south, green south, stand down. We're bringing Thunderchild in. Gold west, cover please."

There was a small Cambridge-blue three-wheel sweeperfloat ahead of him now, its front roller brushes retracted, inclined at forty-five degrees, looking like rusty felt mandibles. The name GUS'S SANITIZING was written down the side in bold yellow letters.

Greg was urged on to the narrow seat in the Perspex-bubble cab, and Des climbed in behind the wheel while Suzy rode shotgun on the footplate. The two Trinities were both wearing jaunty red shirts and matching trousers, complemented with Gus's company caps, burger-bar uniforms.

Des swooped the float into a hard turn and set off back down the quay at a good five kilometers per hour, squirting a thick spray of bubbly detergent in their wake. He fumbled with the dash switches and cut the rain of cleanliness, cursing hotly.

"I've got to go back," Greg said, pinching his nose between thumb and forefinger.

"Fuck that," Des said. "We've blown cover hauling you out. I've gotta get my squad safeguarded. Standard procedure; you should know that, Mr. Military Hotshot. This operation is now over."

"What the hell do you want to go back for?" Suzi asked.

"I have to see something."

They shot out onto the promenade, and Des tilted the joystick sharply left. Pedestrians hopped out of the way, hurling abuse.

"Listen," Des said. "You wanna go back, that's fucking fine by me. I'll stop right now and you can walk. But you're on your own. We've been burning our arses off for you, and I don't see anything to show for it."

"Okay, drop me here."

"Shit." Suzi and Des exchanged anxious befuddled glances. "You can't," said Suzi. "Come on, Greg, you can't hardly walk. We'll bring you back in a couple of days, when it's cooler."

"It has to be now."

"The photon amps are still in place; how about we take you back to Angelica's? You can watch from there."

Greg probed his nose tenderly. It didn't feel broken, and it'd stopped bleeding. "Not that sort of watching, not visual. I want to use my espersense on them."

"Jesus," Des spat. "You Mindstar?"

"Yeah."

"Bloody hell," Suzi muttered. "I knew there was something about you. Father never said nowt."

Greg said nothing. He had always held back from mentioning it to the Trinities. People developed funny attitudes to psychics, kids especially. Let them just think he was lucky; outfits like that put a lot in superstition.

"Jesus," Des said. "Fucking Mindstar active in Peterborough. Think on it. Party always pissed itself over you people. Look, just what is going down on that yacht?"

"If I knew for sure, I wouldn't have to go back."

"Shit, just how close do you have to get?"

They compromised. Des drove into the maze of service alleys behind the promenade shops and swapped clothes with Greg. Then he went off to organize the squad's withdrawal, leaving Suzi to drive

Greg. There'd be no more retrieval posses if Toby and Mike came after them, but the snipers would remain in place until Greg had finished.

Suzi drove back out onto the promenade and deployed the brushes before moving up the quay next to the *Mirriam*'s mooring. Seagull crap dissolved into creamy puddles, frizzy bristles whisking it away into the float's tanks.

"Stop here," Greg told her once they were opposite Kendric's yacht.

She climbed out of the little cab. "Don't be too long," she implored, and lifted the engine cowling.

Greg relaxed, sinking back into the thin cushioning of the bench, and instructed the cortical node to shut out the sharp throbs of pain his nerves were reporting loyally.

The gland: stressed, taut like a marathon runner's calf on the home straight. A sluice of neurohormones bubbled out among his axons.

He wanted a sensory extension that went way beyond his usual short-range emotion perception. To find it he retreated inward, ignoring his blood heat, heartbeats, breathing. The state waited for him right down at the bottom of the mental well, a fragile central pool. Gaseous shapes meandered below its surface. He slipped softly below the interface.

Greg perceived shadows, treacherous gray cobwebs congealing into misleading forms, aching empty gaps of grainy mist. The vision was silent, neither hot nor cold. Through it all, minds shone like diamond-point mirages, a flat cyclonic swirl of fireflies with himself at the tranquil storm eye. He concentrated, seeking the opaque distortion of *Mirriam*, the familiar signature of one mind.

The water resolved as a sheet of black ice, a dead zone; he drifted across it, stretching out close to his absolute limit. *Mirriam*'s hull rose above him, a cliff of insubstantial gauze. Passing through.

The three figures were cloudy alien protrusions into his lonely universe, their shape fuzzy, a pseudo-locus rippling around a solid kernel. Kendric and Hermione slid fluidly over and around Katerina, the three together a tightly knit serpentine coil.

Katerina was a soul in torment, hating herself for what she was doing, unable to refuse. She closed out the degradations Hermione performed, warm with the conviction her reward would come.

Greg observed her arousal growing as Kendric pleasured himself with her, his mind leaking distorted pictures of Julia. Fissures of intense rapture multiplied through her mind, interlacing, spreading to conquer, reducing her to animal abandon. Orgasm brought a blazing concussion of frenzied ecstasy, a neural nova.

Instinct and dusty memory fused within Greg's tarnished cranium, and at last he knew what Kendric had done to her.

The intangible universe twisted, spectral images elongating and spiraling down to a tightly wound vanishing point. The marina's sights and sounds boiled up around him, solid and loud.

"Let's go home," he said weakly. Sustaining such a vast psi-effusion was severely debilitating. Gravity seemed to have quadrupled.

" 'Bout time," Suzi grumbled, slamming down the cowling and locking the catches with a vicious twist. "You look like shit, you know?"

"Thank you." The sky overhead was jaundiced, its turbidity fluctuating in time to his heartbeat.

"That gland must really take it out of you." Her foot pressed down on the accelerator pad.

"It does."

"Thought so. You were thrashing about like you were having a nightmare. Get what you want?"

"Yes."

"Hey, your nose has started bleeding again."

"It'll stop in a minute."

27

O F COURSE KENDRIC WOULDN'T KNOW Wolf's name," Eleanor snapped irritably. "He's the man at the top, the one with the cleanest hands in town. He buys people who buy people who buy Wolf. That's why there was no response to the name; there'll be a whole chain of tekmercs between him and the cutting edge of the operation to get rid of Philip Evans. It's like that precaution you use in gear—what do you call it? And keep still."

"Cutoffs." Greg's voice had a throaty rasp to it.

She'd got his hands spread out on the chalet's kitchen bar, spraying his knuckles with Colman's dermal seal. From her own past experience she knew it stung, but it was the best on the market. The treacly salve fizzed over his grazes, quickly solidifying into a flexible powder blue membrane that would enhance tissue repair, molting after a couple of days.

Eleanor concentrated on keeping her hand steady as she moved the can back and forth, getting an even deposit. Her shoulders ached, and her back was cramped from hunching over him for three-quarters of an hour. She was getting tired, and her temperament showed it.

The lion roar of the Triumph bike trailing the Duo into the Berry-but estate had triggered some kind of premonition in her. She'd come running from the shore as Des helped Greg out of the Duo. There seemed to be blood all over him, his Stewart sweater was torn, and he couldn't walk without leaning on Des.

She'd felt resentful as Suzi and Des carried him into the chalet: an invasion of her personal space. The chalet was symbolic of all that was good in life right now. They were violating that, harbingers of pain and violence. She knew she'd always associate them with disruption now, no matter how much Greg praised them.

They'd seen Greg onto the lounge sofa and departed on the Triumph, Suzi, surprisingly, as awkward as Eleanor herself was. Who would have thought the girl possessed that much sensitivity?

Eleanor had been thankful for her animal husbandry courses; they let her deal with his injuries without the vapors, keeping a rigid leash on her nausea. She'd frozen his nose and clotted the burst blood vessels inside, painted numb-all on his swollen left eye, immobilized his left ankle in a thick sock of quick-set medical polymer, and generally cleaned him up. The clothes would have to go, though; she'd throw them on the bonfire tonight.

"You're right," he said. "Tell you, I thought I'd got it all sussed. I thought Kendric would light up like a Christmas tree when I mentioned Wolf. It was the proof I'd need to convince Morgan Walshaw. And I've got to convince him somehow. Kendric is absolutely jungle crazed about Julia."

"I know," she said. "I reviewed the surveillance memox the Trinities made."

"That's not the half of it. Kendric really is—" He broke off, letting out a long painful breath. "That's why I went on board. I'm worried about Julia, what he'll do. Stupid of me. Breaking all the rules about personal involvement. So you wind up with me looking like this. Sorry. Not a nice sight for you."

She'd never heard him sound so dejected. She leaned over the bar and touched her lips to his face. "I couldn't live with the kind of man who felt nothing for her. You wouldn't be human."

"That's been said before."

"Not by me." She began spraying again. "Besides, this is nothing; superficial apart from the ankle, and that'll be all right in a week."

"Good. Anyway, my visit wasn't a complete disaster. You remember Katerina Cawthorp?"

Eleanor paused, flipping through her mental files. "Friend of Julia's?"

"Got it. Well, right now she's living with Kendric and Hermione."

"And Hermione?"

That brought a weak grin to his lips. "Yeah. That's how Kendric must've found out about Philip Evans's NN core. He would be bound to question Katerina about every aspect of her relationship with Julia, and that includes her time at Wilholm. She told him about the NN core. There is no mole, never has been."

"So how did Kendric get hold of the Zanthus security monitor programs?"

"A top-notch solo hot rod burned into Walshaw's cores. Kendric could afford it."

She finished spraying on the dermal seal and inspected his hand. "But what about the buyout?"

"Yeah," he admitted. "I still don't understand that. But the blitz was definitely a vengeance act. Katerina proves that; she's the link, the common factor. God, Eleanor, you wouldn't believe what he's done to that poor kid. Tell you, she's a virtual cyborg, no messing." He flexed his fingers gingerly, watching the dermal seal stretch over his knuckles.

"Has he drugged her?" she asked.

"Sort of. That's something else we'll have to sort out when this is finished. Christ, as if we didn't have enough to do identifying Wolf and the remaining hot rods."

"You know, if you wanted to flush some compromising evidence out of Kendric's brain, you should've asked him how much the blitz had cost him. Then you'd have seen the guilt, clear-cut and irrefutable. I'll have to bind that forefinger."

"Bugger. Next time I'll take you along. Someone who can think straight."

Her heart fell. "Oh, Greg, you're not thinking of going back there are you? Wasn't this enough?"

"No, I'm not marching up to confront Kendric again; I've learned my lesson. From now on the macho routine is all down to Morgan Walshaw and his hardliners. Hopefully, all I have to do is wait for Royan to backtrack Wolf's payments to O'Donal, find out who the hell he is. Then we can start establishing how Wolf is plugged in with Kendric. The proof's there, somewhere, like you said, another intermediary between Wolf and Kendric, maybe two. But I'm *convinced* it's him at the end of the trail. Does that sound paranoid to you?"

"No, I believe your intuition works, and like you say, having Katerina on his yacht explains how he knew about the NN core." She consulted the Event Horizon terminal. The first-aid kit's diagnostic was plugged into it, the cube showing a white-shadow schematic of Greg's body. His pain points glowed a mild amber; she'd treated all of them. He was relaxed now, growing drowsy from the general tranquilizer she'd given him earlier. She held open his right eyelid, shining the pencil light directly on the pupil, then away, watching the dilation. The terminal said it was within acceptable limits. "Have you been overdoing the gland?"

"Used it a bit, nothing much."

She thought he sounded defensive. Not that she could even begin to give a qualified opinion on neurohormone abuse. Just a feeling, though; he appeared enervated, more than the cuts and sprains could account for. Why did men always try and disguise their weaknesses? "I think you might be slightly concussed. A hospital check-up wouldn't hurt."

"No need to bother them. I'll spend tomorrow resting."

"Promise?"

"All that's scheduled is a trip to Wilholm Manor to check out Gabriel's prediction of a second attack against the NN core."

She peeled the diagnostic pickup from the nape of his neck, where it was interfacing with his cortical node and coiled up the fiber-optic lead. The compact unit slotted neatly into the molded foam of the first-aid kit, a well-worn aluminum case, Army green with a big red cross painted on. Surplus to requirements, Greg had told her. There was a comprehensive range of dressings and medicine inside, all top quality. She'd thought he was a hypochondriac when she first saw it.

"That's all right then," she said, "providing your new billionaire girlfriend doesn't excite you too much."

"Please! Give me a break."

"Oh, I almost forgot. Dr. Ranasfari called this morning, charming man, left a message for you." She licked her lips at the memory. "He made a pass at me."

"Shit."

"Greg!"

"Sorry. You're kidding. Ranasfari? He made a pass at you? Never."

"He did. Men have been known to."

"Impossible, my dear. Ranasfari doesn't like people, any people. We're not rationally precise data packages."

"Don't be so bitchy, or are you just jealous?"

"Neither, simply observant. So what did the good doctor want to tell me?"

"There was definitely an outlaw instruction beamed up to the Merlin, shutting it down. Seven seconds are missing from the up-link's log, an hour before the shutdown. He said it was a very sophisticated interruption. They probably wouldn't have spotted it if you hadn't told them to search for it. They're reviewing the institute's 'ware memory cores to see if someone snatched the Merlin codes. But so far they haven't found any trace of a breach. He says whoever did it must be the best hot rod in existence, covering their tracks like that. The institute 'ware has premier-grade data-guardian programs; the security programmers thought they were unbreakable." Greg was staring at her, confusion and disbelief tugging at his face. Lost. "Something wrong?"

"Ranasfari can't have said that. It doesn't fit."

Seeing him like this, exhausted, wounded, and cripplingly de-spondent, she felt an overwhelming surge of affection for him. The case had been taxing him: punished by the gland, driven by his own ruthless brand of determination, beaten up by Kendric's bastards. Maxed out. All she wanted to do was help, ease the burden. If only he didn't have this stupid code of his, always giving a hundred per-cent. It was too much of him.

"Well, Ranasfari did say it. And it's time you were in bed, Greg Mandel."

"No, no, you don't understand. The blitz was a vengeance attack."

"Yes, you said. You proved Kendric ordered it."

"Yeah, well, sort of."

"The Merlin," she said, beginning to understand.

"If the Merlin was deliberately sabotaged," he said, "then the blitz was part of a *kombinate* spoiler operation."

"You are concussed. There's nothing to say the Merlin shutdown couldn't be vengeance, too. Kendric wanting to wipe Philip Evans and damage Event Horizon at the same time by undermining confi-dence in the gigaconductor cells. Hit Julia from both sides at once. After all, we know he's already used a top-grade hot rod against Event Horizon to pull the security monitors. He probably used the same hot rod to shut down the Merlin."

"Oh, yeah, right."

It was obvious he wasn't convinced. She began to speak with slow deliberation, voicing her thoughts almost as they formed. "The mo-tive for launching the blitz depends on whether Kendric knew of Philip Evans's NN core. If he did, it was him out for vengeance; if not, it was a *kombinate* spoiler. Right?"

"That's about the size of it."

"Good. So, how bright is Katerina?"

"What?"

"Don't you see? It all hangs on her, whether or not she knew about the NN core. And from what you've told me about her before she met Kendric, she sounds like the all-time champion bimbo. Could she have worked out what was going down at Wilholm?"

His eyes closed, face pained. "Dunno. She had a good education."

"Means nothing. Who would know if she's got enough brains?"

"Julia, I suppose. Certainly poor old Adrian. I knew it would hap-pen, that she'd dump him. Should've warned him, given him the ben-efit. He wouldn't have listened."

Eleanor ignored his ramblings. Knowing the sense of excitement derived from solving human intricacies. Finally appreciating how Greg could become so wrapped up in his cases. There was a certain addictive quality to unraveling the carefully crafted deceits of other people; it was a form of conquest, outsmarting them. "Then you'll just have to ask Julia. But not today, I think."

28

W<small>ILHOLM'S LAWN SPRINKLERS WERE WORKING</small> at full strength, their long white plumes adding a faint coppery tang to the dry pollen-clogged air. Julia ran down the garden path, giggling wildly, trying to dodge the spray shooting out of the rotating nozzles. The cotton of her emerald green dress was already damp. She glanced over her shoulder and saw Adrian had almost caught up. A shriek, a last triumphant burst of speed from her legs, and she reached the gravel drive ahead of him.

OtherEyes Access Request.

Adrian yelled behind her, cursing, and she turned, cracking up at the sight of him caught full square in one of the foamy jets. He slopped onto the gravel trailing dark footprints.

"I'm bloody drenched," he wailed, laughing with her.

He was, too, T-shirt and tennis shorts clinging to his skin. She draped her arms round his neck, kissing him exuberantly. "My very own Mr. Wet T-shirt." The giggles set in again, unstoppable.

OtherEyes Priority Access Request.

His hands found her rump, squeezing with interest. "Do we have enough time before he gets here?" His breath was hot in her ear. He'd begun to nuzzle her neck, aiming for that place he'd found that was exceptionally ticklish.

She let out a heartfelt sigh, squirming in his arms as his tongue licked below her ear. "Not this morning. Busy."

"Afternoon?"

She nodded eagerly. Adrian was insatiable. Wonderfully, fabulously insatiable.

Alaka had been disappointed by the nonappearance of their star guest at most of the functions after Friday night. But she didn't give a flying fig about that. This was love.

And Adrian felt the same about her, so enraptured he'd come back to Wilholm with her on Sunday night.

"I'm afraid to let you out of my sight," he'd said. "I can hardly believe a girl like you would even look at someone like me."

So she did her best to convince him, realizing his every wicked fantasy on her big apricot silk bed and in the Jacuzzi, the shower, dresser chair, deep-pile rug. And Adrian could be very wicked indeed.

Her grandfather hadn't said anything about Adrian coming to stay, not a peep. She hoped that meant he'd finally accepted her as an equal. Part of his kindness before, she knew now, had been the type a teacher shows a gifted pupil. That she could be groomed to manage Event Horizon was his driving concern. She forgave him that. Right now she could forgive anybody anything.

OtherEyes Access Request: Please Juliet.

"All afternoon," Adrian growled insistently.

"Absolutely." He was going back to the college in the evening, which would give them a solid six hours to practice yet more of that rapturous sex. Then there was next weekend to look forward to. Thank the Lord Cambridge wasn't far away. Although she would've traveled to Tasmania for him.

Julia heard the sound of tires on the drive and began to disentangle herself, suddenly wondering what the hell she must look like: hair tangled, front of her dress damp from where she'd pressed against Adrian, cheeks flushed, and grinning like a madwoman. Greg would hardly need his empathy to see what she'd been getting up to.

Adrian kept hold of her hand as the little Duo pulled up in front of the portico. The car's arrival frightened Wilholm's flock of snow-white doves into flight above her.

Open Channel to NN Core. Load OtherEyes. Limiter#Three

Sight and hearing only, so her grandfather wouldn't be able to sense her racing heart or experience Adrian's adventurous hands.

Thank you so very much, Philip Evans said. *So sorry to trouble you. In case it's of the remotest interest, we think the Trojan program which Gabriel predicted has been loaded into the Event Horizon datanet. There was a highly sophisticated code melt in our Doncaster silicon-fiber plant 'ware two minutes ago; they are scheduled to squirt their production data to me in another five minutes.*

Julia suddenly hated the real world for intruding on her private happiness. It seemed to delight in conspiring to reduce her time with Adrian—Greg's visit, unseen hackers. Why couldn't they leave her alone? Petty grubbing manipulators, all of them, pissing in the wind. They weren't going to alter society, or bankrupt Event Horizon, or make the Sun revolve around the Earth, turn water into wine. The sum total of their activities was so near to zero as to be derisory. People were so bloody stupid and insensitive: animals that'd learned how to wear clothes.

Her arm tightened instinctively around Adrian. He didn't know how much of a comfort he was.

Don't be so sarcastic, Grandpa; it's very unbecoming. Have Walshaw's security programmers managed to backtrack?

Not yet.

Total surprise.

Give them some credit, Juliet, that melt was hard to spot.

If they'd written a decent guardian program in the first place, there wouldn't have been a melt-through.

Her grandfather answered with a reproachful silence. Surprising what could be read from emptiness.

Greg climbed out of the Duo. Julia let out an involuntary gasp. His left eye was swollen and black, heavily bruised; a molded white surgical dressing covered his nose; his hands seemed to be all blue dermal membrane; he was limping.

Christ!

"What happened?!" she demanded anxiously.

He smiled heavily. "I had a little chat with your friend, Kendric di Girolamo."

"My God! He did this to you?"

"His bodyguards."

"Oh, Greg. You shouldn't even be out of bed. Come along with you, out of this hot sun."

Greg shrugged. "Not as bad as it looks." His eyes were fixed on Adrian. Accusing, Julia thought, certainly not indifferent. My God, could he be jealous?

Adrian stirred uncomfortably under the stare, gripping her hand that little bit tighter.

"Adrian, isn't it?" Greg asked.

"Yes, sir."

They reminded her of two stags, scraping hoofs before they locked antlers. Disturbing to think she might be the cause, but then again it didn't exactly hurt her ego.

Greg's cut lips quirked slightly, breaking the spell. "The name's Greg. Nice to see you again."

Adrian relaxed a little at her side.

She gave him a huge sunny smile. "This conference won't take long, darling. Would you see to Tobias? I've been neglecting him shockingly."

"Sure thing." He pecked her cheek and gave Greg a quick curious glance before heading off toward the stables.

Another thing about him, he understood the way Event Horizon business dominated her life, and made allowance, never making unreasonable demands. There weren't many who'd do that. He was going to make a smashing doctor with that kind of sympathy.

"Nice lad," Greg offered as they reached the shade of the portico. There was sweat on his forehead.

She slipped her arm into his, steadying his walk, glad to have someone trustworthy to confide in. "Nice? Greg, he's gorgeous. And you should see him with his shirt off. Totally hunky!"

"Lucky Adrian."

Doncaster is squirting, now!

Julia nearly groaned aloud. How could she have forgotten about Grandpa? He would've heard every word. That bloody OtherEyes was going to have to be rewritten again.

Greg was looking at her speculatively. A blush was rising up her cheeks.

Morgan Walshaw was waiting for them in the study. He did a double take at Greg's injuries, frowning, then signaled them to sit.

Julia pulled out her chair at the head of the table. The dark polished surface in front of her was cluttered with gear modules and cubes. Morgan Walshaw was devouring information from three cubes fed by an elaborate-looking customized terminal. Next to her grandfather's NN core was a Commodore bioware number cruncher, a maroon hexagonal block fifty centimeters across and twelve high. A thick bundle of fiber-optic cables linked it to the study's communication consoles. Her grandfather called it junior; he'd unplugged his NN core from Event Horizon's datanet, plugging in the Commodore as a replacement. It'd been loaded with a Turing personality responses program, and he'd spent the last three days reformatting it to shuffle Event Horizon's data squirts in a routine fashion.

"Will you look at that." Her grandfather's gruff voice rumbled around the study.

The biggest cube on the table was displaying a schematic of the Commodore's databuses, a nightmare Möbius topology of fine turquoise lines binding together a miniature globular cluster of sparkling jade stars.

A cadaverous pink stain had begun to wash through the image, spreading down the lines and branching at every star, tainting everything in its path.

"Christ, the bugger's expansion rate is phenomenal. About fifth power!" the directionless voice exclaimed.

The cube showed an unhealthy homogenous pink blob.

"Six seconds from reception to total domination. Incredible. Whoever they are, they're serious. I would never have been able to stop it if it'd got into the NN core. That's all down to Gabriel. Where is she, Greg?"

"Her psi-function takes a lot out of her. She's at home recuperating."

"Well, try and get her back here. I want to thank her personally."

If Greg was aware of the irony he didn't show it. "I'll tell her."

"So. Kendric had you roughed up, did he, boy?"

"My fault. I confronted him."

"Why?" Julia asked.

"Taking a shortcut. I wanted to establish that Kendric was the one who paid Wolf."

"Well, of course he is!" she exclaimed.

Greg shook his head gingerly. "No. That's the problem. Kendric isn't directly behind the blitz. Not that I could prove, anyway. My intuition says he's involved in some way, though."

"Well, there you are then," she said.

"I wanted something a little more concrete."

"What for?"

She saw Greg and Walshaw exchange an edgy glance. It was so bloody annoying. Why couldn't they speak in front of her?

"Concrete proof for concrete action," Walshaw said quietly.

"Oh." She put her hands flat on the table, studying the nails intently.

"It wasn't a complete waste of time," Greg said. "I think I can prove Kendric does know about the NN core."

"Ah!" Philip said triumphantly.

Julia suddenly realized Greg was staring right at her.

"Katerina Cawthorp is living with Kendric on his yacht," Greg said.

"Still?" Julia blurted.

"You knew about it?"

"I knew she'd gone off with him; I was there when it happened. I thought Kendric was another of her one-night stands. Kats is like that, you see. Bit of a bed-hopper."

"What I'd like to know is whether or not she's bright enough to work out that your grandfather was planning to translocate his memories into the NN core," Greg said. "She was here for a few days. The opportunity exists."

"A week." Julia stared pensively at the leather-bound books on the wall shelving, not bothering to cut in the processor node. Remembering all those years she and Kats had spent together at school. Only time's perspective gave them a totally different slant, like an old play whose plot she'd forgotten. They'd seemed like great days while they were happening, insufferably tedious now. "Kats never paid any attention to classes, too busy with boys," she said slowly, reluctant to condemn. "But no, she's not stupid. It's just that I find it hard to believe Kats would bother listening to idle business chatter, let alone interpret it."

"She wouldn't have to interpret it; Kendric would do that for himself," Greg said.

"I'm sure I never mentioned the NN core project in front of her. I wouldn't have; there'd be no point: science and finance simply don't fit into her worldview. And Grandpa and I certainly never discussed it at meals."

"She may have overheard it being mentioned. There's a certain thrill in eavesdropping on the conversations of someone as powerful as your grandfather. Even if she couldn't make sense of it at the time, she might remember what was said."

"True enough," said Walshaw. "Though the Kendric connection is still circumstantial."

"Don't be obtuse, Morgan," Julia said. After all Greg had gone through he didn't deserve disparaging observations. "Of course Kendric's guilty. He reeks of it."

"I wasn't disagreeing," the security chief said mildly. "It is the degree of Kendric's involvement which seems to be unresolved."

"Not the exact degree, no," Greg said. "But he's in deep, no messing. And I think we can rule out a mole now that we know about Katerina." He glanced at Walshaw for confirmation.

"Yes."

"Okay, that just leaves the question of why Kendric allowed Julia to buy him out. I still don't understand that, and it bothers me. We know he's in trouble with the family over the money he withdrew from Event Horizon's backing consortium, and he's working on some deals to try and fill the gap, provide the house with an equal return. That's got to be the key, these deals of his. And they're tied up with you somewhere." He shot Julia a fast glance.

She knew he meant his intuition again. It gave her a creepy feeling, the way his suspicions about the spoiler had turned out to be true. Now Kendric was making unknown deals.

"Raw materials?" Walshaw suggested. "Is he buying up the options on the compounds that go into the gigaconductor?"

"No," said Philip. "There aren't any really rare minerals involved in any case. And I've made quite sure we have a safeguarded stockpile of the chemicals we use. That's an elementary precaution; I did that even before we filed the patent."

Greg rubbed the dressing on his nose with a forefinger. "Tell you, my own impression is that Kendric has made some sort of alliance."

"With who?" Julia asked.

He gave her a wan smile. "Don't know. Someone, some organization who would benefit from having your grandfather wiped. Kendric is an influence peddler, you see. Once he established that Philip Evans's memories were stored in the NN core, he could barter the information in exchange for an investment opportunity that'd give the family house money a return equal to the Event Horizon backing consortium. Get someone else to do his dirty work for him and make a profit at the same time. That's his style."

"A *kombinate*?"

"No, I never believed it was a *kombinate* behind the blitz; a month-long delay in introducing the gigaconductor would be a nonsense when you consider their cyber-factories would have to be totally rebuilt to produce the stuff."

"What, then?"

"Sorry, I can't tell you. That's just the feeling I get out of all this." He shrugged. "Kendric definitely has some sort of scheme in mind; the buyout is proof of that, as well as his hatred for you."

"Mutual," Julia said automatically.

"I know."

And the way he said it made her glance at him; he'd sounded disapproving.

"What about this Wolf bloke," Philip said. "He's had two goes at me now. Seems to me, you ought to be concentrating on him, boy."

"I was coming to that. My contact has backtracked O'Donal's payments; he squirted Wolf's identity to me this morning."

"May we know the name?" Walshaw asked.

"Charles Ellis. Currently residing at the Castlewood condominium, New Eastfield, Peterborough."

She couldn't help the little start of interest. "I know that place. Uncle Horace lives there; it's not far from the marina. That proves Ellis is connected to Kendric, doesn't it?"

"Not necessarily. It's a perfectly logical place for someone that rich to gravitate to. Although I admit it's pushing coincidence a long way."

"Rich?" Walshaw inquired. "What is he, a tekmerc?"

"Apparently not," said Greg. "According to my contact, Ellis is a data fence. He normally goes under the handle Medeor. Wolf is a totally new venture for him."

"What do you propose as your next step?" Walshaw asked. His gray eyes had narrowed, contemplating Greg with reserved, vaguely threatening preoccupation.

"Pay Charles Ellis a visit. He's the last link, the connection between the team of hot rods who ran the blitz and whoever paid for it."

"Seeing as how you're so close, I'd like to send one of my operatives along with you," Walshaw said. "I know you prefer to work independently, and I respect that. But the stakes are mounting."

"I wasn't going to object," Greg said. "Just make sure he's briefed not to interrupt."

"He won't."

"One more thing, have you had any luck with the analysis of Tentimes's burns?" Greg asked.

"If you mean is there a single beneficiary, then the answer is no." Walshaw paused, looking concerned. "But seven manufacturing companies have gone under because of O'Donal, and some of the financials are on a sticky wicket, although they'll never admit a thing. And now that we know what to look for, the researchers have spotted several similar victims outside O'Donal's list. It looks like all eight of Wolf's hot rods are very active; they've caused a lot of damage in the last year. It prompts the question why."

"Yes," said Philip. "If that kind of disturbance is being repeated by others like him I'd hate to think of the long-term consequences."

"Perhaps that's Wolf's goal," Greg said. "Trying to sabotage Event Horizon's long-term prospects."

"I don't mean just us, boy. I've run my own analysis on the burns and their fallout. They're totally indiscriminate. If that sort of thing isn't halted soon it'll add at least another couple of points to inflation, and that's already running too high as it is. A further rise would blow the chancellor's budget to pieces."

"You mean even Kendric would suffer?"

"Everybody suffers," Walshaw said bluntly.

"Could it be another government? If England's industrial output goes down, who'd step in to make up the shortfall?"

"Just about everybody," Philip concluded miserably. "Bloody Pacific Rim would be the biggest beneficiaries, of course."

Julia saw the connection without having to kick in her processor nodes. "A finance house," she said firmly. Both men looked at her.

"A finance house would benefit from a change of interest rates, if they knew for sure it would happen."

"That's right, they would. Good girl, Juliet."

"The di Girolamo house?" Walshaw mused.

"Why worry?" she said brightly. "Greg can do his word association thing with Ellis to find out the details. You'll have it all solved for us by tonight, Greg, won't you?"

Greg sat back in his chair, a tired smile playing over his battered face. "How much do you want to bet on that?"

29

GREG KEPT A CAUTIONARY EYE on Julia as she walked out to the car with him. There was a confidence about her that had been absent before; she'd always had poise, but it'd been stilted and formal. This was a natural grace. No doubt Adrian had a lot to do with it. The kind of stability he offered putting her at ease with other people.

Adrian hadn't changed all her habits, though. He thought her emerald broderie anglaise dress was something Maid Marion would've been perfectly at home in; it had puffball cap sleeves, a lace-up bodice, and a skirt hem riding several centimeters above her knees. Nice legs. The girl's clothes sense was the weirdest; nobody else her age wore anything remotely similar. But, of course, she wasn't like anybody else her own age. Just wanted to be.

She lifted the front door's iron latch for him, eager to please. Sparrows, goldfinches, and a couple of hoopoes squabbled underneath the sprinklers' cascade, pecking at the grass for worms that'd risen in the artificial rain. The direct sunlight set off an uncomfortable itch on Greg's face and hands.

"Hop in," he said, as he blipped the Duo doors, "I've got something to say to you."

Her face lit up with mischief. "Greg, really! And Adrian so close by."

He sensed that ghostly extraneous thought current leave her mind with lightning swiftness. Her own thoughts were a fast-paced mixture of excitement and contentment. Julia was one happy girl. He flicked the jammer on, screening the Duo's interior from the manor's security surveillance sensors. "Julia."

Her expression dropped at his tone. "What?"

"Katerina."

"Oh, her. What about her?"

"I'm going to be very nice to you, and I'm not going to put you over my knee and give you a damn good wallop. Although God knows you deserve it, or worse, after what you've done."

"What?" She was spluttering, hauteur and outrage gathering within her mind.

"Your grandfather was quite right about you. You're a sciolist; you know the moves, but not the governing laws."

"I don't know what you mean."

"Oh, you worked it out very nicely on a surface level, I'll grant you that. What you failed to appreciate were the undercurrents."

"Stop talking in euphemisms. It's bloody annoying."

"I've seen inside Kendric's mind," Greg said. "He dreams of you, Julia."

"He does?" She was suddenly very uncertain.

"He hates you and fears you. He wants to destroy you. No. He's obsessed with destroying you. Not merely Event Horizon, but you personally, physically. He wants you beneath him, Julia, spread-eagled and screaming. He's sick in a way you'll never know."

"I do know," she insisted quietly.

"No, not really; you still haven't twigged, have you? Loathing is an abstract to you, a word whose meaning you've looked up in a dictionary. Kendric is its physical embodiment, lethal, and scatological to boot. You will never understand the sheer intensity of his revenge psychosis. It's a monstrous personality dysfunction.

"Tell you, Kendric sets up targets to knock down, fixates on them, devoting himself single-mindedly to their downfall. For the kind of left-hand business he's involved with it's a commendable trait. He'd been pretty successful, too: built up a good reputation for reliability, top man in the field. He'd never really known failure. Then I come along, hired by your grandfather, and we thwart him in what was probably his most ambitious scheme ever: asset-stripping Event Horizon. His first true debacle. Then you followed it up by humiliating him with blackmail. Anyone flying that high is going to be hurt bad by the fall. Small wonder you dominate his thoughts; any normal person would be bitter, but with a wacko like that it was probably the push over the edge. You misjudged him completely, and now Katerina is suffering because of that."

"She went with him," Julia said defiantly. "It was her choice."

"Of course it was, but you engineered it. You and your oh-so-logical nodes, meticulously sketching out all the conceivable scenarios the players could be combined in. You've got Kendric, rich, handsome, an expert in seduction, kinky wife who doesn't object to him playing the field. Katerina, in your eyes naïve, also sex-mad and your close friend, who just happens to have in tow a very desirable stud who you've had your eye on for some time. And finally the poor old stud himself, Adrian, who Katerina had almost tired of anyway.

"You invited Katerina and Adrian to Horace Jepson's party, a real fiesta rave atmosphere complete with the world's greatest rock star. Katerina could no more refuse that than a bee can ignore pollen. And you chose it because that party was the perfect melting pot. Kendric walks in, sees you, the lonely little rich girl with probably her only real friend in the world, who by lucky chance is a real stunner and just as randy as he is. Well, he jumps at it, doesn't he? And he succeeds easily, because he's got the same sex appeal as Adrian, loaded with a suavity Adrian couldn't begin to match, and filthy rich with it. Katerina simply leaps at him.

"Kendric thinks he's scored a double bonus, depriving you of a friend and confidante, and at your age friends like that are terrifically important, plus he gets himself and Hermione a nice chunk of fresh meat to fun around with. You, in the meantime, get rid of Katerina, in whose company any girl will look like one of Cinderella's sisters, and get to console a devastated Adrian, who gratefully repays you with the only currency he's got."

There was a long moment of excruciating silence.

"Kats did, you know." Julia was sitting perfectly still, gazing unseeingly straight down the drive. "School, parties, clubs—nobody even knew I existed. Not with her there. Her bust, her legs, God, even her voice is total audio sex." She sniffed, blinking furiously, neck still rigid. "Do you know why I grew my hair so long? Do you? Because boys like a girl with long hair. Somebody told me that when I was eleven, and I've never had it cut since. I thought it would give me a chance, because there's nothing else to attract them. But of course her hair's long, too, and shiny blond." Julia turned to look straight at him, unrepentant, hot determination shining bright in her mind. "All I've got is my brains. And if brains is the only way I can grab hold of a boy, then by God that's how I'll grab one. And there's nobody, not you, not Grandpa, nobody, who is going to tell me different!"

Greg could see how much pain and loneliness was bottled up behind those stubborn eyes. That was something about her he'd misunderstood, assuming it was brattish cattiness that had provided the motivation behind her conniving. The spoiled rich kid who didn't get the treat she wanted, planning silent revenge on those who'd denied her.

"Oh, Julia, Julia, what are we going to do with you? If you'd sat down and tried to come up with a more harmful goal you couldn't have found anything worse than giving Katerina to Kendric."

"I realize that now," she said miserably. "But how was I to know anyone walking 'round Wilholm could work out what Grandpa intended, or that Kats would be so willing to tell Kendric."

He winced inwardly. "She doesn't have a lot of choice."

"There's something you didn't mention, isn't there? About Kats. I never expected her to stay with Kendric for more than a day or two; not with Hermione insisting on her share. My God, you just can't get any more hetero than Kats. That's why I never felt any remorse, you see. As if one more man would make any difference to her. She said she had her first boy at thirteen. Thirteen! I just wanted their fling to last long enough to disillusion Adrian. But sticking it out like this is way out of character for Kats."

The sprinklers began to die down outside the Duo, leaving the whole front garden glistening under a glacé patina. Tall chrysanthemum stems bowed under the weight of the crystalline droplets that mottled their big bulbous flowers.

"Have you ever heard of something called philter?" Greg asked.

She came as near to embarrassment as he'd ever seen her. "I remember someone mentioning the name once. Some sort of drug?" she said distantly.

"It's not quite a drug. Philter is a symbiotic bacterium which lives in the bloodstream, similar biotechnology principle as the gland. Strictly speaking it's a physiologically benign parasite. The most expensive narcotic ever created, a logical extrapolation from the old Ecstasy drug. It boosts orgasmic pleasure tenfold, a genuine designer high."

"Oh." Julia was studying her nails with minute attention.

"Pavlov would understand what Kendric has done to her. It's the nastiest form of conditioning I've ever come across. If, and only if, she does exactly what he tells her to then he takes her to bed and gives her that superorgasm for a reward. She doesn't know it can happen with anybody.

"I imagine one of the first things he made her do was recount every conversation she'd had with you for the last few months, looking for something to use against you. He really lucked out discovering your grandfather's NN core plans."

Julia was silent for a minute, then said, "Thanks for not saying any of this in front of Grandpa."

He glared at her, feeling his hands ache as his blood rose.

"Now what?" she cried.

"There's just nothing that gets through to you, is there? I tell you that there's a maniac out there who wants your blood, that you're responsible for your best friend being raped twice a day for over a fortnight, that her mind's being systematically destroyed, and all you say is thanks for not telling a swarm of electrons floating around in a mutated vegetable. You fucking ice bitch!"

"Well, for Christ's sake what do you want from me!" she screamed back. "I know all about bloody Kendric. I know more than anybody. I knew he was behind this right from the beginning. But all you cleverdick hardliners did was charge off after moles and hot rods. Nobody ever listens to a word I say; I'm just a nothing. I'm a signature on the bottom of papers. A performing seal. Well I'm not. I'll bloody well show all of you. Nobody's going to treat me like a joke after this. I'm going to kill that bastard di Girolamo for what he's done to me and Grandpa. And you, *gland freak*, you're going to get the proof for me, like you've been paid for. That's all you are, a paid freako let out of the zoo. And if you want to stay out of your cage, freako, you'll do what I bloody well tell you!"

Greg slapped her. Not hard, his hand was still sore. But Julia stared at him for one frozen horrified second, then burst into tears.

Greg raised his eyes heavenward, cursing his own blundering stupidity. He saw the gardeners walking past the Duo, their Wellingtons squelching through the puddles on the lawn. They glanced over at the car, its hot muffled voices, gray misted windows, seeing a figure hunched up in the front seat, face in hands, rocking back and forth. One turned to the other and barked a remark, there was a burst of lusty laughter, and they walked on. The shallow imprints left by their footprints slowly filled with muddy water behind them.

"Greg? I didn't mean it."

"I know. I'm sorry I slapped you."

"Didn't hurt."

Her cheeks were smeared with silver snail's trails of tears, nature's aphrodisiac. She looked terribly fragile and appealing. The ivory-tower princess fallen to earth with a bump, lost and frightened in the world she'd only ever glimpsed from afar. Greg wanted to put his arms around her and give her a big comforting hug. Resistance came hard.

A big teardrop formed on the bottom of her chin. "Greg, he doesn't want me," she said in a tiny voice.

"Julia—"

"No, really." Red-rimmed eyes blinked in anguish. "He's already had me."

She was suddenly in his arms, pressed against him, shivering uncontrollably. He hugged her, stroking her spine to give what reassurance he could. Praying he'd misheard, knowing he hadn't.

"I was fifteen," she said.

"Shush. It's over."

"No, I want to say it."

He studied her face, seeing the need; his espersense slid behind the hot skin and damp eyes. She really was terrified of Kendric. Funny, he'd never noticed that before, but she'd always toughed out any mention of his name. "Then tell me."

"It was my fifteenth birthday party. I'd never been happier: the PSP had just fallen, Grandpa's illness hadn't developed, and me and all my friends were dressed up in such wonderful dresses. Kendric came with a present for me, perfume, all gift wrapped. Uncle Kendric. He and Grandpa hadn't fallen out then, you see. He gave me the perfume and said that was only half of the present. He told me his nieces and nephews were all going to go cruising on the *Mirriam* for a fortnight, a di Girolamo family outing, and would I like to come. I *pleaded* with Grandpa to let me go. Grandpa never can say no to me. And then when I went on board there was only Kendric, no relatives, no family cruise. He was waiting for me. My present. I was too young, too stupidly blind with romance to realize. He was so handsome, the older man, rich and cultured and charming. God was he charming. You can't know what a man like that is capable of doing to the mind of a silly fifteen-year-old. The whole thing was like a channel drama made by the best director in the world, alone together on a yacht, surrounded by sea, shorelines, and golden sunsets. I loved every second of it. Believed every word he said. He hadn't married Hermione then. I thought I was the one. I was going to marry him. I was going to have his babies for him. I didn't believe God could create a monster like Kendric. Not on this world, the Good Earth."

She finished with a limp twitch of her lips. Greg carefully brushed some tangled wisps of hair from her face.

"God," she choked. "You must think I'm bloody worthless."

"I think you're quite beautiful, actually."

Punished eyes widened in surprise.

"Yes," he said. "I never got in touch after you sent all that gear to the chalet, I didn't trust myself."

"With me?"

He gave a slight nod.

"Oh." She wiped the back of her hand across her face, spreading her tears around. Greg smiled, and pulled a paper hankie from the glove compartment.

They drew apart a little. But the spark of intimacy remained. It would always be there, he knew, carried to the grave.

He cleared his throat, resentful that some analytical part of his brain never switched off, not even through this. "Julia, did you tell Kendric about the gigaconductor?"

She wiped the last tear away and crumpled the hankie. "No. All this happened a year before Grandpa told me about Ranasfari and the gigaconductor research project; Ranasfari wasn't even close to a cryogenic gigaconductor then. Kendric didn't have any ulterior motive for seducing me. I was just fun, a notch on his bedpost. He enjoys it, the game he plays in his mind; me and all the other dumb little girls are no different to his business deals. The lies and clever words corrupt us, then we belong to him, worship him. He gets as much satisfaction from our beguilement as he does from the sex. He's a power junkie."

He looked away, trying to lose the terrible image of Julia, a younger, smaller, more delicate Julia, lying below Kendric.

"You will get the proof, won't you, Greg?" she asked urgently. "I'm so scared of him. I've not told anybody that before, but he frightens me."

"I'll provide the proof Morgan Walshaw insists on, no messing." He kneaded his temple with thumb and forefinger. "There's a couple of things I want you to do for me."

She regarded him with comic seriousness. "Anything."

"Firstly, go back into the house and have a word with Walshaw. I want your personal protection stepped up. You're not the only one Kendric frightens; before yesterday I hadn't realized exactly how warped that man is. He is quite capable of having you killed. Especially now that he realizes that his games are over. It's gloves-off time, I'm afraid, Julia."

"Right."

"Secondly, Katerina. I'm going to put a stop to that."

"I don't understand."

"Snatch her from the *Mirriam* and then shove her through detoxification treatment. But that's going to cost."

"Money doesn't bother me."

"Right. I suppose it'll have to be in America or the Caribbean. I haven't looked into it; hell, I don't even know if you can detoxify a philter user. If not, then it'll be a good research project for Event Horizon to undertake."

Julia nodded in relief. "I promise, Greg. Whatever it takes. Event Horizon has a clinic in Austria. They can do anything there."

Greg didn't share her glibness about that, but at least she was genuinely intent on making amends. "Fine. I'll snatch her back tonight."

"Tonight?"

"Yes. I don't want to leave her on the *Mirriam* a minute longer than necessary; I'd develop nightmares. I'll bring her to Event Horizon's finance division offices. Your people can take her from there."

"I'll come."

"No, Julia."

"Yes. The finance division is just as secure as Wilholm. And I want to see her. After all, I'm the one who put her there, and I've had a taste of what she's been through."

He nearly started to say no again, but there wasn't a logical argument against her going. Besides, he could see Julia wasn't going to be moved. Philip Evans wasn't the only one she could wrap around her little finger. "All right, but you get Walshaw to make the travel arrangements, and turn up around midnight prepared for a long wait."

"Do you want the company security hardliners to help you?"

"No. I'm not familiar with their capabilities. I do know all about the people I'm going to be using."

"What people? Tekmercs?" she asked with frank curiosity.

"Tell you sometime."

She gave him a timid smile. "That's a date."

Greg turned the jammer off, and Julia opened her door.

"Julia."

She froze with her legs out of the car.

"Don't try so hard, girl. You're not exactly a frump, you know."

Her smile widened, becoming coquettish. "And Adrian isn't just a lump of muscle, either. He's very bright, and kind. And I like him a lot."

"Then I'm happy for you. See you later."

He didn't rate a wave this time; she simply stood watching him drive off, looking small and sad. He folded the rearview mirror's image up and tucked it away in a corner of his mind. The last thing he needed now was any more guilt rattling around inside his skull.

30

GREG DROVE INTO PETERBOROUGH UNDER a sky that the sun had transformed into a bitter saffron hemisphere raked with the occasional static pillar of cloud. He turned up the windscreen's opacity, muting its eye-smarting intensity. There was a taut thread of pain running through his cortex, the neurohormones' legacy.

It wasn't helped by wondering how he was going to square what he was doing with his promise to Eleanor. And then there was tonight's snatch looming large. Another unforeseen. Events were ganging up on him, dictating his actions.

The conspiracy was unnerving, tenaciously eroding any sensation of control over his life. He was a squaddie back in Turkey, utterly dependent on the wisdom of hidden enigmatic generals and the throw of God's dice. Never again, he'd sworn. Easy to say.

He blended the Duo into the arterial flux of traffic flowing through Peterborough's outlying suburbs, a dawn-to-dusk convoy hauling the city's lifeblood of goods from the industrial sectors to the port and the railway marshaling yard.

Hendaly Street was the same as all the rest in New Eastfield, a long straight gorge of white buildings with grand arched entrances, wide balconies, dark windows, and ranks of flags fluttering on high. Pagoda trees thrust up out of the pavements in the center of brick tubs; people sat on the benches around them, pensioners soaking up the sun, youngsters with VR bands plugged into gamer decks. Eleanor would enjoy living here.

He had to stamp hard on the brake as the red light came on ahead of the Duo. Its meaning had almost been lost down the years. Working traffic lights, by God!

The frontage of the Castlewood condominium was eighty meters long, standing back from the other buildings along the street, and screened with a discreet row of tall caucasian elms. The entrance was below ground level, served by a private loop of road with card-activated barriers at each end.

Greg parked a hundred meters farther down the street and showed his card to the meter, punching in for six hours.

"Six hours?" a voice queried. "I wish I had an expense account like that."

Greg turned and smiled. "Victor. You're looking good."

Victor Tyo's baby-faced good looks smiled back. "Riding high, thanks to you. I was promoted up to captain after our Zanthus excursion, got assigned to the command division down by the estuary. I guess Walshaw must approve of me."

"You're my contact today?"

"Yes. Again. I was at the office when the call came in." He tipped a nod at the Castlewood. "We've had it under observation for twenty-five minutes now."

"We?"

"The rest of my squad. They're covering all possible exits. We wouldn't want our man to filter out without us knowing. I've already checked with the concierge. Ellis is at home right now. A human concierge, by the way; this place is definitely for premier-rankers. I couldn't afford to rent the broom cupboard in there."

Walshaw hadn't actually mentioned anything about a squad, but Greg could appreciate his reasoning. Ellis wasn't the end of the line, but he was near. His confidence rose a fraction. Backup wouldn't come amiss, not if they were as on the ball as young Victor.

"Will this be a long operation?" he was asking. "Some of the observation positions are improvised, temporary."

"It shouldn't take more than an hour, two at the outside."

"Fine. Did you fall down some stairs?"

Greg's hand went to the stiff white mold over his nose. "Not exactly. A run-in with a friend of Mr. Ellis."

"I see. Do you want a weapon before we go in?"

"Are you carrying?"

"Yes. A Lucas laser pistol."

"That ought to be enough. You keep it." Greg began to walk toward the Castlewood's nearest barrier.

"Fine." Victor showed a card to the gate beside the barrier. "Concierge's pass," he explained.

Greg lifted an appreciative eyebrow. And only a twenty-minute head start. Morgan Walshaw ought to start worrying for his job. "Will it open the apartment doors as well?"

Victor did his best not to appear smug. "Of course."

The Castlewood was built in a U shape. The two wings had a conservatory-style glass roof slung between them, curving down to form a transparent wall at the open end. The glass was tinted amber, cooling the sunlight that shone down on a bowling green, tennis courts, an Olympic-size swimming pool, and a separate diving pool. Four tiers of balconies made a giant amphitheater of the enclosure, their long strips of silvered sliding doors staring down on the athletically inclined with blank impersonality.

Charles Ellis owned a penthouse apartment on the fourth story, at the tip of the east wing. One of the most expensive in the condominium. Victor stood outside the door, glancing at Greg for permission.

He held his hand up for the young security captain to wait, and probed with his espersense. There was only one mind inside, a muddled knot of everyday worries and conflicts. Not expecting trouble.

"He's alone," Greg said. "To the right as we go in." He pointed through the wall.

"Fine," Victor acknowledged respectfully. He showed the concierge card to the lock. There was a soft click.

The apartment was five large rooms laid out in parallel, with a hall running along the back of them. Surprisingly, the decor was old-fashioned throughout. Uninspiring, sober prints and dingy Victorian furnishings, all black wood and thick legs draped in cream-colored lace. The internal doors were heavy varnished hardwood, with brass hinges and handles, opening into rooms with dark dressers and tables. Chairs were gilt-edged, upholstered in plain shiny powder blue fabric. Marble-top tables were supported by bronze legs.

The lounge where they found Charles Ellis had six glass-fronted teak wall cabinets exhibiting hundreds of beautifully detailed porcelain figurines. There was a profusion of styles, with animals predominating; whoever owned them was obviously a dedicated collector. Rich, too, though Greg was no real judge, but money had its own special telltale radiance. And it haunted those shelves. He could feel the love and craftsmanship that had been expended in the fashioning of each exquisite piece.

Ellis was a small man in his early fifties, barely over one and a quarter meters tall. His body and limbs didn't quite seem to match, his torso was barrel-shaped, going to fat, but his legs and arms were long and thin, spindly. He had a narrow head, with tight-stretched skin, thin bloodless lips, and a prominent brow overhanging nicotine-yellow eyes. Lank oily hair brushed his collar, leaving a sprinkling of dandruff. He hadn't shaved for a few days, his stubble patchy and gray.

His imbalanced frame was wrapped in a paisley smoking jacket with a quilted green collar. He was sitting in a high-backed Buckingham chair watching a news channel on a big Philips flatscreen, thick velvet drapes hung on either side of it, like theater curtains. The flatscreen was showing a rooftop view of some desert city, indefinably African; its streets were awash with refugee trains, twisters of black smoke rising from shattered temple domes. A chrome-silver fighter flashed overhead, discharging a barrage of area-denial submunitions; tiny parachutes mushroomed in midair, lowering the shoal of AP shrapnel mines gently onto the beleaguered city.

Charles Ellis turned his head toward Greg and Victor, disturbed by the draft as they opened the lounge door. His facial muscles twitched, pulling the skin even tighter over his jawbone.

The flatscreen darkened as he rose from the chair, curtains swishing across it; he had to push hard with his bandy arms to lift himself. "How did you get in?" he asked.

"Door was open," Greg said.

"You're lying. What do you want?"

"Data."

His expression was thunderstruck. "How did you know? Nobody knows I deal in data."

Greg gave him a lopsided apologetic smile. "Somebody does. Cover him."

Ellis swayed backward as Victor produced his Lucas pistol. "No violence, no violence." It was almost a mantra.

Greg walked across the room and looked down on the Castlewood's dark blue diving pool. The lounge was on the corner of the building; two sides of it were glass. The balcony ran all the way around, one-third of it under the condominium's weather-resistant covering.

"Whoever you are, you're an idiot," Ellis said. "You have absolutely no conception of what you've gone and walked into. The kind of people I associate with can tread you back into the mire that gave you birth."

Greg smiled right back at him, baring his teeth. "I know. That's why we came, for your top-rank friends."

Whatever Ellis was going to say died on his tongue.

"Wolf," Greg said. Naked alarm rocked Charles Ellis's already fraught mind. "Medeor." It produced the same response. "Tentimes."

"Never heard of them."

"Wrong. I'm psychic, you see."

Ellis's face hardened, forestalling the onrush of fear and suspicion kindling behind his eyes.

"In fact, you are Wolf, aren't you?"

True, the mind before him blurted helplessly.

"Thank you," said Greg.

Ellis looked at him with revulsion and hatred.

"Do you know what these are?" Greg asked Victor casually. He rested a hand on one of the three gray football-size globes that were sitting on a leather-topped Edwardian writing desk. A Hitachi terminal was plugged into each of them with flat rainbow ribbons of optical cable. "They're Cray hologram memories. You can store half of the British library in one of these."

Greg tapped the Hitachi's power stud. LCDs flipped to black across its pale-brown surface, forming a standard alphanumeric keyboard. The cube lit with the Crays' data storage management menu. "You'll note that they're kept in isolation, not plugged into the English Telecom grid. So nobody can hack in. After all, bytes are money, especially when you know how to market them as well as Medeor here."

"What are you going to do?" Ellis's voice was a grizzled rasp coming from the back of his throat.

"Whatever I have to." Greg read the menu codes and accessed the first Cray. "Sixty-two percent capacity used up," he observed. "That's one fuck of a lot of data. Now, I could go through a whole list of names I'm interested in and see which your mind flinches at, but that would be very time consuming. So I'm just going to ask you to tell me instead. Who paid you to organize the blitz on the Event Horizon datanet?"

Ellis shook his skeletal head, jaw clenched shut. "No."

Greg showed his card to the Hitachi's photon key, using his little finger to activate it. The percentage figure began to unwind at an impressive speed as Royan's data-crash cancer exploded inside the Cray. He hadn't been totally sure it would work on lightware. Admitting now he should've had more faith. The percentage numerals vanished from the cube, sucked away down some electronic black hole. The cube placidly reverted to showing the menu.

"No!" Ellis howled, an unpleasant high-pitched wheezing sound. He ignored Victor's unwavering Lucas pistol to stumble frantically across the lounge to the antique writing desk, looking down in consternation at the cube display. "Oh my God! Do you know what you have done?" His hands came up to claw at Greg, stopping impotently in midair. His face was contorted with fury. "There were seven million personnel files in there, everybody of the remotest interest in the country. Seven million of them! Irreplaceable. God curse you, gland freak."

"Kendric di Girolamo," Greg said calmly.

Stark horror leaped into his mind at the name.

It was very strange; a circle of bright orange flame suddenly burst from Ellis's head to crown him with a blazing halo. For one fleeting moment his mind inveighed utter incomprehension, wild eyes beseeching Greg for an answer. Then the flickering mind was gone, extinguished in an overwhelming gale of pain. The corpse was frozen upright, steaming blood spewing fitfully out of its nose and ears. Its corona evaporated; there was no more hair to burn, the skull blackened, crisping. He heard the iron snap of bone cracking open from thermal stress.

Realization penetrated Greg's numbed thoughts as the reedy legs began to buckle, pitching the body toward him.

"Down!" he screamed. And he was dancing with the corpse, slewing its momentum to keep it between himself and the silvered balcony door as he flung himself on to the fringed Wilton rug. They crashed on to the worn navy blue weave together. There was a drawnout sound of glass smashing as Victor tumbled to the floor behind him.

Greg was flat on his back, the throat-grating stench of singed hair and charred flesh filling his nostrils. A wiry hand twitched on his thigh, not his. Ellis's dense curved weight pressed into his abdomen.

"Jesus," Victor bawled. "Jesus, Jesus."

"Shut up. Keep still."

The air heaved, alive with raucous energy, creaking and groaning as it battled to stabilize itself. A pile of paper forms took flight from the Edwardian desk, rustling eerily as they fluttered about the invisible streamers of boiling ions. The end of the discharge came with an audible crack that jumped the carpet fibers to rigid attention, dousing them in a phosphorescent wash of Saint Elmo's fire.

Greg sent his espersense whirling, perceiving the star sparks of minds swilling through the concrete beehive maze of the Castlewood. Seeing the galvanized ember of victory fleeing.

"Okay, they've gone," he croaked through the backlash of neurohormone pain. Even that sliver of sound seemed distant.

Victor was kneeling beside him, a rictus grimace on his face, rolling Ellis's body off. The back of the skull had cleaved open, a fried jelly offal spilling out.

Victor wrenched aside and vomited, coughing, dry retching, and sobbing for an age. When his convulsions finished he was on all fours, his hair hanging in tassels down his forehead, skin sallow and filmed with cold sweat. "Jesus, what did that to him?"

Greg looked at the wall opposite the balcony door; it was crisscrossed by narrow black scorch marks. Glass fragments from the cabinets were heaped on the carpet; figurines glowed a faint cherry pink on smoldering shelves. "Maser," he said. "Probably a Raytheon or a Minolta, something packing enough power to penetrate the silvering on the glass."

"Bloody hell. What now?"

Greg wriggled his legs from under the small of Ellis's back and propped himself up on his elbows, gulping down air. Looking anywhere but at the ruined flesh at his feet. The world was a mirage, wavering nauseously. "Cover up. Call your squad; this apartment has got to be scrubbed clean. There must be nothing left to prove we ever visited. You'll have to take the body out tonight—cleaning truck, something like that. And get these Crays to Walshaw. Lord knows how long it'll take to go through their contents, though."

"No police?"

"No police. We need the Crays' data. Besides, I'd hate to try and explain what we were doing here. Let Ellis become another unperson; nobody's going to ask questions."

"Oh. Yes." Victor was dazed, moving and thinking with a Saturday-night drunk's shell-shocked apathy.

"Call your squad now."

"Right." He tugged his cybofax out of an inner pocket. "Your nose is bleeding."

Greg dabbed at the flow with some of Ellis's tissues while Victor yammered out increasingly urgent instructions. Flies were beginning to feed on the open skull. Greg pulled a white lace tablecloth over Ellis and collapsed into one of the low chairs, exhausted.

"On their way," said Victor. "You want to flit, find a doctor or something?"

"No. I think I'll just sit here for a minute. Oh, and be sure to have this place swept for bugs." His nose had stopped bleeding.

Victor hovered anxiously, head swiveling around the apartment, missing the body each time. "Bloody hell, what a cock-up."

"Not your fault. But it proves one thing."

"What's that?"

Greg gave him a battle-weary smile. "I'm close."

"Yeah, but Greg . . . what have you got left now?"

"A name. Confirmation."

"That di Girolamo character you mentioned?"

"Yep. It was beautiful the way Ellis's mind funked out. You should've seen it."

"If you say so. This is all way above my head. Surveillance and backup, Walshaw says. You sit there and take it easy for a while. I'll see to the cleanup."

"Sure." Greg drew his cybofax out of his leather jacket's inside pocket, taking care not to make any sudden motions. His brain sloshed from ear to ear each time his head moved.

He flipped the cybofax open and keyed the phone function with difficulty. His fingers were stiff, devoid of feeling.

The cybofax bleeped for an incoming call. Unsurprised, he let it through. *Knowing.*

Gabriel's face appeared on the little screen. "No," she said, with ominous resolution.

"I'm sorry, but you have to. There's no one else."

"No, Gregory."

"Look at me, a proper look. Right now I couldn't even sense a tiger's brain if it was biting me. Tell you, I've got to have psi coverage to get that girl out. You'll be saving lives, Gabriel. The Trinities will bloodbath the *Mirriam* without perfect intelligence information—where Katerina is, where the crew are, and what they're tooled up with."

"You're a bastard, Mandel."

"No messing. See you at the briefing."

After that, it was the difficult call. Eleanor.

31

T RUE TO PREDICTION, ONE OF the yachts docked at the same quay as the *Mirriam* was hosting a party. A brassy, high-wattage rave: hysterical guests spilling out onto the quay itself, dancing, drawing syntho, swilling down champagne. Perfect cover. By two o'clock in the morning it still hadn't peaked.

At five minutes past two Greg walked down the quay with Suzi, the pair of them holding hands and laughing without a care in the world. He wore a dinner jacket that felt as though it was made of canvas, and reeked of starch. Suzi had slipped into a 1920s gold lamé dress, low cut with near invisible straps, a blond bob wig covering her gelled-down spikes. With her size and figure she looked impossibly young—fourteen, fifteen, something like that. He reckoned that as a couple they fit the scene perfectly. Anyone would think it was fathers and daughters night. Thank heavens for café society, immutable in a fluid world.

They infiltrated the party fringes, anthropoid chameleons.

Big Amstrad projectors were mounted on the yacht, firing holographic fireworks into the night. Upturned faces were painted in spicy shades of scarlet and green by carnation bursts of ephemeral meteorites.

Suzi lingered to watch a girl dressed in a sequin bikini and dyed ostrich feathers limbo her way under a boat hook held by two semiparalytic Hoorays.

Greg checked his watch and tugged Suzi's arm with gentle insistence, steering her into the wrap of darkness at the end of the quay. Three minutes before they had to be in position. The snatch had to be performed with exact timing; one mistake, one delay, a hesitation, and they'd be heading down the wrong Tau line and all Gabriel's planning would come to naught. He'd tried to emphasize that to the Trinities, drilling it in.

The limbo girl failed to make it, overbalancing and winding up flat on her back. The flesh of her overripe body quivered with helpless laughter. One of the Hoorays poured champagne into her mouth straight from the magnum. She lapped at the foamy spray spilling down her cheeks, her mind light-years away.

Greg and Suzi tottered away from the revelers. Nobody was paying them a second glance.

"Lady Gee was right," Suzi said from the corner of her mouth. He could sense how tight her small body was wired, rigid with restless tension.

The Trinities had been, to say the least, skeptical when Gabriel began outlining the evening's events. Their agnosticism had been whipped in staggered increments as the prophecies unfurled with uncanny precision—the party, which crewmen would leave the *Mirriam* for the evening, the exact time Kendric and Hermione left for the Blue Ball, the fact that Katerina had been left behind.

Other couples had drifted into the seclusion of the quay beyond the party, exploiting the penumbra of privacy provided by covered gangplanks. Greg kept his eyes firmly on the *Mirriam* ahead; Suzi peeped unashamedly, chortling occasionally.

Mirriam looked deserted, lit only by the intermittent spectral backwash from the Amstrads. Yet Gabriel had said there were seven people on board: two of Kendric's bodyguards, four sailors, and Katerina. She'd even reeled off their locations.

Greg wished he could use his espersense to confirm, but that was a definite no-no. The anemia that the neurohormones had inflicted on the rest of his body had lifted during the afternoon, and physically he was shaping up, but another secretion would cripple his brain.

They reached the *Mirriam*'s gangplank and folded into the midnight shadows it exuded. He checked his watch again.

"How about we go for total realism?" Suzi whispered with a giggle in her voice as she twined her hands round his neck.

"Twelve seconds," he answered. The gangplank was one long pressure pad according to Gabriel.

"Oh, Daddy, give it to me good," she yodeled.

He could feel her shaking with laughter and a crazy burn of exhilaration.

Right on time a voice said, "Hey, sorry folks, but you're gonna have to move along."

Greg was facing the quay so he couldn't see the speaker, but he recognized Toby's baritone rumble. Besides, Gabriel said it would be him. He carried on smooching with Suzi.

There was a faint vibration as Toby walked down the gangplank. "I said—"

Suzi's Armscor stunshot spat a dart of electric-blue flame. Greg heard a startled grunt and turned just in time to catch Toby before he hit the gangplank. Asking himself why the hell he bothered.

Suzi was racing up the gangplank. Greg followed dragging Toby. The bodyguard's breathing was ragged, slitted whites of his eyes showing in the fallout from the silent twinkling light storm overhead.

As always Greg experienced the conviction of operating under divine protection. With Gabriel's guidance he'd become omnipotent.

Suzi ducked into the darker oval of an open hatch, fumbling her photon amp into place as she went.

Greg pulled his own photon amp out of the dinner jacket's pocket. That reassuringly familiar pinching as the band annealed to his skin. *Mirriam* resolved into cold hard reality around him, nebulous leaden shadows stabilizing into sharply defined blue and gray outlines.

02:12:29, flashed the yellow digits.

"At two hours, twelve minutes and thirty-five seconds GMT the crewman will exit the cabin-lounge door onto the afterdeck," Gabriel had said, her voice raised above the Trinities' scoffing.

Greg dumped Toby on the glossy polished decking and ran for the afterdeck, black leather shoes squeaking.

02:12:35.

"At twelve minutes and forty-one seconds GMT he'll move into your line of sight."

02:12:38.

Greg stopped and assumed a marksman stance with his Armscor, lining it up one meter wide of the corner of the superstructure.

02:12:41.

The crewman obviously knew something was amiss; he came around the corner of the superstructure fast, crouched low.

The photon amp showed a monster crab scuttling right at him, meter length of pipe instead of claw. He fired.

"The crewman's name is Nicky."

Metallic clangor as the crab's erratic momentum skated him into the railing, pipe skittering away anarchically. "Bye, Nicky," Greg whispered.

"Radar canceled," Suzi's voice squawked in his earpiece. "God, this place is exactly like Lady Gee described it. Wild!"

Greg finished up at the stern, scanning the glum water of the marina and its flotsam carpet of decaying seaweed. Oily ripples slapped lazily at *Mirriam*'s hull.

"On the taffrail you'll find a control box with six weatherproofed buttons. Press the second from the left."

The box was there. Rigid forefinger pressing. A stifled drone of a motor lowering the diving platform ladder.

The inflatable dinghy surged out of the gloaming, four figures hunched down, muffled engine cutting a hazy wake through the seaweed. It turned a finely judged arc and rode its bow wave to a halt at the foot of the ladder. The first three figures swarmed up the ladder, dressed in combat leathers and helmets. Des and two of his troop, Lynne and Roddy.

They ignored Greg and crossed the deck to the half-open cabin-lounge door. Des slid it right back and the three of them rushed in.

Greg leaned over the taffrail to see Gabriel puffing her way up the ladder. She was wearing a balaclava and a heavy night-camouflage flak jacket, restricting her movements; it was the largest the Trinities had in stock. He put his hand down and diplomatically helped her over the railing.

She tugged the balaclava off, wiping the back of her hand across her perspiring forehead. "We're too old for this Greg, you and I, believe me. If you weren't such a bloody ignorant stubborn bugger." A resigned smile lifted her lips. Shaking her head. "Crazy."

Greg smiled fondly. "Tell you, I have a horrible feeling you may be right."

"That's my boy." A sudden frown wrinkled her plump features. "Damn." She thumbed the communicator set in her breast pocket. "Lynne, it's not that hatch, go to the next one . . . that's right. The crewman is standing behind the cowling."

"Come on," Greg said. "Time for you and I to rescue the damsel."

"You know, Teddy's done a good job with those kids," Gabriel admitted grudgingly as they moved into the lounge.

Greg negotiated the unfamiliar obstacles and found the central companionway. A tube of impenetrably black air, which even the photon amp had difficulty discerning.

"Are we all right for some light?" he asked.

"Yes. One moment."

Greg heard her shut the lounge door; then the biolum strip came on. He peeled the photon amp off. Suzi slithered down a narrow set of stairs from the bridge.

"Mega," she breathed, pulling off her wig and ruffing up her mauve spikes. "You got it spot on, Lady Gee. All of it. Where you said, when you said. It's fucking incredible."

"Thank you, my dear."

The three of them headed for the lower deck. Thick vermilion carpet absorbed their footfalls down the stairs. One of the crewmen was lying on the bottom step, his limbs shivering spastically from the stunshot charge. Des was waiting for them outside the master bedroom's door, helmet off, grinning broadly, his hair a dark sweaty mat.

"All right!" he whooped blithely. "We breezed it, no problem. You ever need a job, Gran, you come'n see me, okay?"

"You're too kind," Gabriel said.

Des missed the mounting testiness, but Suzi winked at Greg, rolling her eyes for his denseness. Lynne and Roddy clattered up the stairs from the crew quarters below.

"Shall we get on with it?" Gabriel said, hurriedly forestalling the compliment Lynne had opened her mouth to begin. She took an infuser tube out of her flak jacket and handed it to Suzi. "You'll need this."

Suzi turned it over, mildly curious. "What for?"

"She's a big girl."

Des and Roddy exchanged a glance.

"Is she armed?" Lynne inquired.

"No."

Greg knew that mood well enough; Gabriel at her most obdurate. There'd be no budging her now.

He opened the bedroom door. There was a subdued pink light inside.

"Hoo boy." Suzi groaned in pawky dismay. Des and Roddy piled in behind her for a look,

Katerina was sprawled across a huge circular water bed, wearing an Arabian harem slave costume, strips of diaphanous lemon chiffon held together with thin gold chains. It was a size too small, strained by the curves of her breasts and hips. The chiffon was so flimsy they could see her large areolas through it, dark purple-brown circles with aroused nipples.

Katerina batted drowsy eyelids at the five faces staring down at her. "I'm ready," was all she said.

Roddy let out a low admiring whistle. "Makes it all kind've worthwhile, doesn't it?"

Des sniggered.

"For God's sake find something to wrap her in," Greg said, annoyed at their abrupt lapse of discipline. Hardly surprised, though. The porno-starlet stage setting sapped any sense of urgency. He let out a hiss of breath, silently cursing Gabriel for not warning him. "Suzi, help me get her up."

Katerina looked up with innocent bewilderment as they each took an arm and tugged her into a sitting position. "I remember you," she said to Greg. "Will you make it happen, too?"

"Not tonight."

"But this is the paradise place. The hurt and the wonder always happens here."

"Bollocks, what's she on?" asked Suzi.

"Philter. Stuff's blowing her brain apart."

Katerina turned her head to focus on Suzi. "Can you make it happen?"

"No way, girl. Come on; let's get you out of here."

Something in Suzi's inflexible tone must've finally penetrated Katerina's befuddled brain. "I don't want to leave, not here, not the wonder. Not ever."

Suzi brought up the infuser in a no-nonsense manner.

Katerina's bare foot lashed out, catching Suzi full in the stomach. She went down with a silent *oof*, curling around herself and fighting for breath. Greg was suddenly left holding a screaming, scratching, biting, kicking she-demon. Gabriel was right: Katerina was big, and strong, and utterly deranged. Tapering lavender nails slashed at his eyes, a knee thudded into his pelvic bone, a tornado of golden hair filled the air. He felt soft flesh, hard flesh. Hampered by not wanting to hurt her. An inhibition rapidly dissolving.

Des made a grab for Katerina's shoulders, succeeding only in ripping her mock slave-costume. All three of them tumbled to the floor in a frenziedly bucking heap. Then Lynne waded in, trying to pin Katerina's arms down. Roddy managed to grab hold of one leg. Finally a wheezing Suzi slammed the infuser on Katerina's neck with unnecessary force. For one horrendous moment Greg thought it wasn't going to have any effect, but a look of outright surprise shot across Katerina's enraged face and she subsided into a limp bundle shrouded in wispy scraps of lemon fog.

"Goddamn . . . ungrateful . . . bitch," Suzi spat between shudders. Her face was chalk white. Greg thought she was going to kick the unconscious body. Probably wouldn't have stopped her.

"She doesn't know what she's doing," he offered in apology. "Hey, you all right?"

Her hands were still clasped tight around her abdomen. "Yeah. Bitch."

Roddy wrapped a toweling robe around Katerina, and Des carried her out in a fireman's lift.

Gabriel stood to one side as they filed out of the master bedroom. "Told you so," she said.

*   *   *

The seven of them rode the dinghy back to Event Horizon's finance division offices, stealing quietly across the Nene's scummy water, making good headway against the outgoing tide. City noises thrummed around them: sirens, horns, the trill of gas-powered traffic, peals of jukebox music from riverside pubs. The sough of the dinghy's electric outboard was lost without trace.

Des dodged the big freighters anchored in the middle of the river outside the port. They were waiting for the early morning tide to provide the draft they needed to take them down the channel to the Wash. Rust-streaked metal giants, sprinkled with tiny navigation lights, their bows a check pattern of hoarfrost where their liquefied gas tanks nestled against the hull. Greg could hear a steady *plop plop plop* as chunks of the mushy rime fell into the water.

Once the freighters were left behind it was a straight ride up the Nene to the Ferry Meadows estuary. The Trinities loosened up, schoolboys returning from a day outing. Their hive-buzz chatter percolated about the inflatable—*Mirriam* crewmen I have zapped.

Des even had a beacon to aim at. Philip Evans had chosen to celebrate his company's triumphant return to solid land with a thirty-five-meter-high sign perched on top of Event Horizon's finance division offices. Its core was a macramé plait of colorful neon tubes orbited by stylized holographic doodles—expanding geometric graphics, cartoon characters, origami birds, and, at Christmas time, a traditional Santa replete with sledge and reindeer. Monumentally vulgar but mesmerizing at the same time.

The deep-throated gurgling of the tidal turbines grew steadily louder as they drew near the little quay jutting out from the steep concrete embankment below the ugly cuboid building.

Victor Tyo was waiting for them, huddled in a parka against the fresh predawn air rising off the estuary. He offered a gentlemanly hand to Gabriel, then grappled a semiconscious Katerina ashore. She groaned as her bare feet touched the cold concrete.

"Why are her hands tied?" Victor asked reasonably as Greg stepped ashore and took some of the weight.

"Coz there wasn't enough rope for her fucking neck," Suzi growled out of the dark.

Victor peered down at the inflatable dinghy with its oblique cargo of well-armed hardliners and an underage girl in a revealing gold party frock. "Bloody hell."

Des gunned the throttle and the little craft surged out into the darkness. "See ya, Greg," Suzi called. "And take care of Lady Gee; she's outta this world."

Walshaw and Julia were waiting in a big corner office on the third floor. Rachel Griffith stood outside. It was a monastically simple room; the walls and ceiling were painted a uniform white, contrasting against the all-black fittings. Greg knew it was Walshaw's office without having to be told. An extension of his personality. Comfortable, efficient, and uncluttered. The furniture was unembellished, two chairs in front of a broad desk, a settee against the wall. Honey-yellow louver blinds shut out a view of what Greg's sense of direction told him would be the estuary. The air was warm and slightly damp, stale, the way it got after people had been breathing it for several hours.

Walshaw was sitting behind the desk when they walked in. Greg was surprised to see the surface covered in little balls of scrunched-up paper.

Julia was rising from the settee, knuckles screwing sleep out of her eyes. She was wearing a V-necked lilac dress with a pleated skirt. A tangerine woollen cobweb shawl was drawn around her shoulders.

She allowed herself a rueful grin. "Midnight, he says. It's gone three."

Then Victor Tyo and one of his squad members carried Katerina in between them. She'd begun to hum tunelessly.

Julia stared at her old schoolfriend, humor and toughness leaching from her face. Whatever zombie incarnation she'd been girding herself for, it wasn't a match for the mental-husk reality provided.

Katerina was lowered onto the settee, utterly uninterested in her environment.

Julia sent Greg a silent desperate plea that this was some awful nightmare, not real.

Walshaw frowned disapprovingly at the grubby rope wrapped around Katerina's wrists. Greg pointed to the fresh scratches on his face.

"See if you can find some padded cuffs," Walshaw told Victor. "And tell Dr. Taylor to stand by. She'll probably need sedating."

Victor nodded crisply and departed, happy to be out of the office.

Julia sank down onto the settee, peering timidly at the beautiful empty shell slumped quiescently beside her. "Kats? Kats, it's me, Julia. Julie. Can you hear me, Kats? Please, Kats. Please."

Katerina's lost eyes swam around. "Julie," she sighed inanely. "Julie. Never thought it would be you. They bring so many others for me, but never you. It's late, isn't it? I can feel it. It's always late when they come for me. We'll be good, won't we, Julie? You and I, when he watches? If we're good then I can go to him afterwards."

"Yeah," Julia stammered. Her eyes had begun to brim with tears. "Yeah, Kats, we'll be good. The best. Promise." She pulled her shawl off and tucked it clumsily around her friend's trembling shoulders. "I'd like you to leave us alone now," she said without looking around.

Greg had known some officers who could speak like that. Commanding instant obedience. Rank had nothing to do with it; their voice plugged directly into the nervous system.

As he left the office he saw Julia tenderly smoothing back Katerina's disheveled tresses.

The corridor was narrow with a high ceiling, built from composite panels that cut up the original open-plan floor into a compartmented maze. A pink-tinged biolum strip ran overhead, its unremitting luminescence showing up the threadbare rut running down the center of the chestnut carpet squares.

Walshaw closed the door behind him. Rachel moved down toward the lift, giving them a degree of privacy.

"I've been doing some checking this afternoon," Walshaw said. "There's a clinic on Granada which claims it can cure philter addiction."

"Successfully?" Greg asked.

"Forty percent of the patients recover. I was wondering. Miss Thompson, isn't it?"

Gabriel was resting with her back flat on the wall, head tilted back, eyes closed, her breathing shallow. Greg recognized the state; he'd seen it in the mirror often enough. That relentless enervation that siphoned the vitality out of every cell.

"Morgan, to someone of your age and ex-rank I'm Gabriel, okay? But no, I can't tell if it works with Katerina. That's too far into the future."

"I don't think Julia will give up," Greg said. "Not now."

"No, I don't suppose she will," Walshaw agreed.

"You know Kendric di Girolamo is going to have to be eliminated, don't you?" Greg said.

Walshaw reached up languidly and began massaging his neck. "Eventually, yes."

"No. Not eventually. You've seen what he's done to that girl, and that was just for *fun*. The guy's an absolute loon. Tell you, I've seen inside his mind. Homicidal psychopath isn't the half of it. Julia needs head-of-state-level protection while he's on the loose, no messing."

"Julia has been badgering me to do the same thing. She is even more intent than you, if anything."

"Hardly surprising, after what she went through with Kendric. Pedophile shit."

Walshaw turned his head very slowly until he was staring directly at Greg. "What?"

"Kendric and Julia; he seduced her. You didn't know?"

"She hates Kendric."

"Not always," Greg said. He couldn't ever remember seeing Walshaw so thrown before, not even the blitz and the possibility of a leak in the gigaconductor project had upset him this much. Another of Julia's secret admirers.

"So that's what is behind this sudden urge for blood," Walshaw said tightly.

"It's not just a wronged girl's *lex talionis*. Kendric is dangerous, believe me."

"I do." For a second the security chief looked heartbroken. Greg was suddenly glad he didn't have the use of his gland at that moment; there were some secrets people were entitled to keep. He guessed Julia had become a surrogate daughter to Walshaw over the years. That strange character flaw of his, the need to have someone to provide him with a purpose in life.

"Kendric can't be eliminated right now, dangerous though he undoubtedly is," Walshaw said. "Your episode with Charles Ellis at the Castlewood condominium confirms there is someone else involved, the organizer of the blitz. Kendric couldn't have arranged for the sniper at Ellis's penthouse because he didn't know Wolf. Which makes Kendric our last link with the organizer. And we have to find out who that is."

"But Wolf knew Kendric," Greg said. "Weird."

"Not really," said Gabriel. "The organizer is their link, a one-way databus who passes on all Kendric's intelligence to Wolf. But there's no return flow; Wolf has nothing Kendric needs to know. And Kendric would've told the organizer that you'd confronted him, that you knew about Wolf. So the organizer fixed for the sniper. Morgan here is right, Greg. We can't get rid of Kendric. He's your only hard lead left. In fact, he ought to watch out; the organizer must realize that, too."

"Shit," Greg muttered in frustration. "Kendric won't take us to the organizer, not now. He's too smart. They'll never contact each other again."

Gabriel opened her eyes. "Snatch him," she said flatly. "That's your only option. Snatch Kendric. Interrogate him. Snuff him."

"Risky," said Walshaw. "A quick clean kill is one thing; snatches have a tendency to get messy no matter how good the hardliners you use. Lots of questions asked."

"My precognition would make sure there's no mess."

"I'll authorize it," Julia said firmly.

Greg hadn't seen her emerge from Walshaw's office. But now she stood in the corridor, head held high, in complete control of herself, as if the bomb blast of Katerina had never happened. No longer the ivory-tower habitué but very much the Princess Regent. Some small part of him mourned the passing of the timid, sweet girl he'd first met on a sunny March day. Innocence was the most appealing of human traits.

Morgan Walshaw shifted uneasily as Julia's chillingly bright gaze turned on him, demanding. "If that's what it takes to sort this out, then that's what'll happen," she said. "It's bad enough having Kendric coming at me like this, but unknown enemies as well, that's totally out. I'm not having it. And the snatch is the way to unmask them. That bastard Kendric has been banking that we won't fight him on his own level. Well, his credit has just run out."

"Julia—," Walshaw said.

"No arguments, just *do* it!"

Greg could see how much effort it took Walshaw to retain control; no espersense needed for that.

"It isn't up to me, Miss Evans."

Julia realized she might've overstepped the limit. "I'm sorry, Morgan. It's Kats, you see. She keeps asking for him. Doesn't say anything else. Bastard. I think she'll have to be sedated."

"Okay." He raised a cybofax and muttered into it. "Doctor's on her way."

"Who then?" Julia asked. "Who is it up to?"

Walshaw looked at Greg. "That's you, Greg. If it's to be done, it's to be done properly. Would you interrogate him?"

Greg had seen it coming, ever since Gabriel blurted the idea of a snatch. It'd given him a few seconds to chew the proposition. He spread his palms wide. "Preparations wouldn't hurt. Mind you, I'd be physically incapable of interrogating anyone for a couple of days anyway. That might give us enough time to analyze the Crays' data. See if we can't find some leads in them. Ellis should've left one."

He noticed Julia's face had gone blank, focusing inward. Must be using her nodes, running their arguments through analysis, battling the pros and cons against each other, trying to reach the conclusions ahead of them. In a way it was a power similar to Gabriel's.

"We're going through the Crays now," said Walshaw. "Although I don't know what the hell you did to one of them; it crashed one of our lightware crunchers when we plugged it in. Bloody thing is so much rubbish now. The other two Crays are clean, although it'll take time to make sure there aren't any concealed wipe instructions buried in them."

"What have you got so far?" Greg asked.

"Ellis had quite an extraordinary accumulation of data, everything from minutely detailed personal dossiers through to industrial templates. Trivia and ultrahush all jumbled together. It's going to take some sifting, even with the lightware crunchers hooked in."

"What did you mean, Ellis should've left a lead?" Julia asked.

"Standard practice," Greg explained. "If you're plugging into those kinds of deals you cover your back. Benign blackmail, to make sure your partners don't get any funny ideas afterwards. There'll be a record of all the burns he arranged as Wolf: money, clients, the names of his hot-rod team, data he bought and sold as Medeor, names, companies. Every damning byte. And it'll be somewhere where it can be found after he's dead. In the Crays, the Hitachi terminal's memory core, his cybofax, public data core on a time delay, hell, even an envelope left with a lawyer."

"Nothing else?" Julia asked.

"Pardon?"

"You don't think there's anything else important in the Crays?"

For some reason her slightly querulous attitude made him aware of how immensely tired he was. He was traveling on buzz energy, had been for hours, and it was running out fast now that they'd got Katerina back.

"I wouldn't know. I expect they're a gold mine of illegal circuit activity."

"That's all?" Julia was leaning forward, studying his face intently. He had the uncomfortable impression he was being judged. Crime unknown. And, frankly, he didn't give a shit.

"All I can think of, yeah."

Dr. Taylor stepped out of the lift, accompanied by Victor, who was carrying her case. She was a young woman wearing a plain cerise trouser suit, her dark hair French pleated. She had a quick word with Morgan Walshaw and went into his office. Julia started to follow, but the security chief laid a light restraining hand on her arm. For a moment she looked like she'd rebel, then nodded meekly. Victor closed the door softly after he'd gone through.

"Thank you for bringing Kats back to me, Greg," Julia said, abruptly all humble contrition.

Greg gave up trying to find motives for her oscillating moods. She was on an emotional roller coaster: depressed by Katerina; frightened by Kendric; trusting in him, Gabriel, and Walshaw to deliver her from evil. Poor kid.

"It hurts so much just seeing her," Julia said. "Serves me right, I suppose." She reached around her neck with both hands and unhooked a slim gold chain. "For you. From me. And you don't even have to give me a kiss for it." She favored him with a sly weary smile.

It was a Saint Christopher pendant, solid gold.

"Well, put it on then," Julia said.

He mimicked a grin, feeling itchy under Gabriel's heartily bemused eye, and fastened it around his own neck. The little disk was warm on his skin as it slithered down beneath the open neck of his crisp dress shirt.

"To keep the demons at bay," Julia said. "Even though you're not a believer."

Greg pulled out of the finance division's nearly deserted car park, turning the Duo west onto the artificial lava surface of the A47. There was a single car in front of them. It wasn't quite dawn. The gross Event Horizon sign splashed the surrounding land with a guttering medley of colored light.

"I feel sorry for that girl, you know," Gabriel said. She was looking out of the window at the clumps of hermes oak scrub along the side of the road. Beyond the bushes was a near-vertical drop to the ruffled waters of the estuary. In the distance were the dark shapes of the hydro-turbine islands, moon-glazed foam rumbling around them.

"Katerina! Who wouldn't?" Greg said.

"No, Katerina is pure survivor breed. I meant Julia; she has no real family, few friends her own age. And you're on the borderline yourself, now, despite her token of esteem."

"How do you figure that?"

"If Ellis hasn't left anything in the Crays, or whatever, about Kendric or the organizer, how do you think she'll feel about you? You've managed to be right all the way so far. She trusts you because of that. Implicitly. Screw up now and it'll all end in tears."

"Not a chance. I know Ellis's type down to his last chromosome. A hyperworrier. He's a little-man intermediary who's lucked into a real superrank underclass operation—elated and terrified all at once.

He'll have taken precautions. That means a way of pointing his finger from beyond the grave."

"Oh yeah?"

"Yep. Ellis's major problem was that he never got around to telling his paymasters he was insured." Greg slowed as the car in front turned off onto the slip road for the bridge ahead, then accelerated again as the cutting walls rose on either side.

Gabriel said, "I still don't think Ellis would take such—"

The front near-side tire blew out.

The Duo veered violently to the left, straight toward the near-vertical slope of the cutting. Greg saw sturdy gray-white saplings, impaled in the headlight beams, lurching toward him. The steering wheel twisted, wrenching at his hands, nearly breaking his grip. He jerked it back as hard as he could, with little or no effect. The Duo's three remaining tires fought for traction on the coarse cellulose surface. It was slewing sideways, screeching hard. A flamboyant fan of orange sparks unfolded across the offside window. That alpine-steep incline was sliding across the windscreen, rushing up on the side of the Duo. Horribly close. They'd spun nearly full circle, and Greg could feel the tilt beginning as the car began to turn turtle. Then there was a bone-shaker impact, a damp thud, and they were disorientingly motionless. Silence crashed down.

Soon broken.

"Shitfire," Gabriel yelped. She was staring wild-eyed out of the windscreen, drawing breath in juddering gulps. "I didn't know!" She whipped round to look at him, frantic, frightened, entreating. Which was something he'd never ever seen in her before. And that alarmed him more than the blowout.

"I didn't know, Greg! There was nothing. Nothing, fuck it! Do you understand?"

"Calm down."

"Nothing!"

"So what! You're tired, and I'm knackered. It's only a bloody tire gone pop; small wonder you didn't see it. Nonevent." Even as he spoke he could feel some submerged memory struggling for recognition. Something about the tire-performance guarantee. Punctureproof? That bonded silicon rubber was tough stuff.

Thankfully, Gabriel subsided into a feverish silence, eyelids tightly shuttered, mind roaming ahead. Did she suffer visions of her gland pumping furiously? He'd never asked.

Greg concentrated on his hands, still clenching the wheel, whiteknuckled. They wouldn't let go.

What appeared to be a eucalyptus branch was lying across the windscreen. Its purple and gray leaves shone dully in the waning rouge emissions from the office block's sign.

Looking out of his side window he could see the bridge nearly directly overhead. They'd only just missed crashing into the concrete support wall.

"Greg—," Gabriel said in a low frightened moan.

Upright shapes were moving purposefully through the dusky shadows outside the sharp cone of light thrown by the Duo's one remaining headlight.

Greg stared disbelievingly at them for one terrible drawn-out second. "Out!" he shouted. His door opened easily enough, and he was diving out, racing for the back of the Duo. A mini-avalanche of loose earth and gravel had digested the rear of the car. His hands flapped across his dinner jacket, hitting every pocket. Panicking. Trying to remember where the fuck he'd left the Armscor stunshot.

There were three of them approaching: two men, one woman. Walking down the middle of the road with a glacial panache, cool and unhurried. A confidence that'd tilted over into sublime arrogance.

The Armscor had gone, swept away by the tide of pitiful sloppiness he was screwing his life with. Given it to Victor? Suzi? Left it in Walshaw's office?

He stuck his head above the Duo's roof, ducking down quickly. The ambush team was closing in remorselessly, empty silhouettes against that idiotic phallic sign and its happy floating Disney projections. They were still carefully avoiding the headlight beam.

Gabriel's door was jammed up against the earth of the cutting; her frantic shoving couldn't budge it more than halfway open. The gap wasn't nearly large enough for her bulk.

One of the men leveled a slender long-barreled rifle at her. Greg squirreled away his profile: leather trousers tucked into calf-high lace-up boots, last-century camouflage jacket, blind plastic band of a photon amp clinging to his face, designer stubble, small ponytail.

"Mine," the man said.

A narrow streak of liquid green flame spewing from the end of the rifle, and Gabriel was jerking about epileptically.

Greg turned and ran for the slope of crumbling earth, clawing at the dense treacherous scrub lassoing his legs, keeping low. The eucalyptus saplings were neatly pruned, a bulbous flare of foliage on top and bare slim boles, providing a meager cover. He grabbed hold of them in a steady swinging rhythm, hauling himself upward, feet scrabbling for purchase. The embankment seemed to stretch out forever.

It was an animal flight. Blind instinct, equating the slip road at the top of the embankment with the grail of sanctuary. Pathetic, some minute core of sanity mocked.

"There," came the triumphant shout from below.

The shot caught him three meters short of the summit, where the saplings and scrub had given way to a bald mat of grass that bordered the slip road. The pain seared down his nerves like a lava flow. He saw his arms windmilling insanely, fingers extended like albino starfish.

As he fell there was just one question looping through his brain. Why hadn't Gabriel known?

GREG WOKE TO FIND HE couldn't move. His toes and fingers were tingling, not so much pins and needles as pokers and knives: the aftermath of a stunshot charge. Arms and legs ached dully. Guts knotted tight, rumbling ominously. A livid collection of aggravated bruises and scrapes.

His cortical node prevented the worst peaks of neural fire from stabbing into his brain, but the cumulative effect was atrocious.

He opened his eyes, seeing grayness distorted by octagonal splash patterns. His whole body was quivering now, drumming against whatever hard surface he was lying on. The tingling bloomed into a sandpaper rasp that the cortical node hurriedly muted.

Consciousness seemed like nothing but constant suffering. He instructed the node to disengage his nerves altogether. Sensation fell away, leaving him alone in gray nothingness. He closed his eyes and slept.

At the second awakening his thoughts were clearer. He'd stopped bucking, still on his back and unable to move. Genuine tactile sensation had replaced the tingling. The surface he was lying on was vibrating faintly. Heavy machinery, somewhere not too far away. A stifled monotonous hum backed the supposition.

He opened his eyes again, focusing slowly.

Gabriel was lying beside him, shuddering, in the throes of stunshot backlash. Her mouth gaped, drooling beads of saliva.

Greg tried to reach out to her, found his hands were immobilized under his back. There was a rigid bracelet about each wrist, bolted to the floor; it was the same for his ankles.

Bloody uncomfortable.

They were in a small empty compartment, metal walls, metal floor, metal ceiling. Painted gray. The only light was coming through a grille in the door.

Greg blinked at that door, haunted by its familiarity. It was rectangular with curved corners, fastened by bulky latches. The last time he'd seen that particular arrangement was on board the *Mirriam*. "Oh, shit." And under way, too, by the sound of it.

Thinking logically, they'd have to be heading down the Nene. Or up? No, the river wasn't deep enough to take the *Mirriam* west of Peterborough. The Wash and the open sea, then.

Next question: why?

Not just to dump them overboard. There were far simpler ways to dispose of bodies. Besides Kendric had gone to a great deal of trouble snatching them alive.

Nothing pleasant, hundred percent cert.

"Greg?" Gabriel's voice was tiny, fearful. "Greg, it's gone."

"What has?" His own voice wasn't much better. "No, wait, think before you speak. Remember they'll probably be listening."

"Bugger that. My precognition won't work. I don't know what's going to happen to us."

"You really gave your gland a workout snatching Katerina, remember? We all have to throttle back occasionally; nature never intended our brains to take the psi strain."

"Shut up and listen, arsehole. There is absolutely nothing. I can't see a second into the future. I don't even know what you're going to say!" He could hear the fright bubbling through her voice. She was holding back a long, terrified scream.

Hear it, but not sense it.

The corrosive throb of overdriven synapses had faded; he must've been out for several hours. He'd recuperated enough to use the gland again. It began to discharge a murky cloud of neurohormones. But that secret gate into the psi universe remained firmly shut. He couldn't even perceive the glow of Gabriel's mind, not fifty centimeters from his own. Impossible. His skin crawled, goose bumps rising at the black sense of deprivation. Mortal again. After fifteen years it was hard.

"Me, too," Greg said. "Not a peep."

The breath came out of her in a woosh. She let her head rest on the decking, staring into a private purgatory. "What have they done to us, Greg?"

"They haven't done anything to us. You were using precognition right up until the Duo crashed. We didn't eat anything dodgy; we certainly weren't infused with anything."

"What then?"

"Must be something which affects psi directly."

"What?" she shouted.

"I don't fucking know. Ask Kendric. He's the one into pilfering new discoveries before they even make it out of the laboratory."

Gabriel closed rheumy eyes in anguish. "Funny, I always thought

I didn't want to see the end coming. Now that I'm sure it is coming I'd like to see it. Not knowing is too much like cold turkey."

"Silly girl. You just want to see which of our escape plans works the best."

"Escape plans," she snorted in a resigned amusement that nudged disapprobation. "Sure, Greg. Sure." After a while she asked, "What do you think they want us for?"

"Information. They want to know what we've discovered of their operation, how much of that we've told Walshaw. Once they know that they'll see what they can salvage. Hopefully that isn't going to be much; we've done a pretty good job up to now."

"Great. That makes me feel one hell of a lot better." She lapsed into sullen silence.

Greg guessed they'd been lying in the blank metal cell for a couple of hours before the hatch swung open.

It was Mark who drew the latches, accompanied by two more of Kendric's bodyguards. A biolum came on above them. After hours of dusk, the glare sent Greg's tear ducts into frantic action.

"Still on your backs?" Mark gloated. "I thought I'd be pulling you off each other by now. Or aren't you up to that? Maybe fancy something different, animals and the like? I heard you gland freaks are kind've warped."

Gabriel glared at him silently, realizing just how nasty things could turn if she started antagonizing him.

Mark bent down and released Greg's legs with a complex-looking mechanical key.

Greg was jerked roughly to his feet. Every ache and pain suddenly doubled in intensity. His legs nearly collapsed as a wave of nausea hit him. He saw the front of his dress shirt was stained by a long ribbon of dried blood; his nose had been bleeding again while he'd been unconscious.

One of the bodyguards supported him as he stumbled out into the corridor. It didn't possess anything like the ostentation of the upper decks. Pipes ran along the walls, red letters were stenciled across small hatches. The engine noise was more pronounced.

Another three bodyguards were waiting for him outside. Including Toby, who glowered with unconcealed menace.

"Christ," Greg croaked. "I must scare you lot shitless."

"Gonna have you, white boy," Toby whispered dangerously. "Gonna take you a-fucking-part."

"Not yet, Toby," Mark said, pushing a shaky Gabriel ahead of him. "When the Man has finished with him."

Greg was marched up and out onto the afterdeck. The sun was nearly full overhead. Well over six hours since they'd been snatched from the Duo. Would Walshaw have noticed? He'd told the security chief he would help to analyze the data in the Crays, but he hadn't given a specific time. Of course, Eleanor would be frantic, but would she ring Walshaw? And even if she did, there was nothing to make him look here.

At least he'd been right about "here." The *Mirriam* was sailing sedately down the Nene.

The course the Nene took for the first thirty kilometers east of Peterborough was a new one. The PSP's delay in authorizing construction of the city's port meant that the old river course had been lost at the start of the Warming, disappearing beneath the water and silt that laid siege to the city boundaries. A couple of years later, when the wharves' foundations were being laid, the dredgers cut a straight line from the port right out to the old estuary at Tydd Gote.

Mirriam was following a huge container freighter out toward the Wash. There was another freighter trailing a couple of kilometers behind. They were the only things moving in a very confined universe. All Greg could see was river, sky, and high gene-tailored coral levees covered in tall stringy reeds.

The tide was full, just beginning to turn, showing a thin line of chocolate mud below the bottom of the reeds.

Mirriam seemed to be losing ground on the freighter in front. Greg glanced over the taffrail to see four crewmen inflating two odd-looking craft on the edge of the diving platform. They were blunt-nosed dinghies with a couple of simple benches strung between the triplex tubing that formed the sides. A loose surplus of leathery fabric ran around the outside. It was only after a big fan, caged in a protective mesh, hinged up to the vertical at the rear of one of the dinghies that Greg realized they were actually hovercraft.

Gabriel nudged him and he turned to see Kendric approaching. *Mirriam*'s owner was wearing olive green tracksuit trousers and a light waterproof jacket. Hermione was at his side, as always, dressed in natty designer equivalents of her husband's attire. But it was the woman keeping a short distance behind who held Greg's attention.

She was in her late twenties with a second chin just beginning to develop; her dumpy face was framed by straight jet-black hair, cut in a fringe along her eyebrows, falling to her shoulders at the sides.

Her skin was dark and leathery, heavily wrinkled from excessive sun exposure.

He was convinced that she was the woman he'd seen at the ambush. He could still see her slightly bulky frame in that trio walking calmly down the road.

Kendric's gaze swept across Greg and Gabriel, utterly unperturbed. A cattleman checking his stock.

"Put them in with Rod and Laurrie," Kendric said to Mark. "You and Toby come with us."

"Yes, sir," Mark replied.

"Postponed," Toby muttered in Greg's ear. "That's all."

"Right, get them down there," Mark was saying.

Kendric and Hermione began to descend the ladder to the diving platform. The crewmen were holding the fully rigged hovercraft steady in Mirriam's wake.

"You'll have to take our cuffs off," Greg pointed out.

"Maybe we'll just throw you down," said Toby.

"Take 'em off," Mark said. "And you two, don't think about jumping."

Greg just managed the climb down the ladder, frightened his weak, trembling hands were going to lose their grip. He flopped down in the bottom of a hovercraft, exhausted and horribly woozy.

Gabriel sat on a bench next to him, breathing heavily. One of the crewmen cuffed them both again.

"Are you all right?" Gabriel asked, her face anxious.

"Yeah."

He heard the fan start up, an incessant droning whine. There was a surge of motion; then the deck tilted up as they climbed the levee wall. The dizziness returned.

When they were down the other side, he struggled into a sitting position against the tough plastic of the gunwale, trying to take an interest in the journey. The sour-faced woman was perched on the rear bench, her waterproof zippered up against the occasional scythe of spray. Her hair was blowing about in the slipstream.

One of the Mirriam's crewmen was up front, steering from behind a little Perspex windshield. A bodyguard was sitting behind him, giving Greg and Gabriel the occasional impersonal glance. At least Toby wasn't on board. He managed to get his eyes above the gunwale.

It'd taken centuries to drain the original fenland marches and turn them into farmland; generations had labored to liberate the rich black loam from the water, rewarded with the most fertile soil in Europe. The polar melt drowned them in eighteen months. The Fens basin wasn't a sea, it was mud: tens of meters thick, with a tackiness gradient that varied from a few centimeters of weed-clogged salt water on the surface down to near solid treacle.

An ex-Fenman living in Oakham had once told Greg that it was possible to tell the age of a Fens house by looking at its doorstep. The older it was, the more the loam would've dried out and contracted beneath it, leaving the doorstep high and dry. Really ancient cottages had a gap below the bottom of the stone and the ground.

Greg couldn't see any doorsteps; on the few lonely farmhouses still visible he was hard pushed even to see the doors. Twelve years of sluggish tidal suction had chewed out their foundations, pulling them down into the absorptive alluvial quagmire. Some of the sturdier buildings had managed to retain their shape, upper floors rising out of the brown-glass surface over which the hovercraft were racing. But the majority had subsided into tiny flattened islands, with juncus rushes growing out of the shattered bricks and skeletal timbers. Ragged felt hems of blue-green algae encircled all of them.

The hovercraft took a gently meandering course, avoiding the solid protrusions and swollen semisubmerged branches of dead copses in wide curves. Greg and Gabriel were following Kendric's craft, slicing through the fine spray its passage whipped up. Behind them, the horizon was marked by a fine green line. The Nene levee. Which meant they were heading approximately south. It didn't make any sense to Greg. There was nothing ahead of them.

Nobody lived in the basin. Crabs and gastropods thrived in the nutrient-rich sludge. But no one could earn a living from catching them. An ordinary fishing boat would stick fast in the mud. Conceivably a very light sail-powered catamaran or trimaran might be able to move about. And the idea of deploying nets or pots was laughable. In fact, hovercraft were just about the only vehicles that could be used successfully on the Fens basin.

From being the most fertile tract of land in Europe the Fens had reverted into a zone of barren desolation rivaling the Sicilian desert for inhospitableness. The sheer sameness of the quagmire was numbing Greg, bleeding away any last reserves of hope and defiance into the stifling atmosphere. Endless kilometers flowed past, compounding the sense of isolation. Gabriel had hunched up in her seat, defeated.

His attention drifted. Analyzing his predicament was suddenly futile, tiresome in the heat and moisture. His thoughts began to freefall, wondering what Eleanor was doing right now. And please don't let Kendric think she was important.

"Greg."

The urgency in Gabriel's voice made him look around quickly. A town was rising out of the horizon's uncompromising interface between brown and blue. It was like a mirage, its base lost in the black and silver ripples of shimmering inflamed air. Kendric's hovercraft was powering straight for it, leading them in.

"Hey."

The bodyguard sitting behind the pilot turned, boredom reigning. "What?"

"Where are we?" Greg asked.

"Wisbech. Why, does it make a difference?"

He should've known. Wisbech was the harbinger. The self-declared capital of the Fens was the first instance of wholesale evacuation in England. At the start of the Warming, excessive rains and record tides had sent the Nene cascading over its banks. And in those days the river ran straight through the center of the town.

Greg had remained glued to the flatscreen for a week while pontoons of news channel cameras chugged through the flooded streets. He remembered the pictures of drowned orchards ringing the town, the sodden refugees slumped apathetically in Royal Marine assault boats, clutching pathetically small bundles of possessions. It was something out of the Third World, not England. The novelty of such scenes had paled rapidly in the months, and then years, that followed, as town after town succumbed to the water.

Wisbech only looked whole from a distance, close-up it was in a sorry state. The outskirts had collapsed completely, leaving a broad inverted moat of rubble, protecting the town's heart from the larger vagaries of the swelling mud tides.

Both hovercraft slowed, maneuvering cautiously around hummocks coated in vigorous growths of reeds. The narrow channels between them were choked with algae, so thick in some places it resembled a green clay. It was stirred up by the hovercraft's downdraft, freeing pockets of rancid gas. Gabriel and the crewmen coughed and swore, clamping their hands over their faces. Greg couldn't smell a thing; his throat began to dry, though.

Five metal street lamps marked one channel for them, miraculously remaining upright after all these years. The conical algal encrustations around them were actually solidifying, turning them into cartoon desert islands. From the height of the poles left above the surface Greg guessed that the street must've been about one and a half meters below the hovercraft.

Farther in, the mounds became more regular, the channels echo-

ing the street pattern they covered. Sections of walls had survived
here, triangular, cracked, and leaning at crooked angles. The brickwork was obscured by a viscid pebble-dash of gull droppings. An
eerie desynchronized harmonic from the electric fans was bouncing
back off them, amplifying their natural soft purr to a vociferous clat-
tering reverberation.

Overhead, hundreds of gulls twisted in devious helices, calling
shrilly, the high-decibel feedback from the entire flock a brazen for-
tissimo rolling across the ruins. Greg realized it was impossible to
creep up on Wisbech.

They swept out of the mounds and into a suburb that was still
standing, two-story houses bordering a light industrial estate. The
mud came halfway up the ground-floor windows. There was no glass
left in them. Second-story windows were shattered, crystalline shark
teeth sticking out of moldering frames. Walls bulged, roofs sagged
alarmingly, shedding tiles like autumn leaves. Gutters were wadded
with grass and bindweed.

Moving on.

The Nene's old course was a serpentine semiliquid desert, 350 meters wide, flat and featureless. All the embankment buildings had
been pulverized by the febrile floodwater, their debris sucked away
by the inexorable vortices generated by the clash between currents
of salt water and fresh water. Since then the eternal mud had oozed
back, a great leveler.

Wisbech used to have a bustling port, the river lined by ugly ware-
houses and towering cranes. Greg had no way of telling where the
iron titans had once stood.

Both hovercraft picked up speed on the flat. The heat pressed
down, magnified by still, heavy air. Even the gulls abandoned the
chase.

Greg received a pernicious impression of waiting *depth*. He was
eager to reach the other side.

Their destination was becoming apparent straight ahead, on the
other side of the old river course. The most prominent building
there was. An old brick mill tower, slightly tapering, stained almost
completely black with age.

Greg didn't understand how it could've possibly survived until
they arrived at its base, riding noisily across the buckled corrugated
roof of a petrol station that was elevated half a meter above the mud.
The tower had been built on the summit of a raised stony mound.
While chaos and ruin had boiled all around, it had remained aloof
and untouched.

Tufts of tough Bermuda grass grew around its base; there was a good two meters of hard-packed earth between the bricks and the mud. The blades in front of the door were trampled down.

Kendric's hovercraft beached itself on the left of the door; Greg's drew up on the right. The pilot kept going until the bow was bumping the filthy brick, then killed the lift.

The tower door opened and a man came out. He was fortyish, dressed in a fawn sweatshirt and olive green Wranglers; his shoes were black leather, polished to a sergeant major's shine. A brown belt holster held a Browning nine-millimeter automatic.

Kendric and Hermione alighted from their hovercraft. Greg was hauled to his feet beside Gabriel. The man from the tower took in the fresh crimson splash down his shirt, the way he kept swaying from side to side.

"You were told: intact," he said to Kendric. There was no deference shown. Kendric seemed to be among equals at last.

"He can walk, he can talk," Kendric retorted indifferently, and marched off into the tower.

"Un-cuff them," said the man, "and get them upstairs. He's waiting."

The crewmen began deflating the hovercraft. Mark unlocked the cuffs and waved them into the tower.

Resignation had settled in long ago. Greg stepped across the door, shuffling like one of the undead, shamed and impotent.

The basement was bare, brick walls and concrete floor, a smack of dampness in the air but not as much as there should've been. He spotted a bright conditioning duct disappearing into the rude wooden plank ceiling. A deflated hovercraft of the same kind they'd arrived in sat in the middle of the floor. There was a cast-iron staircase opposite the door.

"Up," said Mark.

Shiny black shoes were already vanishing through the hole in the ceiling.

The first floor was also one big room, appreciably drier, used for storing crates of food. There were quite a few Harrods hampers stacked beside a small gray metal desk.

The second floor was a living room, carpeted in a thick steel-blue soft pile. Its furniture was modern, matching timber-framed leather chairs and settee, a low ceramic coffee table, and rose-teak executive desk with a recessed Olivetti terminal. Cupboards and a glass-fronted drinks cabinet were fixed to the wall; purpose built, they fit the shallow incline perfectly. Light shone through a single frosted glass window halfway up the wall. The brickwork had been left uncovered, scrubbed clean.

The dumpy woman who'd accompanied Greg on the hovercraft was waiting at the top of the stairs. Which was impossible, because she was following him up. Had to be twins.

But that revelation was blown straight out of his mind by the next person he saw. Kendric was talking earnestly to Leopold Armstrong. And Greg knew he'd finally met the person who'd organized the blitz on Philip Evan's core.

England's ex-president was fifty-seven but still trim and fit; his meaty face had a few more lines than Greg remembered; his mop of neatly cut silver hair was combed back tidily. He wore a simple Shetland cardigan over an open-neck cotton shirt. So ordinary. Almost homely.

Greg had thought he was beyond any further surprises, but he just stood and gawked until Gabriel bumped into his back, and her curse was sliced off in midflow as she caught sight of Armstrong.

He looked both of them over, taking his time. The tip of his tongue moistened his lips. Greg resisted the ridiculous urge to straighten his rumpled dinner jacket.

Mark clattered up the stairs behind them and hustled them forward. The little living room was beginning to get crowded. Hermione had stretched out in one of the two leather chairs, feigning lethargy. In addition to the man who'd met them outside there was another obvious hardliner hovering around Armstrong, just waiting for Greg to try something.

"Sit him down, Neville," he said. "Before he falls."

The man who'd met them outside the tower stabbed his forefinger at the settee, and Greg collapsed into it gratefully. Gabriel joined him after a second thrust.

His name had given Greg the key, placing the face—astonishing the trivia a mind can hold. Neville Turner: junior Home Office minister in the PSP government, second-in-command of the People's Constables, one of the many shadow figures orbiting Armstrong's periphery.

Armstrong now held up Greg's Trinities card, a prosecuting counsel with a bloodstained, fingerprinted knife.

"You're a Mindstar veteran," he said. "What on Earth are you doing consorting with scum like this?"

He was setting the tone, speaking normally, no threats, no gloating dominance charades. The ex-president was concerned only with facts, reality; he didn't possess time to waste on life's inessentials.

"Only a total paranoid would be frightened of ghosts," Greg said. The Trinities card was pocketed. "You mean Philip Evans?" Armstrong asked. "I admit the potential of that fancy NN core of his alarms me. He was remarkable when he only had a human brain. A gigaconductor with a transcendent Evans masterminding its marketing strategy would be a definite setback for me. He's so depressingly efficient at that sort of thing. A clever man. Pity we have opposing political viewpoints. But that's life.

"However, the conflict between Evans and me goes much deeper than that, as I'm sure you're aware."

Greg stared at him dumbly.

"Good Lord, he never told you, did he? Think on it, Mr. Mandel. You've seen Event Horizon's Prowlers at work, I believe?"

"Yes." No ultrahush there; he wasn't giving anything away.

"Military hardware, Mr. Mandel. Good quality American military hardware, as provided by that vicious profiteering little arms merchant, Horace Jepson."

Greg started. And Leopold Armstrong caught it. "Didn't you know? Oh yes, Mr. Mandel, Jepson is a U.S. government convenience. He sells to their allies, discreetly, mark you, and in return their IRS overlooks Globecast's somewhat irregular tax returns." He shook his head. "I don't know what all the fuss about you is. You're not half as good as everyone says. But then Mindstar never did fulfill its promise, did it?"

"You were worried enough, I remember," Greg said. "You and your People's Constables. Never had much joy catching us, though, did you?"

Armstrong pursed his lips. "Quite. Well, now that you have the facts, make the connection."

Greg read the anger in his face, sharp-focused determination, riding him hard. Armstrong was vengeance seeking, said his native intuition, a strong clear message. "My God," he said wonderingly. "Philip Evans blew up Downing Street."

Gabriel threw Greg a quick startled glance, then twisted sharply to look up at Armstrong.

"Very good, Mr. Mandel," said Leopold Armstrong. "The electron-compression warhead was brought into the country by one of his Prowlers, smuggled into Downing Street by his security division's hardliners. Kendric here tells me Evans laughed when the warhead exploded, thinks of himself as a more successful version of Guy Fawkes, no doubt, très romantique. He obliterated me once, Mr. Mandel; just believing I was dead was enough for the country to march in rebellion against the PSP. But now, now that bastard has exploited his money to do it to me again, to do it to all of us. Immortality, Mr. Mandel. He has bought himself immortality, with his imperialist power, his obscene personal wealth. Another twenty years I'm good for, and a lot can be done in that time. But what is a pitiful twenty years to Evans now? He has eternity. He will see me dead again, for real this time. And do you know what the real ball-kicker of it is? He won't even care; my actual death will be of supreme indifference to him. Because to him, secure in his present incarnation, we are all less than nothing. That, Mr. Mandel, cannot be allowed to pass unchallenged. That is why I risked blowing my cover, all my preparations. Because I am not going to allow him to escape death. Death is universal, making us all equal in the end."

"How about you, di Girolamo?" Greg asked. "You believe all this crap? You've got enough obscene personal wealth to translocate your memories like Philip Evans. You going to die when you don't have to?"

Armstrong put on a pained expression. "Please, Mr. Mandel. Kendric and I are not going to be driven apart by your desperation. Our mutual interests are too strong."

"I can't figure you," Greg said to Kendric. "You knew about the gigaconductor, yet you let Julia buy your family house out of the Event Horizon backing consortium. Why? You've kissed good-bye to a fortune."

"A deal," Kendric said thinly. "In return for informing the president of Philip Evans's NN core I will be given Event Horizon on a plate—not some derisory percentage, all of it."

"After it's been nationalized," Armstrong interjected smoothly. "Then naturally an international financier of Kendric's stature would be a perfect choice as chairman. Regretfully, his appointment would have been difficult to justify if Evans junior had exposed his earlier impropriety, which is why he agreed to sever their financial link. But she won't be in a position to issue such paranoiac ultimatums for much longer. After all, we can hardly allow a teenage girl to run a company so important to the country's economic prosperity, now can we?"

"Julia Evans will be stripped of her wealth and power," Kendric said. He looked straight at Greg, smiling mechanically, a slim line of flawless white teeth showing. "You understand, don't you, Mr. Mandel? You know how it is between Julia and me. There was a time when it was a fun game; she was an excellent player. But unfortunately she is too young. She does not fully comprehend the rules of this world.

If I do not take Event Horizon from her, she will use it to harm me, my family house. What would you do in my place?"

"She understands the rules perfectly," Greg retorted. "You just don't like losing. Seventeen years old, and she can outsmart you from dawn till dusk. You shouldn't be worried, Kendric; you should be terrified. But then you are, aren't you."

Kendric's lips closed. "It is not I who will feel terror."

"No?" Greg asked scornfully. "You even misjudged your new partner here. Armstrong isn't interested in vengeance; he's like you. He's after the gigaconductor. You're just his front man, a cheap puppet."

"You do have tenacity, don't you, Mr. Mandel." Armstrong said. "Perhaps that's why Event Horizon hired you. But you're wrong. The money accrued from gigaconductor license production will be split between us. A valuable source of income to further my aspirations."

"Aspirations," said Gabriel. "What aspirations?"

"Ah yes, Miss Thompson, isn't it?" He affected to notice her for the first time. "My return to mainstream politics."

"You can't be serious. You'll never resurrect the PSP."

"Not the old Party, no. It's a fool who doesn't learn from his mistakes. My new organization will be structured along different lines."

"Tentimes," Greg said. "You've been paying for Tentimes and the rest of Charles Ellis's hot-rod team to screw up all those companies."

"Indeed, and my people have been quick to point out the inevitable failings of the free-market system. There is a large groundswell of resentment building against the New Conservatives and their mismanagement of the economy. One I intend to encourage."

"Bollocks," Gabriel snorted. "No matter how bad things get, nobody's going to vote for hard-left policies again. You don't understand just how much people hated everything you stand for."

"Miss Thompson, if you could still see into the future, you'd know that I'm not aiming for the grand slam this time. You can only ever do that once. I was very unlucky in that events beyond my control conspired to put an end to PSP rule. The energy crisis, the Warming, the Credit Crash. No government could withstand that combination. Take a look around at other countries. How many of the leaders of ten years ago remain in power today? We were the ones who were blamed. People don't like to blame their own greed and exorbitant lifestyles. They want someone to hold responsible. And government gets it in the neck every time, from outbreaks of food poisoning to hurricanes. Blame the government."

"From protesters being whipped to death in the street to seed potatoes being dished up on the tables of Party members," Greg said.

"Those kinds of incidents were inevitable to start with. But the abuses were solvable, given time."

"You had ten years," Greg said. "All they ever did was get worse."

"The people who made up the PSP's local committees were un-used to power. If they had been allowed to establish themselves, then we would've seen stability. But of course, Mindstar and that plague of urban predator gangs incited trouble in the cities, goading the Con-stables." He flexed his hands in agitation. "We were . . . misrepre-sented."

Gabriel laughed unsteadily. "What's the matter, Armstrong? Did you think the hard left had a monopoly on political agitators?"

For a moment Greg thought he would hit her, but the ex-president eventually sighed resentfully. "This time I have settled for a more slow-burning form of reformation. There are thousands of my ap-pointees still in place throughout the civil service, primed and wait-ing. The New Conservatives will soon have to order an intervention as the private and denationalized companies begin to falter, bringing them back into the government fold. My people will assume the man-agement duties, with a great deal of success. And I shall direct them, president in all but name and public visibility."

"We'll fight you," Greg said levelly. "We'll fight you with every-thing we've got. Bows and arrows if that's all that's left; we've done it before. And we beat you before."

"Yet here I am. This seems to be the month of miraculous come-backs." He laughed, and grinned around at the faces in the living room. "I do believe I'm talking to a reactionary. However, I don't intend to spend hours justifying my actions to you, Mr. Mandel, nor debating the pros and cons of centrally controlled economies. You were brought here to answer questions. And that is what you will now do."

Greg thought he must've flinched; certainly he stiffened.

"No, no, we don't go around beating confessions out of people here. There are much simpler methods. But understand one thing, Mandel: you are going to die. Just as soon as you have provided me with every byte I require. How you die will be decided by your be-havior. The old easy way or the hard way. You can have a bullet through the head, quick and clean. Alternatively, you can be dumped into the old riverbed, alive and kicking."

"It doesn't make one fuck of a lot of difference in the end, does it?"

Armstrong picked up a cybofax from the coffee table and sat in the last remaining leather chair. "Think about it," he said knowingly.

"*Dwell* on it. You might find your attitude adjusting. Neville, we'll begin now."

Turner opened a drawer in the rose-teak desk and extracted a spaghetti tangle of nylon straps and optical fibers. "Take off your shirt," he told Greg with a doctor's examining-room impartiality.

Greg thought about it. Refusing would be a rather trivial token; the shirt would only be cut or ripped off. Besides, he was thinking of being slung into that bottomless mud. God curse Armstrong. He shrugged out of the jacket and began on the shirt buttons. Flakes of dried blood wedged under his fingernails.

"Good," Armstrong said. "Quite an ironic twist for you, Mr. Mandel, I imagine. On the receiving end of a lie detector for once."

Turner Velcroed a strap around each of Greg's wrists. They prickled, minute needle-tipped sensors probing into his skin, tasting salinity, heat, conductivity, heart rate. The Saint Christopher was flicked to one side, and another strap went around his neck, tightening noose-style.

Leopold Armstrong's fingers drummed on his cybofax. "I have a number of queries. And you'll answer each one honestly. For every lie you make we'll break a bone in Miss Thompson's body. The bigger the lie, the bigger the bone. Understand?" Again, there was no malice; Leopold Armstrong was just telling it the way it was.

"Yeah," Greg replied, as a tiara band was placed on his head. Turner pressed an infuser against his arm. There was a bee sting of pain, turning to an ice spot.

"Relaxant," Turner said, and began plugging the optical cables into a gear module that was already interfaced with the Olivetti deck. The cube lit with scrawling sine waves. He sat in the swivel chair behind the desk and began typing. Data rolled down an LCD display. "Name?" he asked.

The correlation went on for what seemed an age to Greg. The relaxant acted like a gentle influx of rosé wine, pleasantly inebriating, amplifying sounds like squeaking leather and rustling clothes, turning the air warm, drying his throat. Of course, he could still concentrate. If he wanted to.

They seemed to have an encyclopedic knowledge of his life stored in the Olivetti. Stuff he could barely remember: secondary school exam results, Army postings, nicknames of barrack mates, neighbors at the time-share estate. Nothing recent, though. Nothing from the last couple of years.

"He's ready," Turner shouted out eventually.

Armstrong consulted his cybofax. "One. Does anyone on the mainland suspect I am alive?"

Greg had worked out that this was a crux. To answer or not to answer? Watching Gabriel being systematically snapped apart before him. The noise of all those cracking bones would be deafening. But they were going to die anyway. It would be very noble to confound Armstrong.

Decisions. Decisions. Gabriel was silent. Unhelpful as always.

The relaxant's health-spar glow had seeped through his entire body, levitating him. He was back in the womb again, warm, cozy, and untroubled.

"No," he said. "Nobody knows."

Leopold Armstrong's smile illuminated the whole world.

33

Ade O'Donal had discovered that hard cash had its own special weight. Yeah, like no weight at all. He'd filled two Alitalia flight bags with New Sterling and Eurofrancs: thick, hard wads of notes. Kilograms of them, stretching his arms as he walked down the stairs, but he could've carried them for ever. The bags were new, clean, and bright; when people saw them, their exotic foreign logo, they'd know he was for real. One shit-hot guy.

The crappy top stair creaked when he put his foot on it. That was all he needed—Sashy to hear him leaving. He'd waited until late afternoon before scooting, fewer eyes seeing what he was about, and she was still sleeping off an afternoon of *majestic* sex. It'd been one serious way of splitting. He'd been tempted to take her with him. Her compact brown body was the absolute best screw ever, like her brain was loaded with *Kama Sutra* software. But he was traveling light, "Bat Out of Hell" time, breezing down the open road. A woman would hold him back; worse, Sashy was into family in a big way. Brothers, parents, cousins, hundreds of them. Daft girl spent half the day on the phone. She wouldn't understand; he had to get *lost*, out of here, like he'd never existed. Kick loose from the shit glitching his life right now—Wolf, the two Event Horizon bastards.

He'd spent a couple of days collecting the money from cashpoints after that hard guy and the fat slag had turned up, initially terrified they'd pull the money from his Cayman account because of the blitz. Psychics, fucking psychics! Unhumans. Ade O'Donal still got cold burn in his balls thinking about it. His mind being torn open like a paper bag, thoughts held up to the light and examined. That was heavy-duty shit. Wolf must've gone acid crazy thinking they could get away with a burn against Event Horizon. That company was the biggest scene in England, even *kombinates* pissed themselves about Event Horizon.

Ade O'Donal had plugged himself but good into the circuit after the psychics had left, making *serious* connections, a cruise for any hard-core hot rod. Gigaconductor. New word. The circuit was ringing with it. The biggest deal in the known universe was going down, and Wolf had tried to run a spoiler. Shit. He could've been hurt. Hurt bad. Wasted!

The little patch of red blistered skin on his belly where the Event Horizon hardliner had zapped him with the Mulekick was still sore. A good memory. If he ever thought this was one giant curved syntho trip, that patch would set him straight. Might even be a scar. Girls like scars. Scars were macho.

There was a noise down below in the darkened hall. Footsteps clicking on the tiles.

"Brune? Hey, Brune, that you?"

He'd sent Brune out after lunch to top up the BMW, gas and watts. This was going to be one long flight. Cornwall, maybe. Ade O'Donal hadn't made plans. He'd figured just go with the flow was safest. That way no one could load a tracer on him.

Brune was staying here, Brune with his leg in a tube of quick-set polymer. The guy was out of hardlining for a month anyway. Even the BMW would get axed eventually. Then there'd be just him, the money, some of the memoxes, and the Burrows terminal. That Burrows terminal was going to turn him into the circuit's sexiest hot rod.

After the psychics had left, Ade O'Donal had plugged the gate circuits into the Burrows to try and see how the fuck they'd opened it without tripping the alarms. Fifty Richter disaster time. The Burrows had crashed, totally. The only thing left working was the power LED; not even the menu showed. Whatever had been in the gate circuit was hot enough to melt through the hardware core guardian programs Wolf had given him.

That convinced him he had plugged into the biggest underclass operation running. Cancer software that was better than Wolf's! When he settled down he was going to retro that Burrows, no matter what it took. Those bytes were going to earn him megamoney, like what Wolf paid was just small change.

He'd go for a total reincarnation, *plastique*, sign on the circuit as a virgin, build a reputation from scratch. A genuine hot rod, not dependent on anyone. Pity about Tentimes, mind you; it was a slick kind of handle, told the girls all they needed to know out front.

"Brune?"

There was a figure in the hall, bending over a large crumpled bundle on the tiles. It straightened up as he reached the bottom of the stairs. And something about it was megashit wrong. The hospital had shaved Brune's head, coating the back of his skull in dermal membrane. It looked like he was wearing a Jew's skullcap from a distance. Good for a piss-take.

But the guy facing him was albino-white, death-mask face with jet-black lips, a close-cropped Mohican strip of titian hair running from the bridge of his nose over his crown and disappearing below the collar of his biker jacket. Ade O'Donal knew the look. Tribal. The guy was from Stoneygate.

Stoneygate wasn't somewhere Ade O'Donal went even in daytime, loaded with freaked-out psychos. Five tribes protecting Leicester's syntho vats, from the police and from each other; that district was wound up but tight.

Ade O'Donal dropped the Alitalia bags, making a dull slap on the hall tiles. "Brune?" it came out all wavery, like a whimper. And the broken thing on the floor was Brune, a puddle of blood spreading from a jagged rip in the dermal membrane. An ocean of blood, glistening sickly.

"Tentimes?" asked the Stoney.

"Shit, like no way. I ain't never heard of him."

"Lying, O'Donal, dey squirt me yo' file."

"Shit, man, I never told those two nothing, not a byte."

"No crap, Tentimes. No interested."

Ade O'Donal closed his eyes, didn't want to see the gun or knife or whatever. Praying it would be quick.

"Job for yo'."

He risked a peek, ready to slam his eyes shut again. The Stoney was looking at him contemptuously.

"Say what?"

"Job. Burn."

"That's it?"

"Yay."

"All you want is like a fucking burn, and you waste Brune for that! You syntho-crashed shit." Ade O'Donal wanted to smash the Stoney with his fists, pound him into a pulp. His life was exploding into the all-time downer. People out of his nightmares kept coming for him, like every shitty deal in the world was his fault.

There was a tiny click, and a matte gray ten-centimeter blade appeared a centimeter from Ade O'Donal's eye, diamond tip reflecting tiny slivers of cold blue light. "Don' gi' me lip. I slice yo'."

"Sure, okay, no problem, just cool it, man, right?"

"Where yo' terminal?"

The temptation to let the Stoney open the door was near overwhelming. But he was wearing leather gloves; the charge might not be enough to penetrate. Too dangerous. "Down here," Ade O'Donal sighed.

The Stoney took in the wine cellar's hardware with a stoic gaze. "Alien," he murmured.

Ade O'Donal crumpled into his chair behind the table that held his terminals. "What's the burn?"

"Wolf say finish Event Horizon, d' core. Suit yo'?"

"How?"

A shrug.

"Shit."

"Be good. I break cover fo' yo'."

Cover? What the hell did that mean? No way could this arsehole be Wolf in person. This was getting extremely deep, the kind of deep he wasn't likely to climb out from. "Hey, listen, how are you gonna know if I take out the core? I mean, you're gonna leave me alone if I pull this off, right?"

"Friends, dey watching."

"And if it works?"

"Yo' still jiving tomorrow."

Ade O'Donal nodded slowly, as low as he'd ever been. But the Stoney needed him. If he did the burn, there was a chance. Small, though, fucking small. Brune drowning in blood.

There were only two terminals on-line: that psychic hardline bastard had screwed the Hitachi and the Akai; the supercancer from the gate had crashed the Burrows. That just left the Event Horizon and the Honeywell. And no way was he going to use the Event Horizon terminal. That name was too much bad karma right now.

Ade O'Donal tapped the Honeywell's power stud, slipping its throat mike around his neck, muttering, typing, eyes locked into the cube. A melt virus got him into Event Horizon's datanet, disguised as a civil engineering contractor's bid for a new flatscreen factory at Stafford. He loaded a memox Wolf had given him for the blitz, studying company procedure. Bids would be processed by the finance division, the lowest three forwarded to the freaky Turing core for a final decision.

He pulled a memox from the shelves, one he'd planned on taking with him. "This is like the best I've ever written, you know," he said, a sudden urge to explain, to let the Stoney know he was dealing with a real pro hot rod. "It scrambles databus management programs. That's the beauty of it, man; once it's in, you can't access the system to flush it out. Total internal communication shutdown. The core will be sliced right out of the datanet, along with anything it's interfaced with."

"Dat sound sweet."

"Okay." Ade O'Donal pushed the memox into the Honeywell's slot, hands quivering.

The cube showed the bid's data package wrapping around the virus, geometric tentacles choking a crystalline egg. Ade O'Donal probed the finished Trojan with tracer programs. There was no chink in the covering, nothing that hinted at the black treasure beneath the surface. Smooth. And he had made the quotes for the factory ridiculously low; the bid package would be shunted to the core, no sweat.

Idiotically, pride overrode his depression. This was it, his construct, all his own, a solo hot-rod burn. Tentimes had made solo.

O'Donal fed the Trojan an activation code keyed to the core's dump order. It would pass clean through the finance division processors; then once they'd forwarded it to the core, the fucker would detonate, digital H-bomb. Wipe-out time.

Index finger tapped: download.

The cube emptied.

"Might take a while," O'Donal said.

"No matter."

The diamond-tipped blade clicked softly.

34

JULIA HAD INSISTED ON RELIEVING the nurse at Katerina's bedside in the afternoon, keeping a solitary vigil over her brain-wasted friend. She hated every second of it, knowing she deserved it. Pushing Kats toward Kendric had seemed so clever at the time, an elegant solution. Everybody would wind up with what they wanted, no tears, no heartache.

Greg was right—she'd only thought of the deed, never the consequences. Too shallow and self-obsessed. Still a child. Idiot savant.

Katerina stirred, turning, her sleep troubled. Dr. Taylor had given her a trauma suppressor. Short-term amnesiac, the woman had explained. It'll kill the craving for now, but she'd made sure Katerina was infused with tranquilizers throughout the day, only leaving a few periods of brief semilucidity for eating and going to the toilet.

Julia had been the one spooning soup into her. Katerina had swallowed automatically, incapable of coherent speech. Compounding the anguish.

Julia had got three of Event Horizon's premier-grade executives working flat out on securing Katerina that Caribbean treatment, trying to buy a place in the detox clinic. They'd been told there was an eight-month waiting list. Julia refused to let that bother her, pulling in the company's favors, bullying the clinic with financial and political pressure. Dr. Taylor had warned her that Katerina's cranial blood vessels were saturated with the symbiont; if its grip was ever going to be broken, then it would have to be done swiftly.

She'd buy that bloody Caribbean island if necessary. Anything. Anything at all. She just wanted Kats back to her old self. Frivolous, vaguely annoying, and utterly carefree.

The sun had nearly dropped below the horizon, fluorescing a cloud-slashed western sky to a royal gold, fading to black at its zenith. Julia watched it from the bedroom window, seeing the shadows pool in hollows and nooks across Wilholm's grounds, spilling out over the grass. The fountain in the lily pond died down spluttering, its light sensors switching off the pump.

Julia activated a single wall-mounted biolum, then crossed the room and drew the heavy Tudor curtains across both windows. When she'd first left America and the desert she'd been entranced by dawn and dusk in Europe, cool blues and greens gleaming dully under fiery skies, always different. It'd been magical, the expected sadness that she'd miss the desert's beauty never materializing.

Tonight the sight left her totally unmoved. Her emotions seemed to have shut down. The climax would come tonight; she was sure of it. The game had ceased to be a game. And she was responsible, she and Grandpa. Kendric's maneuverings and power ploys had been thwarted at every stage. She'd stalemated him all across the board. There was nothing left to him now but the physical. Kendric would have no qualms about that.

Strangely, even Greg had warned her about the danger. Greg the liar. Greg the betrayer. His name was the only one capable of piercing the wrap of numbness around her feelings. She'd believed in him like nobody before. Worshiped from afar, flirted. Opened her soul to him. Confessed the darkest, most shameful secret.

And he'd *lied* to her.

Just like all the rest. Men must look on her as some kind of victim waiting to be abused. Except for Adrian, a bleak inner voice said, Adrian adored her female side. He was immune to her money. So far. But knowing her luck . . .

She still couldn't believe she'd been so mistaken about Greg. He'd said she was beautiful. And she couldn't be fooled by smooth talk anymore, not after Kendric.

Then why? Why the lie?

Access BlitzCulmination. So called because it brought all aspects of the case together. The homogenized data packages unfolded within her glacial mind, rotating the bedroom and Katerina 180 degrees from her cognizance. Her processor nodes marshaled it into precise channels once more, a construct that incorporated hard facts, assumptions, suspicions.

She ran the logic matrix once more, the fifth time today. It produced a single diamond-hard conviction. No matter how many times she ran it, how much slackness and wishful thinking she incorporated into the matrix channels, the answer was always the same.

Liar. Traitor. Thief. Heartbreaker.

Cancel BlitzCulmination. One thing it never told her was why Greg would do such a thing. She didn't understand human nature well enough to guess. And now she'd probably never know.

Katerina had sunk into an innocent dreamless sleep. Julia pulled the frilly snowdrop-pattern duvet up around her shoulders.

Open Channel to NN Core. Load OtherEyes Limiter#Five.

She felt her grandfather snuggle into her mind, welcoming his touch. The last person on the whole planet she still trusted. And what a sad comment on her life that was.

How are we doing? she asked.

Greg hasn't moved for three hours now. I think Wisbech must be their nesting ground. Clever that. So close, yet so far away. I'm not sure how they got across the Fens basin; too slow for a tilt-fan, possibly a hovercraft.

I trusted him, Grandpa. Really trusted him. Everything he did and said was always right. He made me believe in him. I thought I was safe.

I know you did, Juliet. It must hurt. I'm so sorry.

It doesn't hurt. I don't feel anything. I'm not human anymore.

Course you are, girl. Don't talk nonsense. You're seeing Adrian again this weekend, aren't you? What you do with him is pretty bloody human. And I approve. He's a nice boy.

If I'm still around by the weekend.

Hey, that's no Evans talking. Wilholm is well protected, and I'm hooked into all the security sensors. Ain't nobody going to sneak up on you, girl.

Suppose it's one of the staff, Walshaw even?

No, Juliet, not Morgan. He's been with me for fifteen years, almost since you were born.

Stake your life on it, huh? She let the irony filter back to him.

That's my girl. Keep shining through. But don't you worry; I'm even watching Morgan. No strain on my capacity.

Julia found herself looking down at the wood-paneled study, initially confused by the unusual perspective, a fly on the ceiling. Walshaw was sitting at the long table databasing with his customized terminal; the bald patch on his crown was larger than she'd realized before. Then the incoming squirt from Event Horizon's datanet bloomed in her mind. Walshaw was reviewing the Cray memories as they were being extracted by the security division programming team. All the memories had been run through search and classification programs as they came out, analyzed and indexed. He was running through the categories, accessing every mention of Wolf and Event Horizon, double-checking.

He's been doing that for hours, her grandfather said. *Hunting down that clue Greg was talking about. Hardly the act of a turncoat, now is it?*

I suppose. It would be nice to believe in him at least, Julia thought. But this was her life she was gambling with now. And the list of her mistakes when it came to dealing with people was a long one.

Suddenly she was inundated with a rapid-motion tour of Wilholm through the security sensors, visual, infrared, magnetic, elec-

tromagnetic, UV laser-radar. Millisecond slices of security division
hardliners patroling the corridors; sentinels prowling the grounds;
Tobias in his stables; owls snapped in midflight, wings motionless;
field mice twitching their tiny damp noses in the night air; deserted
tracts of landscape, fields and woodland. A kaleidoscope of bright-
hued luminous colors and conflicting geometries.

See, Juliet? All quiet on the western front.

Her heart began to beat faster. *Why is Walshaw bothering with the
Crays? We know Kendric has plugged in with the PSP, that the card carriers organized the blitz.*

*You and I know, yes, Juliet. But I don't think Morgan has put it together
yet.*

But it's obvious! she exclaimed.

To you.

*Oh, Grandpa! What if Greg hasn't worked it out, either? What if I was
wrong about him? He was so tired, I mean totally run-down. He's been
through hell, and it was Kendric who had him beaten up.*

Relax, girl. First thing I thought of.

What then?

*If he's innocent, why are the two of them in Wisbech? And why didn't
Gabriel warn us about him? She's in it with him.*

Oh.

Sorry, Juliet.

The depression enveloped her again, its return total. She could see
the world simply now, black-and-white, no right, no wrong; there
was just survival that mattered. Instinctive self-preservation,
primeval, the only complexity lay in method. The acceptance decided
her.

When can you hit them? she asked.

*Every hundred and eight minutes, starting in seventy-two minutes—
mark.*

Do it. Her lips synchronized with her thoughts, but no sound
emerged.

*Okay, Juliet. Why don't you take a break? Katerina isn't going any-
where.*

No, I'll stay here. It wouldn't be right leaving her, not now.

I'll give you a status check nearer the time.

"Love you, Grandee."

Wipe OtherEyes Limiter#Five. Exit NN Core.

Julia sat down on the barrel-like Copenhagen chair beside the bed,
hand automatically sliding down the side of the cushion. Her fingers
touched the hard plastic casing, reassuring her. She drew out the

weapon. An ash-gray cylinder thirty centimeters long and three wide, a thin grooved handle at one end. It resembled a fat, long-barreled pistol, weighing about one and a half kilos. The discharge end was solid, with a small circular indentation, gritted with minute carbonized granules. ARMSCOR was printed along the side in black lettering.

She'd stolen it from Greg after he'd brought Kats back to the finance division offices, slipping it off Walshaw's desk and into her bag as soon as the desolating revelation of his betrayal had sunk in. She'd been horribly afraid of him, what he might do.

When she'd got back to Wilholm she'd accessed the manor library's memory core, looking up what she'd got. A stunshot, capable of immobilizing an adult at forty-five meters. Four shots would kill.

The power unit was charged to ninety-five percent capacity, giving her almost two hundred shots. She'd spent the morning familiarizing herself with it—safety catch, grip, aiming. Kept at it until she was satisfied she could do it by touch alone. It tended to wobble unless she used both hands. The library said there was no recoil.

And nobody knew she'd got it, not even Morgan Walshaw. Her last line of defense. Its solidity and weight injecting a primitive kind of confidence into a badly demoralized psyche. She wished it would be Kendric himself who came. There'd be no inhibition holding her back then. Sending all ninety-five percent into his jerking, burning body.

But it would be some tekmerc hardliner, anonymous, a fast-moving shadow in the dark. Her one advantage was that he'd have to come to her, a slight advantage, but it might make the difference between life and death. The odds were impossible for the nodes to compute, too many variables, thank the Lord. That sort of foreknowledge was something she could do without.

Julia sat back in the Copenhagen chair, putting the Armscor on her lap, resting her chin on her hands. Looking at Kats, she realized she'd even been emptied of envy; her friend's beautiful face meant nothing. In fact, when Kats grew older she'd lose far more. You can't lose what you haven't got.

35

T HE WATER-FRUIT FIELD STRETCHED on forever, a perfect example of perspective, parallel rows of creamy-white globes merging at some gray distance. Eleanor felt around underneath the next globe and cut the thick rope root with her knife. Inky sap puffed out, lost in the reservoir's slow current. She lifted the globe and steered it slowly into the neck of her net bag. There were another twenty water-fruit inside. Almost full. Turning back to the row.

A dolphin snout pushed her hand. The knife missed the root. She looked at her hand, puzzled. Tried again. Two hard bumps on the back of her wrist, almost painful.

Annoyance began to register in her sluggish thoughts. She held up her hand, palm outward, pushing twice: back off.

It was Rusty. He didn't budge, guarding the water-fruit. Dark shapes slithered effortlessly through the water behind her, churning up a small cloud of silt. When she turned she saw another pair of dolphins had got hold of the net bag, pulling it away.

Angry now, her steady rhythm had been broken. Hanging a meter off the reservoir bed, motionless, trying to outstare a dolphin. How odd.

Now that the monotony of harvesting was broken she began to realize just how tired she was, muscles whispering their protest into her cortex—arms, legs, shoulders, back, all laced with fatigue toxins.

Exactly how long had she been doing this? The soft green light was fading fast overhead, lowering visibility to less than fifty meters. A cold flash of realization pinched her mind. She hadn't quite fallen into the trap of blue lost, but her soul had migrated, fleeing the memories of guilt and pain. Now they rushed back into her empty brain, unmitigated.

Greg calling, apologetic but firm, ruled by duty. Idiot, she'd answered, trying to disguise a jumble of secret worries and heart-wrenching concern with stiff resolution. He respected toughness. Both refusing to yield.

He'd promised, she'd told him, promised solemnly. But he'd shaken his head, saying it wasn't like that. She'd cried herself to sleep, imagining terrible things happening on the di Girolamo yacht.

How silly it all seemed now. Words spoken, never meant.

Eleanor gave Rusty a submissive thumbs-up and headed for the surface, too weary to rush, a few wriggles with her flippers every couple of meters keeping her ascent steady. Rusty orbited her laggardly.

The hireboats had all returned to the fishing lodge at Whitwell, away down the other prong of the reservoir. Even the windsurfers had packed up. The Berrybut estate's bonfire was sending flames shooting into the neutral sky, a specter-light swarm of sparks lingering above the rectangular clearing in the still air.

Rusty insinuated himself between her legs, and she hugged his dorsal fin gratefully. The ride back to the shore was nothing like the usual turbulent dash. A slow smooth glide. Now, why couldn't people be like dolphins—sympathetic, gentle, perennially happy. Magnificent creatures.

The sun had fallen behind a pearl crescent horizon piled high with lacy clouds when Rusty let her off. She stroked his head and bent to kiss him. Rusty would understand. He chittered wildly and sank below the surface, suddenly leaping up again five meters away, twisting in midair and landing with an almighty splash. She laughed, first time all day.

The pebbles on the drying mud cut into her feet as she walked out of the water, her skin like soft crinkled putty after such a long immersion. It'd been midday when she'd begun harvesting. Greg had sworn he'd be back by early morning. Eleanor had waited until lunchtime for him to return. Then her tolerance had snapped, and she'd dived into the water, sulky and furious.

Duncan was fire warden this evening. He lived two chalets down from number six. Eleanor stopped to say hello, letting the bonfire's ruddy furnace heat dry her puckered skin, welcoming the warmth permeating her limbs. Duncan gave her a couple of baked potatoes out of the raw clay oven-tunnel that ran through the heart of the bonfire, eyeing her chest as the flames threw liquid orange ripples across the dull-sparkle nylon of her one-piece costume. She thanked him, straightfaced, and juggled the hot potatoes back to the chalet. Duncan was sweet. And his covert schoolboy glances started her thinking about how she and Greg could spend the evening making up.

The Duo hadn't returned. Eleanor almost dropped the potatoes. Greg had been gone for thirty hours now. No matter how big their row, he wouldn't have done that without telling her.

She dumped the mirror-lung and the potatoes on the porch, blipping the lock. Inside, and the snug familiarity of the little lounge offered no comfort at all. She activated the Event Horizon terminal, loading Greg's cybofax number.

The delay warned her. Connections never took more than a second. After fifteen seconds the flatscreen printed: THE UNIT YOU HAVE CALLED IS CURRENTLY OUTSIDE EUROCOM'S INTERFACE ZONE.

Now the dark worry she'd held back really began to mount. She didn't even hesitate before loading Gabriel's number.

THE UNIT YOU HAVE CALLED IS CURRENTLY OUTSIDE EURO-COM'S INTERFACE ZONE.

The heart flutter of panic didn't come from fear; it was not knowing what to do next. Instinct cried out to call the police. But snatching that Katerina girl was incredibly illegal. Eleanor wondered if they'd got caught, flung into prison. She could hardly ask. Then she remembered Gabriel had been with him all the time. Nothing could go wrong with Gabriel there to provide advance warning. A doddle, he'd said, a late, lame attempt to reassure her.

Then why wasn't he back here? Her cold mind screamed silently. The ludicrous notion of him running off with Gabriel intruded. Dismissed instantly. She thought for a second, then raced for the bedroom and her cupboard. The Trinities would know—maybe where he was, certainly what to do next.

The card Royan had given her was still in her bag. She showed it to the terminal, praying. The flatscreen remained blank, but she heard scuffling sounds from the speaker.

"Yeah?" The voice was male, flat and uninterested.

"I want to speak to Teddy—Father."

"No shit?"

"Now!"

Eleanor thought she'd blown it; there was only aching silence. Cursing her brittle nerves.

The screen cleared to show Teddy's face. "Eleanor, right? What's up, gal?"

She let out a sob of relief.

Teddy's frown grew as she explained. She wondered if she was coming off like a hysterical jilted girl. He had to realize how important this was.

"Greg didn't leave any message for you at all?" Teddy asked when she finished. And he was taking it seriously. Her confidence rose a fraction; she wasn't alone anymore.

"None."

"That ain't right," Teddy said. "Greg would always cover himself, standard procedure. And Gabriel's cybofax is dead, too?"

"Yes, at least English Telecom says both of them are outside the satellite footprint."

Teddy paused for a moment. "Okay, my people left 'em going into the Event Horizon finance division office. I can't believe the company would waste 'em. They knew they could trust Greg, and it ain't that sort've deal anyway. 'Sides, they let my people get clear. Thing that bothers me is Gabriel. She's like invincible, you know?" He started typing on his terminal keyboard, looking at something off camera. Unintelligible voices stuttered in the background. "Okay, I want you to call that Morgan Walshaw guy for me. You'll get shoved around by secretaries and the like; don't take no shit. Insist on speaking to him. Him only. Ask him if he knows where Greg is. Then call me right back. You'll get straight through this time. I'm gonna see what I can find out about Gabriel, if she ever got back."

"How?"

Teddy's face melted into a fast keen grin. "I got friends everywhere."

"Oh." She felt foolish asking.

"Eleanor, you did good calling me, gal. We'll get him back for you."

And he was gone before she could thank him.

Eleanor tugged on a silk blouse before she called Event Horizon, respectable from the waist up, twisting damp hair into a ponytail. Morgan Walshaw's number was in the terminal's memory core.

The screen lit with a polite-looking young man in a neat powder blue business suit.

Eleanor swallowed. "This is Mandel Investigative Services," she said. "I'm returning Mr. Walshaw's call on a case we're covering for him."

He shrugged; friendly, she thought.

"I'm sorry," he said. "We can't reach Mr. Walshaw at the moment."

"If you check, you'll see our company is cleared for direct access."

"Hey, I'm not giving you the runaround, not someone as pretty as you. Mr. Walshaw really is out of touch."

"Isn't that unusual?"

"Very. There's some big glitch in our communications net right now, really shot it up. It's headless-chicken chaos around here at the moment."

"I see." But she wasn't sure she believed.

"Listen, if it's really urgent, why don't I call you back as soon as the glitch has been debugged? We've got Mandel Investigative Services' number on file. Who shall I ask for?"

"Eleanor, Eleanor Broady."

"Pleased to meet you Eleanor, I'm Bernard Murton."

"That's very kind of you to offer, Bernard. Have you any idea how long it'll take to debug this glitch?"

"Nope, sorry." He smiled ingratiatingly. She wondered if he'd have enough courage to ask her out for a drink. Struck by how bizarre this all was, being chatted up by a randy assistant while God knows what was happening to Greg. Sliding her mind back onto the problem.

"This data package I've got for Walshaw is very important," she said. "I don't suppose you could tell me where he is; I could hand deliver it."

"Er, sure, no ultrahush about that. He's with Miss Evans at her home. But you won't be able to get in. It's sealed up tight, something to do with the communication glitch. They don't tell me anything."

"Thanks, Bernard." She broke the connection before he could say anything else.

There was a number for Wilholm in the terminal memory, listed as private.

Should've done this to start with, Eleanor thought as the connection was placed. Greg always said go straight to the top for real results.

The terminal's flatscreen dissolved into a tricolor snowstorm, red, green, and yellow specks skipping about. The speaker hissed with static.

Eleanor stared at it uncomprehendingly, then cleared the order, ready to try again.

ERROR, flashed the flatscreen as she punched up the menu.

An icy dread settled on her skin, like a fast autumn-morning frost. Piercing clean into her heart. This was something to do with Greg, she *knew* it was. Greg, Event Horizon, Julia, Gabriel, Walshaw, Katerina, all bound together in some devil's tangle. Thoroughly spooked, she punched up the menu again.

ERROR.

ERROR.

ERROR.

The flatscreen went dead, not even that absurd will-o'-the-wisp nebula.

Eleanor snatched up the Trinities card and ran out into the twilight. "Duncan!" People turned to look at her, pale ovals of surprise and concern. "Duncan!"

He was abruptly standing in front of her, face rapt with a mixture of eagerness and trepidation.

"Your terminal, I have to use your terminal!" she cried.

Duncan seemed startled, her frantic urgency taking a moment to sink in. "Right-oh, sure."

Eleanor wanted to grab him and shake him as he fidgeted through his cards, eventually finding the right one for his door with a shy apologetic grimace. "Is it Greg? Is he all right?"

"Yes. No. I'm not sure; that's why I need the terminal."

The door swung open. "Here we go." Duncan had an old Emerson terminal, the keyboard worn, some of the touch tabs completely blank. He tapped the power stud.

Eleanor punched out the phone function with a pulse of anarchic energy, then showed her Trinities card to the key. Duncan's face went white when he saw the bold fist and thorn cross emblem, eyes widening. "I'll er . . . be outside."

Teddy's face appeared, leaning forward, squinting. "Hell, what's happened with you, gal?"

She told him, barely coherent, words falling over each other in her rush to expel them. Made an effort to calm down.

"Not good," he scowled. "Gabriel never made it home either. We wanna find out where they was headed, we gotta talk to Walshaw or that Julia Evans gal."

"Can't. The security man said Wilholm was sealed up, that I wouldn't be able to get in."

"And they ain't taking no calls, neither," Teddy said. "Hostile to 'em, even. Strange. Something in there they don't want no one to see. Ask me and it's something plugged into whatever the Christ is going down. Gotta be. Lay you down good money on that, gal. You know what?"

"What?"

"Reckon we oughta take a look-see." There was a dense gleam of excitement in his eyes, some of his tension draining away.

"Yes, but—how?"

"Ain't nowhere God can't reach, not if he really wants to. Can you get to Wilholm tonight?"

"Yes."

"Okay, I'll round me up a few troops, meet you outside the main entrance in an hour. How's that grab you?"

"Great." And she was lumbered with the problem of transport.

"Everything all right?" Duncan called as she ran down the slope to the water.

"Fine." Lying. Curious eyes tracking her flight.

There were three row boats tied up at the Berrybut estate's little wharf; one of them was Greg's. She unwound the painter from its hoop and hopped in. The floating village was three kilometers away, an impossible distance. Why oh why didn't the marine-adepts even have a cybofax between them? Isolation was fine, but not to that extreme.

Eleanor began to row, lifting one of the oars out every ten or so strokes to slap the water three times.

The marine-adepts had a van, an old Bedford pickup they used to take the water-fruit down to Oakham station. They'd help, and keep silent.

She hadn't gone a hundred meters when the dolphins surfaced around the boat, three of them, agitated, tuning in to her distress. Just in time. The surge of adrenaline that'd got her this far was fading rapidly, arms already leaden.

Eleanor chucked the blouse and dived right into the chilly black water, shockingly aware she'd never been swimming at night before.

The dolphins clustered around, snouts butting her gently. She brought her hands together, making a triangle, then pressing her palms together: home fast. Again.

Loud chittering, then one of the sleek gray bodies rose under her. She hung on grimly and they began to slice through the water, curving round Hambleton peninsula toward the floating village.

36

COLD TURKEY WAS A BITCH. It was convulsive shivering, with hot flushes, cold flushes, dryness burning like vitriol in his gullet. Nothing made sense, light and darkness alternating, noise and silence cartwheeling around each other. Nightmares and nirvana trips entwining, indistinguishable.

It was dark when his fever broke. Greg was sitting uncomfortably on a hard floor, propped up against the wrought iron railings of the tower's stair. His hands had been pushed through the railings and cuffed on the other side. He could slide them a meter and a half up or down, his entire range of possible movement. His bladder ached; his mouth tasted as if it'd been rinsed in copper soap. Somewhere along the line his shirt had got lost; that scratchy dinner jacket was tickling his skin.

When he glanced around he saw he was in the tower's first-floor storage room. Biolum light shone up from the basement and down from the lounge. Murmured conversation drifted out of both holes. The smell of cooking was making his stomach growl.

Gabriel was sitting next to him, her arms embracing the railings. She was asleep, her mouth open.

Greg nudged her with his toe. She shook herself awake, blinking at him.

"Christ, Greg. I was worried about you."

"Yeah, Lord knows what was in that infusion Neville Turner gave me, bloody sight more than a relaxant, though. How come we're still alive?"

She grimaced and shifted closer. He leaned forward as much as his tethered arms let him. They got their heads within a foot and talked in whispers.

"They're checking out what you told them," she said. "From what I can gather, Armstrong has some kind of landline stretching over to Downham Market. He told his apparatchiks to launch another hot-rod attack against Philip Evans's NN core. He reckoned that without me there to warn Evans they'd have a good chance of success this time."

"Figures. What did I tell them?"

Her lips depressed. "Sorry, Greg. Just about everything. Armstrong was fascinated by how you found Tentimes. Made you give him Royan's life story. That really shook them, the way the Trinities have been killing off ex-People's Constables. They thought the Trinities were an ordinary bunch of street punks. Irritants beneath contempt."

"Shit. That'll start a bloody war, no messing. The Blackshirts will be screaming for revenge."

"If Armstrong tells them. He probably doesn't want to draw public attention to PSP remnants right now. Besides, don't write Teddy off so quickly. The Blackshirts would take a hell of a pounding if they ever went into Mucklands Wood."

Depression welled up. Greg felt useless, and worse, he'd betrayed his friends. A real twenty-four-carat Judas. "Did I mention Eleanor?"

"Once or twice. But not in connection with anything important. They never showed any interest in her. She'll be all right, Greg."

One comfort. Bloody small, though.

"Kendric was right pissed off with Julia," Gabriel said. "The way she maneuvered him to clear Katerina from the field so she could nab Adrian for herself. Armstrong had a laugh at that, Kendric outthought by a randy teenager with a crush. That girl isn't stupid."

"I told them that?" Greg was disgusted with himself.

"Yes. They questioned you for over two hours. Don't blame yourself, Greg. Interrogations these days are like punching out a data request in a memory core: the answers pop out quick and clean. There's no way anyone can hold out. You should know that."

"Sure. Thanks." The only hope left now was Morgan Walshaw and anything Ellis might've left behind. "Did I tell them that Walshaw and the Event Horizon security programmers were sifting through the files in Ellis's Crays?"

Gabriel screwed her face up. "I think so, yes."

"Did it kick anything loose? I mean, were they worried about anything he might find?"

"Not especially."

"Bugger." He'd banked everything on Ellis wreaking a silent posthumous vengeance. A folly whose magnitude was now painfully obvious. Even if Ellis had been told exactly who he was working for, he wouldn't have known about this tower hideaway in Wisbech. Need-to-know was an elementary precaution, and Armstrong certainly wouldn't have overlooked anything to do with his personal security. Hindsight must surely be the most useless function of the human brain, torturing yourself over the unalterable past.

Gabriel shifted her knees. "One item which really got them stirred up was the Merlin," she said.

"What about it?"

"Armstrong and Kendric weren't the ones who meddled with it."

"Who did?"

A smile ghosted her lips. "That's what they wanted to know. They asked you three times if you were sure there had been a rogue shutdown instruction squirted up to it."

"I bet I was convincing."

"You were. Armstrong ordered his people to confirm it'd happened; apparently Event Horizon haven't announced the breakdown publicly yet. He said they must make an effort to find out who it was. The enemy of my enemy is my friend, all that crap. Kendric seemed to think it could be one of the rival *kombinates*."

"Kendric's probably right," Greg said. "So when does Armstrong expect the answers to his inquiries?"

"I guess tomorrow morning; there's nothing going on right now. If there are any queries, they'll have another session with you. If not, it'll be straight into the mud."

"No doubt with Toby helping me on my way after his own fashion. Where is he now?"

Gabriel inclined her head. "Kendric's mob are camped out in the basement. Lord and Lady Muck themselves are still upstairs. Maybe Armstrong's got a guest suite."

"Yeah. That Kendric, I'd never have figured on him being plugged into Armstrong and the PSP."

"You think someone like him is going to let a little question of ideology stand in his way when he's been offered the kind of profits which gigaconductor licensing is going to rake in?"

"No," Greg said. "But I'm wondering if Armstrong might just have let himself in for more than he's realized."

"In what way?"

"Tell you, this is all down to Kendric trying to snatch the gigaconductor patent from Julia, right? That's apart from his private psychosexual fixation on her, of course. First the memox spoiler, now feeding Armstrong information in return for a partnership when Event Horizon is nationalized. Lucifer's alliance, but which one is Old Nick? My money's on Kendric."

"Meaning?" Gabriel asked.

"Once Kendric's got the patent in his hands as Event Horizon's chairman I wouldn't like to sell Armstrong any life insurance. Even if his apparatchiks do begin running things again—and I think he's underrating the New Conservative Inquisitors there—he can never return to public life. As he's already dead in everyone's mind there will be absolutely no comeback if Kendric has him killed for real. Hell, the bugger of it is, Kendric would even be a hero for doing it."

"You have a devious nasty mind, Gregory. And I love you for it."

"If I'm so smart, then why are we here?"

"I didn't say you were perfect."

"That's the truth, and no messing."

Gabriel was silent for a minute, contemplative, then, "I think I've worked out why our glands aren't functioning."

"The twins."

"Oh, you know."

"Process of elimination. I'm quite good at that when it's something paltry. I imagine their glands produce some kind of psi null-zone; I remember something like that being mentioned a couple of times back at the Brigade—never really paid attention. Notice that one stayed with Armstrong while we were snatched. No wonder the other Mindstar vets could never find him after the Second Restoration."

"So they won't find us now?"

"No. Morgan Walshaw might put it together eventually. But not by tomorrow morning. And even then, there's nothing to lead him to Wisbech."

Gabriel rested her head on the metal railings, smiling forlornly. "Pity. I was getting quite used to having a human brain again. I could've lived without the gland. Surprising really. I suppose I associate it with childhood."

"Armchair psychiatrist," he teased.

"Greg."

It was going to be bad news, no espersense required. "Yeah."

She took a breath. "Kendric asked you if we had identified his contact in Event Horizon."

For a moment he thought the cold-turkey fever had come back to rattle his bruised brain. "Oh Jesus," he groaned. "There was a mole."

"Yes," she said feebly. "We didn't do very good, did we Greg?"

"No. Shit! Who? We checked everybody. Everybody, Goddamn it!"

"Wish I knew. He must've been the one who fingered us for Kendric's snatch squad. Who knew we were going to the finance office?"

He felt like banging his head against the railing. It certainly wouldn't do any damage; there was nothing inside that bloody worked. No messing. "Julia, Walshaw, that doctor who sorted Katerina out, Victor Tyo."

"Victor Tyo? He's a security programmer, isn't he? Convenient. And he knew you were going to visit Ellis. Somebody was bloody quick off the mark there."

"It can't be Victor." He dived down through a clutter of memories, trying to bring back the day he boarded the *Alabama Spirit*, interviewing a baby-faced man: eager at the opportunity, anxious at the responsibility. "Can't be," he muttered.

"Who then? Even you and I aren't infallible, not the whole time. Take a look around if you don't believe me."

"I interviewed Victor one-on-one. Tell you, I might miss peripheral tension, like he's forgotten his girl's birthday card, but that kind of treachery I can spot straightaway."

"Whatever you say."

He shifted his legs, trying to ease the stiff aching muscles. "Could we have missed someone?"

"Unlikely."

"The security headquarters staff," he said, ticking them off in his mind. "Both research teams, the manor staff—Christ, I even asked Julia and Walshaw." He felt an icy spike of fright penetrate his heart. "Oh Jesus," he whispered. "Walshaw."

"Walshaw?" She was openly scornful.

"No," he snapped. "Course not. But Walshaw didn't know Kendric had seduced Julia. Why not?"

"What do you mean? Why should be know?"

"Because Julia has a bodyguard with her twenty-four hours a day, no matter where she goes outside Wilholm. Remember, there was even one in the corridor outside Walshaw's office at the finance center. That hardline woman. God, what was her name? Rachel. She was at Wilholm, too. A bodyguard who reports directly to Walshaw, who should have told Walshaw what happened on the *Mirriam*."

Gabriel bowed her head. "A bodyguard: top-rank security, close to every executive decision ever made, knew Julia was going to the finance center. But a bodyguard isn't part of the security headquarters staff, nor on the manor's staff. Oh, Greg, we are a pair of fuckups, aren't we? She was standing next to Julia the whole time, and we never even bloody saw her."

"Yeah," he said. Then gave a start. "Yeah, the whole time. That's strange."

"What is?"

"I've only ever seen the one bodyguard: Rachel. Every time I've visited Julia, it's been Rachel on duty. Doesn't that strike you as odd? There's got to be more than one."

"Did you always let them know you were coming in advance?"

He nodded silently. The death chill hadn't left his heart. "Whoever he is, he is still with Julia. Tonight. Now. A hardliner taking orders from Kendric. And Armstrong has already ordered an attack on Philip Evans's NN core."

Gabriel stared at him with destitute eyes. "Oh, God."

He pulled at his cuffs, slowly increasing the strength until his wrists were circles of hot pain. Forearm muscles trembled with the strain. Nothing gave, not the cuff locks, not the iron stair rail. Nothing. "Shit." He let go, graze marks livid on his skin. The futility hurt as much as the failure.

"That's it, isn't it?" Gabriel said quietly. "End of the road. Philip Evans wiped, Julia snuffed by her own bodyguard, and you and I into the mud."

He couldn't answer. His own death he could handle, even Gabriel's. But Julia. Her whole life had been devoid of any normality, ruined by money, by grudges and power struggles that had been going on before she was born. When he closed his eyes he could see a young oval face with the most trusting expression he'd ever known. Soft eyes regarded him with a belief that bordered on devotion.

He should have fought the drug, should have sacrificed Gabriel's bones. Anything to give Julia a chance at life.

"We had some good times, didn't we, Greg?" Gabriel said vacantly. "Even in this screwed-up world."

"Yeah. Good times." They hadn't outweighed the bad, though. Not even close.

Gabriel's eyes drooped.

Greg leaned his shoulder on the railings, as near to comfortable as he'd ever get. Muscles were cramping at the back of his neck. He knew he really ought to have been looking for a way out. Jailer's keys dangling on a nail, within reach of an improvised hook on the end of his belt. The iron stair railing that was loose. That carelessly discarded loop of monolattice filament in among the food crates that he could use to saw through the iron with. Keep dreaming, he told himself.

He did. Waking dreams. Mostly of Eleanor. Now, those were good times. They must've been, they hurt.

37

KATS WAS DREAMING. JULIA WATCHED her eyelids fluttering, shoulders restless below the duvet, the occasional sighs, half-formed words.

It would probably be Kendric who filled her thoughts. She doubted the amnesia infusion could reach down into the subconscious to root him out. And that was exactly the kind of arcane universe where Kendric would lurk, his home ground.

To this day his phantom still stole into Julia's sleep-loosened mind, a dark oneiromancer calling her back to the velvet shadows of *Mirriam's* cabin, soft silk sheets, hot hard flesh. That handsome face poised inches above her, smiling as she moaned in erotic delirium. Not even the freshness of Adrian could banish the quondam ecstasy. First loves never die. They just . . . haunt.

She gave Kats a dry smile. Maybe she should go through the detoxification with her, get rid of Kendric that way. Concerned professional doctors prizing him out of her mind. Nothing else seemed to work.

OtherEyes Emergency Access Request.

Open Channel to NN Core. Load OtherEyes Limiter#Five. It was a reflexive acknowledgment; her nerves were stretched taut, ready to jump at figments. She sat bolt upright in the chair, grabbing the Armscor.

Juliet. Christ, virus virus, they've Trojaned a virus into me!

Wilholm's banshee klaxon went off outside.

"Grandpa!" she yelled.

Losing my capacity. Some kind of interface scrambler. Bugger, security sensor access went down. The NN core's internal channels are crashing, Juliet. Childhood gone. It's accelerating. I've failed you, girl. My memory patterns are being disconnected. Management routines gone.

"No, Grandpa," she sobbed. "You couldn't fail me. Not you."

You're all that's left, girl. Datanet's cut. Unlock me in a century. Trust Walshaw, Juliet. Trust him. My girl. Love you. Take care, Kendric will come for you. Integrity stasis, beat it at its own game. Shutting down. Limbo.

And he was gone. But there was something else intruding into her mind, a smooth, grotesque presence oozing in to corrupt her thoughts. Julia jammed her knuckles in her wide, silently screaming mouth. The horror pulled at her memories, prizing them out of their neat processor-assigned stacks. She could see them tumbling away from her: stained-glass rosettes, each one a billion-picture mosaic. Her life encapsulated, ruptured, pouring away into some infinite insatiable sink point.

Data Error.

She felt herself falling to the floor, howling in psychosomatic agony, Armscor dropping from deadened fingers. Vision lost in the blinding sparkle of vivid memories flashing by, people, buildings, school games, countryside, mathematical formulas, lists of words.

Memory Node One Index Error.

Her mind was contracting, conscious thoughts slowing as they passed through the processor nodes. The presence was everywhere, tainting the entire contents of her cerebrum and memory nodes, eviscerating her own personality and replacing it with its own implacable insentient logic.

She began to claw wildly at her head.

Memory Node Two Interface Error.

The virus, it was in her nodes, Trojaned into her through OtherEyes. She should've realized instantly. Her intellect was crumbling, the supporting experience-based reasoning mentality denuded of references, blocking her ability to think. Only a vestigial essence of bloody-minded stubbornness remained, that fundamental aspect of human ego that the virus was unable to subsume.

Memory Node Three Interface Error.

Fight back, Julia pleaded with herself. Stop it spreading.

Processor Node Two Format Loss.

Disengage Memory Node One, she ordered. The command was terribly slow to formulate.

Her subconscious rose ominously to fill the vacuous gulf left in the virus's wake. Wounded pictures of a world peopled by caricatures of those who walked through her natural universe. It was the alternate she lived in fear of, nightmares fully expressed. Black idolatry, so hard and bright her remaining rationality nearly disintegrated under its impact.

Disengage Memory Node Two.

Floating without weight, seeing herself and Kendric coupling like frenzied rampant beasts. Loving it, hating it. Grandpa watching them, frail, poised, ready to die, tears streaming down his cheeks.

Disengage Memory Node Three.

Primate Marcus offering her benediction inside a suffocating bubble of rock. Herself supplicant, putting Event Horizon on the burnished silver collection platter for him. Dropping it, seeing it shatter into splinters of pure data, profit and loss. All important. Grandpa shook his head in dismay and died.

Shut Down Processor Nodes One and Two.

The exorcism. Julia felt the virus withdraw, retreating into the nodes. Then the synaptic interfaces sealed, cutting her free, trapping it in isolation.

There was no physical pain, only loss, all that wondrous knowledge she'd taken for granted had been snatched beyond reach. Her own thoughts and memories, once so ordered, now a tangled seething wreckage.

A sound in her gullet. Struggling to place it. Ah yes. Weeping.

Julia rolled onto her back, drawing breath in shallow gasps. Her dress was cold and damp from sweat.

Vacant watery eyes set in the center of a golden cloud of hair blinked at her. "Julie?"

Julia rummaged round for the name. So difficult, surely human brains weren't this inefficient. "Hi, Kats," she said weakly.

"I want to go for a pee."

Laughter and tears got dreadfully muddled in her throat.

"It's not funny," Katerina said in a wounded tone. "I'm bursting."

"Sure thing, Kats. Sorry." Julia was rather surprised to find her limbs doing what she told them. She managed to clamber to her feet, using the bed for support. The Armscor was lying on the carpet. The sight of it jolted her slowly coalescing thoughts. The klaxon was silent now. She was sure she'd heard it going off. Tried to consult her event timer without thinking, a null request. But it could only have been seconds ago.

Somebody had penetrated Wilholm's defensive cordon. A two-pronged attack, then. Her and Grandpa, and they'd nearly got very lucky.

The door handle rattled. "Julia? Julia, you in there?"

Kendric. Kendric will come for you.

"Morgan?" she called.

"It's Steven; open up, Julia." There was a thump followed by a muffled curse.

"Get Morgan," she told him. *Trust Walshaw, Juliet. Trust him.*

"Julia, open up." A louder thump, a shoulder hitting the door. She could see it quiver in the frame.

"Morgan, get Morgan here."

A third blow. She heard the sound of wood splitting.

"Morgan!" Julia grabbed hold of Kats and yanked her off the bed in one almighty burst of strength. Kats squealed and floundered about in the duvet.

"Stay down," Julia commanded.

She crouched next to Kats, bringing the Armscor up in a smooth arc, thumb flicking off the safety catch. Immensely glad she'd taken the time to learn the weapon.

The door crashed open, frame splintering.

"Morgan!" she screamed.

Pink-white light from the corridor shone into the dimly lit bedroom. A lone figure was silhouetted in the open doorway, Uzi hand laser held ready, stumbling forward. Definitely male.

Kendric.

The maw of the Uzi swung down toward them, a malignant smile behind it.

Julia jerked her forefinger back on the trigger, holding it down. Bullet-size pulses of intense blue lightning streamed out of the Armscor, so close together they were almost a continuous flare. They hit the wall around the door, splashing open with a loud crack. Wallpaper ignited in tight balls of garish orange flame. The bedroom was alive with strobing light, huge distorted shadows leaped up across the walls and ceiling.

"Shit!" yelled the silhouette. He was diving to one side, not quite making it.

One of the Armscor's pulses caught his leg as he was still going down. Beautiful. There was an agonized grunt, swiftly choked off. His whole body convulsed, hit by an invisible fist, buffeting him back into the corridor.

Got you, you bastard!

A bright ruby laser beam stabbed out from somewhere down the corridor, striking him on the side of his neck. His body jerked again, keeling over. The laser fired a second time. Blue-white flame flared out of his chest.

Julia sent another barrage of blazing pulses out through the flame-wreathed door. Her retinas were scarred with long purple after-images.

"Julia, for Christ's sake!"

Julia could barely hear the voice above Kats' soprano wailing, but somewhere in her whirling mind the sound connected; that same

voice was lodged in tenuous memories. She let go of the trigger, peering along the barrel, bewildered.

"Rachel?"

"Yes, for Christ's sake! Now, will you put the fucking gun down.
Please!"

"Where's Morgan!" she cried.

"He's coming, Julia. I promise."

"I . . ." Julia stared at the Armscor as her wrists drooped, letting
it fall onto the bed. And all she could do after that was watch, because anything else was just too much. Her fate was all down to
Rachel now. Could everybody in the world be against her?

Rachel appeared in the doorway, her face furious as she stood over
the prone smoldering body, Uzi hand laser held in a professional
double-handed grip, pointing straight down. She pumped two more
slices of red energy into his head.

Their eyes met. It seemed as though time were stretching out.
Then Rachel gave a little sigh of relief. "It's all over now."

After that, events became kind of remote, out of focus. All the biolums were activated as the bedroom filled with people. Excited
babbling shouts echoed around her. Someone used a fire extin-
guisher on the burning wall, filling the air with chemicals and soot.
Three people held onto poor old Kats, who was having blue-fit hys-
terics. Morgan Walshaw arrived at a dead run, face ashen.

Julia put her arms to the security chief, as she used to do for her
mother years past remembering, too weak to rise from the bed. He
sat beside her as Dr. Taylor discharged an infuser tube into Kats's
neck, his own arms going around her, squeezing tight, rocking her
gently. Cheeks pressed together, his stubble. He held her for a long
time, until everything in her mind quieted down and the world didn't
hurt anymore.

Trust. And it worked, for the very first time.

The shower was revitalizing, washing away the smell of sweat and
fear. Julia felt herself come alive again under the sharp spray, hot
lime-soaped water thrumming against her shoulders and back. It was
a physical punctuation mark, she decided, separating out the past and
future. She turned off the soap and let the suddenly icy water rinse
her down.

The two would be different, she thought determinedly, as she
stepped out onto the bathroom's rich shag carpet.

Rachel was standing right outside the shower cubicle, still holding her Uzi, jaw set. She hadn't been more than two meters away from Julia since she killed Steven.

A real live avenging angel.

After Julia toweled herself down, she chose a plain black cotton vest dress from her wardrobe; it seemed apt somehow, right for a born-again human, one with faith in herself, her pure self, unaugmented.

A big man called Ben was waiting for her in the bedroom when she came out of the bathroom, ruthlessly combing knots from her still-damp hair. She gave him a tight smile and he responded with a brief nod. Polite and respectful, perfect for a personal bodyguard. But then with Morgan choosing them, they all were.

"How are you feeling?" Rachel asked.

"Still a bit dazed. It's fading, though. Remembering things isn't so difficult now." Julia slipped a couple of big butterfly clips into her hair. "Let's go."

Her bedroom door was splintered around the lock. All Wilholm's locks had been glitched by the virus. She nearly got the shakes again when she thought about that. If they hadn't been glitched, Steven would have just walked straight in. Luck or chance. Fate.

Rachel walked beside her, Ben taking up position a couple of paces behind. At least she didn't have to be shown the way to the study, that was too ingrained. But she simply couldn't match a name to the face of one of the manor's anxious-looking domestic staff as they walked past. It was definitely a member of the staff, though. That was something.

"Thank you, Rachel," she said, suddenly shy.

"What for? You did all the work. Even after all you'd been through you held it together just perfect. Most of us would've gone completely to pieces. By rights you ought to sack the lot of us. Some bodyguard I turned out to be."

"No. Steven wasn't your fault. How could we have known?"

"It's my job to be suspicious. All that sudden calling in sick every time your psychic friend Mandel turned up. I should have known."

Julia frowned. That couldn't be right. Greg and Steven were both working for Kendric. Weren't they? She requested a logic matrix. "Oh," she sighed in disappointment. The loss of the nodes was going to take some getting used to.

"I don't want you to worry anymore," Rachel said. "No greasy little hardline tekmerc is going to get near you. Not with us here."

Julia could see Rachel was bottling up a core of hearty excitement, almost as if she relished the prospect of a tekmerc attack. It sent little roots of doubt into Julia's mood because it made her seem like nothing more than an excuse for the two sides to let fly at one another. They enjoyed it.

"Isn't that right, Ben?" Rachel called over her shoulder.

"God's honest truth, Miss Evans."

Julia turned at the unexpectedly mellow voice, giving an embarrassed little grin. "That's just Julia, please."

He nodded warmly.

Rachel tipped her a wink as she pushed the study door open. The lock had disappeared, leaving a rough semicircle of charred wood. Morgan had been in a *hurry*.

She walked in feeling better than she had any right to. Rachel had never spoken to her like that before. Friendly. Who'd have thought it?

There were about ten people in the study, four of them sitting at the paper-littered table. She could name seven: five in security, two manor staff. The buzz of conversation faded out, all heads turning to look at her. She saw concern and relief register in their faces. They cared about her.

Morgan rose from his seat and she went to his side.

"Okay now?" he asked tenderly.

"Yeah. Thank you." She cleared her throat. "I'd like to thank all of you, actually. I'm really very grateful for your support." She sat quickly, not meeting eyes. The chair was the one next to Morgan's; she'd always sat at the head of the table before, or opposite him. No more. She sensed Rachel take up position behind her. "What happened?"

"Ha, you tell me," Morgan said.

"Grandpa said someone had managed to squirt a Trojan into him." Julia glanced up at the rustle of sounds, smiling faintly at the curious glances thrown at her. Her finger lined up on the NN core. Ultrahush belonged in the past, too. These were her people; they had a right to know. "His memories are in there, translocated before he died. Still are from what I can gather. He shut himself down to stop the virus spreading. Once we write an antithesis program we can unlock him." She stopped, pleased with herself: gear terminology had all been node-referenced.

"The NN core's still drawing power," Morgan said. "Small but constant."

"Great. What do we do in the meantime?"

"Stay put, I'm afraid. We don't have a lot of choice."

"What do you mean?"

"Piers will tell you."

Julia knew that name. Piers Ryder, one of the security division staff, technical.

He was sitting on the other side of the table from her, none too happy at being the center of attention, reflected in a slightly strained voice. "One of the assault methods we anticipated was an attempt to knock out the defense gear around the manor with a virus program as a prelude to hardliner physical penetration. Consequently, the gear is all designed to revert to a fully autonomous mode if such a virus is detected in the security datanet. And that's exactly what has happened. For all its power, this virus is easily detectable; in fact, you can't fail to notice it. From what I've managed to ascertain it only attacks databus management programs. The 'ware processors themselves are left unscathed. Basically it's a spoiler virus; it can't do any actual damage."

"Really?"

Piers Ryder shifted at the irony in her drawl, dislodging some of the sheets of hard copy he'd covered in thin wavery handwriting. "I mean, not long-term damage."

"So it was aimed at the security gear rather than Grandpa's NN core?" Julia asked.

"That's what I think. There would be no point in directing it at a bioware core; as you've seen, the programs stored inside won't actually suffer any damage. The hot rod who squirted it in must have known that."

"Which implies that we're going to have visitors sometime soon," Morgan Walshaw said.

"Then why are we still here?" she asked. "The finance division offices are just as secure. And they won't know I'm there if we move fast."

Ryder took an awkward breath. "Miss Evans, Wilholm's defenses will shoot anything larger than a rabbit which moves inside the grounds, apart from the sentinels."

"Including us?" Julia asked incredulously.

"If anyone were to step outside, then yes."

"We're perfectly safe," Morgan Walshaw said. "Just can't get out, that's all."

"All!"

"And no one can get in. The attack has failed, Julia."

"You hope."

"We're patroling the manor on the inside. I've got lookouts with photon amps scanning the gardens. If anyone does get past the sentinels and the defense gear, they'll be sitting ducks for our hand lasers."

"Oh." Julia tried to spot a flaw in his reasoning and couldn't, to her immense relief. "Guess we're going to be all right, then."

"Good girl. We'll just sit it out in here for the rest of the night."

Julia realized that there was something Ryder hadn't said. "How long before your team finishes the antithesis program?" she asked him.

"There's only me here," Piers Ryder replied. "I can't do anything by myself; you need a lightware cruncher to write an antithesis."

"Haven't they even given you an estimate?"

"We can't talk to anyone outside, Julia," Morgan said.

"Why not?"

"The virus has contaminated all the communications consoles. Your grandfather's NN core was plugged into every landline, ours and English Telecom's."

"Well, what about the satellite uplinks?"

"Same problem," said Piers Ryder. "Even the dish servos are glitched."

"So use a cybofax."

Piers Ryder looked crestfallen. He glanced at Morgan Walshaw for support. The security chief responded with an empty wave.

"One of the security systems protecting the manor is an all-spectrum electromagnetic jammer," said Piers Ryder. "We thought a tekmerc penetration squad would have to be equipped with some kind of military-grade communication gear to coordinate their assault. A commercial cybofax couldn't possibly break through the jamming blanket. I'm sorry."

Julia felt a pang of sympathy for Ryder. "Don't apologize; I had no idea I was so well protected."

"The security office in Peterborough will know exactly what's happened," Morgan said smoothly. "They'll be working on it now."

"All they need is the antithesis," Ryder said earnestly. "Once they've cracked it, they'll load it into the company datanet and send it into our communications consoles through the optical cables. It'll flush the virus in seconds."

"Right then." Julia gave them all a bright smile.

Morgan sensed her agitation had ebbed, and relaxed into his chair. He'd already drawn up schedules for the patrols on the back of hardcopy sheets. Even his terminal's dot-matrix printer was glitched.

The security people began marshaling Wilholm's domestic staff into a bedroom near the study. Morgan said he didn't want anyone but the patrols moving through the manor. Julia stayed in the study, where there would always be at least four security hardliners in the room with her.

Tea arrived in an ornate silver pot and she went around silently, pouring for everyone. Morgan smiled fondly as she offered him the biscuits. Ginger nuts, his favorite. Now, she remembered that. Funny what had stuck.

38

THE MARINE-ADEPTS' BEDFORD VAN stank of stale water-fruit and pig shit; its thirty-year-old combustion engine wheezed asthmatically from the methane it was burning, a fuel it'd never been designed to run on. Eleanor neither noticed nor cared about its failings. The van moved, and that was all that mattered right now.

Nicole drove, hunched forward over the steering wheel, staring myopically down the weak beams its headlights threw along the narrow uneven road. There weren't any doors; wind whipped through the cab, frosting Eleanor's legs.

"Should be along here somewhere," the marine-adept woman said.

"Greg said it looks just like a farm road."

"Right." Nicole leaned even farther forward, nose almost touching the cracked windscreen. "What the hell's this?"

As they turned a corner Eleanor saw about fifteen cars and four methane-fueled Transit vans parked along both sides of the road; all of them had flashing lights on top, blue and orange in equal numbers. "Police?" The ever-present fear increased its hold.

"Some of them."

Nicole slowed. A uniformed bobby was standing in the middle of the road, flagging them down. The headlights of the parked vehicles had been left on, casting pale beams of light along the tall hedgerows, turning the leaves gray. There were a lot of people milling about on the road; less than half were wearing police uniforms. The rest had green nylon windcheater jackets with Event Horizon's logo across the back.

The bobby looked into the cab and smiled. "Evening, ladies. Won't keep you a moment. There's a C9 division van backing off the road up ahead."

"I have to get to Wilholm manor," Eleanor said. "I've got an appointment with Julia Evans."

The bobby looked her slowly up and down. Eleanor had thrown a thick lumberjack shirt over her swimsuit, and there were some borrowed trainers on her feet. His eyes tracked her long bare legs. "Oh yes, ma'am?"

Nicole didn't turn her head, gripping the wheel tighter.

"Please, I really do."

"Name?"

"Eleanor Broady."

The bobby pulled out a slim cybofax and typed quickly. Eleanor's heart sank.

"I don't think you do, Miss Broady," he said.

"Well, its really Morgan Walshaw I'm booked to see."

He began to walk away. "Drive straight through when the road's clear."

"Arsehole," Nicole muttered.

"What is going on here?" Eleanor could see the big van ahead, creeping into a gap between two powerful Vauxhall groundcruisers with the Event Horizon logo on their sides; there were armed men inside.

"Lotta heavy shit going down."

They both jumped at the voice. There was a young man standing on the running board next to Nicole, dressed in a black jumpsuit with a rubbery collar that came up to his chin.

Familiar face, unpleasant memory. "Des, isn't it?" Eleanor asked.

Des grinned wolfishly. "Kinda memorable, right? Listen, Father's hung out a hundred meters past the last of the pigs. See ya there." He jumped off.

Nicole grunted and shoved the Bedford into gear, and they growled slowly between the lines of stationary vehicles. Eleanor saw what must've been Wilholm's entrance, a cattle grid that opened into the fields of sugarcane. It was illuminated from below by a harsh orange light, as though something were burning beneath it. Several people were standing watching it, none venturing particularly close.

It was Suzi they saw first, standing in the middle of the road, hands planted firmly on her hips. She was wearing the same kind of jumpsuit as Des, a photon amp across her eyes, and a maroon beret on her head. She waved them onto the grass verge.

Nicole pulled over and switched off the engine and lights. Eleanor looked around to see Suzi marching determinedly down the road toward the ant's-nest commotion outside the manor's entrance.

Teddy swarmed into the cab, sitting beside Eleanor. " 'Lo there, Nicole. Thanks for bringing her."

"No problem. Good seeing you again, Ted."

Eleanor hadn't known they knew each other. The military mates thing again.

"Okay, we've got problems," Teddy said. "Royan can't access

Wilholm to see what the hell's going down; the manor's 'ware has been burned by a virus. Event Horizon and English Telecom have both physically unplugged it from their networks—it was doing too much damage hooked in. Half of Peterborough's telephones have already been glitched by the fallout." His thumb jerked back toward the entrance. "That's why the cavalry's here."

"Someone's attacked the manor's 'ware again?" Eleanor asked.

"Yeah, third time. Persistent buggers."

"Why are the police waiting out here?" she asked. "Why haven't they gone in?"

"Can't," said Teddy. "All the manor's defense gear is running loose. They've got to deactivate it first, which ain't gonna happen before morning; some of that stuff is seriously hazardous. And when they do get in, the likes of you and I aren't gonna be first on the guest list."

"But we've got to find out about Greg. It's been hours!" Eleanor felt Nicole's restraining hand on her shoulder, sympathetic, alleviating some of the anguish.

"I know, gal. Looks like we're gonna have to go in ourselves if we want some answers."

"Hey, Father." Suzi calling with soft urgency.

Teddy and Eleanor climbed out of the cab.

Suzi had a man in tow, Asian-looking with a young face, wearing one of the Event Horizon jackets. "Man here is Victor Tyo," Suzi said. "Met him last night, one of Julia's security people. Captain no less."

"I know you," Eleanor said quickly. "You went up to Zanthus with Greg."

Victor Tyo seemed puzzled. "That's right, although can't say I remember you. I'm sure I would, though."

"Greg's my man," she said simply.

"And we'd like to know what's happened to him," Suzi said.

"Happened?"

"Yeah," said Teddy. "He never got back home after snatching that philter junkie from the di Girolamo yacht. Eleanor here is loaded up with grief about that. You know anything about it?"

Victor glanced around at the circle of faces. "I don't understand. Greg left the finance division offices right ahead of Miss Evans's convoy."

"When?"

"About half past four this morning."

"You saw him leave?"

"Yes. He had Miss Thompson with him in the Duo. He said he'd be back later to help analyze some holomemories we'd acquired."

"The Crays from Ellis?" Teddy asked.

"How did you know?"

"Always cover yourself, Victor. Someone you trust. And don't sweat yourself, man; I ain't interested in no corporate politics. So Greg never showed today at all, right?"

"Not at the finance offices, no. But the programming team assigned to crack the Crays squirted all the data they pulled out up here to the manor. I thought he must be here."

"Don't get it," said Suzi. "Nothing could happen to Greg, not with that Lady Gee in tow. She's in-fucking-credible, like nothing happens without her seeing it first. Nothing!"

"Then why did this virus get into the manor's gear?" Eleanor said. They all looked at her, faces gusted by random beams of blue and orange light from the vehicles in the distance. "Gabriel predicted the second hot-rod attack against Wilholm, why not the third?"

"Shit," from Suzi.

"Okay, so strike Gabriel," said Teddy. "She and Greg have been zapped—" He flinched, glanced at Eleanor, started again. "Least, we don't know what's happened to 'em; same time Wilholm gets burned again. You like maybe see a connection there, Victor?"

The security captain nodded earnestly. "I'll make absolutely sure that you get to the manor right after we debug the defense gear."

Teddy snorted. Eleanor was struck by just how menacing he'd become, nothing like the directionless thuggishness of Des. He focused his energy and anger with deadly precision. And she was very glad she wasn't on the receiving end of it. Victor Tyo was wilting under his stare, unable to look away.

"You're not reading me right, man," Teddy said softly. "The answers are in that fancy mansion your lady boss lives in, and we want them. Tonight. Now."

Victor spread his arms helplessly. "We're calling in all our security programmers, but it's the middle of the night. They'll produce an antithesis, but it's going to take time. There is nothing I can do that'll get us in there any sooner."

"Wrong, man. We're going in now, and you're coming with us."

"What?"

"Think about it. Security hardliners inside see us coming at them, it's gonna be target-practice time. We need you out in front to show them we ain't hostile."

"You're insane," Victor Tyo said. "Do you have any idea what kind of hardware is guarding that manor?"

Teddy grinned and beckoned.

There were five electric Honda bikes behind the hedgerow. Des was waiting with them, along with Roddy and another Trinity called Jules. All of them wearing the same black jumpsuit. Eleanor began to think it must be more than just a uniform.

Teddy flipped open a cybofax, showing it to Victor Tyo. "See this? List of Wilholm's defense gear. We know what they're loaded with, where it is, line of fire. Got our approach figured out. We can handle the automatics; all we need now is some way of convincing the security hardliners not to shoot after we've broken through. That's you, man."

Victor Tyo took the cybofax, holding it gently as he read down the screen, dismay growing on his face. "Where in Christ's name did you get this from? Every byte here is ultrahush."

"Snatched right out of your security division cores," Teddy said. "Now you believe we're serious?"

Royan, Eleanor knew. The thought that he was behind them, an intangible general, bolstered her in a way she couldn't define. She actually began to believe there might be hope after all.

The Hondas took them across country, heading for the back of the Wilholm estate in a long, flat curve to avoid the police patrols checking the perimeter. Eleanor rode pillion behind Suzi, clinging tenaciously to the wiry Trinities girl, sugarcane beating at her legs and arms. She could see the front wheel fork's chrome suspension springs hammering up and down as the bike bounced over the compacted furrows of sandy red soil. They were traveling in single file, with Teddy leading; Nicole was his passenger.

There'd never been any question over the marine-adept woman joining the break-in team, which irked Eleanor because Teddy hadn't wanted to take her along.

"No offense, gal," he'd said calmly. "But you ain't used to this kind of heat."

"So how many times have you broken into a place like this?" she'd retorted.

"That ain't the point. My troops, they got the discipline, know weapons."

"I used shotguns and rifles at my kibbutz. And I'll just follow you after you go in."

"Shit, okay, gal, but Greg'll have my arse if he ever finds out. Guess there's more to you than—well, you check out neat."

More than tits 'n" ass, Eleanor had filled in silently. But Teddy had stopped objecting after that. Some part of her wished he hadn't.

It was Suzi who'd given Eleanor one of the jumpsuits to put on. "It's an energy dissipater," she'd explained intently. "It can hold out against a hand laser for a good twelve seconds. But with those Bofors masers they've got up at the manor, you've got maybe three, four seconds to skip out of the beam before burn-through."

Along with Victor and Nicole, Eleanor had stripped off before pulling the heavy garment on, its slippery, spongy lining clinging to her skin. When it had adjusted to her figure there was virtually no restriction of movement. A tight cap held her hair down, and a hood with an integral photon amp came over her face, sealing to the collar.

Once it was on she became appreciably colder, the thermal shunt fibers siphoning out her body heat.

"It's no use against bullets," Suzy went on. "Then, you can't have everything. 'Sides, Wilholm only has beam weapons. So Son says. Better be fucking right."

The world as seen through the photon amp was a place of ghostly shadows, shaded blue and gray. Eleanor was gradually growing used to it; depth perception was a little misleading, but as long as she remembered that, there'd be no trouble. Suzi had shown her how to up the magnification, bleed in infrared. There was a throat-mike activated graphic overlay, the jumpsuit's internal gear already loaded with the route Royan had devised into Wilholm. Eleanor ran through an articulation acceptance check and practiced calling up the various data projections.

The Hondas were riding down a slight incline. Teddy's bike was slowing up ahead. Eleanor searched her mind, but there was no fear, only determination. A sense of inevitability.

Teddy pulled up beside a broad fast-flowing stream at the bottom of the slope; sugarcane had given way to thick reedy grass. Suzi braked beside him.

They all gathered together at the water's edge. "We'll use a diamond formation," Teddy said in a low steady voice. "Eleanor and Victor at the center; you two will carry the Rockwell cannon and its power units. It's heavy, but we're gonna need its firepower to take out the manor's Bofors masers when we get within range. The rest of you are gonna provide us a three-sixty cover. Now, you look out for those sentinel panthers, okay? You ain't never been up against 'em before, but I have. They're not simple modifications like police assault dogs—they're gene-tailored. Hazards don't come any bigger. They don't behave like animals; they're smart and sneaky with it.

Your AKs can handle 'em, but it's gonna take more than one hit. Okay, now remember, we stick to the water. The estate's got lotsa ground traps. They're listed, but in these conditions you're gonna have trouble matching the graphics to the landscape. The streambed's safe. Jules, you stay out here; see to the receiver."

"Hey, screw that, Father."

"It's important, boy. Might all wind up depending on that receiver before tonight's out. Gotta be done properly."

Jules looked away across the fields, anger showing in the set of his shoulders. Eleanor wondered if he was blaming her.

"Radio communications to the manor are out," Victor said. "There's a jammer blocking all frequencies."

"Yeah, I know, a Grumman ECM788," Teddy said. "We got us a tactical message laser. Nothing gonna interfere with that. Jules'll take the receiver up to the top of the valley; Son says we'll have direct line of sight from there to the manor."

"Christ," Victor muttered in an undertone. "Walshaw's going to kill somebody when this is over."

"Anything else?" Teddy asked. "Okay. We'll ask the Lord for his blessing."

The Trinities bowed their heads. Eleanor saw Victor look around in surprise. She lowered her own head.

"Lord, we ask for your guidance and protection in our task ahead. We're going to see if we can help our lost brother and sister, and we believe our cause is right and just. If in your wisdom you could grant us success, we will remain thankful for such mercy for the remainder of our mortal life. Amen."

"Amen," the Trinities whispered in chorus.

"Amen," Eleanor added.

"Okay. Tool up. Move out."

The Rockwell was a wound monolattice-filament tube one and a half meters long and twenty centimeters wide. It had a broad leather strap so Eleanor could carry it across her back. She lifted it up and realized just how dependent she was going to be on the Trinities for protection from the sentinels. She was confident she could carry it to the manor, but the weight was going to slow her down.

After she'd settled the cannon into place, Suzi clipped a Braun laser pistol onto her belt. "Twenty-five shots or a five-second continuous burn," Suzi said. "Don't fret yourself none about getting it wet; it's waterproof." Five power magazines were added. Eleanor felt like protesting about the extra weight but held her tongue. Suzi's normally infallible barbed humor had evaporated.

The seven of them splashed into the middle of the stream. Teddy and Suzi paired at the front; Roddy took up station on Eleanor's right-hand side. On her left was Victor, who was carrying a couple of high-density power units for the Rockwell along with the message laser. Nicole was on his left, and Des brought up the rear.

The graphics display had reproduced a perfect profile of the stream's winding course for her, a memory loaded straight from the security core Royan had burned. It'd been built by the landscape team who had fashioned the manor's grounds; they had made the actual bed from fine, hard-packed sand, then layered it with long strips of worn limestone pebbles. The width was a nearly constant four meters where she stepped in, with the water coming halfway up her shins. After a minute she managed to find the best rhythm for walking, not quite lifting her sole out of the water. At least they were going in the direction of the flow. Heat was draining out of her feet. Her toes were already numb.

Teddy held his hand up. "Okay, people. Hoods on."

Eleanor reached back and pulled it over her head. A circle of skin around her eye sockets tingled briefly. The photon amp fed its monochrome image into her retinas, suit graphics confirming the neck seal's integrity. She breathed air through the filters, dry and metallic.

She took it as an offhand compliment that nobody checked to see if she'd fixed her hood properly.

The stream ran through a thick braided cassia hedge ten meters ahead, the dividing line between the sugarcane fields and a broad tract of undulating meadowland. Eleanor saw a line of posts spaced seven or eight meters apart had risen up in front of the hedge, two meters high and featureless except for a small red light flashing away on top. The earth around them had been torn as they'd pushed their way up out of their recesses.

Her photon amp picked out a band of forest about eight hundred meters past the hedge. She didn't like to think about lugging the Rockwell all that way. And how far was the manor beyond the forest?

THREE HUNDRED METERS, the graphics told her. Oh well.

"Boundary," Teddy said. His voice was muffled by his hood filters. "Now is when it starts to hit the fan. Okay, Suzi."

Both of them brought up their AK carbines. There was a bass stutter and the two posts on either side of the stream disintegrated. They switched their aim to the next pair.

In the end they took out eight before Teddy was satisfied. His arm signaled the advance.

Eleanor meshed the infrared into her image, alert for any sign of the sentinels. The function fuzzed the outlines a little, but she saw a couple of pink spots pelting away from the stream. Stoats, invisible before.

The meadowland here offered little or no cover. The grass was knee-high, laced with weeds and keck. Nothing had grazed on it for months.

Two hundred meters past the boundary markers and Teddy stopped them again. He plucked one of the smallest spherical grenades dangling from his waist and twisted the timer. "Down."

Eleanor squatted, her backside below the surface of the water. Growing cold. Teddy lobbed the grenade out across the meadowland. Crouching down. Five seconds later there was a barely audible thud.

Another line of posts rose out of the ground ahead of them. Eleanor could hear grass and soil ripping. This time there were no red lights on top.

Suzi and Teddy took aim with their AKs.

PRESSURE-SENSITIVE PICKET, said the graphics when she asked. There were another two picket lines between them and the forest. The memory core didn't have any information about what they did if you walked between them. Presumably, if you were talented enough to be on this kind of mission, you ought to know.

They yomped on.

The stream's banks were growing perceptibly steeper. Eleanor thought the water was getting deeper, too. Her view across the meadowland was shrinking. Thick patches of watercress choked both sides of the stream. Roddy and Nicole had to walk through it, kicking away a tangled wrap of tendrils from their legs every few paces.

Eleanor was glad of the brief rest when they came to the next picket line.

Victor pressed his head up to hers. "You okay?"

The AKs demolished another set of pillars.

"Fine."

There was a quick squeeze on her upper arm.

Suzi and Teddy reloaded their carbines, jamming in fresh magazines with hard snaps.

The stream fell on harder rock. It was narrower now, deeper. The water came up to Eleanor's knees. Teddy slowed the pace, edging cautiously around the sharper turns.

"How about a couple of us walk along the side?" Suzi said. The banks had risen until they were level with Eleanor's head. She couldn't see much of the meadowland now. What was visible seemed to be small deep hollows and ground-hugging bushes. There could've been anything hidden out there. Her breathing was coming faster.

"No," Teddy said.

Suzi didn't argue. Discipline. Eleanor thought it would've made a lot of sense to have someone who could look out over the meadowland.

They rounded a bend and saw the last line of picket pillars had already emerged from the earth. Five AK carbines came up in reflex. There was a moment's pause.

The sentinel came at them through the air like a guided missile. Eleanor saw it as a pink streak arcing overhead, forelegs at full stretch, an angel of death reaching for Des. All five AKs opened up, filling the air with a guttural roar. Des was falling backward, still firing. The sentinel's heavy streamlined body juddered in midflight, its edges distorting as the slugs chewed it apart. Momentum kept it going. Des hit the water. Eleanor's image was suddenly degraded by a spray of blood painting her hood's photon-amp receptors. The sentinel landed almost on top of Des, already dead.

"Keep watching!" Teddy bellowed as they all began to move toward the carcass.

Des still hadn't surfaced. Eleanor felt vomit about to rise from her belly. Forced herself to hold it down. She'd drown if she puked with the hood on.

"Eleanor, Victor, see to him." Teddy's words became lost in a strident whistle; already piercing, it was rapidly broaching her pain threshold. Eleanor jammed her hands over her ears and floundered toward the dark soggy hump that was the sentinel.

The four pillars nearest the stream had begun to glow violet. Eleanor's photon amp hurriedly faded them down. She felt her bones beginning to shake from the noise.

Victor was at her side, shoving at the bulky sentinel. She helped him, pushing its hindquarters. It began to move with desperate slowness. The sound from the pillars had turned to fire, drilling into her ears. Concentration was becoming impossible. The dead cat rolled over, and Des thrashed to the surface. Victor pulled at his hood, breaking the neck seal. Des was choking, squirting water, and gasping for air.

The hideous sound level had begun to reduce. Eleanor risked a glance around. Teddy and Suzi were blasting away at the brilliant pillars. Nicole and Roddy were poised in a half crouch, AKs held ready, scanning the top of the banks.

Des's desperate coughing subsided. The last violet pillar crumpled. Eleanor found she was trembling violently.

Silence closed about them.

Victor shook Eleanor's arm.

"What?" She couldn't even hear her own voice.

He was jabbing a finger at Des's arm. She saw the jumpsuit fabric was torn above the elbow, slashed by the sentinel's claws. Blood was streaming out of the wound.

The sight snapped Eleanor out of her daze. She made Victor clamp his hand around the wound, reducing the flow of blood. Nicole was carrying the field first-aid kit. She let Eleanor take it from her without ever breaking her vigilance.

Teddy fished the Rockwell and its power units from the water while Eleanor pulled an elasticated sheath up around Des's wound. It ballooned out as she touched the inflation stud, analgesic foam setting in seconds. She helped Des to his feet. Even with the photon amp's peculiar vague shading she could tell his face was chalk white.

Teddy handed an AK to Victor and hung one of the power units on Des. He gave the second power unit to Eleanor after she'd lifted the Rockwell again, taking the message laser himself.

"Come on. Outta here."

Eleanor knew Teddy must've shouted it, but she barely heard the sound over the occlusive ringing in her ears. The weight of the weaponry was tormenting her spine. Her mind chucked out stupid irrelevances like cold feet and keeping watch across the meadowland to concentrate on the important: thrusting one foot at a time through the churning water. Her flesh was going through the routine, disjointed from her mind. Solitude's anguish unraveling around her. Alone with people she didn't know, walking to a place she didn't want to go to.

They were fifty meters from the forest when Nicole opened fire, her AK a subliminal rumble. The sentinel was hunkered down behind a bush, a clenched shadow, coiled up waiting to leap. It managed a short jump before the slugs bit into its skull. Crashing down into the watercress.

Teddy never even broke stride.

Eleanor trudged past the sentinel, dimly acknowledging how stately its huge head was, humiliated by cracked bone and ripped flesh. There was no honor in death, and it wasn't even a true enemy.

We malign life, she thought, suborning its grace and majesty to our own purpose, mocking it. Even the reservoir dolphins were a sin, so far from their true home, tame, unable to return. She knew water would never be a refuge for her again, not after tonight.

The stream's banks dipped down as they reached the forest, but the water remained knee-high. Tall acacias and virginciana trees threw boughs right across the stream; black heart leaves interlaced above Eleanor, blocking even the ashen phosphorescence of moonlit clouds. The trunks were knotted columns coiled by ivy and ipomoea vines; grape-cluster flower cascades dangled down, brushing against her head. A thick carpet of fleshy flowers covered the forest floor, tiny star shapes closed against the night, light gray in her image feed. She imagined the air would be thick with their scent if she removed her hood.

The forest had to be a human concoction, a designer ideal of fey woodland wilderness. Eleanor was staggered by how much it must've cost.

"Okay," said Teddy. And she could hear him better this time. "So far, so good. Now we've got a couple of lasers overlooking the stream before we reach the lake. Suzi, you trailblaze, clean 'em out. The rest of you keep watching for sentinels. This here is prime ambush country. When you leave the tree cover remember to keep yourselves below the water before you reach the lake; means crawling, but make fucking sure you don't let more than your head show. Those Bofors masers will zap anything over fifty centimeters in diameter. If you do get hit, dive fast, wind up cannibal lunch otherwise."

"What about the people inside Wilholm?" Victor asked. "They've got to know we're here after the racket the pickets kicked up."

Teddy patted the message laser. "We put this on wide-beam and use Morse code to rap with 'em."

"Morse code!"

"Sure, man. Walshaw's ex-military, isn't he?"

"Yes," Victor agreed.

"Then he'll know Morse. Tell him to take a look at you. Means your hood's gotta come off, though. You be careful."

"Careful. Christ."

"Okay, let's move," Teddy barked.

Suzi took the lead, walking down the living wooden tunnel a couple of meters in front of Teddy.

The forest was alive with creatures, picked out by the infrared as quick-moving pink blotches snaking around the trees. Squirrels, Eleanor guessed. More pink spots slipped across the ground, not even disturbing the flowers. It was faintly macabre, seeing the unseen. Distracting.

The stream began to change; big quarried rocks had been used to line the banks, similar to marble. Water was frothing around their rough-hewn edges. It was getting slippery underfoot. Eleanor's soles were sliding over loose oval stones. The water was climbing up over her knees.

Suzi stopped in midstride, her jumpsuit glaring an all-over claret, rising swiftly toward vermilion. Eleanor marveled at the girl's cool as the AK carbine swung around slowly, picking out the laser hidden in the tree. She could never have done that, more likely scream and run around in circles. Finally understanding what Teddy meant by discipline: far more than following orders. Curlicues of steam were rising from the stream around Suzi's legs, the water bubbling. The girl had found the laser, taking sight, pulling the carbine's trigger.

A sentinel landed on Roddy's back. Jaw clamped on his neck, hind legs raking his lower back with daggerlike claws.

Eleanor screamed.

Roddy pitched forward, ridden down by the sentinel. Foaming water fountained up as the two writhed about beside her.

"Behind you!" someone yelled.

Victor began firing his carbine back up the stream.

Teddy was pointing his at Roddy and the sentinel, unable to shoot. The sentinel was tossing the man about as though he were a doll.

Eleanor yanked the Braun from her belt, leaning forward. Saturated black fur twisted into view below her outstretched hand. She jabbed the laser down until it hit something solid and tugged the trigger. There was a blur of infrared energy, flash of singeing fur.

Hot pain smashed into her belly, ripping. Oblivion was smothering in soft black velvet—

". . . coming outta it."

"Come on, gal, up you get."

Swirling pearl gray mists resolved into two figures wearing energy dissipater jumpsuits. Hard lumpy stone pressed into Eleanor's back. Water was gurgling around her feet.

"The sentinel!" she cried.

"Dead," Teddy answered.

There was absolutely no sensation coming from her abdomen, no cold, warmth, pain. Nothing. That frightened her more than having a nagging pain. She glanced down: a cauliflower oval of analgesic foam was clinging to the front of her jumpsuit. "Roddy?"

"Giving Saint Peter a hard time. Come on, gal. Up."

Strong hands gripped under her shoulders, lifting. She stood, fighting the dizziness that blanked out her vision for a moment.

"Can you carry anything?"

"I—yes, I'll try." Eleanor was curiously unmoved by Roddy's death. His body had been dragged out of the stream, lying on the rocky bank, limbs bent oddly, head kinked at an impossible angle. They must've infused her with something, and she didn't particularly mind; it was nice having thoughts this peaceful.

Teddy handed her the Rockwell again, Nicole taking the second power unit. Suzi took up position on her flank. When Eleanor looked around she saw Victor limping behind her, a ring of analgesic foam around his left thigh.

One dead, three walking wounded. If it wasn't for the drug, she knew she'd have given up right there and then.

Teddy led them on.

The stream continued its inexorable advance up Eleanor's legs. Solid footing was hard to find, the fast current pushing insistently at the back of her knees. A raggedy curtain of pigtail ivy ribbons hung from the gnarled branches above her, long enough to trail in the water, an irritant she was constantly having to sweep aside. There were big boulders in the stream now, creating a turbulent white-water surface. The stone-lined banks were closing in, becoming steeper. She and Des were pressing together, Suzi occasionally bumping into her. The stream was being channeled for some reason.

Teddy made them stop, then walked on alone, struggling to keep his balance. The second laser found him, inflaming his jumpsuit to a lambent crimson. His AK sent a burst of slugs back along the beam. A pyrotechnic shower of sparks erupted from a big acacia tree.

"Okay, people, last stage. Easy does it." Teddy waited for the others to reach him, and they began to move off together.

Eleanor heard a low rumbling coming from somewhere ahead. Couldn't quite place the sound; her ears still had a residual ringing from the pickets. The water reached her waist.

"Hey—," Victor began.

Teddy snarled a curse and vanished from view. Eleanor took a step forward and found the streambed falling away. Instinct made her tighten her grip on the Rockwell. She knew she'd never be able to fight the water; she had to let it take her. Her feet were swept from under her, dunking her below the water. She breathed out, expelling air from the filter nozzle until she broke surface. Bobbing around like a piece of driftwood. The stone banks were like cliffs whizzing by. Ivy fronds slapped at her. She shifted the Rockwell around, hugging it to her numb chest. The rumbling was growing steadily louder. Memory placed it: waterfall.

Eleanor twisted desperately, getting her feet out in front, locking her legs straight. Slaloming around the last bend, she saw Wilholm manor dead ahead. The building was floodlit, its roof blanked out, hidden in shadow. Biolum lights glared from the windows of the top two stories; the ground floor was a featureless slate-gray band. There was a vast expanse of flat exposed lawn surrounding it. Killing ground, she thought. Then she went over the lip.

The waterfall wasn't high, three meters. She seemed to hang in the air, floating down.

MASER ATTACK, shouted scarlet graphics. The photon-amp image dimmed. Thick fog exploded around her.

Eleanor hit the lake hard, her backside taking the impact. The Rockwell knocked the breath out of her. *Don't drop it*, her only thought.

The weight of the weapon and the jumpsuit held her down. Rising with terrible slowness, her lungs bursting. Water had defeated the photon amp, all she could see was a uniform powder blue mist.

Eleanor surfaced, keeping the water level above her shoulders, bracing herself for the graphic warning again. It remained off. Treading water. Somehow she'd turned around to face the waterfall. A dark figure shot over the lip, arms flapping at the air. The curving torrent of water behind it boiled furiously again as the manor's Bofors masers fired.

"Check in," a voice called out.

"Teddy? Teddy, I'm here. It's Eleanor."

"Christ, gal. Okay, you still got the Rockwell?"

Eleanor patted her one free hand, cumbersome in the thick garment, turning until she spotted him, a small mound protruding from the lake's gently rippling surface. "I've got it."

"Thank you, sweet Jesus."

"Father. Suzi here."

"Victor held the power unit."

"Terrific."

Eleanor saw Teddy bring the message laser out of the water.

"Shit." Des's voice, high and panicky. "Being lasered."

There was a splash somewhere off to Eleanor's left.

"Nicole, 'nother unit."

The facade of the manor seemed to flicker, its brightness oscillating. Tiny points of bright-red light twinkled from the second-story windows.

LASER ATTACK. The photon-amp image went completely white.

Eleanor drew a deep breath and sank below the surface. The photon-amp image reverted to blue with slashes of black. This time she could make slightly more sense of it: three intense dots of brighter blue above her, where the lasers from the manor were striking the surface, bubbles fizzing up around her. She kicked with her feet, moving away.

"—look you bastards," Teddy was shouting as Eleanor came up. "Christ." He ducked below the lake.

White. LASER ATTACK.

The blueness was speckled with red and green, throbbing. Her lungs burned. Can't do this many more times.

Up again.

Droplets of water came in with the air. Eleanor coughed, swallowing some. It tasted foul.

"They've stopped," Suzi called out.

"Now what?" Des asked.

"Wait," said Teddy. "Eleanor, you and Victor come over to me, slow and easy. I wanna get that Rockwell sorted."

Eleanor rolled over, letting herself float on her back with the water lapping around her chin. Waving her feet, creeping toward Teddy. Will they think grouping together is hostile?

Eleanor was about five meters short of Teddy when a voice boomed out from the manor. "Who the hell are you people?" It sounded angry.

Teddy began to flash the laser again. Eleanor stopped moving. Whatever Morse code was, it seemed incredibly ponderous.

"You want to come in and talk about Mandel? Who've you got as a guarantee?"

"Do your thing, Victor," Teddy grunted.

"Right." He submerged.

Eleanor felt insufferably weary. Just wanted it all to be over. The infusion must be wearing off, she thought.

Victor came up without his hood, hair plastered across his forehead.

"Smile, man."

"Victor," the voice blared. "Hell, it is you. Are these people genuine? We've got them covered if they try and force you. Nod for yes. Shake for no."

"Jesus wept," said Teddy. "Paranoid or what."

"All right," said the voice. "And just how do you reckon on getting across the lawn? We can't shut off the masers, and the ground floor's sealed tight."

The message laser flashed out a long complicated story.

"No way!" the voice called.

"Screw you, arsehole," Suzi shouted.

"Throttle down, gal," said Teddy, and even he sounded tired. The message laser flashed once more.

"All right," said the voice. "Listen good. Only Victor may use the cannon. If one of those plasma shots lands anywhere but on a maser, you are dead."

"And up yours, too," said Teddy. "Okay, let's get the Rockwell together."

Eleanor started kicking again, her legs like lead. Teddy and Victor were moving forward, toward the shore.

"Touching ground," Teddy said. He was five meters short of the lawn.

Eleanor came up beside him, toes prodding the viscous lake bed. "Let's have it, gal."

Victor drifted up on the other side. He and Teddy started muttering at each other as they mated the Rockwell's cable to the power unit by touch alone.

With the Rockwell gone, Eleanor thought she'd be able to fly. She weighed nothing at all.

Victor stuck the Rockwell's targeting imager over his right eye, its cable coiling down below the water.

"Ready," he said.

Eleanor saw that Des, Suzi, and Nicole had swum up level with her. Unidentifiable, blind tumors of crepe fabric. Behind them, on the shore where the trees bordered the lawn, were two swift-moving red blobs. No, her mind cried. Enough, we've had enough. "Sentinels," she called out, voice rasping in her throat. "Sentinels, they're coming."

Victor fired the first plasma bolt. A solar-bright fireball tearing through the night, overloading Eleanor's photon amp. A nearly ultrasonic whine ending in a stentorian thunderclap. One of the manor's chimney stacks exploded.

The sentinels were sprinting for the lake shore. Eleanor watched the two people closest to them churn about, trying to reach their weapons. Steam billowed up around one of them as the frantic motion lifted their shoulders out of the water. Eleanor started to swim breaststroke. Suzi had said the Braun was waterproof, although she had no idea if it would work in the water.

Both sentinels leaped together.

MASER ATTACK. Eleanor duck-dived fast.

Surfacing, just in time to hear the second concussion as more of the manor's masonry was vaporized. Three more to go. A locust swarm of slate fragments tumbled through the air high above Wilholm.

The sentinels were in the water, two whirlpools of surf. Des was screaming. Eleanor headed for the nearest conflagration. Couldn't even remember if she'd recharged the Braun.

MASER ATTACK. Plunging.

A sentinel shrieked in mortal terror, a keening that sliced right through Eleanor. The sound electrified, freezing her limbs. What in God's name could a sentinel possibly fear? She saw it disappear below the surface of the lake, sucked down backward in a maelstrom of bubbles. Something was floating inertly where it'd vanished, undulating with the swell.

The third plasma bolt speared a small ornate rotunda, its detonation shockwave flinging smoking chunks of stone halfway across the lawn.

Eleanor was looking straight at a sentinel three meters away. Its jaws were open, showing a double layer of shark teeth, huge eyes staring at her. Powerful bands of muscle rippled along its back as it paddled toward her.

Cats can't swim!

Her feet sank into muck up to her ankles and she stood. MASER ATTACK. Counting off the seconds. One. A storm cloud of steam raged around her. Two. THERMAL INPUT APPROACHING MAXIMUM SHUT CAPACITY. The sentinel was a meter and a half from her when its fur ignited. It yowled in pain, skin crisping, cracking, thick fluid oozing out. Three. Eleanor could feel her skin beginning to blister as a wave of searing heat poured through the jumpsuit insulation. The sentinel gave a convulsive shudder; its back was flayed down to its rib cage, skull exposed, eyes roasted. Blood gushed out of its mouth, splattering on her suit. Four. THERMAL SATURATION ALERT. Dead.

Eleanor collapsed back into the lake, her own body on fire. Somewhere inside her belly she could feel dampness. The sentinel's corpse sank as she floated up.

A plasma bolt flashed overhead. Part of a very distant universe.

Something shot up out of the water nearby. "Got the bastard!" Nicole.

The marine-adept woman swam clumsily over to the floating shape. "Eleanor, hey, Eleanor, give me a hand with Suzi. Think she's still alive."

"Go on, gal," Teddy called. "Masers are out."

Eleanor moved sluggishly. Between them they dragged Suzi onto the lawn. The girl's jumpsuit was in tatters, blood soaking the grass. Eleanor kneeled beside her and tugged her hood off. Water flooded out. Suzi's tongue protruded.

Victor appeared and bent to breathe air into her. Eleanor was thankful; she certainly didn't have the strength left to resuscitate her.

"Lost the aid kit," Nicole said dully. Her forearms were lacerated, tatters of skin hanging loosely.

"They'll have something for her in the manor," said Teddy.

Suzi spluttered weakly, liquids gurgling inside her.

There was no sign of Des.

"Okay, let's move," Teddy urged. "Remember the ground traps."

Eleanor slowly pulled her own hood off, sobbing softly. Proper colors deluged her eyes. The foam across her abdomen was flaking off, blood mingling with water in her lap.

"Come on, gal," Teddy said. "You made it now. Jesus must really love you." He handed her his AK. "Safety's off. Cover us if any more sentinels show."

Rabbits, she'd shot rabbits back at the kibbutz.

Victor hoisted Suzi onto Teddy's back, and the big man set off toward the manor, message laser banging against his side. They followed in single file as he traced a path across the lawn, Wilholm's floodlights casting long spidery shadows as they wove around the traps.

Flat metal slabs had slid out of the manor's stonework to seal the ground floor's doors and windows. Teddy set Suzi down against the wall and unslung a small pack.

Eleanor and Victor watched the grounds, AKs held ready, as Teddy slapped a thermal-slice tape on the slab of metal covering a window. It was a thick flexible tube that hissed as it adhered to the slab.

"Okay, don't look."

Startlingly bright blue-white light glared out, buzzing and sizzling. Eleanor saw sparks skipping along the paving slabs around her feet. She could feel its warmth on the back of her neck.

"Here it comes." The light dimmed, and there was a loud resonant clang, smashing glass. A fan of milder biolum light spilled out across the grass.

Eleanor kept looking over the lawn, her nerves raw-edged. She expected to see a mass charge of sentinels coming at her. They'll never let us get in. Not those devils.

There was grunting and shuffling from behind her. "Don't touch the edge," she heard Teddy warning. He was shoving Suzi through the hole. "Got her? Okay, for Christ's sake go easy. You next, Nicole."

Eleanor began to back toward the window, shivering uncontrollably.

"You make it with that leg, Victor? Okay, I'll boost you." Silence. Eleanor knew she was alone. Sweeping the AK in wild arcs. Nothing moved on the lawn.

"Move it, Eleanor."

The jagged hole was roughly square, one and a half meters high, its lower rim a meter off the ground. She put a leg through.

"All right, lady, hands where we can see them, and moving real slow."

The room inside was huge, its floor an intricate mosaic of olive green and cream tiles; there were chandeliers hanging on gold chains, pastel frescoes of waterfowl on the walls, Regency furniture, a grand piano. Smoke layered the air; two people were using fire extinguishers on the window frame; glass crunched under her foot. A small army was pointing Uzi hand lasers at her.

Standing in the middle of the room was a dignified gray-haired man whose face was stiff with tension and suspicion. Had to be Walshaw.

Suzi was lying on the floor, chest a mass of gore, blood pooling on the shiny tiles. There was a woman kneeling beside her, working frantically. Medical gear modules were scattered around, red and amber LEDs flashing, their needle sensors jabbing through the remnants of the jumpsuit. The woman slapped a bioware mask over Suzi's face, a rubbery sac concertinaed out of it and began palpitating.

Nicole was slumped motionless against a wall. Two of the security people were covering her with Uzis while a third wrapped fluffy aquamarine towels around her shredded arms, blood staining them brown.

Victor was standing, hands on head, eyes red with pain. A grim-faced woman was frisking him with expert thoroughness.

Three security people surrounded Teddy. He was facedown on the floor, spread-eagled, his hood thrown back, an Uzi pressed against the back of his bare neck.

Right at the back of the room Eleanor saw a tall teenage girl with a pretty oval face and long straight chestnut hair wearing an expensive black dress. Julia Evans—shouldering her way past a big man and an imposing woman, arm rising to point a rigid accusing forefinger straight at Eleanor.

"SIT!" Julia barked in a voice so commanding that Eleanor's nerves went dead.

She heard a quiet sighing sound at her back and turned to see a sentinel folding onto its haunches not a meter behind her. It licked its muzzle with a long pink tongue.

"Good girl," Julia enthused warmly. "Who's a good girl, then?"

Eleanor's legs gave out.

39

G<small>REG!"</small>

"Huh, yeah?"

Monastic silence had enveloped the tower, the light diffusing into their makeshift prison reduced to the minutest candle glimmer from above. The basement was inky black.

Gabriel's strained face was ghostly pale. "Greg, we're going to die."

"Come on, Gabriel. Don't give the bastards the satisfaction."

"Screw you, Mandel," she hissed. "I'm not cracking up. I've got it back again, thank Christ. The future. It's all fuzzy. But I can see it, and it all comes to an end in about forty minutes."

Greg's cuffs clanged loudly against the rail as her words penetrated. He squirmed round to look at her, trepidation and hope heating his blood. Psi meant crushing Armstrong's mind inside his skull, raping every thought with obscene distortions, drowning him in his own agonizing insanity. Making him love his own death.

Greg hadn't known he could hate someone that much. But he could do it. For Armstrong, he could do it. No messing.

The gland: quavering like a cardiac victim. He waited in a funk of anticipation for the tower to fade from sight, for his thoughts to levitate, liberating him from the confines of his own skull. But there was nothing, only the bitter sense of frustration.

"Are you sure?" he hissed back testily. "I still can't sense your mind."

"Sure? Course I'm fucking sure," Gabriel raged. The *old* Gabriel. Fabulous. But why hadn't his own ability returned?

"Can you see a Tau line which has us escaping?" Greg demanded.

"It's not like that. Not my usual ability. No Tau lines. There's only the one vision. Christ, Greg, the whole tower's just going to blow. Like an atom bomb or something."

"A nuke?" he asked incredulously. He was picking up on the rising panic pulling at her thorax. He believed without the espersense. An event so powerful it'd burst through the twins' nullifying blockade. Which meant it was all too real.

There was the weirdest tickle at the back of Greg's throat. He knew if he opened his mouth it would burst out as a giddy laugh.

"I don't know," Gabriel protested. "There's no details, just a bloody great bang."

"Electron compression," Greg said, half to himself. "Has to be." Doubt rotted the upspring of bold conviction. Philip Evans had been given a warhead once. For one specific task. The American government wouldn't hand them out like sweets. And yet . . . the original warhead had been intended for Armstrong. Could Julia or Walshaw have got hold of another one from Horace Jepson? They would have to prove Armstrong was still alive first. Concrete proof.

"Ellis," Greg said excitedly. "Lord bless that skinny little fart. He came through." But uncertainty still nagged malevolently. Even if Ellis had left details about Armstrong in the Crays, someone had moved bloody fast to mount a strike by tonight. Perhaps it was just a colossal conventional bomb. Julia had Prowlers, maybe she'd got a B5 stashed away somewhere, too. Or a Hades. Or a Tochka. Now that was an interesting way to spend your last half hour, he mocked himself. See how many tactical weapon systems you can name that could blow you out of existence.

At least anything powerful enough to take out the entire tower promised to be quick. Not for Gabriel, though. She had half an hour of mental torment left. Better than being beaten to a pulp for his heroism or thrashing about in the mud's embrace.

"This attack must mean Armstrong and Kendric aren't having it all their own way," he said with a barely suppressed excitement. "Maybe Julia survived. Yeah. And Walshaw interrogated the mole. They're hitting back, Gabriel."

Gabriel's breathing was coming in ragged gasps. "But what do we do?" she whined.

Greg took an iron grip on his nerves. "Say nothing. At least this way we'll take Armstrong and Kendric with us."

"Is that all you can think of?"

"Well, what the hell else is there?" Greg snapped back, suddenly furious. Despising his own fear because it would be so easy to let it win.

"You want to shout a warning?" he asked. "Is that what you want to do? Is it? Wake them up, tell them what you can see, let them get clear? Silence is all we've got left, Gabriel, our vengeance weapon. This way we get our revenge. It doesn't matter that we don't get to see it; we're dead anyway."

Gabriel bit her lower lip, trembling. He caught a glimpse of moisture glinting in her eyes as she hugged the railings hard.

40

E<small>LEANOR SAT ON A HARD</small> wooden chair in Wilholm's study. Someone had put a bone china breakfast cup of tea in front of her. She hadn't drunk any. The air was warm and stuffy from too many people breathing it. Six Event Horizon security hardliners were standing watching her and Teddy, four on the other side of the table, two behind them.

Stupid. Farcical. But Eleanor hadn't complained. Didn't have the energy. Her belly was cold now, colder than ice.

A harassed Dr. Taylor had broken off attending to Suzi long enough to give Eleanor an infusion that'd taken her down to a state where peripheries, like injuries and the manor's fabulous wall-to-wall glitter, didn't register much. Then some kind of bioware dressing had been stuck over the claw wounds, and a salve was sprayed over skin that was red raw where the maser had leaked through the dissipater jumpsuit. Dr. Taylor wanted her to lie down for a more elaborate treatment. She refused point-blank.

Eleanor had to know about Greg, persuade the Evans girl and Morgan Walshaw to help find him. Except they didn't seem to be getting anywhere. She was wrapped in a jade toweling-robe, sitting beside Teddy, who was also in a robe, one that was too small for him. Julia Evans and Morgan Walshaw sat opposite them. Matched contrasts.

Julia was quiet, sticking to Walshaw wherever he went. Mouse timid. Nothing like the way Greg had described her.

Further up the table a man called Piers Ryder had opened up the squat cylindrical message laser, much to Teddy's impotent fury. Ryder had plugged a cybofax into the laser's hardware with optical cable, looking for bugs on Walshaw's orders.

There was no trust in the study. And after all the horror they'd endured, Eleanor could've wept, except it wouldn't have changed anything.

Teddy and Walshaw were doing all the talking. Arguing, actually. All down to Walshaw's totally unbelievable statement that Greg had gone somewhere with Kendric di Girolamo.

"You think Greg's sold out, you outta your ballsed-up mind," Teddy said, loud but not shouting, his anger a dangerous undercurrent.

"Even I find it difficult to believe," Walshaw said. "But nonetheless, he did leave with di Girolamo on the *Mirriam*."

"Going where?"

"Does it matter? The complicity exists."

"Fucking right it matters. He ain't with that arsehole di Girolamo outta free will. Once we find him my troops gonna snatch him back."

"You can't," said Julia. It was the first time she'd spoken.

"Why not, gal?" Teddy asked. He wasn't quite so abusive to her.

"I'm not quite sure of his exact position anymore."

"Way they was headed will do. We'll pick 'em up soon as they put into port."

Julia consulted Walshaw silently. The security chief shrugged.

"Last time I checked, Greg was in Wisbech," Julia said.

"Wisbech?" Teddy asked.

"Yeah."

"What, Wisbech in the basin? How the fuck did he get there?"

"I'm not sure. It wasn't fast enough to be a plane; we thought perhaps a hovercraft."

Teddy narrowed his eyes. "How come you know that? You weren't following him."

"I gave him my Saint Christopher. It's got a transmitter in it, a very complex frequency hopper. Event Horizon's Earth Resource satellite platforms are equipped with sensors which can pick up the signal anywhere on the planet. I wear it in case I get kidnapped."

"And you gave it to Greg? Why, for Christ's sake?"

"I wanted to know what he was doing, where he was. You see, Kendric has done a deal with the PSP and Greg didn't tell me."

"PSP?" Teddy half rose from the chair. "You telling me PSP is plugged in on this?"

"Yeah," Julia said.

"Then, gal, you are way, way outta line saying Greg ain't on the level. While rich bitches like you were living it up abroad, that rat-prick Armstrong was screwing us into the ground. Me and my troops, we were fighting his Constables. We fucking died so you could swan back here and make money outta us. Eight years Greg was out on those streets. Hardest there is, and they nearly broke him. But he stood and fought. So don't you ever sit in front of me and tell me he's gone and done a deal with no fucking Armstrong relics. You ain't good enough to shovel up his shit. You hear me!"

Julia shrank back in the seat, her tawny eyes wide. "I wasn't sure," she pleaded. "That's why I gave him the transmitter. Because I didn't understand."

"Understand what?"

She swallowed hard, looking around the room in desperation. "Victor. You were there at Ellis's flat. Ellis told you that the Cray which Greg crashed was loaded with millions of personal files. Everyone important in England, that's what he said."

"Yes," Victor agreed cautiously.

"See?" Julia asked Teddy.

"See what?"

Julia covered her face in her hands, veiling the sting of misery in her eyes. "Nobody sees. It's me. Those bloody nodes. I kept looking at it until I had the answer." Her hands dropped to the table, palms down, fingers wide. "Who? Who, in this whole wide world is going to compile millions of files on people living in this country?"

"Goddamn." The anger fled from Teddy; his chair creaked as it took his full weight again. "PSP."

"The amount of data in even one of the Crays was far too much for anyone to snatch from a mainframe; the squirt would last for days. Ellis had to have direct access to the Ministry of Public Order mainframe at some time before the circuit hot rods crashed it and the PSP fell. The one explanation which fits is that he was an ex-apparatchik; and only a high ranker would have an authority code that'd clear duplication copying on that scale. And he was running a team of hackers that are disrupting the English economy. That's the oldest trick in the political book; cause dissatisfaction with the current government, and people always turn to the opposition. It had to mean that Ellis was still actively working for the PSP."

"Okay," Teddy said. "So maybe Greg ain't so fast these days, didn't see the connection straight off. Don't mean he's turned."

"I know that," Julia shot back. "I didn't want to believe he'd do that to me, not Greg. I trusted him, like nobody else. That's why I slipped him the Saint Christopher. To find out what he was doing. Then he went with Kendric, and I had to believe."

"It's all down to Gabriel Thompson," Walshaw said. "Her precognition ability would suggest it is impossible to snatch or even surprise her. Therefore she and Greg went with di Girolamo out of their own choice."

"Christ, man, I don't know about that. Gabriel is one hotshot gal, but that psi gland messes her about something serious. You've only ever seen her on the up. In Turkey I seen her down, and you just can't get any lower and still be human." Teddy made a fist and rapped on the table with it. "Okay, listen; you count Gabriel and her precog outta all this, you gotta scene where Greg's in deep shit. Right? Ain't I right?"

Julia turned to Walshaw, face tilted up with hope.

"Yes, all right," said the security chief. "Psi was always looked on as a wild card when I was in active service. I just thought they'd improved it since my day. Greg and Gabriel seemed to have it down pat."

Teddy gave a fast grin. "Now we are getting somewhere." He looked at Julia. "Okay, gal, you work your magic spy trick on Greg again, tell us exactly where he is, and we'll squirt the coords out to my troops." He glared at Ryder. "That's if you ain't screwed my laser. And maybe Event Horizon can loan the Trinities a couple of Prowlers to jump 'em out to wherever Greg is now. I wanna get this settled soon as possible."

Julia became fluttery with concern. "I can't find out where Greg is now. Grandpa was plugged into every piece of gear Wilholm has. It's all glitched by the virus. We have to wait until the company security people outside write an antithesis."

Teddy's face wound up with pain. "Jesus. They've had Greg for hours. You got any idea what they could've done to him by now? That bimbo friend of yours wasn't the half of it. They were being nice to her."

"The situation is hardly Miss Evans's fault," Walshaw said smartly.

Julia had closed tortured eyes.

"Yeah, okay," said Teddy. "So let me use the message laser, plug it into the man's NN core. I got someone who can write an anti-thing in zero time."

"There is nobody better than our experts," Walshaw said.

"Bullshit! Son is the best there's ever been. Melted through your security core guardians like butter to get at the manor defense specs, didn't he? We wouldn't have been here if it wasn't for him. How the hell do you think Greg found Tentimes? Who backtracked Ellis for you?"

"You expect me to allow some kind of super hacker to plug directly into Philip Evans's NN core?" Walshaw asked. "The heart of the entire company? Not a chance. I'm more than willing to do whatever I can to help Greg, once the virus is broken. But that is out."

"You *owe* us, man. You owe us so bad it's gonna take you a couple of centuries to kick your debt. You are responsible for Greg being where he is now. You hired him; you put him there."

Eleanor watched Walshaw stare up at the ceiling, brows knotted with furious concentration. Greg's life was being decided inside his skull, she realized. It was obvious that Julia would follow his decision. The girl looked dreadfully unhappy.

"Miss Evans?" Eleanor said. She was distantly bemused by how such an awfully reedy voice as hers had become could attract everyone's rapt attention. They all wanted someone to produce a miracle, blow away their dilemma. She couldn't, of course. "You don't know me, Miss Evans, but I live with Greg, and I love him. He would never betray you. I suppose you think of him as a hard man, never showing much feeling. He is in a way. I have only ever seen him let emotion overrun common sense on one occasion. That was when he found out what di Girolamo had done to your friend, Katerina. All he could think about was getting her out. He cared about her, a girl he'd only ever met for a few minutes before. Does that tell you anything about him? I have also met Royan, the hacker Teddy wants to plug into your grandfather's NN core. I was sick to my stomach for a day after I met him, I couldn't eat, couldn't drink. Royan doesn't even have any legs, Miss Evans. He doesn't have any arms. He doesn't even have eyes. To look at him you wouldn't even believe he was a human being. Physically he is a lump of flesh with a digestive system and a brain which is plugged into some gear. The PSP did that to him, their People's Constables. But I've talked with him, had coffee with him. He's one of the most decent, bravest people in the world. He knows what pain really is; he isn't about to harm you or your grandfather."

Julia might've been carved from stone, staring at Eleanor with fascinated revulsion, unable to look away.

"Right now there are two people lying dead on your grounds," Eleanor went on. "The only reason they came to Wilholm was to help Greg. I'm going to wake up screaming every night for the rest of my life remembering that trip. But I'm glad I will, because I thought coming here meant there would be a chance of getting Greg back. All of us, Miss Evans, we all believe in Greg. Even you did once, I think. He's just an ordinary man, nothing special in the way of the world. But I'd be very grateful if you could do what you can to bring him back to me. Thank you."

The speech exhausted the last of her strength; she withered back in the chair, spent. Someone gripped her freezing hand in a viselike hold that verged on the painful. She knew it must be Teddy.

Julia turned to Ryder. "Plug it in."

41

"WHAT ARE YOU DOING?" Gabriel asked tersely.

Greg had crouched down, squashing his face against the cold banister, trying to bend a wrist double to reach his dinner jacket's breast pocket. "What I should've done hours ago. Getting us out of here."

"How?" she squeaked.

"Tell you, it's not going to be easy, all right? At the moment, we're already dead, so a bit of damage now isn't going to make a whole load of difference. Handcuffs are a bureaucrat's fallacy to the condemned. Especially the condemned fitted with cortical nodes."

"Oh." Gabriel's eyes widened in comprehension.

"Yeah," he said, suddenly disquieted. "Besides, you should've thought of this, too; you went to the same tactics courses as me."

"Tactics courses! Christ, Greg, I was a flaming nurse before Mindstar dragooned me."

Greg's scrabbling fingertips found the top of the handkerchief sticking out of his breast pocket, and he tugged the square of white silk out into the air. It wasn't as big as he'd have liked, but it would have to do. "Listen, this is going to look bad, okay? But self-mutilation is a damn sight better than dying. If you've got a different solution, now's the time."

She shook her head silently. Very pale now.

Greg outlined what he wanted her to do and stretched out to give her the handkerchief. Her hands were shaking when she took it.

She leaned forward to press her face into a gap between the stair rails and bit into the handkerchief, chewing it into her mouth. Her cheeks bulged out.

"Bite hard," he instructed.

She ducked her head in acknowledgment.

"Okay. Now let's get into position."

They faced the tower's curving wall, as though they were praying at an altar, Greg thought. He held Gabriel's eyes as she knelt on the floorboards, willing her on. She pulled the cuffs right up to the railing and rested her hands on the ten-centimeter lip of solid oak planking. Her fingers stuck out over the edge, but her knuckles remained on the wood.

Greg went the other way, sliding his arms right up to the banister and standing on his left foot. He pushed his right leg through the gap in the railings above Gabriel's left hand.

"Fist your right hand," he told her. "Then disengage all the nerves below the left elbow."

She looked up at him, her shoulders quivering, dry weeping. The sight nearly broke his determination.

Slowly her right hand clenched into a fist, leaving the left open.

"Can you feel your left hand?" he asked.

She shook her head.

"Are you sure?" He was worried about the stunshot charge they'd both been hit with; if there was any damage to the cortical node, there'd be no chance of pulling this off.

She glared at him.

"Look away," Greg said.

Her head turned.

"Right away," he said, deliberately harsh. He couldn't risk her flinching.

She jerked her head forcibly aside.

He concentrated on the leg he'd stuck through the railings. He had to get it perfect first time. If he didn't, he doubted she would ever allow him a second go.

He was wearing sturdy leather shoes. Grubby and scuffed now, but with a hard, flat sole.

Lining the heel up in the funereal glimmer of light.

Greg pushed up with his hands, as though he were trying to lift the banister off the top of the railings. Bunched muscles tightened the jacket fabric across his shoulders. His left foot was pressed hard onto the floor. He could even hear a feeble groan from the oak as it adjusted to the new stress pattern. Praying the strength he'd built filling up the chalet's water tank would be sufficient.

Ready.

He stamped down.

The heel smashed down onto the top of Gabriel's knuckles, *giving.* Bone snapped, a liquid-dulled crack.

She convulsed, slumping forward into the railings, her puling muted by the ball of silk.

Greg tugged his leg back out of the railings and hooked the back of his calf inside Gabriel's left elbow. Her head twisted around; there was a small tail of cloth sticking out of her mouth. Shock-wide eyes screamed up at him in pure terror. He jerked his leg back savagely.

Her arm moved with sickening slowness. Then suddenly there was no more resistance, and Greg was swinging wildly, left foot slipping, backside coming down fast. The cuffs made an excruciatingly loud racket scraping down the railing. He sat heavily, his coccyx trying to punch its way up into his throat.

But Gabriel was free. She lay facedown on the floor, right hand still through the railing, left arm curled limply at her side, its pulped hand brushing her hair. Her whole body was quaking softly. The handkerchief had begun to emerge out of her mouth like some vile glistening imago escaping from its chrysalis.

She rolled over, gulping, a half-choke. A trail of thin vomit ran down her chin. She wore the expression of the torturer's victim, an utter incomprehension of how one person could do this to another. Frightened eyes found her left hand. She drew it up to her face, mesmerized, and began to cry.

"Gabriel?"

She was curling up into a fetal ball, sucking down air in shallow gulps.

"Gabriel, did the cortical node work?"

"Yes."

"Gabriel, you have to get up."

A shiver ran down her spine. "I want to go home," she whispered through clenched teeth.

"We are going home. Now get up."

Gabriel rocked back onto her knees, cradling her left hand. Tears streaked her cheeks. "Oh, Christ, Greg."

"I know," he said. "Now look round and find something you can use as a club."

"No. No, I can't do that. Don't make me do that. Please, Greg. Please."

"You can't leave me here." Greg deliberately let a note of desperation filter into his voice. Bullying her with guilt. "There's only about thirty minutes left before the tower blows."

She clambered to her feet in slow motion stages, never allowing her arm to leave her side. He could see the film of sweat on her forehead, and felt clammy apprehension rise. The grisly snap of cracking bone seemed to be echoing around the room.

She tottered off behind him, rummaging through the stacks of food crates. He didn't look, keeping still, eyes on the ancient worn brickwork on the other side of the stairs.

"Will this do?" she asked. She couldn't think for herself. Shock numbness had set in.

The length of wood she'd found was a meter long, four or five centimeters wide. Three rusty screws jutted out of the middle. It ought to be heavy enough, he thought.

"It'll do." With grim horror he realized that after she'd smashed his hand, he'd have to yank it free through the handcuff himself. She could never manage that.

"Gabriel, you must be hard. Swing the club real hard, no messing. Imagine it's Armstrong's hand or something. Don't do it to me twice. Promise?"

"Right."

He put his left hand on the ledge of wood, then instructed his cortical node to disengage the nerves of his left arm. From the elbow down he could feel nothing, not even the dead meat coldness of anesthetic, the buoyant release of morphine. His forearm and hand had ceased to exist.

"Okay," he said, finding out just how much it'd cost Gabriel to say that.

Gabriel pushed the handkerchief into his mouth. It was disgusting. Soggy, tasting of sour acidic stomach juices. Good. Focus on the revulsion. Shutting out the sight of Gabriel steadying herself on the second step. Knuckles whitening as she clenched the makeshift club. Her face mimicking the intense concentration he'd once seen on a golf pro's face as he lined up his putter for an albatross.

Greg heard the swish of air.

Shock was worse than pain in its own way. His brain seemed to expand time, letting him see the full horror of his flesh being triturated, every detail slamming into his mind. The sight flushing away the intention to pull with all his strength. It took the animal fear of impending death to twist his mind back, overriding reluctance. Greg pulled.

He felt the scream rising inside him as he watched his ruined hand squeezing through a metal circle that was two centimeters too small. It was obscenely malleable, damp cracking sounds marking its progress.

His hand came free, and a lungful of air blasted the handkerchief from his mouth. There was nothing to stop the scream that would vent some of his anguish. He hovered on the brink for one eternal second. Closed his gaping mouth, contracting the throat muscles that would've formed the blissful release of sound.

Gabriel: laughing, crying, whimpering. "We've done it." Wiping tears from her face. "We've fucking done it."

Greg drank down liters of fresh clean air. His right hand was still on the other side of the railing. He turned it slowly and brought it and the cuff through the gap. His left hand was something from a butcher's stall, crushed, swelling with blood, pussy fluid leaking from the graze where the club had struck.

Greg shared a long glance with Gabriel, a love that wasn't physical, didn't need to be. They were blood siblings, a far stronger bond. "Time to go," he said. It broke the spell.

She went to work on the storeroom's central biolum panel, easing it away from its clips. He started on the Harrods hampers and found a case of three-star brandy.

He clamped the first bottle between his knees and unscrewed the cap with his right hand. The aroma set up a satanic craving in his maltreated stomach.

After opening five bottles, Greg tiptoed around the room, soaking the kelpboard cases with the liquor. Taking care not to spill any on the floor with its wide cracks.

"The window's behind this lot," Gabriel whispered, poking a tall stack of cases. "It'll take an age to shift them."

"Forget shifting them. Our exit isn't going to be stealthy. You got the biolum?"

"Yeah." She'd cracked the back open, exposing the activation trigger. A finger-size pewter cylinder with enough charge to activate the motes' bias. There was also enough charge to spark—two, maybe three times if their luck was in.

He impaled a wad of paper on the screws of Gabriel's club, sloshing brandy over it. She put it on the desk, eagerness animating her features, dulling the pain.

He put his shoulders to the stack of crates, tensing. Nodded.

Two idiot smiles.

A minute blue spark sizzled between the cylinder electrodes and one of the screws. The paper caught at once, a bright yellow tongue of flame that left sharp purple after-images on his retinas.

Gabriel picked up her torch and thrust it against some of the cases he'd doused. Flames bloomed wherever it touched. She carried it around in a triumphal circuit.

The room was becoming dazzlingly bright to Greg's gloaming-acclimatized eyes, but he waited until the fire began to crackle noisily before heaving at the cases. The stack toppled with a crash that seemed deafeningly loud in the small room. Cases burst open, scattering tins of meat with Brazilian labels across the oak floorboards.

Greg jumped onto the two remaining cases below the window, kicking out the glass. It shattered into wicked ice daggers, scything off into the galactic-deep night outside.

"Out," he yelled, and used his good hand to haul Gabriel up onto the cases. She balanced on the narrow dirt-ingrained window ledge, crouching down for the jump. There were shouts coming from the basement. The fire had really taken hold now. Greg could feel its heat on his face and his right hand.

Gabriel had already gone. And someone was pounding up the stairs. Greg flexed his knees and leaped into the cool damp air.

42

Processor Node One Status: Loading Basic Management Program.

Julia's head jerked up. She hand't actually been sleeping, just allowing her rattled, abused thoughts some peace.

Processor Node Two Status: Loading Basic Management Program.

"What?" asked Walshaw.

Memory Node One: File Codes Loaded.

The huge black man, Teddy, was giving her that eagle-eyed stare again, as if he were examining her soul. Finding it flawed.

Memory Node Two: File Codes Loaded.

"Lord Jesus." She clapped her hands in excited delight. "He's done it. Royan. He's in the 'ware."

Memory Node Three: File Codes Loaded.

The fabric of the nodes' artificial mentality rose out of nowhere to fortify and enrich her own thoughts. Dictionaries, language and technical lexicons, encyclopedias, logic matrices, all returned to their warm familiar places.

Neural Augmentation On-line.

Walshaw was leaning over his terminal, hands reaching for the keyboard. The cubes were full of crazed graphics, slowly returning to equilibrium.

Hello, Juliet.

"Grandpa!"

Her view of the study was suddenly riddled with cracks, it fragmented and whirled away. She was looking down on Earth from a great height. But the picture was wrong; there were no half-shades. The colors were all primary: an amorphous jigsaw of emerald, crimson, turquoise, and rose-gold oil patterns. It was overlaid by regular grid lines. False-Color Thematic Image, supplied the nodes. There was a town at the center of the image, one that was curiously blurred around its outskirts.

Wisbech, Julia said, intuitively. There was no sound to hear, no tactile sensation present in this flat universe that had captured her, only the image itself. She could sense her grandfather's presence by her side. They weren't alone.

Juliet, I'd like you to meet a very smart young lad. Goes by the name of Royan.

Pleased to meet you, Miss Juliet. I've never met an heiress before.

Thank you for unlocking my grandpa, Royan.

It was a breeze; whoever wrote the virus was dumb.

It didn't seem that way when I was on the receiving end.

I'm not surprised. You know, you ought to load some proper protection into your nodes. They're terrific pieces of gear; wish I had some. But the guardian bytes you're using leave them wide open.

I used to think I had proper protection.

I could write you some. I wouldn't want anything bad to happen to you; you're a friend of Greg's. And the PSP hates you. That makes you an A-one person in my book.

I'd take him up on that, Juliet, if I were you. Royan and I have been having a long chat. Boy knows what he's talking about.

Long? she asked.

You're operating in 'ware time now, Miss Juliet. Fast fast fast.

Oh. Thanks for the offer, Royan. But I think we'd better do what we can for Greg first.

Yeah, said Philip. *Misjudged him in a big way. Jumping the gun. Never would've done that in the flesh. Really shouldn't have done it now. But we can make amends soon enough.*

Julia concentrated on the thematic image. Her grandfather was squirting a solid stream of binary pulses up to a company Earth Resources platform through Wilholm's one remaining uplink, a hum in the background of her consciousness.

Greg's moving, look, he said.

A diamond star had appeared on the thematic image. The magnification leaped up. Wisbech's outskirts disappeared. The town was slashed in two by a broad meandering band of deep turquoise. Like a rain-swollen river, Julia thought, even though she knew the whole place was mud-locked. Her grandfather jumped the magnification again. Then again. The star was gleaming a few hundred meters east of the turquoise band. A small dot of crimson on the edge of the turquoise band was turning a brighter scarlet.

Something is warming up down there, Philip said.

I think I can help, said Royan.

A crude transparent map was superimposed on the thematic image.

Ordnance Survey, Royan explained. *The last one before the PSP came to power. Nothing much changed between then and the start of the Warming.*

The map rotated slowly clockwise until the two sets of grid lines meshed, then it swam in and out of focus, matching up the street patterns.

Close as we'll get.

Disused mill, Julia read. The dot had become a fluorescent ruby.

Thermal emission rising sharply, said Philip. *It's on fire. And Greg's moving away, dead slow. Means the boy's on foot, swimming rather, in that gunk.*

Escaping, said Royan.

Could well be. I wonder if Gabriel is with him.

If she's alive, she'll be with him, Royan censured.

Julia sensed the adoration verging on love that Royan had somehow managed to convey into their inanimate medium. His belief was unshakable. And she knew he was right; Greg didn't desert people to save his own skin.

Grandpa?

I know, Juliet. The strike window ends in ninety seconds—mark. Decision time.

Mr. Philip told me about that, Miss Juliet. It's a grand idea. He said it was your suggestion.

Certainly was, boy. She's an Evans, through and through. And we don't do anything by halves. No sir.

I wonder who's in that tower, Royan asked.

Someone big, Julia said. *Someone important, important enough to make Kendric visit him, not the other way round. And if you knew Kendric like I do, you'd know how few people in the world would be granted that concession.*

The first instance of sensation invaded their private universe, an electric tingle reminding her of far-off nerves. Julia looked down on the mill, judging it with the dispassion of some Olympian goddess.

Could it really be? Philip asked.

There was never anybody, said Royan. *Never any real proof. Not even Mindstar knew.*

We'd have to hurry. The timing is tight, very tight.

No, Julia said, bold with conviction. *The timing is perfect. Synchronized.*

Gabriel? Philip inquired.

I expect so, she said. *Whatever the reason, we cannot ignore this opportunity.*

I agree, said Royan.

That makes it unanimous, then. Access the Ordnance Survey's memory core and download that mill's coords, m'boy, accurate as you can get. We've only got the one satellite uplink left after your friends came a-knocking. I would've preferred to keep watching Wisbech, just in case we need to update. But we'll simply have to make do.

You're lucky you've still got that one. Father is efficient.

Julia's awareness shifted as the thematic image faded. She was plugged directly into Wilholm's myriad gear systems, a brightly glowing three-dimensional cobweb of data channels. New strands were coming on-line at a phenomenal rate as the antithesis poured through it, purging the virus.

A quick status check showed her that there were only three functional servos out of the eight that steered Wilholm's one remaining satellite dish. Accelerated time stretched for what seemed like aeons as the dish swiveled round on its axis to point at the western horizon. Her grandfather had overridden the servos' safety limiters, allowing them to take a double load. Temperature sensors relayed the heat from overloaded motors straight into her medulla, interpreted as scalding hands.

Sorry, Juliet.

Her pain vanished.

The dish's rotation halted. Smaller azimuth servos began tracking it across the sky.

Coords ready for loading, Mr. Philip. Got them down to half a meter.

Anything within three hundred meters would be enough, Julia said.

Don't brag so, girl, Philip said as he loaded the figures into an OtherEyes personality package. But a sliver of pride escaped from his thoughts.

So, that just leaves the reactivation code. Juliet, your honor.

She allowed herself one moment of supremely self-indulgent satisfaction.

Access AvengingAngel. The long string of binary digits emerged from her nodes to hang between the three of them. Her grandfather integrated it into the OtherEyes personality package. The completed data construct squirted into the dish transmitter, streaming upward at lightspeed.

This time, you bastard, this time I'll get you.

43

IN HIS MIND THE THEORY was perfect. They weren't particularly high up, and the mud around the tower shouldn't have been deep. Of course, there was no way of actually testing it in advance.

Greg hit the thin coating of surface water and kept on going, his momentum only slowing when the water reached his thighs. He let his knees bend, absorbing inertia. Thick viscous goo rose up his shins, embedding them. That was the point where his left hand thumped into the water, finally overloading his beleaguered cortical node. Greg screamed at the lancets of pain its faltering barricade let through. Brilliant starbursts of light danced across his vision.

His feet were resting on something solid. He could see guttering orange light washing across a big clump of reeds about three meters in front of him, marking the perimeter of a low mound of rubble. A gable end was sticking up in the middle of it, inclined at forty-five degrees, supported by a buttress of rafters that resembled some bizarre geometric whale skeleton.

The water had come up to the bottom of his rib cage, leaving his folded legs entirely under the mud. Greg tried to straighten his knees. It took an age before even the faintest tremble of motion began. The mud refused to let go.

Panic churned his gut. He had absolutely nothing to grip, nothing he could use to drag himself out. His legs muscles had to do all the work. And any second now Kendric's crewmen would be storming out of the tower.

"Where are you, Greg?" Gabriel called.

"I'm coming." Was he rising fractionally faster? The pain from his left hand had been suppressed again, making it easier to concentrate. He could feel the mud sliding down his thighs. "Get into the reeds. Go on! Move."

His buttocks left the mud behind, and he stood up. There was water up to the top of his legs; the mud still incarcerated his knees. Greg brought his left foot out of the mud's suction clutch, standing stork-style, then fell forward, windmilling his arms.

The strain on his right knee was incredible: his body weight was

trying to bend it in exactly the opposite direction to which it was designed to hinge. He grabbed at the reeds with his right hand, pulling
himself along toward the cover of the mound. The mud relinquished
its hold on his right leg with extreme reluctance.

A chorus of wild shouting broke out behind him. Mark's voice
rose above the others, bawling to bring some lights.

Greg grasped at another clump of reeds. His progress was a combination of swimming, slithering, and crawling, all at a snail's pace.
He was completely hampered by his desperation to avoid any commotion. Thankfully, the reeds began to get thicker and higher.

He heard a long erratic stutter of muffled thuds from behind him
and guessed at food cans rupturing in the fire.

A quick glance around let him see the tower, a black phallic mono-
lith probing a cloud-smeared night sky. The first floor's broken window was a glaring yellow rectangle, while others glowed with biolum's softer pink-white radiance; sketchy shadows were moving
about inside. Several people were dashing about on the grass ring
around the tower's base; three were splashing through the shallows
but not venturing far. If they wanted to get across to the reeds, they'd
have to get down on their bellies and squirm; it was the only way.
They didn't have the motivation. A couple of intense torch beams
stabbed out, scouring the reeds.

Greg rolled back onto his stomach and began his serpent wriggle
again. Thirty seconds later there was hard ground under his elbows.
Reeds competing with stiff blades of grass. He was using his knees
as well as his elbows now, scuttling toward the gable end, and cover.
He knew exactly what Kendric and Armstrong would do next. Flinty
pebbles and rapier grass lacerated his skin. Somewhere over to his
left another heavy body was burrowing through the vegetation.

An electromagnetic rifle opened up, warbling loudly. Bullets thudded into the mound, pinged against the brickwork, ricocheted off,
whining. Greg kept going.

"Get over there." That was Kendric's unmistakably enraged voice.
Murmurs of argument followed.

The white torchlight trimmed the tips of the reeds around Greg.
Tiny reddish-brown ovate flowers glowed lambently. Midges formed
a silver galaxy overhead. The light passed on. The electromagnetic
rifle had fallen silent.

Greg reached the sloping brickwork. Gabriel was ahead of him,
panting heavily at the end of a streaky mud trail.

"God, the smell!" she exclaimed.

"What smell?"

"Some people."

He climbed gingerly to his feet. The island they were on was about twenty meters at its widest. Greg had cherished a half-notion that the mounds would all be connected. But the next one was a good forty meters away. Algae-curdled water sloshed like crude oil between the two. It didn't look as though there was much of it on top of the mud.

"Clothes off," Greg said, then flinched as the electromagnetic rifle poured another fusillade of bullets into the gable end.

"Do what?" Gabriel asked. She was cradling her left hand again. Her face was haggard, totally lethargic.

"We've got a lot of swimming to do. Clothes are going to drag us under."

"Swim where?"

"Clear of the tower, remember? Kilometer at least. How long have we got?"

Gabriel closed her eyes. "About twenty minutes, maybe less."

"Do we survive?"

"Some of us do, some of us don't." She sounded completely disinterested.

Greg ducked his head around the side of the bricks, bringing it back fast. "Bugger!"

"Now what?"

"They've put the fire out. I was hoping it would be a beacon to the ships on the Nene. Somebody might report it."

That brought a half-hysterical giggle from Gabriel, ending in a gurgling cough. "Don't you worry, Greg. Lots of people are going to see your tower before tonight's out. You betcha."

"Oh, yeah." He felt stupid. "Let's go." He started shrugging out of the dinner jacket, clenching his teeth as his left hand dragged through the arm. It'd swollen badly, skin stretched taut, pulling open the grazes. Trousers followed, and the discovery that buckles are tricky one-handed.

More shouting had broken out from the tower. Lots of conflicting orders interwound with Kendric's repeated urgings and Armstrong's controlled barks.

Gabriel gave him a remorseful stare before starting halfheartedly on the buttons of her blouse. Greg peeled his trousers off and helped her pull her blouse gingerly over her inflated left hand.

"Put your shoes back on," he said.

A third burst of rifle fire lashed the bricks.

They bent double, keeping the bulk of the small pyramid between themselves and the tower as they crept down to the gray slime. The stuff was semiliquid, a thick gelatin that squelched and undulated alarmingly as Greg immersed himself. It closed around him, finding its way into every orifice. But he didn't sink. In fact the worst of it was on the surface. A sixty-centimeter stratum of water had been sandwiched between the spongy mud and lathery algae.

Gabriel groaned as she lowered herself behind him and the cold mire enveloped her.

Greg began to move, a tortuously slow sidestroke, kicking hard with his feet. Big fecal gobs of the pulpy algae clotted his right arm, splattering over his face. He had to stop every four or five strokes and wipe it off. His eyes were stung raw. Gabriel had it easier. He was pathbreaking for her, clearing a ragged channel.

When they reached the second island, Greg began to worry about what kind of chase was being organized back at the tower. He looked over his shoulder and saw that someone had opened the tower's top-floor window; they were raking the torch beam over the first island and the surrounding water. The light wasn't powerful enough to reach him, but he made Gabriel keep below the wavering tops of the thin reeds as the pair of them crossed over to the island's opposite side.

Away to the right, Greg could see the bloated humps of decomposing tree trunks protruding from the algae like surfaced whales. The number, about thirty, implied some sort of park, which ruled out that direction. They needed to move fast now. Build distance before the tower blew. The park would be genuine swamp, impossible to traverse.

One hundred fifty meters ahead were the first ranks of buildings recognizable as such: detached houses, their walls partially collapsed and roofs concave, but remaining upright. Bridging the gap was a pockmarked landscape of ash-green atolls separated by hoary stretches of slough.

"Any preference direction-wise?" Greg asked.

Gabriel shook her head. "No. But you were right about getting clear. That explosion is a brute. I hope I can make it."

She was a state. Loose folds of flab were caked in thick sable mud; her hair was a tangle of ossifying dreadlocks. Every breath was asthmatic, a battle against coagulating catarrh. She twitched like a palsy victim.

"No problem," he said, wishing to God he meant it.

They waded into the first slough channel.

The fifth island they came to was much larger than the previous four. Iron girders were sticking out among the sedges. There was more grass than reeds on the crest. Soil had begun to accumulate in the crevices between the fragments of stone and cement. Greg cut his calf on something jagged. Cursed.

The island's far shore brought them to within thirty meters of the houses. One more immersion and back onto solid ground. This time it was a long straight ridge parallel to the row of houses. It was cluttered with twisted, drooping chimney stacks and buckled rafter apexes gnarled with scabby lichens; slate tiles formed a loose flaky shingle beneath their feet, making the going hard.

Just as he reached the summit, Greg heard the sound. A low-volume hum in the background. But rising in pitch and intensity, in menace. A note he was irksomely familiar with.

"Move out, double time," he said. "The bastards have inflated the hovercraft."

"No more," Gabriel said wretchedly.

"One last time. That's all. Then it'll all be over."

"Yes. Yes, you're right. Only a few minutes left. It's clearing, Greg. So much clearer now."

Realization struck. He could sense her mind. A pale disconsolate mist of disjointed thoughts, fluttering aimlessly, corrupted with coarse threads of harrowing pain. Gabriel was animated by adrenaline alone, and her endocrine glands were virtually exhausted.

They'd escaped the twins' nullifying effect. Greg let his gland run riot, charging his cerebellum to overload, and screw the risk. Synapses vibrated shrilly under the stress, delusional ripping sounds filtered into his ears, coming from inside his skull, neurone membranes splitting open. His espersense swept out. It was a heady boost. Whole once more.

Two hovercraft were curving away from the tower, each containing three minds, radiant hard-wound balls of mercurial malevolence. Greg recognized Toby riding in one of them, along with a couple of crewmen he couldn't place. Mark and Kendric were paired in the second, along with its pilot. There was no sign of the other minds Greg knew to be out there—Armstrong and Turner, not even Hermione. The tower was an empty shell to his espersense, which meant at least one twin had remained behind. The big question was whether the third hovercraft had been inflated.

A faint haze of small minds glowed around the wavering perimeter of his espersense, occasional twinkles within. Animals of some sort, clinging to a dour existence amid the ruins. Abandoned pets reverted to their true feral nature, rodents scrabbling to stay above the mud, an invasion of reptiles.

He pulled Gabriel roughly down the slope and into the bog that covered the street, ignoring her weepy cries of protest. They didn't have to swim. The syrupy mud drowning the tarmac was only a few centimeters deep, lapping over his feet like slushed snow. It was possible to wade. The raft of algae came up to midthigh.

Greg was nearly tempted to hide in one of the houses. None of them had doors or windows left. Pick one at random and cower down. Unless the hovercraft boasted some pretty sophisticated sensors, Kendric and Toby would never find him in time. But the dangerously dilapidated condition of the walls stopped him. If the tower went up with anything like the violence Gabriel claimed, the friable houses would collapse on top of them.

They reached a moldering dune that had once been a leylandii hedge, and squelched over it. Greg saw two white aureoles sliding fluidly across the horizon behind them, winding down through the slough channels. The drone of the hovercraft propellers drifted in and out of audibility. Kendric and Toby were fanning out, their search pattern carrying them farther apart. At least it was only two.

He steered Gabriel down the narrow dank gully between two houses. There were animals on the other side of the walls, more than he'd originally thought, scurrying around frantically. The garden at the rear of the house backed onto another garden. Head-high panel fencing marked out the boundary, putrefying laths drooping under their own weight. In one corner was a greenhouse whose panes were pasted with hand-size valentine leaves. Some abandoned horticultural treasure had thrived in the heat and abundant nutrient-soaked mud, making it look as though the aluminum-framed structure were about to burst apart at the seams.

Caustic fingers of silver-white light probed through a gap between a couple of houses a hundred meters away. The propeller noise was loud, fluctuating in strident piccolo whistles. Greg sensed Toby's churlish mind; the man was spite-laden, yearning to be the one who found the quarry. Instinct chafed at him. He knew Greg was nearby. A nature-ordained hunter.

The bulk of the houses blocked off the light as the hovercraft glided down the street. Then the questing fingers reappeared, closer this time, three houses away.

Greg urged Gabriel behind the greenhouse and waited until the searchlight fluoresced the verdant avocado-green leaves.

The green corona died as the hovercraft moved on, but Greg knew that knot of determination in Toby's mind. He'd order the pilot to take the hovercraft down the gardens once he reached the end of the street.

His espersense tracked Kendric, who was still patroling the slough channels. They couldn't go back, and the blast would turn the confined gardens into a death trap of flying masonry.

"Through there." Greg pointed ahead. The row of houses in front of them were virtually identical to the ones behind, only in slightly better condition. Gabriel moved like an automaton.

Greg kicked at the panel fence, tearing through it like tissue paper. There was a fruit cage on the other side, a box made from galvanized steel poles wrapped in a tattered cobweb of black nylon netting. The sight of it sparked an idea.

He reached up to one of the crossbeams with his right hand and began to tug. The pole was held in place between the uprights by two molded plastic sockets at each end, both of them fractured and bleached by the decade-long torrent of UV-infested sunlight. One of the sockets crackled at the pressure he applied, then snapped abruptly. Greg yanked the other end of the pole out of its socket with a burst of ebullient strength, tearing the netting as it came free. The pole was three meters long, in good condition; the zinc coating had whitened down the years, but it'd protected the steel from rust.

"What's happening?" Gabriel asked.

"I'm improvising a little present for Toby." There was no longer any vindictiveness at the prospect, or even malice. This was an intrinsic fight for survival now, nothing more. His mind had relegated Toby to an obstacle that had to be tackled. Hatred was all the other man's problem.

Greg clamped the pole between his knees and tied on a strip of the ripped nylon mesh. It was a laborious job; he had to use his teeth to grip the end of the strip while his fingers formed the knot. Spears didn't come any more primitive, but the rudimentary tail ought to keep its trajectory stable for a few meters.

They slogged toward a narrow alleyway between the two houses ahead. The disturbingly concave walls had so many bricks missing, they looked like two vertical checkerboards. There was an unstable aggregation of brick chunks and sandy earth in the gap, rising half a meter above the algae. Greg had lost his shoes somewhere in the slough channels; his feet were unrecognizable lumps of gummy tar that ached abominably. If he stood on anything sharp, they'd go completely numb as the pain breached the cortical node's threshold. When they reached the small front garden they were knee-deep in the greasy mire again.

The street they found themselves on was virtually intact. Greg could almost believe he'd walked out into a predawn autumn morning of fifteen years ago. Rusted, windowless hulks of petrol-driven cars were parked along the road. Barren trees stood tall; low brick walls were topped by fanciful wrought-iron railings; the lampposts were still vertical. It was a well-ordered slice of middle-class suburbia. Only the algae-matted water shattered the illusion of normality.

A curtain of light streaked out at the far end of the houses 150 meters away. Toby's hovercraft had turned down into the gardens. Greg sensed the excitement rising in the man's mind. Toby's native instinct was telling him his prey was nearby.

Greg found it uncanny to observe, almost as though his own ability was being turned against him. He and Toby must share the same mental genotype.

"I want you to walk down to the other end of the street," he told Gabriel.

She didn't reply, standing with shoulders drooping, arms dangling at her side. Her left hand looked appalling, tumescent and inflamed. Mud had dried and cracked on it, as though she were shedding a hardened outer skin, allowing new, blue-tender flesh to break through. He refused the impulse to check his own.

"Listen, Gabriel. You must walk down the street. And when the hovercraft comes, you fall down. Okay? That's all. Can you manage that for me?"

A confused frown puckered her forehead. "Walk?"

"Yes." Greg pressed his hand on her back, starting her off. "And when the light shines, you go for cover."

Gabriel's feet had found a shuffling rhythm. "Fall down?"

"That's right."

"Orders," she mumbled vaguely. "I won't let you down, Greg. I won't."

Greg left her doing her apathetic sleepwalk, feeling a prize turd for using her as bait, and headed back up the street toward the wide beam of light that kept shooting out, documenting the hovercraft's progress. Algae foamed around his knees. Slithery mud tried to pull his feet from under him. Sometimes he thought he could feel the hardness of the tarmac.

The light shone out of the gap in front of him. Greg stood still, listening to the drone of the propeller growing louder, echoing back and forth across the street. The light was extinguished. A faint trace of it rippled along the roof of the house.

Toby's hovercraft drew level with him. Light slammed out of the gap, transfixing him like a rabbit in a headlamp.

A scream of ecstatic triumph burst from Toby's mind. Greg's vision was wiped out in a sparkling pink mist as his retinas were overwhelmed by a targeting laser. He lurched forward. The warbling of electromagnetic rifle fire punctured the night. Bullets stitched a line of small craters in the algae behind him. The propeller drone rose to a crescendo as the pilot fought to turn the hovercraft.

Greg was dumped into the darkness again. The laser impact abated, and he saw a smattering of stars through the shredded gauze of cirrus clouds. He could hear the ripping sounds of the hovercraft riding roughshod over fences.

Greg felt his nerves cooling, heartbeat slowing, tension abating. Going with the flow.

He sensed the hovercraft racing down the gardens, heading back the way it'd come.

A final visual check on Gabriel showed him a forlorn figure bumbling through the mire. His espersense showed her mind was operating with cyborg simplicity, completely absorbed by the mechanics of walking.

He lowered himself into the algae.

The hovercraft had reached the end of the gardens now, rounding the last house in the row. Greg caught a glimpse of its insect eye array of lights sliding into view as he dropped below the surface.

Espersense revealed all he needed, real and hypersense universes entwining smoothly. Toby leaning against the prow, fists clenched, eyes bugging, slipstream plucking at him. The merciless lights finding Gabriel. Her legs buckling, sending her toppling forward. Toby's howl of revenge consummation.

Greg could hear a throbbing sound transmitted through the filthy water, getting louder.

Toby's mind was a lurid spew-point of animus thoughts zooming toward him.

Greg pressed his feet down hard as the hovercraft rumbled directly overhead. He broke surface, bringing a cloying cone of algae with him. A blast of desert-air wind escaping from beneath the hovercraft skirt ablated the mucus from his face. He kept rising like a shabby tenth-rate Neptune, galvanized spear in his hand, already drawn back for the throw. Aiming. The pole steady. And *fling*.

It shot through the wide mesh of the protective carbon-fiber grille at the rear of the hovercraft, hitting the spinning propeller full on. The trajectory bent then as the tip was chopped by the blade's leading edge, tugging it down and round. That, by itself, wasn't disas-

trous; the blade edge was designed to handle bird impacts. But the
length of the pole meant it was deflected right into the mounting. The
propeller's axle-bearing sheared off instantly under the terrible impact stress. And a two-meter-diameter five-hundred-r.p.m. buzz saw
exploded out of the grille to digest the rear of the pneumatic hovercraft.

There was a thunderclap blowout, and the prow of the hovercraft
bucked up into the air, losing rigidity, light beams strafing the sky.
Three bodies and pieces of loose equipment were catapulted in a
short arc. A tremendous spume of water jetted up as the propeller
hit the algae, chewing through. One of the bodies fell into its base.
The shredded hovercraft hull flopped back down. The lights went
out, and the spume died.

It began to rain gobs of mud and algae, pattering down over a wide
area.

One mind had survived, the body that housed it writhing feebly.
Another body was facedown in the water, Toby. Of the third there
was no sign.

Greg waded forward. It was easy going. A vast patch of the street
had been stripped of its covering of algae.

Gabriel was floating on her back, half submerged. Greg got his
hand under her head and lifted her. She coughed weakly. "I did it,
didn't I, Greg? Just like you wanted."

"Sure did, and no messing."

"Did you get 'em?"

"Yeah, they aren't going to hazard anyone again."

Four light beams pinioned him. Kendric's hovercraft was turning
down onto the street. He froze into place. Too exhausted to run. Besides, he could never have left Gabriel.

The hovercraft approached at a cautious unhurried pace. Greg
shielded his eyes against the glare. Kendric was standing in the prow,
in front of the Perspex windscreen. The epitome of the great white
hunter, electromagnetic rifle cradled in a light grip, one foot on the
gunwale.

Greg saw it coming, reading it straight from Gabriel's mind. Genuine telepathy. His mouth gaped, and he pointed high into the western sky.

Kendric's mind registered sublime contempt that Greg would try
such a pathetic stunt. Then vacillation set in, precisely because it was
so unlikely. He looked around to follow the direction of Greg's accusing finger, just in time to see a frigid saffron dawn expand across
the sky above Wisbech.

The light source was directly above them, a cold dazzling star that crawled through the genuine constellations at an infinitesimal pace. Its radiance was throwing shadows as sharp-edged as daylight. Greg could see wisps of fluffy cloud gusting high overhead; they must've been kilometers away.

Gabriel began to laugh.

The false star was as intense as noonday sunlight, then brighter. It began to elongate. Brick walls glared scarlet. Dew-mottled algae sparkled like a diamanté ice floe.

Intuition whispered into Greg's brain. He *knew*. The Merlin. Then his far-flung espersense delivered the final shock, a single band of incendiary thought originating from the space probe's bioware nodes: Philip Evans's unholy vengeance glee as he hurtled inexorably toward Leopold Armstrong.

The Merlin descended at orbital velocity, boring a vacuum-tunnel through the lower atmosphere. A purple-white plasma comet with a rigid incandescent tail of superionized air, stabbing down like some monstrously overpowered strategic defense laser.

Greg flung his arms desperately over his face, trying to save his eyes. There was carmine blood-light, then sable blackness.

The blast wave was a white-noise tsunami. It plucked Greg out of the mire and sent him spinning through space. He could see the street's houses disintegrating, slates taking flight, bricks avalanching. The air had become a blizzard of giant splinters and powdery fragments.

He saw the tower. Rather, where the tower had been: a thick column of fusion-hot air fountaining up into the darkening sky. Its flickering vermilion fluorescence was sheathed by ragged braids of ebony soot clouds. Garish blue-green static webs discharged around its mushrooming crown.

For a liquid, the water was incredibly hard.

44

GREG WOKE TO PEACE, BODY and mind. Blissful. He could feel his entire body except for his left hand, and nothing hurt, nothing felt abused. There was just warmth and softness.

Makes a bloody change.

He opened his eyes. Even the light was gentle, pale pearl. Rapid blinking resolved the blurred shapes around him.

He was lying on his back looking up at an ivory-colored ceiling with inset biolum strips. A young man in a white medical-style coat was removing an electrode hoop from his forehead.

"Welcome back, Mr. Mandel," he said.

That humorless tone, his intent professionalism. He had to belong to Event Horizon.

"There is no need to worry," the doctor assured Greg. "You are a patient in Event Horizon's Liezen clinic—that's in Austria."

"Who's worrying?"

The doctor nodded earnestly. "Ah, good. Sometimes there is disorientation following a prolonged somnolence induction."

"What do you call prolonged?"

"Eight days. In addition to your physical injuries you were suffering from advanced cerebral stress due to an overdose of neurohormones. I've loaded a prohibition order into your cortical node preventing any gland secretions. Come back in three months, and I'll wipe the order, or you might consider having the gland itself extracted." His nose twitched. "I don't approve of them, personally."

"Thank you, Doctor." Julia's cut-crystal voice chopped off any further admonishments. "That will be all."

The doctor sighed resignedly and backed away.

Greg turned his head. He was in a small tidy room with plenty of medical gear modules stacked beside the bed. A picture window looked out over sunny parkland dotted with grazing llamas.

The bed was elevating him smoothly into a sitting position. His arms lay outside the ocher blankets. A chalky-colored bioware bladder had been inflated around his left hand, trailing scores of fine fiber-optic cables to the gear modules, its nutrient fluid veins pulsing rhythmically. Just as well; he didn't particularly fancy looking at the hand.

Julia was wearing a crinkled navy blue sundress. The skirt was shorter than her usual, its hem hovering well above her knees. She was watching him with silent diligence.

"The hair's nice," Greg told her. Tiny corkscrew curls had fluffed it out into a candyfloss cloud. A chain of minute blue flowers formed a delicate tiara above her brow. Given a posy of primroses she would've made a good bridesmaid, he thought.

"Oh, you think so?" A dainty long-fingered hand lifted to pat a few of the more wayward strands. "Adrian likes it this way."

"Lucky old Adrian."

The door closed behind the doctor.

Julia's face fell, giving him a woeful stare. "I'm so sorry, Greg. Really I am. None of this need have happened. It's all my fault."

"Don't be silly."

"But it is."

Greg listened as she launched into an explanation about the Cray files, her mistrust, the Saint Christopher. There was no energy in him to power any strong feelings about it, one way or the other, anger or despair. The issue seemed an abstract. It was over; all it could ever be now was an exercise in "what if." The whole bloody great cockup was down to his overreliance on mystic intuition, treating it as infallible, giving logical thought the big elbow. His own stupid fault.

He let out a long dispirited sigh and said, "Forgiven. Besides, you were right: I should've seen Ellis's connection with the PSP. And I missed Steven as well. That's got to make us quits."

"Really? Did you really mean you forgive me?" She was studying his face, trepidation lurking in her expressive tawny eyes.

Julia wanted absolution, so he smiled and said, "Yeah, I really do. No messing." He'd sought it for himself often enough. He could hardly deny her.

She flashed him a hundred-watt grin and sat on the edge of the bed. "I've been terrified of you waking up all week. You were the last loose end. I've made my peace with everyone else."

"Everyone?" His thoughts moved slowly. "Hey, what about Gabriel?"

"She's all right. Everyone is all right now. Treating you all at the clinic was the least I could do." Her lips came together pensively. "They took Gabriel's gland out two days ago. She insisted, said it was part of her deal."

That would take a while to sink in, Greg knew. Gabriel without her gland would be interesting. Maybe she'd even get back into shape, take part in life. Nice idea.

"How did you get us out?" Greg asked.

"Oh, Teddy and Morgan Walshaw jumped a Prowler over to Wisbech about twenty minutes after the blast. I wanted to go." Her face hardened slightly at the memory. "They both said no. Only thing those two ever did agree on."

"Teddy? How do you know Teddy?"

Julia's smile was taunting. "You've got a bit of catching up to do. I'll let Eleanor explain. I pulled rank to be here when they woke you, but I'd better not stay much longer or she'll be bashing the door down to get at you. She's good at that." The smile turned devilish. "I might've known you'd prefer the buxom type. And you're lucky to have her, Greg. We've spent a lot of time talking this last week. I've got to know her quite well. She's a smashing girl."

"You think I don't know?"

Julia nodded in satisfaction. "Good. You'll be quite all right to have children, by the way. The Merlin's isotopes were left in orbit; there was no radioactive fallout."

"You did it. You shut it down."

"Yeah. It was all I had, Greg. I told you I knew it was Kendric who was behind the blitz; somehow, somewhere along the line, he'd be there. I didn't know who to trust. The Merlin was the one global-range weapon which was totally under my direct control; I didn't have to go through anyone, ask anyone's permission. My executive code gave me unlimited access to the Astronautics Institute's memory cores. I pulled the Merlin's command codes and used them to put it into stasis. I was going to kill Kendric with it. When he was out at sea on the *Mirriam*, where no one else could get hurt. The Merlin can fly twelve million kilometers and find a rock two hundred meters across; dropping it three and half thousand kilometers onto a sixty-meter target is no problem. All I'd need to do was place a satellite call to Kendric, and I'd have *Mirriam*'s position down to a meter, constantly updated. Not that I needed a direct hit; even with its isotopes and ninety percent of its fuel dumped, the Merlin still masses over a ton. And, well, you saw how big a kinetic punch it packed traveling at that velocity."

"Yeah, I saw. What did happen to Kendric? I survived."

Julia glanced out at the grassland beyond the window, expression neutral. "They only brought you and Gabriel back. I didn't ask. You can if you want."

"No. Not necessary." Not with Teddy in the rescue party. Walshaw, too, come to that; maybe especially Walshaw.

Julia bent over and touched her lips to his, a soft dry kiss. "First time," she murmured huskily. "Thank you, Greg." There was a draft of some expensive Parisian scent, then she was standing up briskly. "Memento for you." She hung the Saint Christopher on the bedpost. "Don't worry; it doesn't work anymore."

"Pity, I'd feel safer."

"Must dash. Got a lesson with Royan. He's teaching me to write proper hot-rod software."

Greg almost asked. But settled for hearing it from Eleanor instead.

Julia opened the door. Eleanor stood outside, looking grand even in the shapeless white clinic robe she was wearing. There was something not quite right about the way she walked, and the skin on her face seemed to be peeling, except for two patches around her eyes.

The two girls exchanged a glance as they passed. Smiled knowingly.

"All yours," said Julia.